FANGIRL CONFESSIONS COLLECTION

KIRSTEN S. BLACKETER

FANGIRL CONFESSIONS

THE COSPLAYER
THE ARTIST
THE BODYGUARD
THE DIRECTOR
THE AUTHOR

Printed in the United States of America.
First Printing, October 2025
ISBN: 9781966905202

Written by Kirsten S. Blacketer.
Published by BlackShip Press
Kirsten.blacketer@gmail.com

Cover Design: **The Midnight Muse**

https://kirstensblacketer.com

Dedication

Fangirls, this is for you.

To all the fangirls I've met over the years.
Thanks for all the feels.

To my Philly Fangirls 2015.
Thanks for the memories.

To Madre, my sister from another mister.
You're STUCK with me forever.

Table of Contents

The Cosplayer

The Artist

THE BODYGUARD

THE DIRECTOR

THE AUTHOR

The Cosplayer
Fangirl Confessions
Book 1
KIRSTEN S. BLACKETER

CHAPTER ONE

"No way—Nathan Burke was *born* to play Commander Colton," Jessica says, fixing the pass around her neck.

I wait with a small group by the convention center entrance.

"Absolutely not." Ginger vehemently shakes her head. "That role should have gone to Vince Parker. He was fantastic in that film with Tom Cruise."

"*Space Vendetta* is the biggest franchise next to *Star Wars* and *Marvel.* They would miss out on a huge opportunity by casting someone like Parker." Jessica snaps her gum. "Burke *is* Commander Colton."

Ignoring their debate, I lean against the wall and rifle through the emergency kit on my hip. There are always cosplayers at these conventions who have epic costume fails, and I learned long ago to pack the necessities to get them patched up and on their way. No one pays for my services. I enjoy doing it. Working in costume design has given me all kinds of insight into how to quickly fix wardrobe malfunctions.

"Vicky, you're a *Vendetta* girl. Who do you think would be a better Commander Colton?" Ginger nudges me with her elbow. "Parker or Burke?"

I zip the bag closed, readjust it over my shoulder, and sigh. I hate these types of debates. They're pointless, but it's not like I don't have an opinion. "Neither."

Both Ginger and Jessica gape at me.

"You have to pick one," Jessica demands, her blue eyes wide, her blonde ringlets bouncing.

Just then, the line starts moving. We slowly make our way

toward the entrance, where security is checking bags and tickets before fans enter the convention center. I've been waiting for this con for months. This small group of women I befriended on Tumblr are members of the same fandoms as me. We write fan fiction and binge everything with our favorite actors. This is the first time we've met in person, and my introverted self already regrets the decision.

The two women standing beside me will never let me escape without answering their question. I steel myself before speaking. "Burke was a decent choice, and Parker would have been amazing, but neither of them have the depth to play a conflicted character like Commander Colton." I regard them with a level stare.

"Then who would you cast?" Ginger asks, folding her arms across her chest. The summer sun highlights her auburn hair and sets it on fire.

I know exactly who I would cast for the role, and this time, I don't hesitate. "Jason Hunt."

"The guy from *Throne of Ashes*?" Jessica sounds surprised. "Really?"

"Yeah. He's got depth and range." I shrug as we near the entrance. "Plus, he's a damn chameleon. I've seen nearly every movie he's ever been in, and each role is so different. He's versatile and seamlessly embodies any character."

"I didn't realize you're a *Throne of Ashes* fan." Ginger smiles. "That's a great show. I can't wait for next season."

"Should be out early next year." I turn just as we reach the security guard.

He doesn't smile as he takes my bag, checks the contents, scans my badge, and steps aside to admit me into the building. Dark hair, dark eyes, no sense of humor. I pity the idiot who crosses him. Security is a thankless job. Poor guy.

"Have a good day." I beam at him as I walk past.

He grunts in response while repeating the process with the cosplayer behind me.

"Well, he's a ray of sunshine," I mutter to Jessica, who laughs when she stops alongside me.

Ginger joins us, breathless, grinning from ear to ear. "Where to first?"

Jessica lingers behind as we wander deeper into the sea of fans heading toward the inner sanctum of the convention center.

"What did you think of the last season of *Throne of Ashes*?" Ginger squeezes me.

"It needed more scenes with the Forgotten Knight."

Ginger laughs, and the sound draws the attention of passing fans dressed in varying levels of cosplay. "You may be right about Hunt, though. He would have been a fantastic Commander Colton."

"But then he wouldn't be Phinneas Bannon, the Forgotten Knight."

"That long dark hair and those piercing ice-blue eyes." Ginger shivers with a longing sigh. "I think it's his voice that does it for me. Deep, gruff…*ugh*, sinful."

Ginger falls back to check on Jessica and I lose myself in a daydream about the Forgotten Knight.

Since I started watching *Throne of Ashes* and fell down the Forgotten Knight rabbit hole, I've been obsessed with watching anything and everything with Jason Hunt. His voice in *Throne of Ashes* is the character's voice, not the one I've heard in countless interviews and other productions.

But the Forgotten Knight's voice is by far my favorite. The things I would let that man do to me if he asked in that voice…*holy shit.*

When we reach the vendor area, Beth is impatiently tapping

her foot by the Pokémon stand. She's wearing a cute little modified cosplay from an animated series called *SteamedPunk*. The pint-sized hat atop her black hair sits at a jaunty angle, completely at odds with her scowl and narrowed dark eyes.

Beth butts into Jessica and Ginger's conversation immediately. I shake my head.

"Just trying to get a plan of attack." Ginger redirects the topic, and I shoot her a grateful look. "I know some of us have photo ops and autograph signings today."

"Jen and Madre will be hanging out in the signing area today." Ginger pulls a map from her bag. "We have the group chat. Just check in around one, and we'll see where everyone is."

"I don't think Jessica heard you." Beth points at me and then to her ears.

"I heard everything. Thanks." Jessica smiles, but it doesn't reach her eyes. "Ronnie is waiting for me by the escalator. I'll catch you guys later."

"What's got your panties in a twist?" Ginger asks Beth after Jessica disappears into the crowd.

"One of the security guards was an asshole." Beth sniffed and fluffed her skirt. "Threatened to ban me if I cause any trouble."

"What did you do?" I blink at her.

Beth's fandom persona is Mistress Viper, and her comments are as sharp and injurious as her namesake's bite. She isn't very well liked by our band of online fangirls because of her critical nature, but she's a fantastic author. We've just learned to take her in small doses.

"I didn't do a damn thing," she snaps. "Doesn't matter. It's not like I'll see the asshole again. Fuck him."

Ginger snorts.

"Let's go." Beth leads the way, Ginger following and casting me an imploring look over her shoulder.

We make a point to stop at nearly every vendor stall. I love supporting small artists, and events like this are the best way to network with other creatives.

"Oh no! My strap broke." A woman sobs behind me.

I turn, already fumbling through my bag for a small metal container full of safety pins. "I can help."

Her eyes fill with tears as I pull a pin from the case.

"Thank you." She clutches the broken strap to her shoulder to keep it from falling and causing a scene.

"Here, let me..." I take the strap from her hand and locate the broken piece hanging down her back. Within a few moments, I have them fastened together, a pin securing them from underneath. No one will ever know. "There. That should hold until you get a chance to fix it."

"You're a lifesaver." She throws her arms around me. "Thank you so much."

When she finally lets go, I hand her one of my cards. "Just text this number if you need me again."

"I will." She reads the card. "Vicky, thanks again."

"Go. Enjoy the con." I smile as she bounds to her friends, free of tears.

Pride fills me. This is why I do this. It makes me happy to know I've helped someone avert a cosplay crisis. It's my calling.

"That was sweet of you," Ginger says, joining me. "I bet that happens a lot."

"More than you know." I sigh and close the bag. "Where's Be—"

The question dies in my throat when *he* rounds the corner.

The Forgotten Knight. Phinneas Bannon.

I shake my head and press my hand over my racing heart.

No. It *can't* be him.

This is a comic convention. There are bound to be many people dressed as characters from *Throne of Ashes*. It's the most popular show on TV right now.

"She's over there." Ginger points to a booth to our right but stops when she notices my stare. "Are you okay?" Then she sees the hulking knight stalking toward us. "Oh…damn. He's good." She purrs. "That's the best fucking cosplay I've ever seen. He looks just like him."

His crimson hair reflects the light. This must be a recent adaptation of the character. The "Blessing" episode caught him in a curse and turned his dark auburn hair white in thick streaks. Whoever designed this cosplay has done their homework—it's nearly an exact reproduction of the character's wig. Not to mention the intricate detail of the armor on his chest and the maroon tunic underneath.

He stalks through the crowd, his head bowed, eyes focused on the floor. Piercing blue eyes, I would guess. Only contacts could create the vibrant blue on the show, but that's showbiz. A longsword drapes across his back, the hilt peeking over his broad shoulders.

The closer he comes, the larger he seems. I blink twice as he strides toward me. His attention is focused, his eyes unblinking.

Ginger steps out of the way as he approaches, skirting around me. As he passes, she nudges me. "Ask him for a picture."

I turn toward him. He's massive. I inhale deeply, building my courage. His cologne hits me, a warm wave of invitation. It's intoxicating, drawing me to him.

Then I notice the strap holding his great sword is barely tethered. Only one thread remains, threatening to snap with the slightest motion.

My conscience kicks in. "Sir." I reach out to tap his shoulder. "Excuse me."

He spins, and blue eyes narrow on me. Not winter blue, but wary sky blue.

"Your strap. It's frayed…the sword will fall." I open my bag and dig through the contents, searching for something strong enough to hold leather. "I can fix it, just give me a minute."

"Fix it?" The gruffness of his voice mirrors the character's. A flawless imitation.

I brace a hand on his shoulder to steady myself. It's probably the worst thing I can do because it brings me closer to him.

Oh god, what am I doing? Inside, I'm freaking out. *Just fix the strap. Focus.*

I locate the proper thread and needle. "Take it off, please."

His brow rises. "I beg your pardon."

"The sword…take it off so I can fix the strap." I meet his gaze. Parties of bees and butterflies take flight in my stomach. "Please."

His jaw flexes as he considers my words before he relents and pulls the strap over his head. The moment he does, the final thread breaks free.

"Huh." He touches it with a gloved finger and sighs. "You were right."

He hands it to me, and I take it with a smile, ignoring the way his hand brushes mine. "Won't take long."

We stand in silence as I thread a needle, then use the holes in the leather as a guide. He holds the sword as I work on the sheath and strap. Within minutes, I've repaired it, and I beam with pride when I return it to his oversized hand.

God, this man is massive. I stare up at him as he puts the sheath in place and positions the sword on his shoulder.

"My thanks, dear lady." He remains in character with a small bow. "You saved me from disaster."

My grin widens. "I am at your service, good sir." I hand him a card. "Take this and call upon me should you happen to require my services once more."

The lightness of the banter takes away the remaining nerves fluttering in my stomach. Whoever this cosplayer is, he's fucking amazing.

"Do you do this professionally?" I ask, reaching out to touch the breastplate. "The craftsmanship of this cosplay is truly spectacular."

"It's more of a hobby…" He clears his throat. "Thank you."

"I'm a costume designer, and I know quality work when I see it." I grin. "Your Forgotten Knight is…well, unforgettable. Bravo."

"Would you like a photo for your wall of conquests?" His cheeks pinken. "I mean your averted cosplay crises."

I gasp playfully. "How do you know about that wall? It's a secret."

"Your secret's safe with me." He winks.

I hold my phone out for a selfie. He's leaning in close when Ginger appears.

"I'll take it."

She snatches the phone from my hand, and I link my arm through the knight's. His warmth sinks into me, and the dizzying scent of him fills my head with wicked thoughts. I smile and lean against his shoulder.

Ginger snaps a few photos. "Got it."

I feel the heat of his breath on my cheek as I draw away.

"Thank you again." The deep rumble of his voice ignites longing deep inside me.

My response catches in my throat as Ginger hands back the

phone. "Seriously, that cosplay is amazing."

He nods to Ginger, then looks at me. "Until we meet again." And with a bow, he takes his leave.

The Forgotten Knight disappears into the crowd, drawing stares with every step. I stand there watching him until Ginger tugs at my arm.

"Girl, you should have asked for his number." She sighs. "Damn, he is fine."

I shrug and unlock my phone. There, our picture is immortalized in pixels. I look ridiculous with my peace sign, clinging to his arm like an insipid lovesick fan.

Which would have been true if he were the real deal, but there's no way in hell Jason Hunt would come to Philly for a fan convention…in cosplay of his own character. No fucking way.

"Come on, Beth is waiting for us." Ginger tugs my arm.

"One sec." I murmur before uploading the photo to Instagram.

Saved another cosplay today! Isn't this one amazing? I type the caption with a few hashtags, then post it.

After I tuck my phone away, I take one last look through the shifting crowd.

He's gone.

Damn it. Ginger is right. I should have asked for his number. Too late now. Maybe I'll run into him later.

Pushing regret aside, I join Ginger and Beth to search for our fangirl companions.

CHAPTER TWO

The rest of the day passes in a blur. I vaguely recall wandering the narrow galleries of vendors before following Beth and Ginger to meet up with the rest of our group.

There had been quite a few cosplayers in need of my services, and I happily jumped into my role as seamstress savior. Their gratitude warmed my heart, though as the day wore on, I couldn't help but scan the passing crowd for any sign of *him*. But the enigmatic Forgotten Knight cosplayer had vanished.

I frown, and a heavy sigh of longing escapes me.

"Hey, you okay?" Ginger gently elbows me in the side.

"Yeah." I sway into her as she links her arm through mine.

Beth is two steps ahead, leading us down the street toward a restaurant after our full convention day. My stomach growls, but honestly, I'd be fine grabbing something to take back to the hotel. Just the thought of returning to the convention tomorrow has my stomach in knots.

Will *he* be there? Who *is* he?

"You're thinking way too hard," Ginger teases me. "I can see smoke rolling out of your ears."

I chuckle at the imagery.

"Were the cosplayers too much today?" she asks as we round the corner.

"Not really." I shrug, wondering if I should share the thoughts pinging around in my head. I'm not normally this fixated, but seeing the *Throne of Ashes* cosplayer has me all twisted up.

Especially the way he whispered in my ear. I shiver.

"Girl…" Ginger shakes me. "You look like you're about to burst. Spill it."

"I…*ugh*, this is going to sound stupid."

Beth opens the door to the restaurant, holding it for us. The warm scent of fresh bread and bar fare hits me as I step into the small Irish pub. We ate here last night, but it was so good we came back for a second round. God, I need a drink.

"What's going to sound stupid?" Beth asks, coming alongside us as we wait to be seated.

"Well, I—"

My mouth snaps shut as the waitress greets us, grabs three menus, and shows us to a booth tucked in the back corner. I continue biting my tongue until she leaves, promising to bring our drinks as soon as possible.

We quickly scan the menu and ultimately pick the same food we had the night before. Once the waitress returns with our cocktails and takes our order, I inhale to steady myself before launching into a confession.

"I can't stop thinking about him."

Beth snorts into her Cosmo. "Who?"

"A cosplayer." Ginger's lips curl in a knowing smile. "The Forgotten Knight."

I nod as Ginger fills Beth in on the details. By the time she finishes, I know my face is six shades of red.

Both of them face me and grin.

"So, did you get his number?" Beth asks. "It wouldn't be the first time I've heard of people hooking up at a convention due to a mutual fandom bond."

"I'm not hooking up with him," I manage to choke out.

My face has heated up even more—I didn't think it was physically possible. I want to crawl under the table for even thinking about doing something so out of character. Instead, I hide behind my mojito and sip the minty rum concoction. Alcohol only fans the flames.

"Maybe you should." Beth smirks. "Sounds like all of us need to get laid."

"Did you get the security guard's number?" Ginger turns it on Beth. "You two can fuck it out of your systems."

Beth snarls at the mention of the man and waves her hand. "He's not worth my time." Her gaze fixes on me. "You never answered...*did* you get his number?"

"No." I frown and pull out my phone, holding up the picture of us together. "All I got was a photo."

"Let me see." Beth takes the phone from my hand and stares at it. Her eyes narrow. She zooms in and out on different parts of the photo. "You two look pretty cozy."

"They were." Ginger snickers before taking a sip of her lemon drop martini, avoiding my glare. "They were so cute together."

"Wait..."

I nearly drop my drink at Beth's choked gasp. "What?"

Her gaze meets mine, her eyes wide. "Did you post this online?"

"Yeah, why?"

"Girl...I don't know how to tell you this, but that's not a cosplayer." Beth turns the photo back toward me. "That's Jason Hunt."

"Get the fuck out of here!" Ginger snatches the phone and stares at it. "Oh. My. God. No fucking way!"

My heart jumps into my throat, and I can't breathe. "What are you talking about?"

"See here?" Beth points to a spot on his throat where she zoomed in. "There's a scar."

"Wasn't he injured during filming last fall?" Ginger spins to me. "A sword nicked his throat while they were shooting a fight scene. He had to get stitches and everything."

I remember reading an article and seeing the bandage on his neck during the following weeks while he did interviews for a film's release. My eyes lose focus the longer I stare at the picture of the two of us.

No. It can't be him. Why would he be in Philadelphia? At a comic and fandom convention?

He seemed startled when I stopped him, but he humored me. Let me fix his cosplay. Then he held me close and let Ginger take a picture of us together. He whispered in my ear.

My breath hitches, and my pulse pounds in my ears.

Holy shit.

"It's him," I mutter.

"Uh, Vicky? You might want to check your Instagram." Beth bites her lip as she scrolls on her phone.

"What?" I snatch my phone from Ginger and open the app.

Five thousand notifications in the last four hours. I slump back in the booth as I skim through the list. Comments. Likes. Reposts.

"Holy fuck." Beth grins at me. "Your little pic with Hunt went viral. You're famous now, babe."

"Oh, no." I groan as the reality of the situation sinks in. I tagged the location. Everyone knows Jason Hunt was in cosplay as his own fucking character at the Philly convention. "Shit. Shit. *Shit.*"

"What's wrong?" Ginger asks. "Isn't this a good thing?"

"For him, no." I scramble to hit the delete button, but there's no point. The damage is done. It's been screenshot and shared so many times, there's no way in hell I can undo what I've done. "Oh god. I fucked up."

"I don't understand." Ginger frowns and glances at Beth.

They aren't Jason Hunt fangirls, at least not to the extent I am. They haven't watched his interviews. They don't know he prefers a low profile and anonymity.

But why the hell did he come to an event of this size in his own cosplay then?

"A few years ago, he did an interview with one of the major magazines—I can't remember which one, but they asked him if he would ever do a public appearance, like a fan convention." I somehow manage to get the words out, even as panic infuses me. "He swore he never would. He doesn't like the spotlight, and the rapid growth of his fan base made attending events more of a hindrance than a help to his career."

"I remember that." Ginger snaps her fingers. "*FilmTalk* magazine did the interview. He's an introvert, prefers gaming to going out."

"Nerd." Beth chuckles. "Hot nerd."

"I have to delete this." I pull up the Instagram post again.

"Why?"

I pause at Beth's question, my finger hovering over the button.

"Did he ask you not to post it on social media?"

"No, but—"

"But nothing. If he didn't want it getting out that he was here, he would've hidden his identity better and asked you not to post the photo." Beth sips her drink like it's obvious.

"I know, but I should've asked before I posted it." I bite my lip as panic coalesces into guilt.

"You're right." Ginger rests her arm around my shoulders and pulls me to her with a side hug. "You should have asked, but you can't take it back now. Even if you delete this picture, it's already viral, baby!"

I bury my head in her shoulder. "Oh god, what have I done?"

"You didn't do anything," Beth reassures me. "He's a big boy. He can handle it."

"But I stirred up a hornet's nest." I drop the phone onto the table and finish my mojito with one self-deprecating gulp.

A snort escapes Beth. "For who? He's got a publicist for this shit. They'll handle it."

"I ruined everything."

"Did you though?" Beth leans forward, resting her elbows on the table. Her stare burns into me. "Listen—he came to a public fan convention wearing cosplay of his character. That's tempting fate if you ask me. He was going to get caught one way or another."

"Beth is right." Ginger nudges me. "If you hadn't recognized him, someone else would have. Hell, there are probably hundreds of photos of him floating around the internet from today."

"You think?" I push my empty glass aside.

"I *know*."

I reach for my phone, but Ginger stops me as the waitress arrives with our food.

"Let's eat, then we'll head back to the hotel and you can look it up on my laptop."

Warmth rises from my vegetable soup, and a knot in my chest eases at her words. I pick up my spoon and take a deep breath. "Okay."

"Good. Now can we discuss tomorrow's schedule?" Beth picks up her sandwich and takes a bite.

"Yes. My panel starts at eleven."

Ginger lays out her itinerary to sit in on the *Space Vendetta* panel the next day with the director of the franchise. Beth outlines her photo ops with two cast members of another show, but I'm lost in thought, barely picking up anything either of them is saying.

I eat my soup and wallow in regret. Posting the photo was the stupidest thing I have ever done. I should have printed it and hung it on my wall at home.

No one would know. His secret would be safe.

But I feel like an asshole for exposing him to thousands of fans around the world.

Damn, I'm an idiot.

CHAPTER THREE

I delete the Instagram post, but the damage has already been done. And even though Beth and Ginger reassure me I did nothing wrong, I feel guilty as hell.

The girls are getting together to go to another bar, but I just want a moment alone.

In the quiet space of my hotel room, I flop down on the bed. Ginger is sharing a room with me, but since she chose to venture out with the other fangirls, I have the chance I need to get my thoughts in order. Not that it matters.

Cursed with a guilty conscience and insomnia, I scroll through my feed. My followers have quadrupled since I last checked, even with the photo removed from my page. *Shit.*

A text message dings in my purse—not on my personal phone but the one I use for cosplay emergencies. I sigh. Someone must have been too rough on their costume. Thankful for the distraction, I grab the phone and open the message.

(Unknown): I have a problem. Can you call me?

I blink twice at the message. Whoever it is, they must have a mess on their hands. I call the number. It rings only once before connecting.

"Hi." A deep voice rumbles through the line. "I'm sorry to interrupt your evening, but I have a problem."

It's *him.* I shoot to my feet. The phone nearly slips from my hand. "A problem?" I play it off like I have no idea who is contacting me. "It's nothing I can't fix."

"Yes."

A brief pause.

"You deleted the post."

Pinching my eyes closed, I sigh. "Yeah, I…I'm sorry. I had no idea. If I'd known—"

"Don't apologize." He interrupts me. "I should have said something."

"I feel terrible." My fingers twist the fabric of my skirt.

"Don't." A deep breath fills the silence. "Can we talk in person?"

My heart skips a beat. "You want to meet with me? Now?"

"Yeah. Are you still in town?"

"Of course. I'm in my hotel room."

"Does your hotel have a bar?"

I nod, then quickly realize he can't see me. "Yeah."

"Which hotel?"

His sinful question lingers between us.

This is the most reckless and stupid thing I've ever done in my life. I can't believe I'm actually considering giving a total stranger this information. Not only that, there's no one to know if I go missing.

Fuck. Don't do it. Don't become a crime statistic.

"The Weston." Wow. I'm weak. So weak.

"I'll meet you there in ten minutes."

He ends the call, and I shoot into panic.

Rapid-fire, I send three text messages, praying they go through. Ginger, Beth, and Jessica have my information now. If something happens to me, they'll know. I share my location with all of them, just in case. I've seen enough crime documentaries to know to leave breadcrumbs for investigators.

Get a grip, Vicky. I shake my head going into the bathroom. I manage to fix my makeup and hair, but I'm still wearing my cosplay. Will he care? Does it matter? He's probably going to hand me a lawsuit for being an idiot. Or worse…

"He's not going to kidnap you and harvest your organs. He's not going to sue you. He just wants to *talk*," I tell my reflection.

My quick pep talk does nothing for the nerves fluttering like a flock of birds in my gut. I take a deep breath. Then another.

"Just be calm."

Once I tuck both phones into my purse, I sling it over my shoulder and head for the elevator. At nearly ten, the lobby is deserted except for a few guests coming in the main door. I turn the corner and spy the entrance to the restaurant. There's a bar along the far wall with two occupants. One is an older man who ignores me as I walk past.

The other turns, and my whole world implodes. *Holy shit. It's Jason Hunt.*

A lopsided smile curves his sinful mouth when I stop beside him.

"I didn't think you'd actually show up."

"Well…I'm here."

"I see that." He pulls out a barstool beside him. "Have a seat. Let me buy you a drink."

His voice is softer, more friendly than that of the Forgotten Knight. Much more relaxed than the tone I've heard in interviews. I can't help but wonder if this is the *true* Jason Hunt. A thrill ripples through me, making my legs unsteady.

"I outed your secret on social media and you want to buy me a drink?" I scoff, sliding into the seat. My thigh brushes his as he turns toward me. I manage to stifle a squeak of surprise just before it escapes my traitorous lips.

"It was only a matter of time before someone figured it out." He waves to the bartender.

"Mojito and a water, please." I hang my purse on a hook

beneath the bar as the bartender nods and leaves.

My gaze slides to the man beside me. He's even more handsome in person. Tall and broad in cosplay, he exudes the same energy in character as he does now. His dark hair is smoothed back—damp from a shower, it looks like—and a day's worth of stubble lines his strong jaw. I clench my hands in fists to keep from reaching out and touching him.

Contain yourself, woman.

"Mr. Hunt, let me apologize. I—"

"Jason." He sets down his rocks glass and holds up his hand. "You don't have to apologize. You didn't do anything wrong. For all you knew, I was a fan in cosplay."

My face warms under his intense gaze as he studies me.

"I didn't expect you to be *you.*" I cringe at my shitty explanation.

"I know what you mean." He chuckles, and the sound warms me. "*No one* expects it." He shrugs. "That's why I took the chance. Guess it backfired, huh?"

"I guess so." Tension eases out of my shoulders. When the bartender sets down my drink, I raise it in a toast. "Cheers."

"Cheers." He taps his glass to mine and we drink.

The liquor numbs my self-consciousness, and I find what remains of my courage. "You said you have a problem. I already deleted the post, so I don't know how much more help I can be."

"Oh." He grins. "Don't worry about it. My publicist is already handling the fallout. He'll have it figured out by morning."

"Sorry." I cringe again.

Jason shoots me a pointed look. "I didn't invite you here for a guilt trip." He reaches into his jacket pocket and withdraws a deep red swath of fabric. "My sash ripped. I was hoping you could fix it."

I take the garment, admiring the weight and texture of the cotton cloth. As I inspect it, I find the rip. An easy fix. My eyes narrow, and I look at him. "Even *you* could fix this with a needle and some thread."

"I don't have the supplies. Besides, you did such a good job with my leather sheath, I figured this would be right up your alley."

"*This* is your emergency?" I drop the sash in my lap and gape at him.

"Well, yes…but I also didn't get a chance to tell you how much I appreciate your kindness today."

"Even after my social media fumble?"

"Water under the bridge." Jason smiles, and I'm struck again by how gorgeous he is.

"Is this your *thing*?" I call him out. "You dress in cosplay and find enamored fans to seduce them?"

He stares at me, mouth agape.

"Do you make them sign an NDA when they figure it out?" Indignation rises, and I do my best to maintain my composure, even through the sting of betrayal. "Is it a game to you, *Jason*?" I bite off his name, like it leaves a sour taste on my tongue.

His brows rise in his stunned silence.

"I'm not some insipid fangirl who throws herself at the nearest celebrity, hoping she'll get laid and have a story she can never tell." I toss the sash at him and slide off the seat before snatching up my bag. "Thanks for the drink, asshole."

Halfway through the restaurant, I stop at the firm grasp of his hand around my wrist. I'm about to tell him off when his gruff voice surrounds me.

"Vicky, wait. Please."

I extract my hand from his grasp and fold my arms across

my chest. "You have sixty seconds."

"I'm terrible at this." He rakes his fingers through his hair, messing up the neat strands, and a lock falls across his forehead. His blue eyes are pleading, even while his shoulders slump.

"Terrible at what? Hiding your identity? Lying about your intentions?" I stand my ground, though I soften at his posture. "Look, it doesn't matter. You could have any woman you want. Go chase someone who will put up with your bullshit."

"Vicky—"

"You know what? You're right. I don't regret posting that picture." I choke on rising tears. "I do regret being one of your fangirls."

His expression falls. "You're entitled to think the worst of me, and you're more than welcome to walk out of here right now and never look back. I won't think less of you if you leave."

I take a fortifying breath, bracing for whatever he says next.

"I just…today, when you helped me at the convention, you didn't do it because of who I am. You did it out of the goodness of your heart." He sighs, dropping his hand to his side. "It was the first time someone saw *me* and not the actor…not my status."

I swear beneath my breath. His words seem sincere, but how can I be sure this isn't a ploy to gain my trust only to betray me later?

"Why were you at the convention today?" I ask, unable to stop the curiosity burning in my soul.

"I was in town, and it seemed like a good idea." He shrugs. "In hindsight, it wasn't the best execution. I should have gone as someone other than the character I play. Maybe a full face mask." A self-deprecating laugh punctuates his statement. "Not that it matters. Everyone knows about my outing, so I won't be doing it again anytime soon."

"But *why* did you do it?"

"I love the fandom." He stuffs his hands in his pockets. "I read the books years ago, and I play the video game. When the chance to be part of the show came along, I jumped at the opportunity to play my favorite character. I was a fan long before I took on the role."

The edge of my fury fades. He's said as much in interviews over the years, but none of them portrayed this level of vulnerability.

"This was my chance to go as a *fan*, not as a celebrity." Jason gives me a half smile. "Looking back, it wasn't the best decision, was it?"

"Probably not." My arms uncross, and I fix the strap of my purse on my shoulder.

"If you still want to leave, I won't stop you, but you deserve to know I'm not being a pervert or taking advantage of my status. And you're right, it wasn't a cosplay emergency."

"Then why did you call me?" My mouth goes dry.

"Because you were lovely and caring…and you appreciated the detail I went to with my cosplay."

My eyes widen. "*You* made that?"

"You seem surprised?"

"I am." My curiosity wins, and I offer my hand.

"What's this?" He eyes my hand for a moment before taking it in his.

The warmth of his touch burns through me, lighting sparks of pleasure in my brain.

"A chance to start over." I shake his hand. "I'm Vicky, seamstress, costume designer, avid fangirl."

A smile blooms across his face. I nearly swoon.

"I'm Jason, cosplayer, gamer, avid fanboy." He shakes my hand. "Lovely to meet you."

"You left something out," I tease.

"Did I?" A mischievous sparkle lights his eyes.

"Actor?"

"Not tonight." He chuckles. "For the rest of tonight, I'm only a fan, just like you."

"Well then, Jason." I drop his hand before I do something stupid, like tell him how sexy he is. *None of that. Bad, Vicky.* "Can I buy you a drink?"

"I'd like that." With a sweep of his arm, he allows me to lead the way to our seats at the bar.

Awareness pulses through me as he follows. The scent of his cologne teases my wicked thoughts, but I succeed in pushing them aside when we resume our seats.

"So tell me, Jason, which book in the *Space Vendetta* series is your favorite and why?"

He grins at my question, relaxing as he launches into an animated response.

I still don't completely trust him, but the more he talks, the more I realize I might have to eat my words.

He's more attractive as a regular guy than as a celebrity.

How is that even possible?

CHAPTER FOUR

Jason Hunt is a fanboy. One hundred percent. That knowledge is a dangerous aphrodisiac.

I'm alarmingly close to admitting I may be smitten. I mean, I was enamored before, but there was distance between us, the divide between creator and fan. A line rarely crossed.

Now I've jumped over it without a second thought. What the hell am I thinking?

"How did you get sucked into the fandom?" he asks, taking a drink of water.

"Fan art." I push aside my empty water glass, hoping the dim light hides my blush. "It was…well, enlightening."

"Rule thirty-four, huh?" Jason chuckles.

"'If it exists, there's porn of it.'" I recite the basic concept and lick my lips. "Does it make you uncomfortable, knowing there's art of you as your character in…erotic situations?"

He sucks in a breath and exhales sharply, laughing. "I will admit, it's a little weird. I stopped Googling myself after I found a crack ship between the Forbidden Knight and the King of Ashes."

I clap my hand over my mouth. "They haven't even met in the series!"

"I know." He shrugs. "Fans love what they love. Who am I to take the dream away?"

"Yeah, I don't go that far. I mean…the closest I get is fan fiction I wrote where I shipped the Forgotten Knight with the Crimson Priestess."

His brows rise. "Wait. You ship those two?"

"Yeah, I mean…I know they've only had one scene together, but the chemistry is undeniable." I swoon at the thought. It's my favorite pairing, and I've written a half a dozen fanfics about the two characters. No one appreciates it. The fools.

Jason laughs. "I won't tell you about filming then. I don't want to ruin the TV magic for you."

"Is there really chemistry between you and Lana?" I ask about the actress who filmed the scene in question.

"Maybe a little, but only because she's a phenomenal actress. She's happily married of course, and I would never presume to create waves…but she's hot, I won't deny it." Jason waves to the bartender for another round.

"Have you ever hooked up with a costar?" The question bursts free, and I clap my hand over my mouth.

"That's a rather personal question." Jason arches a brow at me and smiles. "I'll answer under one condition." His smile turns into a confident smirk. "You answer my question."

"What question?" I swallow a lump in my throat, wondering what the hell I am getting myself into.

"What name do you publish your fan fiction under?"

Those blue eyes burn into me, and I sputter, unable to form a coherent response.

He wants to know what my fanfic author name is?

Oh…this is a bad idea. A really bad fucking idea.

If I tell him, he'll read it.

Do I really want to know the answer to my question? Or am I just hyped up playing a dangerous game with a man I only know through interviews and biographies?

"JustMyStarShip."

Jason drops his hand against the bar. "Wait…*you're*

JustMyStarShip?"

"Yeah…"

He rubs his eyes and looks skyward, studying the ceiling for a moment, as though collecting himself.

"Why?" I ask.

With a deep breath, he faces me, his eyes darker, more focused. "I…" He scoffs and shakes his head. "I've read all of your fics."

"You've what?"

He rubs his hand over his face, and a choked laugh escapes as he shifts uncomfortably on the stool. "I love your Forgotten Knight fics."

I blink three times before I'm able to form words. "You…what?"

"I typically avoid media, but I'm a sucker for fan fiction. I can't stay away." He hangs his head sheepishly. "I don't leave stars or kudos, but I read…a lot."

"I'm sorry." I shake my head to clear the cotton lodged between my eardrums and my brain. "Did you just say you *like* my fan fiction?"

"No." He meets my gaze. "I *love* it."

"Really?"

"Yes. Really." He leans back and picks up the whiskey the bartender delivered without commentary. "Is that so hard to believe?"

"Actually…yes. It is."

"Why?" He holds my gaze with an intensity that has me feeling self-conscious.

"I'm not a writer. I just post stories for fun." I roll my shoulders. "It helps me relax."

A smirk tugs his sensual mouth. "Writing smut relaxes you?"

My resistance falters. "It does."

"I see." He takes a drink. "Why do you love the Forgotten Knight?"

Jason redirects the conversation, leaving me breathless and unsteady. Still, I'm invested and intrigued.

"That's a complicated answer."

"We have time." He sets his glass down. "Unless you'd rather call it a night?"

"No." I cradle the full mojito between my hands. "But we've just met. I mean…this feels kind of intimate."

"Just two fans, having a drink after a convention." He swirls the liquid in his glass.

"You're good at this."

"At what?"

"Putting people at ease."

"Am I?" He takes a sip. "Normally, I'm dreadfully awkward."

"And it's different with me?"

"Strangely enough, yes." He holds up a hand. "That's a compliment."

"Is it?" I smother a laugh behind my hand. "You're awkward, and yet, I find it charming."

"You do?" He preens, straightening in his chair.

"Only a little." I hold up two fingers with a small gap between them. "Jury's still out on whether or not you're a player."

"I can promise you, I'm not." Jason presses his hand to his heart.

"Spoken like a true player."

"Touché." He salutes me with his glass before taking another sip.

"You never answered my question."

"Have I hooked up with any of my coworkers?" He hisses and sets the half-full glass aside. "I have, though it was a long time ago, when I first started acting. I was young and full of dreams…" His voice trails off.

"So it's not all starlight and rainbows?"

"Hardly." He scoffs, unable to meet my gaze.

"Why continue acting?"

"Because I love it." He finally looks at me, and his eyes glow with passion. "It gives me purpose." He licks his lips. "And the fans keep me going. I might not interact with them online, but I see them. I appreciate them…more than they know."

A response catches in my throat. I can't tease him. Not about this. Sincerity laces every word, and I feel it deep in the marrow of my bones.

I reach out and rest my hand on his. "I understand."

Surprised, he glances at my hand before turning to me. "You're too kind."

"What can I say?" I laugh before removing my hand. "I've been told I'm too nice."

"No." He catches my hand with his and holds it. The warmth of his touch seeps through his fingers, setting me ablaze. "You're lovely. Thank you."

"For what?"

"Humoring me." He lifts my hand to his lips and presses a soft kiss to my knuckles.

Every warning bell and celebration whistle goes off in my head. *What's going on?* I'm too stunned to speak.

His eyes darken when he catches my shocked gaze. "Thank you."

"You-you're welcome," I stutter, unable to form a coherent thought.

He drops my hand. "If there's anything I can do for you,

please let me know."

"How will I do that?"

He slides a piece of paper across the bar. "For emergencies."

I tuck the paper in my pocket as he stands. "Jason?"

"Yes?" He turns toward me.

My courage falters, but I manage to refortify before he disappears from my life forever. "Can I ask for a crazy favor?"

"Whatever you want."

I melt at his smile, and he leans against the bar, crowding my space.

"A kiss."

Both his brows shoot up in surprise. "A kiss?"

Way to go, stupid. Asking him to kiss you. What are you thinking? I silence the voice in my head and nod. "It doesn't have to be anythi—"

Jason closes the gap between us and cradles my jaw in his hand, then his warm lips cover mine. I barely register a growl deep in his throat as he caresses the seam of my lips with his tongue.

I open for him, and I'm lost.

Complete surrender.

CHAPTER FIVE

Kissing Jason Hunt should be illegal. He draws me closer until the heat of him sinks into me. Whiskey and sin linger on his lips, making me wonder if I'm in over my head.

Somewhere behind me, a throat clears, and I'm torn from the moment. Jason breaks the kiss with visible reluctance. His hands remain firmly on my shoulders, and I can't tell if it's because he can't pull away or he's ensuring we keep a little distance.

"That was…unexpected." Jason smiles before relinquishing his hold on me. He removes his wallet from his back pocket.

I run my hands over my face, trying to cool the heat. There's no way I can even look at the bartender, and Jason hands him a hundred-dollar bill.

"I'll walk you to your room." Jason presses a hand to the small of my back as we weave through the empty bar.

All I can think about is that kiss. Had I really been bold enough to ask him for it? Who am I?

By the time we reach the lobby, it's after midnight.

I turn to him at the elevator. "Thank you. For everything."

"My pleasure." His eyes linger on my lips for a moment. "Vicky…"

"Yeah?" I push the call button for the elevator.

"I don't…" He groans, as though pained to speak. "I don't normally do this kind of thing…"

"Neither do I."

"I can't tell if it's the rush of something new or if I'm just crazy…" He rakes his fingers through his hair.

"Conventions always give me a rush." I rest a hand on his arm. "I feel like I can be anyone, and no one will judge me."

Jason exhales sharply. "Yeah, something like that."

"It felt good to be on the floor in costume and unrecognizable, didn't it?"

"Yes."

"I'm sorry I ruined it."

Jason shakes his head. "You didn't ruin anything. In fact, meeting you was the best thing to happen all day."

"Feels like something out of a fan fiction."

The door to the elevator dings open behind me. I step back into the car, resting my hand on the door.

"Speaking of fan fiction." His eyes darken, and his tone dips low as he follows me into the elevator. "I wanted to tell you how much I enjoy yours."

My eyes widen as the doors close behind him, trapping us together in this small space.

"You don't have to say that to be nice," I squeak.

"I'm not just being nice."

"How did you find it?" I ask, desperately trying to hide my trembling hands.

"I stumbled across it one night when I searched my favorite pairing." His voice deepens. "Red on Red. You're a woman of many talents, Vicky."

"Thanks." I reach behind him to press the floor for my room, but he catches my wrist in his hand. "Jason?"

"Why did you ask me to kiss you?"

He holds my gaze. I gasp at a flicker of need in his blue eyes.

"I…" My voice catches in my throat. "I knew if I walked away without asking, I would regret it."

"If I asked you to come to my room, would you?" He rubs

the inside of my wrist, my thoughts scrambling in a sea of need.

"You're staying *here*?"

"Yes."

I bite my lip. This could be the craziest thing I've ever done. But just like the kiss, I can't say no to the curiosity burning inside me. Even if it's only one night, it's one night with Jason Hunt.

"Are you asking me to spend the night with you?" I step into his space and rest my palm on his jaw.

"Yes." His breathless reply twists my insides with excitement. "If I don't ask, I'll regret it for the rest of my life."

"Any woman would kill for a night with you."

"I don't want *any* woman." He leans closer, his breath caressing my lips. "I want you."

"Why?"

"Is it so hard to believe I'm attracted to you?"

"No," I murmur softly. "But…"

"But what?"

"What if I prefer the fantasy?"

His brows furrow. "I don't understand."

"Part of the fun of being a fangirl is indulging in fantasies, sexy ones." I drop my hand to my side. "If I stay with you, it's not a fantasy anymore."

"Are you worried reality won't live up to fantasy?" He chuckles.

"In my experience, it never does." I study his stunned expression. "Am I wrong?"

"You're not wrong." He steps back and releases my wrist. "It's days like this I wish I were some random guy who loved the fandom."

"Jason." I grab his hand. "I didn't say no…it's just…I like you. I don't want this to be something both of us regret in the morning."

"Sounds like there could be regrets either way." He sighs. "We're damned if we do, damned if we don't."

"What floor?" I reach past him, my finger hovering above the panel.

Jason swallows hard. "Twelve."

I push the button, and the elevator lurches into motion.

It takes every effort to not reach for him as we ascend. I pull out my phone to shoot a quick text to my weekend roommate, letting them know I won't be coming back with a winking emoji.

Jason takes my hand the moment the elevator stops on his floor. We're only halfway down the hall when butterflies take flight in the pit of my stomach. I can't believe I'm actually doing this. Never in a million years would I even entertain a one-night stand.

Yet here I am.

He pauses outside room 1235 to press a card to the lock panel. When he pushes the door open, Jason gestures for me to enter ahead of him. The reality of the moment hits me as I step across the threshold, past the point of no return.

It's a standard room, not a fancy suite. The king-size bed sits near a window overlooking Philly, a vast spread of twinkling lights on the midnight horizon. The door clicks closed behind me, and I turn around.

Jason leans on the door, his blue shirt tight across his chest. "We can just talk if you're uncomfortable."

"Who says I'm uncomfortable?" I set my purse next to the television.

He laughs and steps close, stopping just out of reach. "I told you. I'm really bad at this."

"Bad at seducing women?" I can't hide a smirk playing on my lips.

"You still think I'm a playboy?" He shakes his head.

"It's how you're portrayed." I study his face, searching for deception. He's all openness and honesty. "But I've listened to your interviews. You don't *sound* like a playboy."

"What do I sound like?" He's in my space now, crowding me with his intoxicating scent, with his heat.

"A nerd."

His laughter washes over me, and I'm smitten by the brilliance of his humor.

"Good thing I'm a sucker for nerds." I grab a handful of his shirt and drag him to me.

When my lips touch his, fire ignites inside me.

His growl reverberates through me as he pulls me into his arms. We're a tangle of limbs. I wrap my arms around his neck. His hands tug my skirt. Cool air brushes my bare legs as he tugs it up to my waist.

Slowly, he maneuvers me back until I hit the wall. I gasp when he pins me against it, then presses his thigh between my legs. I moan into his mouth as he delves deeper, tasting and teasing. His firm grip keeps me steady, but I want his hands everywhere.

"Jason…" I plead between kisses. "Please."

"What do you need, Vicky?" His mouth trails along my jaw.

"Make me come," I murmur, threading my fingers through his hair.

"And how do you prefer I accomplish that?" He nuzzles my neck, his touch stilling at my waist, his hands holding my skirt. "My mouth?" A kiss on my throat. "My fingers?" He hums against my skin. "My cock?"

"Oh god," I whimper. I'm not one for dirty talk, but hearing those words from Jason's lips liquefies what remains of my reservation. "Your mouth."

"Thank fuck." He groans. "I've been dying to taste *all* of you."

Jason hooks me at the waist and lifts me off the ground. He crosses the short space to the bed to place me on the edge. When he drops to his knees, his eyes dark, his kiss-bruised lips twist in a grin as he spreads my legs.

I bite back a moan when he glides his hands over my thighs. His fingers hook into my underwear, and without effort, he tugs them over my hips and tosses them aside.

"You look good enough to eat." Jason pulls me to the edge of the bed. His hot breath caresses my pussy.

I hold my breath, and his tongue darts out.

His dark eyes fix on mine the moment he presses it to my aching center.

"Fuck me." I grab a fistful of his hair as he delves deep, tasting all of me.

"I intend to." He growls into my slick pussy, then returns all of his attention to it.

My head drops onto the bed, one hand tangling in his hair while the other grasps the blanket by my hip. I drown in sensation as he draws his tongue up and down, teasing with every stroke. My hips buck as he pulls my clit into his mouth, sucking with firm but gentle pressure.

I might explode if he keeps this up.

When he slides two fingers inside me, a guttural moan rips free. He strokes deeper, matching the rhythm of my hips with his mouth, creating an unrelenting, cresting pleasure. It spirals higher and higher, leading me to a peak I could never reach with a vibrator.

Nothing will match this. Ever. My hold on him tightens as my body spins toward release.

His tongue flicks over my clit, back and forth, as he finger fucks me. Whatever thoughts I had fly away in the summer night as my orgasm takes hold. Fireworks flash behind my lids. I pinch my eyes closed and ride the wave of pleasure. I pulse around his fingers, pulling him deeper, wanting more. He presses gentle kisses to my pussy as I slowly come down from my high.

When I finally open my eyes, I'm limp on the blankets, staring at an amused Jason Hunt, his grin glistening with the evidence of my climax. He wipes his mouth with the back of his hand and rises to his feet.

Jason readjusts the front of his jeans, and I see the hard ridge of his cock nestled beneath the denim.

"Holy shit," I manage to say as he pulls his shirt off and tosses it aside, revealing the solid abs of a man dedicated to his physique for the sake of his craft. "How are you real?"

He laughs. "I was wondering the same about you."

Heat creeps into my cheeks, and I manage to sit up. He pulls me to my feet. My hand rests on his warm, solid chest. I swallow a curse of surprise when he doesn't disappear.

Jason tugs my shirt. "Take this off. I want to see what you're hiding."

I unbutton my collar and pull the striped top over my head. His hand rests on my rib cage. He teases the curve of my breast with his thumb.

"Fuck, you're smart and gorgeous." He bites his lip. "That's a heady combination."

My fingers trail and rest at his belt. "Still too many clothes."

He unfastens my skirt zipper while I pull his belt free. We scramble to undress, him grasping at my clothing, me pushing at his. Panting and desperate, we somehow get our clothes off in a flurry of flailing limbs and heated kisses. His hands roam across my bare skin, tracing my hips, up to cup my breasts.

His cock brushes my thigh as he pulls me down to him.

Sprawled out on the center of the bed, he settles me against his chest and kisses me hard. I wrap myself around him, savoring the press of his naked body to mine.

I love this. Skin to skin. Heat and need exchanging between us like the steady beat of my heart pressed to his.

"Take what you want, sweetheart." He grins against my mouth. "I'm all yours."

I wiggle my hips, enjoying the press of his hard cock on my stomach. My hand wraps around it, and he hisses in a breath as his eyes drift closed. He's hard and thick in my hand. I stroke him twice, earning a guttural groan from deep inside his chest.

"Protection?"

"Fuck." His eyes fly open.

"Don't worry." I climb off the bed and retrieve my purse. From inside, I grab a condom and hold it up between two fingers. "I'm always prepared."

His brow arches. "I thought…never mind."

"I always carry them." I climb back on top of him and tear open the packet. His body tenses as I slide the condom over his cock. He closes his eyes when I cup his sack.

The moment I position him at my entrance, his eyes fly open. He watches as I take him deep, easing down on his cock, filling myself until I'm fully seated.

"Fuck, you're big." I readjust, shifting and sliding over him.

"You feel so fucking good." His hands grasp my hips, holding me steady. "Just give me a minute…"

I go still. "Too much for you?"

"It's…been a while."

My heart stops at his unfiltered confession. "Do you want me to…" I try to move, but he holds me firmly in place.

"Just…hold still."

Careful not to shift my hips, I lean down and kiss him softly.

"It's okay. We have all night."

He wraps his arms around my waist and rotates us, pinning me to the bed beneath him. His hips drive into mine. I savor the burst of sensation at his thrust. My legs lock around his back. My fingers dig into his shoulders. He kisses me as he fucks me, hard and fast. I'm still riding the high from the orgasm he gave me with his wicked mouth and talented fingers as he drives his cock deeper.

When he comes, I cling tight to him, savoring the power I have over his pleasure.

He buries his face in my neck. "I…I'm sorry."

"Why are you sorry?" I ask, smoothing his hair.

"I didn't let you finish."

"You can make it up to me next time," I whisper in his ear.

He draws back and smiles at me. "Next time?"

I shrug. "Mind if I shower?"

"Can I join you?" he asks, slowly sliding his cock free.

"Of course." I cup his cheek and kiss him, letting the moment linger. "Let me take care of something first."

When I manage to climb from the bed, I make my way to the bathroom, careful to hide the grin on my lips.

CHAPTER SIX

Holy shit. I close the bathroom door. Did that just happen? I clap my hand over my mouth and catch my own stunned expression in the mirror.

My whole body is flushed, rosy and pink. I admire the shades of color and snort when the red in my face burns brighter at the reminder of what just happened.

I never do things like this. *Ever.* What the hell am I thinking?

It's insanely obvious. I'm not thinking.

I try to be rational, but being near him, seeing the man beneath the celebrity has my brain short-circuiting.

No one will believe me, but there's no going back on it now.

Not that it matters. I'm fully committed to this decision. A laugh escapes me. I straighten and take a deep breath. Until morning, Jason Hunt is *mine.*

With little elegance, I use the toilet and wash before turning on the shower. Warm spray fills the air with steam, fogging the mirror. Stealing a moment of solitude before Jason joins me, I step into the tub and let the hot water revitalize me.

There's barely enough room for me in here, let alone him. But I can't stop my growing anticipation from crowding out the logistics. My body is humming.

I wash with a sweet-smelling soap supplied by the hotel, wishing I had my own on hand. It's back in my room, along with Ginger. Guilt floods me. I should have given her and Beth more details, but I didn't want them to freak out. They know I'm with someone, but I didn't tell them who. Guess it won't be a secret in the morning after they bombard me with questions.

Tomorrow, he'll go his way and I'll go mine.

Shaking the thought free, I dip my head under the spray and let the nagging concerns wash down the drain. Beyond the shower curtain, the door opens, and a broad shadow steps into view.

"Any room for me?" Jason asks, peering around the edge of the fabric curtain.

"Not much, but we can make it work."

I rinse the soap off as he steps into the tub. His broad shoulders fill the width.

It's tight, and we get cozy beneath the water's gentle spray. I switch positions, allowing him to step under the warm jet.

His blue eyes darken as he watches me lean against the far wall. I've seen him damn near naked in his films, but nothing has prepared me for the sight of him bare and soaking wet, just out of arm's reach.

"You're too far away." He stretches his arm out with an open hand. "Come here."

I take his hand, and he pulls me against him. Warm water sluices over both of us as he nuzzles his face in the crook of my neck.

Gripping his forearms, I lean into him and brace myself. I might melt into a puddle and slide down the drain if I stay here too long.

He makes me feel warm, safe, wanted.

How can I have such a feeling with someone I literally just met? It defies logic.

"This is crazy," I murmur when he tips my chin up.

"What is?"

"This." My heart beats faster. "Us."

"What's crazy about it?"

"We just met. You're…well, *you*." I drop my gaze to his chest, lost in whirls of dark hair dotted with beads of water. "I'm just me."

"Vicky." The way he says my name, so soft, makes my breath catch. I meet his heated gaze, and the temperature of the room seems to increase ten degrees. "You're lovely and funny. Meeting you is worth being exposed on social media."

"Don't tease me. I still feel bad about that." I nudge him, but he holds me tight.

"I'm not teasing you, and you have no reason to feel bad." He smiles, and my heart constricts at how handsome he is. "It was my dumb fault for thinking I could cosplay as my own character at a comic convention and *not* be recognized."

"It was a really good cosplay." I return the smile, and the tension between us shifts to something more intimate.

"I'm sure you could make it better." He runs a hand over my shoulder, and I shiver. "That's what you do, isn't it?"

"Make things better?" I blink up at him, distracted by the press of his naked body against me, the delicate caress of his fingertips tracing my collarbone.

He chuckles. "Well, that…but I was talking about costume design."

"Oh, yeah." Good thing it's warm in here. The steam and heat of the shower hide my embarrassed flush.

"I believe I owe you an orgasm." Jason grins and slides his fingers between my breasts, drifting lower, shifting slightly to cup my pussy with his warm hand. The heel of his palm grinds against my clit as he dips his fingers inside me.

My grip on his arms tightens, and I'm afraid my nails will leave indentations in his skin. He spins me around, pulling me flush to him, his fingertips playing along the seam of my pussy.

He nudges my thighs apart. "Open for me, baby."

I prop my foot on the edge of the tub, praying I don't slip and kill the mood with an untimely demise. His satisfied groan caresses my cheek as he slides in two fingers, deep, curling them against my G-spot. The gentle pressure of his thumb against my clit makes me whimper.

I bite my lip to keep quiet.

"I want to hear every moan." He fucks me slowly with those wicked fingers. "I want to hear my name from your lips when you come."

His cock rubs my ass as he thrusts, meeting the motion of his fingers with the gyration of his hips. I collapse into him, praying he holds me up. I'm like sugar in the summer rain, melting into a puddle of sticky sweet delight.

Every time the sensation starts to peak, he shifts his fingers and slows to a decadent slide against the most sensitive areas.

After five minutes, I'm squirming in his hold.

"Please, Jason..." I gasp, feeling pressure build. "I'm close...so...close."

"Do you want to come, baby?"

"God, yes." I moan as he adds another finger, stretching me wider, driving deeper.

The hand resting on my hip moves to my neck. The gentle but steady pressure of his hand at the base of my throat sends my arousal through the roof.

"Come for me, Vicky." He growls in my ear as he curls his fingers, adding pressure to satisfy the orgasmic gods.

I buck against his hold as it washes over me in waves of pleasure. He holds me tighter with every pulse. I've never come this hard on my own, let alone with a partner. Fuck—it's like he knew exactly what I need to reach that peak.

The pressure of his hold eases, but he cradles me beneath the lukewarm spray of water as I regain my composure.

"That was fucking hot," he murmurs into my ear with a tender kiss on my cheek.

I turn and grin. "Yeah, it was."

He kisses me, sliding his tongue across my lips before delving between them and stealing my breath. The kiss is unhurried and lingering. I groan with disappointment when he pulls away.

"I'll let you rinse off." He kisses the tip of my nose. "Are you hungry?"

"A little."

"I'll order something." He grins and steps out of the tub, leaving me alone. "Anything particular?"

"Whatever. I'm flexible."

"Got it." He closes the curtain.

I stare at his shadow as he dries off, and a million questions race through my mind. What happens after tonight? Is this a one-night stand or are we friends now? What if I want more? I bite my lip as thoughts snowball in my mind.

"Hey, Jason?"

"Yeah?" he says from the other side of the fabric.

The questions die on my lips. "Pizza would be fantastic."

He peers around the curtain and grins. "Pizza sounds great."

Once he disappears from the bathroom, I lean my head on the shower wall. What the hell am I thinking? I'm not built for one-night stands. My heart can't take it.

I like him. A lot. But this isn't meant to be anything. It's just fun.

Right?

By the time I finish in the shower and dry off, I'm more composed, but worry has burrowed into my brain and refuses to let go.

When I step into the room, the scent of melted cheese and pepperoni hits me. My stomach growls.

Jason's wearing a pair of shorts slung low on his hips and no shirt. He tosses me one of his shirts. His gaze rakes over me as I remove the towel and button his shirt over my naked breasts.

"Looks good on you." He offers me some pizza, and I collapse on the bed beside him, taking it with glee.

"Thanks." I devour the slice and two more after.

We eat in relative silence, pushing away the empty box once we've had our fill.

"That was amazing."

He opens his arm and invites me to curl against him. I nestle into his chest and sigh with contentment. This is nice. It's more than nice. The simmer of worry rises to the surface, but I stuff it down as he turns on the television.

The gentle caress of his hand on my shoulder lulls me into a peaceful doze. Between the sex and the pizza, I'm sated, and sleep crashes over me in an unexpected rush, the television droning in the background.

When I finally wake, there's a steady stream of light coming through the window. I sit up and look around.

The room is empty except for my discarded clothes and a note on his pillow.

I'm sorry I left without saying goodbye. I had an early flight and you needed to rest. Here's my number. Thanks for everything. – Jason

His phone number stares at me from the small square of paper. Should I text him? Call him?

With a sigh, I retrieve my phone to find thirty missed texts. *Shit.* It's nearly nine thirty! Ginger and Beth must be out of their minds. We're supposed to go to the convention at ten.

I jump out of bed and pull on yesterday's clothes. Then I cradle the shirt he let me borrow against my chest as I bolt from his hotel room to the elevator.

They will demand answers. I run through dozens of scenarios in my head before I reach my floor. By the time I stop outside our shared hotel room, I know I can't tell the truth.

I can't tell anyone.

I hold his shirt close and inhale his lingering scent.

This was *our* night together. *Our* secret.

The moment I open the hotel door, questions come fast and furious.

CHAPTER SEVEN

"What the hell happened to you?" Ginger eyes me the moment I walk in the door. "We were worried."

I tuck the shirt under my arm, trying not to look suspicious, although I feel guilty as hell for not telling them where I was or who I was with. I shouldn't feel bad; I should feel absolutely amazing after last night. The details lay hidden in the back of my mind, a secret tucked away for only me.

Before I respond, Beth pops her head around the corner and narrows her eyes. "Someone got *lucky*."

Warmth stains my cheeks, and I duck my head as I push past Ginger, heading for my suitcase tucked against the wall.

"Your silence speaks louder than the glow on your face." Ginger comes beside me as I tuck his shirt into the bottom of my suitcase and pull out some fresh clothes.

"Who was he?" Beth leans on the doorway leading to the bathroom. "Someone you met at the con yesterday?"

I bite the inside of my cheek. I can't lie to them, but I can't tell them the truth. While this is the first time I've officially met Beth and Ginger in person, I know them. We've talked endlessly online, shared secrets and hopes and dreams. They're my fandom family.

I can trust them, can't I?

Ginger sighs and slumps onto the bed. "If you won't tell us *who*, will you at least tell us what happened? I mean, you vanished after dinner. We were worried someone snatched you."

"Yeah…I mean, the text was appreciated, but how the hell

are we supposed to come to your rescue if you don't give us deets, girl?" Beth tosses her brush to the bed.

"You had my location. I didn't leave the hotel." I smooth my fingers over my cotton blouse, unable to meet their curious stares.

"So he was staying *here*?" Beth arches her brow.

"Yeah."

Ginger thoughtfully rubs a hand over her jaw before jumping to her feet. "Shit—what time is it?"

"Nine forty-five," Beth says. "We're supposed to meet the rest of the girls in the lobby at ten before we head over."

"My panel starts at eleven." Ginger squares her shoulders. "John Martigan will get a piece of my mind today."

Beth whistles low. "Don't go crazy. They'll kick you out and ban you from conventions for life. You don't want to be on *that* no-fly list."

I breathe easy as the conversation shifts away from my night toward the events scheduled for the day.

It's hard to keep my night a secret. I want to scream it from the roof of the hotel, but I promised myself I wouldn't.

"Well, after your stunt yesterday with that guard, I'm surprised you weren't put on that list." Ginger rests a hand on her hip. "If you cross him today, he'll kick your ass out for good."

"I'd like to see him fucking try." Beth crosses her arms. "Grumpy asshole. They shouldn't let miserable people work conventions. It's supposed to be a happy place."

"If you guys want, head down. I'm going to get ready."

"We'll wait for you, if you want." Ginger reaches for her bag.

"No, go ahead. I'll be down in ten."

"Okay." Ginger pulls the strap over her shoulder. "I'm gonna grab a coffee from the lobby café. You want anything?"

"Caramel latte sounds great."

"You got it." Ginger grabs Beth's sleeve.

"I'm coming." Beth tugs her skirt and drapes a badge around her neck. Her cute costume is loosely based on a science fiction series—she reimagined one of the villains as a sexy showgirl. The dress looks amazing, but my passion for costuming and design is dimmed by the heaviness settling around my shoulders.

The two women continue their discussion as they exit the room, leaving me alone to dress. Once the door clicks shut behind them, I collapse on the bed. I don't know if I can go today.

"No, you're here. You're going," I tell myself out loud. "Get dressed and get moving."

Somehow I manage to change into clean clothes and wrangle my hair into a braid over my shoulder. Ten minutes later, I've applied light makeup and restocked my cosplay medic kit. I tuck both phones into my purse and take a deep breath.

"It was one amazing night. That's it." I exhale to clear my mind. "Let it go and move on."

But I can't. Jason Hunt has branded me. Ruined me.

Fuck.

The rest of the convention passes in a blur. Ginger somehow managed to single-handedly disrupt the *Space Vendetta* panel and piss off director John Martigan. Beth got into an altercation with one of the guards and has been permanently banned from future conventions in Philly. Between the drama caused by those two and Jen's abrupt disappearance, I didn't have time to dwell on Jason.

There was no sign of him all day. Of course there wasn't. He was all over social media—Jason Hunt dressed in cosplay as the character he plays in *Throne of Ashes.* Hell, he was trending.

#TheCosplayer led every social media outlet for a week.

It was weird seeing my face all over the place, but no one paid me any attention. Everyone was focused on him.

There are comments. Hateful, hurtful, spiteful comments. I ignore them.

Or try to ignore them, at least. The longer the discourse lasts, the more toxic the environment becomes. I could feel myself being pulled into an endless void of negativity. Finally, after the second week, I take a hiatus from all social media. It feels good to unplug for a while. I don't have time for it. I have a life to get back to. I have work to do.

When I show up at the warehouse to prepare for the next show, my heart stops at an eight-by-eleven photo tacked to the bulletin board in the break room. The photo that started a scandal. Jason as the Forgotten Knight, his arm wrapped around me.

Seeing it again—taking up such space—twists the guilt and longing in my heart. Memories rush back to me, and my heart pounds. I miss him. My hand clenches around my phone. I want to text him, but I can't. I won't.

No. We had an agreement. It was one night. Nothing more. Jason Hunt is the next big action star. There's no room for me in his future. I have my own dreams, my own goals. It was fun while it lasted, but it's over.

I want to tear the photo down, but my coworkers burst into the room and all hell breaks loose.

Of course they have a million questions. I do my best to answer as plainly as I can without giving any hint to there being something more than a fan encounter at a convention. They seem pacified by my responses, but the whole encounter leaves me hollow.

I sneak to the bathroom and pull up his official Instagram

account. Ignoring the fifteen hundred notifications of my own, I click the link and his smile fills my screen.

It's not a true smile. I've glimpsed the Jason behind the curtain, and this is Jason Hunt, the actor, not Jason Hunt the fanboy. Not the man who kissed me like I was the last woman on the planet. The man who took my pleasure as his own personal mission.

Where are you? What are you doing right now? I sigh.

Swallowing my rising frustration, I close the app and pocket my phone. I can't keep doing this. Pining over a one-night stand, a man I can never have. It's unhealthy…and unrealistic.

With a big production coming in three months, I have my work cut out for me. There's a lot to be done, and I can't waste any time on fangirl fantasies. It's back to reality.

No matter how much it hurts.

My phone pings. I unlock it to find a message from Ginger.

(Ginger): Chicago just dropped their lineup. You're never gonna believe who they got.

My grip tightens on the phone. My breath catches.

Heart pounding, I watch three dots play on the screen. I know what she's going to say before she even hits send.

An image pops up. I read it aloud. "Now attending Chicago Comic Fandimonium, Jason Hunt." My voice drifts off as I scan the information beneath his name. It's in two months.

I bite my lip when another message comes through.

(Ginger): Are you going?

I wasn't planning on it, but this changes things. He doesn't do appearances like this. Ever. Why the sudden change of heart?

(Me): Let me think about it.

(Ginger): Okay. I'm there if you need me.

Her reply warms my heart.

I open my saved numbers, and my finger hovers over his

name for a half a second before reality sets in.

No. I'm not going to go off half-cocked. If I'm going to the convention, I'm doing it for me. Not him.

After locking the screen, I tuck the phone into my pocket and return to my chaotic workspace.

Inspiration strikes, and I grab my sketchbook.

Two months is more than enough time to make the *perfect* cosplay.

CHAPTER EIGHT

Two months of pure torment pass in a flash.

Chicago Comic Fandimonium is this weekend, and I'm freaking out. My cosplay looks amazing. My cosplay medic bag is packed and ready to rock. My pass is good for Saturday and Sunday.

Tomorrow. I take a deep breath.

Standing outside the hotel, I start hyperventilating. *What if he doesn't want to see me? What if this is a huge mistake? I'm going to look like an idiot.*

I should've texted him. For the last two and a half months, I've thought about texting him every single day. But whenever I pick up my phone, I panic and talk myself out of it. He doesn't need me bothering him. Not with how busy his shooting schedule is. It's better this way.

At least I think it is. I mean, until I see him on the floor tomorrow, surrounded by fans.

Will he even remember me?

I'm two seconds from talking myself out of it when I hear a familiar voice. "Vicky!"

Heart racing, I turn to see Ginger rushing toward me. She wraps her arms around me in a huge hug.

"Oh my god! You made it." She holds me at arm's length and beams. "I'm so glad. You look amazing."

"Me?" I laugh. "Look at you. You're practically glowing."

"Oh, girl, you're never going to believe what's happened. It's insane." Ginger hooks her arm through mine and pulls me into the hotel. "Let's check in. I'll tell you all about it over dinner."

I set my bags down at the front desk and ring the bell. "I can't wait."

"I can't wait to see your cosplay." She squeals and bounces on her toes, making her wavy hair shimmer like an auburn waterfall. "Tomorrow is going to be epic."

"Yeah," I murmur under my breath. Thankfully, the receptionist shows up to check us in.

The evening is a whirlwind of activity. Ginger and I deposit our bags in our room, then head for the hotel restaurant. I'm starving. For some reason, I forget to eat when I travel, and that's never a good thing. Not only that, it's made me a lightweight.

I sip my second cocktail, and I'm feeling it…hard. My head is fuzzy. I'm more relaxed than I should be, considering tomorrow is the freaking convention. Where is my food?

"Did you bring your cosplay medic kit?" Ginger asks, picking at the small basket of chips in the center of the table.

"Yeah. I never come to a convention without it." I nibble on a chip and sip my water, ignoring the tempting, delicious cocktail. "You wouldn't believe how many people come to conventions without proper emergency kits."

"You're a damned saint, Vicky." Ginger winks. "Did you post on your socials to let your followers know you're available if they have need of your services?"

"Yeah. I did a whole lead-up to convention week with a series of posts dedicated to cosplay basics and what-to-do scenarios."

"You're so good at that stuff."

"Thanks." I shift at the compliment, but it doesn't make me uncomfortable. Pride fills me at her words.

"Did you ever hear from him again?" Ginger asks, her voice

low.

"Who?" I blink at her a moment until it hits me. "Ohh…Jason Hunt?" I shake my head. "No, I mean…after we spent the night together, I hoped he would call, but…" My voice drifts off.

"I still can't believe you hooked up with Jason fucking Hunt." Ginger's attention fixes on me with the intensity of a laser harnessed velociraptor. Green eyes wide, she keeps her voice steady. "And you didn't trust us enough to tell us the next morning."

"Yes, well." I scoot my chair closer and clear my throat. "It just kind of…happened. I promised him I wouldn't tell anyone. It was a one-night thing. I didn't anticipate it even getting this far."

"Holy shit, Vicky!" Ginger downs the rest of her lemon drop martini and motions for another to a passing waiter, then she's back on me like a mountain lion scenting prey. "You'd better give me the whole story this time."

The liquor makes me bold. If I'm spilling my story, I'm also pulling the thread on hers.

"Fine." I cross my arms and pin her with my best no-bullshit stare. "But only if you tell me what happened at the panel in Philly and what happened after security escorted you from the *Space Vendetta* panel."

"I wasn't the *only* one who got in trouble at the Philly convention." She smirks. "But Beth isn't here to defend herself, so I guess it's only fair to leave her story for another day."

"Oh, Beth will get a call as soon as we get back to our room, but right now, I want to know what happened with the director after the panel."

"He was acting like a dick. I called him out on it." Ginger lifts her drink in salute. "Simple."

"Uh-huh."

"You first though."

Mischief dances in her eyes, and I sigh.

"Fine." I recap the events at the Philly con when Ginger and the rest of the fangirls were absent. It's hard to keep excitement from creeping into my voice as I talk about my sexy, steamy night with Jason. Just the thought of our evening together has me warm and tingling.

We take a break to eat, but soon I'm back to the story, and as I tell it, something unravels inside me. A longing I can't explain, a regret I can't quite place.

"So when you told me he was going to make an appearance in Chicago, I almost said no."

"Why the hell would you say *no*?" Ginger blinks in confusion. "Doesn't sound like he was done with you, sweetie."

"It doesn't?"

"Hell no." She snags the last French fry off her plate. "Why didn't you call him?"

"He was shooting the new season. I couldn't—"

"Let *him* decide that." Ginger sighs. "Listen. He gave you his number. That's an invitation if I ever heard one."

"Yeah, but—"

"But nothing." Ginger pushes her plate aside. "He was into you. You were into him. I fail to see a problem."

"What if it was a mistake? He's probably forgotten all about me." I try to play it off, but this conversation has my heart twisting and dinner churning in my gut.

"Text him." She points to my phone. "Right now. Tell him you're in Chicago and you want to see him."

I unlock the phone and pull up his contact information. I've done this a million times.

"Do it." Ginger leans forward, her gaze intent. When her

phone rings, she startles and jumps back. A smile brightens her face as she reads the screen. "Be right back. I have to take this."

She bounds out of the restaurant to answer the call.

That's definitely suspicious. I make a mental note to ask her about it once we get back to the room, but right now, I can't stop nervous butterflies from swarming in the pit of my gut.

I can do this. It's a text. No big deal.

With a deep breath, I type out a quick message. Erase it. Type another one. It takes me ten tries before I'm happy. I check it one more time for errors.

My finger hovers over the send button.

I press it, and off it goes into the vast interweb void.

(Me): Hey Jason. It's Vicky. I'm in Chicago. See you at the con tomorrow.

My bubble fills the screen with the sent time. It shifts to *Read.* Panic surfaces.

There are no dots. No sign of response. Only receipt.

My hands get clammy. I set the phone aside and pick up my drink.

"Sorry about that." Ginger returns to the table. She's fucking glowing.

"Who was it?" I ask, hiding a grin behind my glass.

"Oh…a work thing." She waves her hand.

"Your job makes you glow like a firecracker on the Fourth of July?" I tease, and she turns three shades of red.

"You remember how I got kicked out of the convention in Philly?" She bites her lip and scrunches her nose. "Well…"

I sit back in disbelief as I listen to her story. How the hell did I not know any of this?

Then I remember. I had kept Jason Hunt from her. I'm sure there are all kinds of secrets and stories to uncover after two months apart.

By the time we retire to our room, it's well after midnight. Ginger takes a quick shower as I lay out my cosplay. Staring at the vibrant crimson velvet and gilded stitching along the floor-length bell sleeves, I picture the actress playing the high priestess in the medieval series. The character I've shipped with Jason's character since the series started. The characters I've written copious amounts of smut about and posted on fan fiction websites.

The same stories Jason admitted to reading…and enjoying.

No one would know the connection.

No one but *him*.

I glance at my phone. Still no response. Fuck.

Maybe this is a bad idea. There's still time to go home. No reason to show my face tomorrow and have my heart crushed.

Ginger comes out, and I retreat to the steamy bathroom, ignoring the memories it brings to the surface and the nagging regret tugging at my brain.

It was one night. Nothing more.

CHAPTER NINE

The moment I walk through the convention doors, I'm drawn into that world again. Excitement pulses through me like an energy beam…a lightning current humming through my veins. I can't tell if it's because I'm at a convention—the first time since Philly—or if it's the anticipation of seeing him again, even from a distance.

I compulsively check my phone every five minutes to make sure I haven't missed a text. It looks odd and out of place with the cosplay I've created, so I tuck it into my leather bag with my sewing supplies.

"The Crimson Priestess!" someone shouts from across the room.

I pull up short and grasp Ginger's sleeve. She stands steadfast beside me as a few fans rush toward us, their cosplays easily recognizable from a popular anime series my brother adores.

"Oh my god! You look *just* like her," one of the younger girls says, her eyes wide. "Did you make it?"

"I did." With a little flourish, I spin around, letting the skirt flounce around my legs.

The three girls simper at the movement, their eyes glittering. If heart eyes were a real thing, they'd have them. I blush under their admiration.

"I could never make something so intricate." The tall one with black hair reaches out to touch my sleeve. "You've got mad skills, girl. You should be, like, a costume designer or something."

"Actually, I am." I laugh when they gasp.

"Seriously?" they ask in unison.

"Seriously. I work for a theater in Boston. My job is to design and sew costumes for the productions we put on there."

"Well, you're freaking amazing!" the youngest one says. "Can we get our picture with you?"

"Sure."

Without missing a beat, Ginger snatches their phones and takes a series of pictures of me with the three eager fans. We chat a bit longer, and I give them my card in case they have a cosplay emergency. Their enthusiasm reminds me why I do this, why I come to the conventions and carry my kit. Why I design my own costumes.

I fucking *love* helping people find their own passion in fandom.

The girls wave as they venture into the growing crowd. It's getting close to noon, and the photo ops will be opening for those who bought passes. To my right, I see a sign directing traffic to the photo staging areas and the autograph booths.

"Cheer up." Ginger nudges me. "Somewhere beyond those curtains is your Forgotten Knight."

"Yeah, but I don't think I'll have a chance to see him." I resist the urge to reach into my bag and pull out my phone. *No.* He's had his opportunity to text me, to set a time for us to meet.

"He hasn't texted you back?" Ginger asks, her green eyes sympathetic.

"No." I bite my lip. "Maybe this was just a one-night thing."

"He left his number." My friend takes me by the arm. "That's not something someone does after a one-night stand."

"It's been months. Maybe he found someone else."

"That could be." She nods. "Or he's been busy filming. I've

heard their schedules are horrific. They have to do research and training beforehand, then they're required to do all the marketing and interviews."

"I know." Inside, a twist of uncertainty plunges into my brain and impostor syndrome takes root. "It's just…I don't know. Am I crazy to think there might be something between us?"

"First of all…" Ginger stops me and takes ahold of my shoulders. "You're not crazy. And second, he's an idiot if he lets you get away."

"But—"

"Vicky, listen to me." She sighs and her gaze softens. "You are fucking amazing and incredibly talented. Any man would be *lucky* to have you in his life. If he doesn't see that, he's a total fucking moron and you're better off without him." A smile curves her lips. "Trust me, you dodged a bullet. These Hollywood types are nothing but drama."

"But aren't you…?" I drift off at the pointed look she gives me and clear my throat.

"We're not talking about me. This trip is about *you* reuniting with your long-lost knight in shining armor."

"More like tarnished tin." I chuckle as we start walking again.

"Exactly." She waves her hand. "No more talk of him. Let's grab a snack and make the rounds. I saw some amazing fan art, and I want to see if they have any *Space Vendetta* goodies."

As we wander through the artist galleries, Ginger points out the awesome pieces, and slowly I'm pulled into a familiar mental place. The thrumming heartbeat of the convention surrounds me, and I remember why I come.

These are my people. This is my tribe. When I'm here, I'm home.

There's something missing though. It's not Philly. A once in a lifetime adventure, when a group of fangirls meet in person for the first time to indulge in a wild weekend of revelry. We all found something special that weekend. While Chicago is fun and being with Ginger is a blast, I miss the other fangirls. I miss the camaraderie.

I miss *him*.

While we meander through the crowd, I spy familiar faces and amazing cosplays. There are a few people who flag me down after recognizing me from my blogs and social media. I patch them up and get them back on their way. They gush over my cosplay, and I'm once again reminded *why* I came in this dress.

My gaze drifts to the curtained area where visiting celebrities are signing autographs and taking photos with fans.

Ginger leans close. "Want to take a peek? We can always just walk around. There's no rule against looking."

"You sure?"

"We've got all day tomorrow too. Let's go." She takes me by the hand and drags me to the designated area.

Giggling and pointing, we walk down narrow paths for curious onlookers. There are quite a few celebs I recognize. Several of them are from *Throne of Ashes* and *Space Vendetta.*

"The other girls would *love* this," I murmur.

"They would," Ginger agrees. "I tried to invite them, but they were all busy."

"I mean, we all have lives outside of fandom," I point out with a solemn nod. "It's not like we can live the fantasy every day."

"Can't we?" Ginger grins as we round a corner.

I stop when I see his name in oversized letters above the booth. There's a line of fans at least fifty deep, winding through a cattle chute to his table. From this angle, I can't see him, but he's there. I know he is. I can make out the dark heads of the bodyguards standing around his booth.

My hand grips Ginger's arm, nails biting into her skin. She rests her hand over mine.

"It's okay. Let's get a closer look." She walks toward his booth, dragging me by the hand.

Deep in my chest, my heart is pounding. My mouth is dry. I can't draw enough breath.

Maybe this is a bad idea. What if he sees me? What if he *ignores* me?

I pinch my eyes closed and take several deep, steadying breaths.

"What the hell am I doing?" I mutter as she pulls me to the right and stops.

"There." Satisfied, she places me in front of her.

He looks as handsome as he did at the bar in Philly. Every memory of our stolen night together comes to me in a rush.

Jason glances at the fan on the other side of the table. He hands a photo to her and smiles. My fucking heart stops beating. *That smile.* I know what it feels like to have it trained on me. It's fucking intoxicating. It's like I'm the only woman in the world.

My cheeks heat, and I can't quite close my mouth.

Am I panting? Am I having a heart attack?

No, a panic attack.

Ginger nudges me forward. I stumble a few steps before catching myself and straighten quickly.

Jason's attention shifts from the gushing fan to me. His eyes darken. His smile drops.

Shit. He doesn't want to see me. Fuck. Everything stops moving as he motions the nearest bodyguard to come closer.

"Let's go." I turn, snatch Ginger by the wrist, and dart into the crowd of people.

"Why?" she whines, stumbling behind me. "What the fuck happened?"

I don't stop until we reach the artist gallery again. There are twice as many people here, and I feel the anonymity of the crowd slowly surround me, protecting me.

"Vicky!"

Ginger pulls me close, her gaze boring into mine. I'm on the verge of tears, but I manage to find stability in her presence.

"Girl, what the hell happened back there?"

"He doesn't want to see me." I choke on the words. "This is a mistake."

"What are you talking about? He didn't see you."

"Oh, he saw me all right." The brief flash of his intensity left me burning with shame. "I shouldn't have worn this. I shouldn't have come." Panic infuses me again, and I fan my face to chase embarrassment away.

"Whoa, girl. Back that train up." Ginger shakes her head. "You look like you're going to pass out."

"I might." Panic grabs me by the throat.

"Wait here. I'll get you some water. Don't move." Ginger disappears into the crowd.

I lean against a concrete wall, careful to stay out of the way. Maybe I should just leave.

"Miss?" A deep voice echoes behind me.

Startled, I turn to find two tall, broad men wearing black polo shirts and earpieces. Security guards.

Fuck.

"Yes?" I reply innocently, my gaze searching the crowd for Ginger.

"We're going to need you to come with us."

Fear settles in the pit of my gut. "What's wrong?"

"Just come."

I bite my lip and point into the crowd where I watched Ginger disappear. "But my friend…"

"We'll let her know," the dark-haired man says, his expression serious. "You need to come with us now."

"O-okay," I stutter.

I fall into step ahead of him, and he murmurs something into his headset. With every step, I can't help but feel like I'm walking to my own execution…like the Crimson Priestess in *Throne of Ashes.*

Banishment from a fandom convention is the same thing, isn't it? A type of death.

I lift my head high and turn toward the entrance. If they're going to kick me out, I'm leaving on my own terms, not theirs.

A firm grip on my elbow brings me to a stop.

"Not that way, miss." The man gestures to a narrow hallway. "This way."

I blink at him, unable to speak. Before I realize it, I'm halfway down the hall and in the middle of a full-blown panic attack.

Shit.

CHAPTER TEN

Where the hell are they taking me? A riot of nerves in my stomach explodes into a five-alarm fire in a house full of hornets.

Am I under arrest? Did I do something illegal?

Oh god, what if they called the FBI and I'm about to find out what happens when they check your search history? I stifle a sob with a gasp at the realization—they'll never believe it was research or just straight-up curiosity. I'm one hundred percent fucked now.

We turn the corner, and I see signs pointing to VIP lounges. I blink twice as we pass two open doors before stopping at a closed door. What in the hell?

The man leading the way knocks twice before looking at me. "Inside."

Before I can respond, the two men disappear down the hall. My mouth is halfway open to call after them when the door swings wide.

"Come in," an unfamiliar voice drifts out of the room.

I step over the threshold, expecting to find five men in black suits with guns trained on me. Somewhere deep inside, I know I'm overreacting, but with the way my heart is beating, you'd think I'd been arrested for a felony.

A tall thin man in a gray pinstripe suit turns, hands in his pockets, and assesses me for a long moment. His gaze narrows as he takes in my costume from head to toe.

"You made this yourself?"

I nod, unsure who this man is or what he wants with me.

"Impressive." He strokes his jaw and sighs before smiling. "He said you're talented, but he forgot to mention how lovely you are."

The wheels in my brain aren't clicking into gear, and I'm spinning in confusion. "Wait? Who are you?"

"Archer Donfeld." He extends his hand and I shake it. "I'm Jason Hunt's agent."

My arm freezes midshake. Before I can extract it, he releases me.

"Am I in trouble?"

He laughs, which lightens the mood but doesn't quell the swirling anxiety coursing through my body.

"No, Vicky, you're not in trouble." He rakes his fingers through his hair. "Although you *did* cause quite a mess with your social media post."

"It was a complete misunderstanding…I didn't know—"

Archer holds up a hand. "I get it, and I've placed the blame fully on Jason for even considering such a crazy stunt…like his fans wouldn't recognize him in his own damned costume." He huffs, as though the whole situation is more irritation than problem. "He wouldn't believe me, but now he knows he can't go around half-cocked and expect no one to notice."

"It's hard *not* to notice him," I say, unable to keep from smiling.

"That's true." Archer assesses me for another long moment. I shift my weight from foot to foot.

"Why am I here?" I blurt, unable to bear it a moment longer.

"You two make a handsome couple." Archer's smile appears again. "The rising star with a sweet girl next door, who just happens to be a talented artist…and a fan." His eyes sparkle. "That's marketing dynamite right there."

"Wait? What?" I shake my head. "We had a…moment." I redirect the conversation, not sure if the details of our association were clear to anyone else. "But I haven't spoken to him since the Philly convention." Guilt pricks me even though I texted him yesterday. And heard nothing in return. "The phone works both ways."

"You're right." A deep, familiar voice rumbles behind me.

Stunned, I turn to find Jason standing in the doorway. He looks exactly how I remember him from the bar…handsome, untouchable. I take a step back as he enters the room, his gaze fixed on me, filled with hunger I hadn't anticipated. Not after the brief encounter on the signing floor what felt like hours ago.

"Thanks, Arch." Jason turns to his agent, hand extended.

"Jason." Archer shakes it. "She's all yours."

I stare at Jason, dumbfounded, as Archer leaves the room, pulling the door closed behind him. My mouth refuses to cooperate with my brain, and somewhere between the chaos-induced electrical storm in my mind and my tongue, I'm rendered speechless.

"I got your text." His soothing baritone glides over me, and long dormant desire moves to the forefront. "I apologize for not responding."

"It's…" *Okay*, I want to say, but irritation slips in, commandeering my senses. "Understandable." I sniff, maintaining distance between us. "You're a hot commodity right now. I'm sure your schedule is packed. It would be ridiculous for you to put everything on hold to talk to me." Disappointment twists in my chest, making it ache.

"Don't do that, Vicky." He keeps his voice even, soothing my ruffled nerves.

"Don't do what?"

I stand my ground as he closes the distance between us in

two strides.

"Dismiss your own value." His gaze drops to the glass ruby at my throat. "When I saw you in the crowd earlier, I forgot where I was." Those blue eyes lock on mine again, dark as midnight, burning with unspoken need. "I wanted to call you a hundred times, but I...couldn't bring myself to burden you."

"Burden me?" I ask, stunned by his confession. "With what?"

"If they knew..." His brow furrows before he shakes his head.

"Jason, I'm so confused."

He cradles my face in his hands. It's the first time we've touched in months. My skin burns beneath his fingertips, igniting heat through my whole body. I *crave* him with a desperation that terrifies me.

"My fans." He sighs, licking his full lips. "If they knew how much I want you, how much I want to be with you, they—"

Through the haze of desire, I can't help but laugh. The sound seems to confuse him.

"What's funny?"

"You think I don't know about your fans?" I laugh again. "I'm one of your most ardent supporters. I've been in your fandom since your career began. If anyone knows your fans, it's me."

"I...just want to protect you."

"From what? Hateful comments?" I rest my hand on his, still against my cheek. "Where were you when I was in high school?" I chuckle when he grins. "One thing I've learned, haters are always going to exist. If they can't be happy for you—for *us*—that's their problem. Not ours."

"I knew you were as brilliant as you are beautiful."

I lean closer, allowing my body to press into his. "Is this

your way of saying 'I'm an idiot and I should have texted you back'?"

"No." His right hand slides to the back of my neck while the other dips to my waist. "I'm an idiot who put too much thought into what could go wrong. I didn't think about how I could hurt you by not responding. I'm sorry about that."

Every fiber of my being thrums beneath his touch. "I guess we were both idiots."

"What a way to start a relationship, huh?" he asks, his breath brushing my lips.

"Wait." I press my hand to his chest. "Are you—?"

"Serious about you?" Jason nods. "As a heart attack."

I snort-laugh. "You're so corny."

A lopsided smile appears on his handsome face. I'm so smitten.

"Does that mean you're interested?" he asks.

"How the hell are we going to make this work?"

"Well, typically, when two people are interested in each other—"

"You know what I'm asking." I'm still in his embrace, holding his gaze with breathless anticipation.

"We'll figure it out." His fingertips stroke the nape of my neck.

A shiver of need pulses like a lightning strike. Without meaning to, I sway into him and notice the insistent erection pressed against my thigh. "Jason, I—"

His mouth covers mine, and I'm lost in the sensation of his kiss. It pulls me back to that night in Philly. But knowing what I know now, having him here against all odds and expectations, it's like a dam has been released. All the pressure slides away as he pulls me into a tight embrace.

Fuck, I missed this. I missed *him*.

My fingers thread through his hair, gripping tighter than I mean to. His groan echoes in my mouth, and he delves deeper, devouring me like a starved beast.

I arch into him, needing to be close, wanting skin to skin. Whatever restraint I had vanishes. I don't care where I am or who sees us, I just need him inside me.

We're alone and the door is locked…the remaining reservation slips into the void.

"Jason, please…" I pant into his mouth between breaths and frenzied kisses.

His hand slides to my hip and gathers my skirt in a fist, dragging it up until cool air brushes my inner thighs. Whenever I'm in costume, I wear my most comfortable undergarments, but right now, I'd let him shred them just to get his hands on me.

Jason palms my pussy over the fabric and groans when he finds me soaking wet. "Sugar, you're killing me." He licks his lips and pushes the fabric down, leaving me bare. When he rises, his fingertips glide through the evidence of my need. "Have you been walking around like this all day?"

I nod, unable to breathe let alone speak.

"Thinking about me?" He pushes a thick finger inside me.

"Yes," I gasp, rocking into his hand. I need more, damn it, but he's content to tease me into confessing my soul.

"When I saw you clad in crimson velvet, looking like you'd just stepped off the set of *Throne of Ashes…*" His growl reverberates through me. "It took every ounce of strength not to claim you right there in front of everyone."

"Fuck." I moan as he adds another finger, holding me to him, pushing deeper with slow, agile strokes.

"Is that what you want me to do?" He murmurs in my ear. "Make you sit on my lap and show everyone you are *mine.*" The last word comes out in a possessive growl.

My body tightens at the sound, spiraling toward orgasm.

I've heard that voice, that word. It was a line in his show, but the context was different.

This time, it's meant for me. And *only* me.

"I–I—" Words stutter and catch in my throat as his thumb circles my clit. I'm so fucking close, and he knows it.

"Tell me what you want." His deep voice weaves a spell around me. "Let me give you what you need." His hand stills, allowing me a moment to catch my breath.

"I need to come all over your cock." The words barely leave my lips before I'm spinning in his arms. He steals my breath with another kiss as he lifts me off the ground.

Thankfully, the slit on the skirt is long, and it doesn't tear when he gathers the fabric around my waist. How the hell is he so strong? I cling to his shoulders as he carries me to the sofa and sits, placing me perfectly on his lap, my thighs straddling his on the soft cushions.

Jason rests his hands on my hips, pushing the skirt away. "Remember this scene?"

Through the haze of lust, I blink at him in confusion. "What scene?"

Eyes level, he holds my gaze, and a smile slowly curves his sinful mouth. "In your fic, when the Forgotten Knight is seduced by the Crimson Priestess?"

The scene clicks into place, making me hot and flustered. He chuckles and the sound pulses straight to my clit.

"What did you call it? Red on Red?"

"You remember?" I rest my hands on his chest, lost in his blue eyes.

"I've read it every night since Philly." His voice drops impossibly deep. "I've imagined you and I recreating that scene in costume, on set."

My body is aflame. His words arouse me even further. He's tormenting me with this visual, and I want it. More than anything I've ever wanted before.

"I can't tell you how many times I've gotten off thinking of it." His breathy confession leaves me aching and feverish.

"You're not in costume," I manage. "We're not on set." Leaning closer, I let my breasts spill forward, giving him an eyeful before he groans and shifts beneath me. "But I can indulge your fantasies since you've indulged in mine."

"Are you saying a one-night stand with your favorite actor is one of your fantasies?" He caresses my hip with his thumb.

"No." I slide my arms around his neck and bring my lips to hover above his. "But falling in love with him is at the top of the list."

"Wait." He stills beneath me. "You have a *list*?"

I laugh. "That's what you focused on in that sentence?"

"No. I heard exactly what you said." He grins and places a tender kiss on my lips. "Falling in love with a fan wasn't on my bingo card, but here we are."

"People will think we're crazy," I murmur as he trails kisses along my jaw.

"Then we'll own it." He kisses me hard.

Desire sparks again. I remember my position…and his request.

My hands drift down his chest until they come to rest at his belt. Holding his gaze, I unfasten it and unzip his pants. He shifts and we shimmy together until he's seated in only his boxers. With a bold touch, I trace the outline of his cock through the fabric, making it jump beneath my fingers.

"Did you bring a condom?" I ask, taking him in my grip.

"Back pocket." He nods toward his discarded pants on the floor.

I grab them, rip open the foil, and free his cock. His eyes glaze over as I roll the condom down his thick length. When I tease the head against my pussy, his eyes shutter closed and a curse rips from his throat.

Slowly, I lower myself onto his cock. Warmth radiates through me as he stretches me.

Bracing my hands on his shoulders, I grind my hips against him as I seat myself fully. Another string of curses pours from his wicked mouth.

Lost in a haze of lust, the lines I wrote years ago pour from my lips. "*My knight. I am yours. Bound in blood, Red on red.*"

"*A man is honored,*" Jason murmurs the response as he thrusts deep. His hands hold fast to my hips, guiding and stroking as I move over him, every movement filling me, teasing him.

Together, we fall into rhythm as I ride his cock. Push and pull, an endless battle for pleasure.

I cling to his shoulders, fisting the fabric in my hands as he teases my clit with his fingers and whispers encouragement against my throat.

"Come for me, sweet priestess."

Heat spirals inside me until it finally burst in an explosion of pleasure. Sensations ripple through me in waves as he coaxes me through my orgasm, stroking my clit with softening pressure. I clench around him and rock once more.

His groan rips through me as he comes, his left hand grasping my thigh, his panting breaths echoing in my ear.

I grin with satisfaction as he rests his head on my shoulder. "You—"

A knock shakes us from our blissful sedation.

"Jason? You need to be on stage in five minutes. Wrap it up." Archer's voice comes from the other side of the door.

"Coming," he replies.

I smother laughter behind my hand. "If he only knew."

"Oh, he knows." Jason grins. "He's been on the other side of the door since he left the room."

Horror fills me. "He heard *everything*?"

I shove Jason before climbing off his lap, acutely aware of our disheveled state. The lingering postsex bliss fades quickly as I straighten my dress. I can still feel him between my thighs, but I ignore the persistent reminder of his touch.

"Probably." Jason disposes of the condom and retrieves his pants. "Does that bother you?"

"Yes. No. Uh…I don't know." I run my hand over my hair, which is probably falling out of the braids. "He probably thinks I'm some psycho fan—"

"Stop." Jason drops his belt and takes my hands. "Listen to me. He knows this isn't a fling for me, okay? He never would have brought you back here if he didn't support my decision."

"So it was a test to see if I was a match for his rising star?" His words lessen the sting, but it still hurts.

"No. I told him I wanted you brought to the VIP room. He's just protective and doesn't want anyone to take advantage of me."

"As if I would take advantage of you." I huff.

"I wouldn't mind if you took a *little* advantage." Jason winks and tugs me close.

I laugh as he presses a kiss to my forehead. "If you're trying to make me feel better about this, it's working."

"Good." His warm hug wraps me in confidence. "I have to do this panel for *Throne of Ashes*, and I may do something stupid and reckless."

"Like what?" I rear back and stare at his handsome, smirking face.

"You'll have to wait and see." He disappears into the bathroom.

I stare at the floor for a moment, lost in thought. What does he mean, *something stupid*? Is he quitting the show?

The sound of running water fills the room, and I follow it until I see his reflection in a mirror where he's bent over a sink washing his hands.

"I'll give you a few to clean up." He dries his hands and draws me close for a quick kiss. "Archer will bring you to the panel when you're ready."

"You want me at the panel?" I stare blankly, a nugget of fear lodging in my chest.

"Of course." His smile is practically glowing. "You'll want to be there for my announcement."

"Your…what?"

"You'll see." With a parting grin, he vanishes through the door.

I turn in disbelief and stare at my reflection. Then I realize the true mess he made of me. Makeup smeared. Red marks trailing my throat. My skin pink and warm, awash with an after-sex glow. Yup, my hair is an absolute disaster.

Taking a few minutes to compose myself, I manage to wrangle my wig into some semblance of order and fix my makeup with my kit. Good thing I always bring it to cons for other people. This is the first time I've needed to use it for myself.

When I step back into the VIP room, Archer is waiting for me with a knowing smile.

"Don't say a word," I warn him.

"I wouldn't dream of it." He extends a hand toward the exit. "Shall we?"

As we walk down the corridor, I can't help feeling like I'm

walking into a trap…or worse, an execution.

"Don't worry. It'll be fine," Archer says with a kind smile. "They don't bite…hard."

"Wait, what?" Panic infuses me.

When we round the corner, I'm at the edge of the room. The stage is directly in front of me, and the panel has already started. The room is packed. Every seat in the audience is filled, and there are people standing along the walls, watching with rapt attention.

The host stands to the side asking questions, and Jason sits with his costars in a row across the stage, microphones in hand.

Archer leads me closer, and that's when I see Jason turn to me. His charming grin transforms his typically stoic face, and he winks.

I sit in an empty seat next to the stage, directly in front of Jason.

"Jason, there have been rumors floating around over the past few months—is there a new love in your life?"

His costars exchange uneasy glances, and a soft excited murmur hums through the crowd. I bite my lip and rub my sweaty palms on my skirt. He's never discussed his love life in public before. Our incident in Philly only made him more secretive.

I cringe, waiting for the moment he shuts down the question.

"I'm glad you asked, Matt." Jason shifts forward, leaning on his knees, his eyes boring into mine. "The rumors are true."

A collective gasp ripples through the crowd and across the stage. His costars are equally as stunned as the fans. Chatter fills the room as whispers start.

"Would you like to meet her?" Jason asks, and the crowd ignites into applause.

If I could, I would have melted into a puddle of embarrassed goo. Straight through the floorboards.

"Come up here, sweetheart." Jason's words are for me alone, and they add fuel to the excited inferno consuming the fans.

Archer takes my arm and gently pulls me to my feet. Squeals and shouts of encouragement explode around me as I slowly make my way to the stairs.

Jason meets me at the edge of the stage and wraps an arm around my waist. His eyes sparkle as he dips me and kisses me in front of everyone.

The crowd's reaction is deafening. It's a volcanic eruption, and we're caught in the center of it. I cling to his shirt as he brings me back to my feet. His smile grounds me.

"Well now. I wasn't expecting that today." The host fans himself with the notecards in his hand.

Jason leads me to where an empty chair has been placed beside his. He picks up the mic he left on the seat. When I try to sit on the chair beside his, I nearly stumble, and Jason catches me by the waist to pull me into his lap.

Another riot of cheers radiates from the crowd, and I bury my face into his chest in embarrassment, uncaring of my makeup. His costars join the ruckus.

"Does she have a name? Or shall we call her the Crimson Priestess?" the host asks, his question met with laughter.

"Vicky." Jason says simply, and the crowd goes silent.

"And how did you two meet?"

"We met in Philly." He holds me close, showing everyone in attendance the sincerity of his words. "She fixed my costume."

"That's Vicky, the Cosplay Medic." A woman's voice rises from the crowd, causing a ripple of curious murmurs.

My gaze searches the audience for the person who just

outed me to the world. As if I didn't do that myself months ago when I posted the now infamous photograph with Jason in cosplay at the Philly convention.

"I love you, girl," the voice adds, causing more murmurs.

Then I see her. Ginger is in the third row, her red hair a beacon in the dim light. She's grinning from ear to ear.

"Friend of yours?" Jason whispers against my cheek.

I nod.

"Looks like we made a scene." He chuckles, and I shiver with need. "I told you I was going to do something reckless."

The crowd's applause dims in the background as he kisses me in front of the world again, marking me as his and him as mine. When he pulls away, he carefully guides me to the seat beside his and takes my hand.

As the questions pour in and the panel continues, the conversation and spotlight shift away from us. I'm grateful for the reprieve, for the steadfast presence of the man beside me. He holds my hand until the host dismisses the panel. Even then, he keeps me close until we leave the convention through a back door and into a black town car.

Looks like we both did something stupid…like fall in love.

I can't say I'm mad about it though.

CHAPTER ELEVEN

Once we slide into a booth at the hotel restaurant, I'm finally able to breathe easy and calm my erratic heartbeat. The rush of adrenaline wears off as the waiter takes our order.

Ginger sent me a text right after the panel, telling me she had a flight to catch. *You're in good hands*, she added. I smile at the words and tuck my phone into my pocket.

Jason lifts his whiskey. "To new beginnings."

I salute him with my mojito before taking a sip. Unease begins to settle around me as the excitement of the day fades away.

"Something wrong?" he asks, setting his drink down.

"How do we make this work?" I gesture between us. "We don't even live in the same city."

"We make it work the same way any other long-distance couple makes it work." His brow furrows. "Unless that's not something you want?"

"Lots of phone calls, missed opportunities, layovers in random airports…not really." I sigh and push my drink aside when his expression falls.

When I take his hand, he looks up and I see hurt in his expression.

Finally, he shrugs. "I struggled with this for weeks after we met. Convinced myself you'd never want to pursue a relationship because we live so far apart and have our own careers. But…I held out hope we could find a balance, make it work."

"Unless one of us is willing to make a change, a relationship is going to be hard to maintain in the long term." I run my fingers over his knuckles in a soothing motion. "Some people can do it, but—"

"You want more than a long-distance relationship?"

I nod. "If we're going to do this, I want to give it the best possible chance of survival."

"How do we do that?"

"Well…" I take a deep breath. "How long is your contract with *Throne of Ashes*?"

"Three more seasons."

"So a few years at least." I make the mental calculations. "I'm committed to the theater until the end of December."

"Come to LA. There have to be places who would love to have a costume designer as talented as you on their team. I can make a few phone calls."

"Jason, I appreciate it, really, but I can't ask you to do that."

"Why not? It would put us in the same state, the same house."

"Are you asking me to give up my job and come *live* with you in LA?" I stare at him in stunned surprise.

"Why does it sound crazy when you say it like that?" He smiles. "I think it's a perfectly logical next step."

"We barely know each other, Jason."

"And how are we supposed to get to know each other if it's only over the phone or during quick visits on weekends?" His smile disappears, and guilt stabs me.

"I don't want to rush into something." I stand and slide into the bench beside him. His arm immediately comes around my shoulders. "We should take it slow."

"I've already made my intentions clear, if today wasn't obvious enough."

"The entertainment world is abuzz with your big reveal

today. I may never forgive you for that public display of affection, thank you."

"I wanted you to know I'm serious about this…about us." He kisses my forehead, and I melt into him.

"I know." My heart aches. "I want this too…but what if it falls apart?"

"We'll never know unless we try." He holds me tighter. "I'm willing to try. Whatever it takes. However long it takes."

"Really?" I grab his hand and squeeze.

"Absolutely." He brings my hand to his lips and kisses my knuckles like a true knight. "You're worth it, Vicky."

Uncertainty and excitement fill me. This could be one of the craziest things I've ever done, but the way this year is going, it only makes sense to ride the crazy train and see where it leads.

"Six months."

He blinks at me. "What?"

"Let's try long-distance for six months and go from there. Deal?"

His eyes narrow before a grin splits his lips. "Deal."

We shake on it. I have six months to figure shit out, to see if this will work.

"Neither of us should have to give up our dreams," I say when our food arrives.

"I completely agree." He inhales deeply. "Maybe we can find some new dreams to share."

"That sounds like a great idea." I stab a piece of broccoli.

"What's your dream?" he asks suddenly.

"You first." I chew my veggies as I watch his mind spin.

"Believe it or not, my dream wasn't to become an actor." He chuckles. "I went to school for writing."

"You want to write a bestselling novel?"

"Something like that." He takes a bite of potato. "You?"

"I want to design a clothing line, something with a vintage flair."

His eyes darken. "I bet you'd look stunning in a swing dress and pearls."

"How 1950s of y—"

"As you ride my cock," he finishes, his voice low, full of sensual promise.

My mouth rounds into an O of surprise, and I take a drink to keep from choking on a response.

"So…when do you leave for LA?" I hedge with an innocent question.

"Tomorrow at noon."

"My flight for Boston leaves at ten a.m."

"We have all night then." He winks. "I brought my cosplay."

Warmth fills my face. "How much of my fan fiction have you read?"

"Everything, love." Jason grins. "I plan on reenacting every single scene."

My heart stops. I immediately regret writing over fifty fics with the Red-on-Red pairing. But when I see hunger in his eyes, my own desire ignites along with my long dormant fantasies.

"Bring it on." I offer him a bawdy wink. "And when we're done, I'll show you the ones I didn't publish."

I laugh at the surprise on his face, but it's soon replaced by the same hunger I feel deep in my bones.

We can make this work. I *know* we can.

CHAPTER TWELVE

One Year After Philly

"Are you sure this is okay?" Jason asks, tugging the collar of his suit.

"Absolutely," I reassure him as we walk through the crowded hotel lobby. "Jen said it's a *Space Vendetta* themed wedding."

"Yes, but the bride also mentioned she and the groom will be dressed as Ranger Lynnea Stark and Commander Colton." He shoots me a look as we pass under the floral archway.

"I already asked if it was okay if you wore a *different* Commander Colton costume." I sigh at his dramatics. "Besides, I favor a different pairing for this series than she does."

"Fangirls. Whatever would we do without them?" He lovingly squeezes my arm as we step into the throng of wedding guests.

"Waste away into a meaningless void," I respond with a grin, and he matches it with his own.

I gasp, clinging tighter to Jason as we walk into the grand ballroom. It's decorated according to theme, bearing sigils of the famous science fiction factions, and feels like a fantastical romance ceremony in some faraway land. I can't stop staring at the intricate details, from small starships in the floral arrangements to streamers glittering like shooting stars overhead. It's amazing. I can't believe Jen invited me to participate in her special day.

After her hurried exit at the Philly convention last year, I was worried we'd done something to upset her, but after talking to Madre, I understood the extent of her fangirl obsession. Truly, I sympathized. I was like that once too, but since meeting Jason, I realize even if we find love with the actual man of our dreams, life is far from a fairy tale. Relationships take tons of work.

After Chicago, we each went home to our respective lives. Jason came to visit when he could, and I spent Christmas and New Years with him in LA. His filming schedule and my theater responsibilities kept us busy, but not a day went by when we didn't talk…or sext.

It's fine. We made it work.

I'm not going to lie, it wasn't easy. Not only was I in a constant state of panic and anxiety about whether this was the real deal, but I had to constantly remind myself this was a good test to see if there was something substantial between us.

Then in February, he got an offer for a bigger, more prominent role in an upcoming franchise. The catch was filming wouldn't start until his *Throne of Ashes* contract ended. So we had time.

Truth was, I couldn't stand being so far away from him.

After spending Christmas week with him, I put in my resignation at the theater. Jason doesn't know. I've been working on commission to make ends meet while sending out my resume to as many places in LA as I can. So far, there haven't been any takers. I'm starting to worry. I want to make this work—make *us* work—but I don't want him to use his influence to get me a position in LA. I want to earn it.

But today isn't about me or us.

It's Jen and Shaun's big day.

We wander in as the ceremony begins, and it's everything I could hope for in a fandom themed wedding, complete with mood music and cosplaying guests. I dab away a few tears during the ceremony, earning a questioning look from Jason. I nudge my elbow into his ribs to remind him to pay attention.

I'm taking notes, because I have every intention of having my own themed wedding…if this works out. The press will have a field day, but I don't care. It's *my* day, not theirs.

Shaking my daydream free, I admire Jen and Shaun as they exchange vows at the front of the room. He looks every inch the part of Commander Colton, standing next to Jen's Lynnea. I hazard a sly side-eye at Jason's profile.

Fucking swoon. I can't get enough of this man. I stand by what I told Ginger and Beth at the con last year—Jason Hunt is my *ideal* Commander Colton. But it's only because I have this strange desire to see him paired with the insatiable companion, Viann. She's a space hooker, for lack of a better term, but I see her and Commander Colton as the perfect pair. Her razor-sharp wit and his dashing charm would make for some interesting interactions. Alas, they've only met twice on screen. I keep hoping for more, but I'm in the minority.

That's okay. I have my own Commander Colton today, and I'm dressed as Viann. Two pairings, not wrong, not cannon.

Both perfect in the eyes of fandom.

After the ceremony, we find our table and mingle with the other guests. There are a few other fangirls from our Philly excursion. Ginger and her husband, which honestly left me stunned since she told me nothing of her hasty marriage. Madre, of course, who flew in from Iowa, and Jessica with her boyfriend, Alex. It's fantastic seeing the fangirls all together again. The only ones missing are Ronnie, who had prior plans, and Beth, who probably didn't get an invitation since she pissed Jen off in our group forum last year.

No one seems surprised by my date. Ginger gives me two

enthusiastic thumbs-up with a wink when she spots us together. I still haven't forgiven her for her outburst during the convention panel in Chicago, when she outed me to the crowd. Might not happen today either, but there's hope for redemption.

Long after the bridal party returns with a grand entrance and the toasts have been completed, Jason ventures to the bar to get us drinks. I spy Jen wandering among the guests, greeting friends and family. She squeals in excitement when she sees me and the other fangirls at a table together.

"Oh my god! I'm so glad you guys made it." Jen takes my hand as she comes to a stop. Madre, Ginger, Jessica, and I all huddle around her. "Thank you so much for coming. I know it was a big ask, but you guys are family."

"We're happy to come." Madre speaks for all of us. "Plus, it gave me a chance to get away from the Midwest for a long weekend."

Laughter surrounds us. "I've missed you all," I say, caught up in the moment. "So much has happened since Philly."

"I should say so." Jen's gaze drifts across the group. "Ginger's married, Jessica snagged an artist, Vicky's living the dream with a superstar boyfriend, and Madre published a novel."

"Not everything is centered around men here." Madre winks.

Jen turns to me with wide, glittering eyes. "How in the hell did you manage to catch the eye of a stud like Jason Hunt?"

"Luck?" I laugh. They join me, but the truth is deeper. I don't want to go into it. Not today. This is Jen's day.

"Well, thank you all for coming. I appreciate you being here," Jen says as Shaun joins her, wrapping an arm around her waist. "Speak of the devil."

"I heard you whispering about me," Shaun teases.

"My thoughts exactly."

At the sound of a deep voice, I turn to find Jason standing behind me. "Babe, you scared me."

"I'm sorry, love." He kisses my forehead. I swear an echoing *aw* surrounds us.

My face turns six shades of red when I see all their eyes on me. "Everyone, meet Jason." I introduce him to my companions one at a time and watch their starstruck expressions shift from awe to pure pleasure. He has that effect on people, I've noticed.

Even Shaun seems awed. "Eh, thanks for coming today. We're honored to have you."

"We wouldn't have missed it for the world," Jason says smoothly, his charm on full display.

"Love your cosplay." Shaun gestures to Jason's navy blue Commander Colton uniform. "I'm glad we don't clash." He motions to his own bright red suit.

"Now, gentlemen, there's enough room for *two* dashing Commander Coltons in this room." Jen laughs.

The rest of us join her. There's no animosity, only teasing banter among friends. I sigh in relief. We chat for a few more minutes before scattering in different directions.

Jen and Shaun head for the main floor for the first dance. I watch in silence for a few moments, admiring the loving way they lock in a singular embrace. A tear runs down my cheek. I'm happy for them. Truly. And I'm honored they chose to include me in this momentous occasion.

"Would you like to dance?" Jason whispers in my ear, breaking me from my thoughts.

I take his hand. "I'd love to."

Jason leads me to the dance floor and places his hand on my waist, pulling me against him. I'm swept up in the romantic moment, in the schmaltzy ballad playing through the speakers, but my gaze is riveted on him. I never imagined this moment.

How could I? It was always a dream. A fantasy.

As he spins me in a circle, he smiles, and I realize this isn't a fairytale. It isn't a dream. This is my life. Jason Fucking Hunt is dancing with me, looking at me like I'm the only person in the world who means anything.

"I love you." The words slip free before I can think better of it. We've hinted at it before, but this…it's brutal honesty. It's fucking terrifying.

"I love you too," he responds without hesitation, and every thread of anxiety disintegrates immediately.

We spin to the music for a few more seconds before he continues. "Does this mean you're finally moving to LA?"

"I–I'm trying to find a job there." I bite my lip, ashamed at my inability to adequately adult when I've done quite well so far. "The market is tight in LA when it comes to costume design."

"You're right. There's a lot of competition." Jason nods, his fingers climbing higher on my waist. "If you need a referral, I can always—"

"No, Jason. I told you. I'm doing this on my own. No handouts from the big superstar."

"I understand, but my offer remains." He sighs. "I just…I miss you, Vicky."

"I miss you too." I sigh. "But I refuse to be some little wife you keep hidden away."

Jason laughs. "I doubt there's any way I could keep you hidden away. Remember Chicago?"

"How could I forget?" I groan. "The whole theater troupe had a coronary wanting all the details when I returned from that trip."

"Did you give them *all* the details?" He winks.

"Absolutely not." I stiffen against him.

"You don't have to find a job right away," Jason adds softly.

"You'll find something eventually."

"I'd go crazy cooped up at home."

"Then take on commissions. You can bring all your sewing gear. I have a spare room you can use as your workshop." His invitation is enticing…it's downright wicked temptation.

"No. I won't be a burden." My stance is adamant. Even in the midst of a romantic dance during a friend's wedding, I will not be swayed. "No."

"Fine." He shrugs, dismissing it without a thought.

Another song begins, but Jason doesn't relinquish his hold. I'm pulled into the 80s ballad—I've always been a Bon Jovi kind of girl. It's romantic, seductive. And he knows it.

I can feel my irritation drifting away. Soon, I'm leaning on his shoulder, swaying to the irresistible beat, lost in my own reverie.

"Marry me, Vicky."

Wait, did I hear him right?

I pull back and stare up at him. His blue eyes glitter under the false twinkling starlight.

"What did you say?" My voice is small and squeaky.

"I'm asking you to marry me." The lopsided grin I've come to love appears in earnest. "I can't stand being apart from you for a moment longer."

"But…I need work…"

"We'll figure it out." He takes my hand and presses a kiss to my knuckles. "This new contract."

"What about it?"

"I told them I would only do it if I could pick my own costume designer."

I blanche. "You what?"

"I stated in my response, I would only accept the position if they brought on a designer of my choosing to handle my wardrobe for the films," he responds simply.

"You didn't?" I gape at him…at his audacity.

"I did."

"You know what you are?" I jab him in the center of his chest.

"No. What am I, love?" He smirks.

"A diva." I scoff. "You've become a fucking diva. All this fame has gone to your head."

He grabs my wrist and brings it to his lips, licking the small spot where my pulse beats hot and fast.

"No, I'm a businessman." He chuckles. "If they want me, they'll give me what I want."

"That's pretty arrogant of you."

"That's showbiz, baby." He draws back with a grin. "If they want me, they get us both. Otherwise, there's no deal."

"Why would you say that?" I stare at him, dumbfounded.

"Because I want you by my side." He takes both my hands in his and stops in the middle of the dance floor. "Without you, I'm nothing. I want you…no, *need* you by my side. We're a package deal from here on out."

"You're insane." I scoff at him, even as my heart swells with pride and love for this insane man and his crazy ideas. "You know you're crazy, right?"

"I'd be crazy to let someone as fantastic as you get away."

My face warms at his praise. "You-you're just saying that."

"No. It's true." He holds me close, his expression deadly serious. "From the first moment I saw you in Philly, I knew there was something special about you, a quality I couldn't ignore."

"Is that why you asked me to fix your costume?" I tease.

"No." He shakes his head. "That's why you stopped me to fix my costume without knowing who I was…or what was in it for you." Jason softly strokes my cheek with his fingertips. "You are an artisan who uses her gifts for good without thought for compensation or reward. You're an angel."

His smile breaks me, and tears spill free. I sniffle, trying to stop the flow of emotion.

Jason wipes away the tears with a white handkerchief. "What do you say, love? Will you join me on this next adventure?"

"Yes." I sob, clinging to his lapels. "I'll follow you to the ends of the galaxy and beyond."

When he kisses me, I barely hear the soft gasps and applause around us.

It's just him and me.

That's all it needs to be.

THE END Book 1

The Artist
Fangirl Confessions
Book 2
KIRSTEN S. BLACKETER

CHAPTER ONE

Fandom conventions should have an introvert recovery room, a quiet space to recharge before diving into the chaos and excitement.

It's taking all my effort to smile and nod along to the animated discussion with Ginger and Vicky as we pass through the security entrance. They're discussing the best actor for the lead character in the *Space Vendetta* Series while we filter through the growing crowd inside the convention center. It's overwhelming, and we haven't even been here twenty minutes.

I really need time to adjust, to steady myself. My head is spinning with all the people, the commotion, the noise. I could go back to the hotel room I'm sharing with Ronnie and take a few minutes to collect my bearings.

No, damn it.

I'm here. I'm doing this.

After months of planning and cajoling from the other fangirls, I've made it to a convention. We all agreed Philly would be the place our little online group finally meet in person. I love my fellow fangirls, but for an anxious introvert, this is way outside my comfort zone.

I square my shoulders and fish the specially designed earplugs out of my purse. They take the edge off the noise and let me breathe when I'm in public. A genius invention. Never leave home without them.

"What are those?" Ginger asks, noting the little silver rings sitting comfortably in my ears.

"They're called Loops." I gesture to the crowd, growing by the moment as people enter the convention. "They dull the noise so I can keep my sanity."

"Yeah, this can be a lot." Ginger's expression softens. "If you need a break, we can find a quiet spot."

The noise eases around me, and my nerves slowly find a steady state.

I shake my head. "Thanks. I'm good now."

"Can you still hear me with those things?"

"Yeah. They filter out loud noises, but I'm able to have a conversation with no problem."

"Cool. I'll have to check them out."

"What are you two talking about?" Beth worms her way into the conversation the moment we come to a stop beside the Pokémon stand where she's waiting for us.

"Just trying to get a plan of attack." Ginger redirects the topic, and I shoot her a grateful look. "I know some of us have photo ops and autograph signings today."

I drop my gaze to the floor. While I love a lot of the actors attending this con, I don't have extra cash to splurge on photos and autographs. I'd rather spend my money supporting local artists selling their wares.

"Jen and Madre will be hanging out in the signing area today." Ginger pulls a map from her bag as she discusses the plan of attack. "We have the group chat. Just check in around one, and we'll see where everyone is."

"I don't think Jessica heard you." Beth points at me and then to her ears.

Irritation bites at me. "I heard everything. Thanks." I plaster on a fake smile and glance at my phone where a notification appears. It's hard to ignore the way she burrows under my skin.

"Ronnie is waiting for me by the escalator. I'll catch you guys later."

Beth, known as MistressViper in the fangirl community, has a snarky, sarcastic humor and is often a bully. I honestly don't think she has a filter. I try to give her a wide berth and not take her comments to heart. She has moments of kindness, but they're few and far between. Ginger seems to balance her out well.

Meeting Beth in person seems to have added fuel to her fire. I don't know who peed in her cereal today, but she's on the warpath and it isn't even ten o'clock. I have no interest in sticking around to find out why.

As I make my way toward the far end of the room, another text comes through.

(Ginger): *Don't worry about Beth. She had a run-in with a security guard this morning and it put her in a mood.*

I chuckle and type out a response.

(Me): *Did she take a swing at him?*

(Ginger): *No, but I thought there might be fireworks. *flame emoji**

I can picture Beth's death glare at my inelegant snort laugh.

"There you are!" Ronnie tosses her black curls over her shoulder and fixes a bra strap peeking out from beneath the *Space Vendetta* tee she's sporting. "Sorry I bailed on you this morning, but I had to run to the Reading Market Terminal. They have the most amazing pastries!"

"That sounds delicious."

"Here, I got you a Danish." She hands me a small brown paper bag.

"Thanks." I tuck it into my purse for later.

"You're never going to believe this." Ronnie's eyes glitter with unrestrained excitement as we head toward the line forming by the escalator. "This morning, I saw a post from Michael

DeHart saying he'll be signing new copies of the latest *Space Vendetta* novel all day." She squeals with delight, and I swear there are hearts floating in her eyes.

"Girl, I've read every book, watched every film and interview…I am *obsessed* with *Space Vendetta*." She presses a hand to her pink cheek.

"Who's Michael DeHart?" I'm unfamiliar with the name. "I've only watched the movies, though I know they're based on books."

Ronnie gapes at me, blue eyes wide. "He's the creator of the *Space Vendetta* universe! A true genius." She launches into the history of *Space Vendetta*, and despite her passion, I'm completely lost.

I may be part of the *Space Vendetta* fandom, but it's purely coincidental. I enjoy the films. I dabble in the fan fiction. That's about it. I stumbled into the online fangirl group by accident, and they welcomed me without question. So, I stuck around.

While Ronnie chatters, we pause at the top of the escalator, joining the crowd and stepping onto the mechanical death trap. I hate these things. Ronnie pushes forward, paving a path in the way only a single-minded, determined curvy goddess can.

I hesitate at the top, and when I take a step, my shoe catches the edge of the metal guard. I pitch forward, my breath whooshing out as I nearly tumble into the line of attendees to create a domino collision down the escalator.

I brace for impact, but a solid, warm body pulls me back. I manage to right myself and lean against the railing.

"Th-thank you," I sputter, breathless, my heart racing a mile a minute. I press a hand to my chest as the warmth disappears, replaced by the subtle, spicy scent of men's cologne.

"You're welcome."

I turn toward my rescuer and stifle a laugh. A man dressed

as Daredevil.

"Those things are dangerous," he says, gesturing to the escalator. "The stairs may be a safer option."

"I agree completely."

"Are you okay?" He inclines his head, but it's disconcerting because of his mask—I can't see his eyes or half his face. His voice is warm and soothing though.

Somehow, I nod. My heart isn't racing from fear anymore. It's shifted rhythm to something more alluring and unexpected.

"You just nodded, didn't you?"

"Yeah, I'm fine." I blink. "Sorry."

I mentally kick myself. I'm working on becoming more articulate with my needs and not assuming people can read my moods and thoughts. It's a process.

"No apology needed." He bows with a flourish. "I'm glad you're okay. Enjoy the convention."

"Thanks," I say before taking my chances with the escalator. When I turn back, Daredevil is gone.

I curse myself when I realize I didn't even ask his name.

At the bottom, Ronnie is waiting for me. "Oh my God—I saw the whole thing. Are you okay?"

"I'm fine." I fall into step beside her, looking back for another glimpse of my hero.

"Good thing Daredevil came to your rescue." Ronnie sighs. "There's something about a man in a mask, isn't there?"

My vision fills with the masked vigilante, and I have to agree. I've always been partial to those characters, the ones who hide their faces, who cling to the shadows. They don't do it for recognition or glory. They do it because they want to help people and right wrongs.

"Yeah. There is." I readjust the earplug until the noise around us has faded again.

"Maybe you'll run into him again." Ronnie nudges me. "Did you get his number?"

I shake my head and again curse myself for it before verbalizing my response. "No. I didn't even get his name."

"Well, in a getup like that, he'll be easy to spot." She winks. "We'll find him."

"What if he doesn't want to be found?" I murmur the question more to myself than to her.

"Honey, he's wearing a red bodysuit. Trust me, he *wants* to be seen in this crowd."

"If he were Deadpool, I'd agree." I scan the crowd as we enter the vendor area. "But we're talking about Daredevil."

"Look, girl, if he doesn't come looking for you, then he's blind. You're a knockout!" She huffs and rolls her eyes. "Men."

My face heats at her statement. I've never thought of myself as *a knockout*, but with girl-next-door blonde ringlets and blue eyes, I'm passably cute. Obviously not enough to tempt a man, but looks aren't everything, right? Personality makes up for it.

If only I could let that part shine through.

I pull myself together and weave into the crowd beside Ronnie, who commands presence with every step. She's a force of nature, and part of me is glad she decided to come with me on this adventure.

"First time at a con?" Ronnie asks, looking at a booth full of Funko Pop! figurines.

"What gave it away?" I laugh.

"Nothing gave it away." She pauses. "I can tell you're overwhelmed by the crowd."

"A little." I sidestep a passing cosplayer whose wings nearly clip my shoulder. "I'm working through it."

"Well, if you need a break, let me know."

"I appreciate it." I rest my hand on her arm, then retrieve a map from my bag. "Where's that author's booth?"

Ronnie's eyes sparkle. "I think it's on the other side of the room."

"Let's head that way then." I link my arm through hers, and we make our way down the aisle, perusing booths and admiring cosplays along the way. Her steady presence allows me to ground myself.

Even though we'd never met before this weekend, these fangirls are giving me a safe opportunity to venture outside of my comfort zone. Aside from the escalator trying to kill me, I'm glad I came. Who knows what else will happen?

I'd normally be scared of that unknown, but honestly, after my run-in with Daredevil, I find myself eagerly scanning the crowd for the masked vigilante. I'm determined to get his name…if I can find him.

If I don't psych myself out in the process…damn my brain.

CHAPTER TWO

Surrounded by a million new sights and sounds, my brain just won't turn off. It's like he's burrowed into my thoughts, and I can't shake him free.

It's insane, pining over a man I just met, a man whose face I haven't even seen. But his kindness and concern left an imprint on my thoughts. I can't help but have questions, and I want to know more about him. Cursing myself for going blank and letting the moment get away from me won't solve anything. But finding him in this chaotic crowd is like searching for a single bloom in a thousand-acre field of sunflowers.

I pass three Deadpools and a Matthew Murdoch before I give up hope of finding the elusive Daredevil. My heart may never recover from the whiplash of this impossible search.

When Ronnie and I find the table she's been searching for, she squeals with excitement and rushes to it. I hang back, watching her interact with her favorite author. Judging by his wide eyes and slack jaw, I'm guessing he's stunned by her passion. When he stands and comes around the table to pose for a picture, I admire the touching scene between artist and fan.

I sidestep so I'm practically hiding in the neighboring vendor's display of plushie backpacks and tufted hats as I study Ronnie and the author. He's handsome…and younger than I'd imagined. For some reason, I assumed a grizzled old man with a cigarette hanging out of his mouth came up with all of those wild space pirate adventures. Seeing Michael DeHart in person alters my interpretation of the universe he created.

I don't want to interrupt Ronnie's animated discussion with him, so I wander through the booth beside them, admiring the custom plushie artistry. The vibrant colors lure me in, and I reach out to touch the soft velvet fabric. It's nice, not abrasive or rough. Almost comforting.

I'm stepping back to check out the items on the other side of the display when a pack of gargoyles walks by and a wing knocks me in the head. Spinning, I reach out to brace myself for the fall…only to have a familiar sensation surround me, followed by the haunting spice of his scent.

"We really need to stop meeting this way." His laugh ripples through me as he sets me back on my feet.

Once I'm confident I have my footing, I turn and smile. "That's the second time you've come to my rescue today."

"I guess I've been at the right place at the right time." The mask covering half his face does nothing to hide his brilliant smile.

My heart flutters. "Well, thank you again, Daredevil."

"Alex." He extends his hand.

"Jessica." I take it, savoring the warmth of his touch through his glove. "Thanks again for saving me."

"My pleasure." His grip is firm as he shakes my hand. There's a swift sense of loss when he lets go, but it's replaced with anticipation as he reaches for the mask.

He pulls it off, releasing thick dark hair, the tousled waves framing his handsome face. He's sporting a day's worth of stubble and an easy grin. His eyes are vibrant caramel brown.

"Wow," I mutter under my breath as I admire the striking man beside me.

"Not what you expected?" he asks, his eyes unfocused on a point over my shoulder. "I'm sure my hair is a mess. Damn mask." He tries to smooth his hair down but only ruffles it in irritation, then laughs. "Hopeless really, and a mirror is useless."

He's blind.

"Oh…shit. I'm sorry I didn't know…" My words drift off. I'm uncertain how to continue the thought without sounding like a total dick.

"No apologies necessary. Happens all the time." He laughs. "I get it. No one actually expects a Daredevil cosplayer to share a core trait with the character. I'm blind, not helpless. Just like Matt Murdoch."

His humor softens my embarrassment. "Again, I'm…well, I'm a clumsy mess, as you can tell. I've been told I'm not very observant when I'm overstimulated."

"It happens a lot, huh?" He nods with understanding. "I get it. These events can be overwhelming if you're not used to them."

"How do you…" My face heats and I backtrack. "Sorry. Never mind."

"How do I get around without help?" He chuckles. "I get that question a lot. I always have a friend nearby to nudge me in the right direction when I don't have my cane."

"But you caught me on the escalator…" My mind spins with questions. "How?"

Alex leans closer, his scent wrapping around me in a delicious distraction. "I was behind you. I heard you trip and your breath catch. You were within arm's reach. It was a gut reaction. I relied on instinct."

"So you got lucky?"

"One hundred percent. Either I would save you or we'd both go down." He inclines his head thoughtfully. "And I couldn't pass up the chance to meet you."

"Meet me?" I blink twice. "But—"

"Your scent…shampoo, perfume, *something*…whatever it is,

it had me in a chokehold the moment you stepped into my world."

A full-on blush consumes me, my face on fire at his simple confession. He's charming *and* handsome—a dangerous combination. I stutter and clamp my mouth shut, unable to respond.

"Do you like art?" he asks, pulling me from my spiraling thoughts.

"I love it."

He offers his arm, and I take it. With a few agile steps, he leads me to a booth beside the plushies. There are circular towers inside the twelve-by-twelve space, and vibrant neon paintings cover every surface. I lean in to inspect them one by one.

Gorgeous landscapes. Detailed animal renderings. Vibrant portraits of people in varying states of emotion. All are rendered in rich, deep hues and highlighted with neon colors. They're enchanting, and I gasp at the way they capture light and glow with depth and life.

"These are gorgeous." I turn to him. "Do you know the artist?"

"I should." Alex turns to me with a grin. "Look at the signature."

Squinting, I lean toward one of the paintings to assess the flourish of letters in the bottom right corner. "Alex Vernon." My gaze flashes to the sign over the booth, then back to him. "You're the artist?"

"Shocking, I know."

"How in the world…?" I shake my head and curse myself. "Sorry."

Alex rests his hand on mine. "First of all, stop apologizing. I want you to ask whatever question comes to mind. I promise, I won't be offended."

Shame lifts as his words take root. "Okay. I'll try."

"No *try*. Do it." He squeezes my hand. "Don't be embarrassed. I'm used to these questions. It's hard to believe a blind man can paint…let alone with this level of detail and skill."

"Not hard to believe." I study the paintings again. "It's amazing. Honestly, I'm impressed."

"Thanks." Alex puffs up his chest a little. "I can't take all the credit. I have amazing friends who help me prepare canvases and keep my studio organized. I couldn't do it without them."

"That's fantastic." My heart warms. "It's wonderful you have a supportive network."

"Everyone needs a supportive network." He tugs my hand. "Would you like to meet mine?"

"Absolutely." I round the corner to see a couple sitting behind the table. A short brunette with a pixie cut turns as we appear. A broad, bearded man narrows his eyes at me but smiles.

"There you are, Alex." She brightens, her eyes sparkling when she sees him holding my hand.

I warm as I note her observation. When did he take my hand? And why does it feel so grounding?

"Mindy, Sam, this is Jessica." He gestures between us. "Jessica, this is my team."

Alex releases my hand, and I greet them both with a firm handshake.

"Nice to meet you." I step to the side of the table.

Mindy opens her mouth but turns quickly as a customer approaches the table.

"Are you the artist?" he asks.

"No." She gestures to Alex. "This is our master artist."

"Oh." The gentleman turns in surprise. "These are amazing. I'm writing an article for my blog. Can I ask you a few questions?"

"Absolutely." Alex guides the newcomer to where he and I had just been standing. Their conversation fades to a soft murmur.

I shift my weight from foot to foot, unsure of whether to stay or go. I don't want to take up space when there are other people waiting to talk to them. To buy something. Thankfully, I'm saved when Mindy appears beside me.

"I'm glad to see you survived the escalator."

"How do you know that was me?" I ask, my face burning.

"I was with Alex when he came to your rescue." She sighs. "He's always been hyper aware of his surroundings even before he lost his sight."

"Oh." I squeak, unable to find words that aren't a barrage of personal questions.

"The moment we walked away from you, he wanted to know exactly what you look like and demanded I commit it to memory."

"Why?" I'm genuinely confused.

"He said you inspired him." Mindy shrugs, but a knowing smile plays on her lips.

Another customer interrupts us, and I take the opportunity to look at the paintings at the other side of the booth. As I study the whorls of color and ink, I let my mind wander.

What did she mean, I *inspired* him? How?

Shaking my head, I push the questions aside. The noise around me fades again, dulled by my earplugs and the fluttering in my chest. I scan the pieces hanging on the makeshift walls.

Then I see it.

A piece so beautiful, it grabs my heart with both hands. Its peaceful serenity leaves me breathless. It's a scenic portrait of a city park and a pathway lined with trees. A woman standing in the foreground draws me in. It's like I'm in the painting.

I am *her*.

I glance at the price and choke. As much as I love it, there's no way I can afford it. Though he deserves that price for that piece. It's fucking breathtaking.

Alex isn't just an artist. He's a master of his craft.

Pride fills me. Even though we just met, I can't help but feel the strong emotion. Without knowing anything about his history or his journey, I admire the amazing work he's done and the way he shares it with the world.

A kernel of doubt settles in my stomach and spreads, weighing me down. I've struggled with self-doubt and insecurity my whole life. And it's stopped me from creating, from doing what I love.

If anyone's an inspiration, it's Alex.

Me? I'm a disappointment. A mediocre fangirl with no direction and only pathetic attempts at fan fiction.

I can't even afford to support the artists I love, let alone pursue my own passion. And the sad part is, I don't even know what my passion is because I'm too terrified of failing to try anything. It's why I don't do relationships and don't have a lot of friends. The possibility of rejection is too overwhelming. Why does it have to be so hard?

Maybe I should walk away.

Guilt stabs me. Alex and his friends have been kind. He came to my rescue. I can't just ditch them because impostor syndrome is pulling me into another spiraling funk.

I take a deep breath and exhale, staring at the woman in the painting. I put myself in her shoes. Let the image draw me in. Slowly, the negativity fades and I can feel my surroundings again. The noise. The crowds. The laughter.

With a shaky laugh, I'm able to ground myself.

I was wrong.

Alex isn't a master; he's a wizard.

And I'm smitten.

CHAPTER THREE

"Find a favorite?" Alex's soft chuckle pulls me from my thoughts.

I cast one last lingering glance at the painting before looking at him. He's facing me. Gone is the Daredevil mask, but he still wears the signature red-and-black suit. His chocolate brown eyes are hidden behind sunglasses, and I warm at his kind smile as he waits for my response.

"I did."

"Which one?" he asks, his attention fixed solely on me.

"This one." I point to the painting of the woman in the park, then realize I've done it again. Kicking myself, I sputter, "Sorry…I, uh—"

Alex responds with a soft chuckle.

I read the tag beneath it and recover my composure. "It's titled *A Walk in Spring*."

"Describe it to me."

"What?" I blink twice, unsure of what he expects from me.

"The painting. Describe it to me. I want to see it through your eyes."

I shift uncomfortably. "I don't—"

"Everyone views art differently." He elaborates, excitement building in his voice. "When you walk through a museum, you're overwhelmed by the amount of art surrounding you, but there are always pieces that make you stop. They call to you, draw you in, invite you to stay a while, to admire the view. To *feel* something."

The way he describes it hits me right in the chest. I've been there, in that specific moment, experiencing a connection to a piece of art I couldn't explain. Like now. "Exactly."

"So tell me." He licks his lips and smiles again. "It called to you. What did it say?"

My heart flutters as he steps closer, taking up the space beside me. His scent, spicy and warm, washes over me. Clove and…lemongrass.

I shake my head and focus on the painting.

"There's…serenity." I inhale deeply to ease the uncertainty of my thoughts, then exhale. Tension ebbs away, and all I see is the painted scene on the canvas. "The woman walking alone through the park, beneath brightly colored trees, I put myself in her shoes. I've been there. Alone in nature, with only birdsong and wind ruffling the leaves for conversation. It's peaceful here." A ripple of relaxation washes over me, and I sigh. "There's no crowds. No commotion. No loud conversations or arguments." My lip trembles. "It's like…I'm the only person in the world."

Beside me, Alex removes his glasses to rub his eyes with the back of his hand. He sniffs and drops his hand, turning toward me. His dark eyes are unfocused, but they're full of understanding. "Thank you." He murmurs with a nod. "For humoring me."

"Your work is magical." The words come out in a near whisper.

"You think so?" He leans even closer, and I'm distracted by his strong presence as it shuts out the commotion around us.

"How do you do it?"

"Do what? Paint?" He chuckles when my breath catches. "To find out that answer, you'll have to visit my studio."

"I…" Is he messing with me? "Are you inviting me to watch you work?"

"Yeah. You seem genuinely interested in my art." He shrugs. "And I like talking with you."

"How do I know you're not a serial killer? Or a—"

"A secret, crime-fighting vigilante?" He laughs. "It's a chance you'll have to take."

I nod, studying his unbothered expression. "Where's your studio?"

"Small town outside of Newark. Train goes right through." He pulls out a card and hands it to me. "Text me and I'll send you the address. You can stop by if you're in the area."

My fingertips brush his as I take the card. A thrill shoots through me at the innocent touch, warming the pit of my stomach. There's something here…a spark of chemistry. I could flirt, maybe say something witty or cute, but my anxiety wires my mouth closed and no words can escape.

Why am I like this? Why can't I say what's in my head?

"Here's one for the road."

Alex opens his hand, and I laugh at the lemon drop candy hiding there. I take it. His hand closes around mine, and the butterflies take flight again. I watch, stunned, as he lifts my fingers to his lips to place a soft kiss on the back of my knuckles. The butterflies turn into fireworks, and every fiber of my being ignites at his chivalrous gesture.

"Alex," his companion calls from the table behind the art wall.

"It's been a pleasure." With a crooked grin, he releases my hand and backs away. Just before tipping his glasses down, he winks and disappears around the corner.

I'm rooted to the spot. What just happened? Was he flirting with me? Did he…no, that can't be right. I shake my head and take a deep breath before sliding his card into my purse.

Ensuring my earplugs are tucked in my ears, I step back into the convention crowd, the colors and sounds muted outside his vibrant booth. My thoughts twist with possibilities about the artist I just met.

I search the immediate area for Ronnie's familiar face and find her still at the table with the author. They seem to be locked in animated discussion, and I'm in no headspace to join. I need to find a place to just gather my thoughts, but it's so loud here.

"There you are," Ginger calls from across the aisle, Vicky and Beth trailing behind her. "Everything okay?" she asks, resting her hand on my arm.

"Oh. Yeah. I'm good." My head nods, but inside, my heart is pounding and my nerves are alight with the memory of his lips on my skin. "Is there a water fountain around here?"

"Yeah." Ginger links her arm through mine. "We passed one back there."

She turns to tell Beth and Vicky we'll meet up with them in a few minutes, then resolutely leads me through the crowd until we reach a hallway with restrooms and water fountains.

I ignore the hum of the crowd and the heat clawing my neck. Ginger stands beside me as I bend to take a drink.

The water is cooling, granting me a momentary reprieve. I think I've overdone it.

Coming to this convention is a huge step for me—the crowds, the noise. I'm overstimulated and flustered. While the earplugs helped to keep me here longer than I typically would have stayed, I think I'm done for the day. At this point, all I can think about is the quiet of my air-conditioned hotel room and the handsome artist who gave me his number. I grasp the edges of the water fountain.

"You doing okay, hon?" Ginger asks again.

"Actually, I'm a little overwhelmed." I look at her with guilt churning in my stomach, but she offers a kind smile and nods sympathetically.

"Totally understand. Conventions can be intense." She rests a hand on my shoulder. "I'll walk you back to the hotel."

"No, I don't want to put you out. Stay. Enjoy the afternoon."

"The panel I want to crash isn't until tomorrow, and I've already scoped out the best vendors." Ginger takes my arm and leads the way back through the crowd. "We can grab a drink at the hotel bar, and you can tell me about your first day at the con."

My heart swells with gratitude. "Thanks, Ginger. I appreciate it."

"No problem." She pulls out her phone. "I'm just going to text the group to let them know."

By the time she sends the message, we're halfway across the floor, and I can see the exit sign ahead. Mustering the last of my energy, I push through the breakdown looming on my horizon.

Once we step out to the street and away from the convention traffic, I feel my stress start to ease. But it's not until we slide into a booth in the bar that I'm finally able to breathe.

It's nearly one in the afternoon, and the bar is empty except for two women across the room. Soft music plays through overhead speakers, and the lighting is dim and relaxing.

Ginger orders iced tea and a mixed appetizer for both of us. I'm grateful for her thoughtfulness. My head is still spinning with convention chaos.

"So…" Ginger rests her hands on the table. "Aside from overstimulation, how was it?"

"The convention?" I clarify.

She nods.

"It's a lot." I sigh. "Sorry, I'm not a fan of crowds and people. Coming here was a test for me…I think I failed miserably."

"I don't think you failed." She thanks the server who delivers our drinks. "I'm proud of you for putting yourself out there."

"Thank you." I hide my blush by taking a sip of the refreshing iced tea.

"Did you get a chance to mingle? Make new friends?" Ginger's green eyes search me, curious and kind.

"I…yeah, I met some people."

"Anyone famous?"

"No." I laugh. "But there's this artist…" Reaching into my purse, I search for the card Alex gave me.

"Ohh, let me see." She takes the card and does a quick search on her phone. "His art is amazing." Ginger opens another window, and Alex's picture fills the screen. "Lord, girl, you didn't tell me he's a fox." She hands me the card. "And he gave you his digits."

"He invited me to visit his studio," I say absently as I tuck the card away again.

"On a date?" She grins.

"No. He was just being nice." I sip my tea and ignore the doubt clawing at my brain. These intrusive thoughts must be my anxiety brain creeping in. No matter how hard I try to work through it, negativity always seems to win. I can't help but always remember what went wrong instead of what went right.

"Jessica, he was *not* just being nice." Ginger shakes her head.

"He saved me from falling down the escalator." A laugh escapes me.

"So he came to your rescue, then invited you to his place? I fail to see how that's just being nice." She winks. "He sees something special in you."

"Yeah—a klutz who can't stand being in crowds."

Ginger leans forward and takes my hand. "Don't talk that

way about yourself, hon. You're allowed to give yourself grace. Cons are huge, intimidating events. Even those of us who can handle noise and chaos often break down. It happens. Don't beat yourself up."

"Why me then?" I ask seriously. "I mean, he can't really want to get to know *me* better…right? I'm just…me. I'm nothing special."

"You're wrong. You are special. I've read your fics. I've seen your art. You may be quiet and keep to yourself, but that doesn't mean you're not worth getting to know." Ginger's words sink deep into my soul. "Give him a chance. You never know…he may be the *one*."

I scoff. "I don't date. The last time I tried, it didn't end well. I'm not looking for a relationship."

"Well, at least give him a chance to get to know you. Friendship can be just as rewarding."

"I don't know." I bite my lip.

"Just text him. See where it leads."

"Fine," I relent, uncertainty filling my head with a hundred scenarios where this doesn't end well.

Fortunately, the appetizer arrives, and I take the opportunity to change the topic of conversation. Ginger mentioned a panel she wants to crash tomorrow, so I ask her about it.

Her eyes light up, and all thought of the artist disappear from her head. I'm thankful for the reprieve.

By the time I reach my hotel room, I'm completely spent. I have no energy left.

After a long shower, I curl up in bed and scroll through my phone. With a sigh, I pull the card from my purse and add his number to my contacts.

(Me): *Thanks for saving me today, Daredevil.*

I hit send.

(Alex): *My pleasure.*

His first message is quickly followed by another.

(Alex): *Call anytime.*

A smile crosses my lips. Maybe Ginger is right. Maybe he's *not* just being nice.

CHAPTER FOUR

I've been home for a week, and I can't stop thinking about my experience at the convention. The wonderful fangirls I met in person. Pushing myself outside my comfort zone. Putting my introverted, anxiety-ridden self in a chaotic environment.

Every thought circles back to Alex. The blind artist who touched my soul with his work. Not just him, but the way he treated me. Like he understood how hard it was for me to be there.

The connection between us had been instantaneous, a gentle humming undercurrent of delicious tension. Maybe I read too much into the situation. I probably did. And now I'm hyperfixated. Rolling over our interaction in my head again and again, searching for hints of his interest…or for something I did wrong.

But that's just it. I didn't do anything wrong. His response to my text proved it.

Call anytime.

I stare at those words on my screen and bite my lip. Steam curls above my hot tea, and the sweet scent of honey, lavender, and chamomile fills the apartment. An insistent rumbling meow echoes behind me, and a soft bump against my sloppy bun shakes me from my thoughts.

"I know, Jax." I turn and scratch under the tabby's jaw. He purrs in response, his amber eyes fixed on mine. "I'm overthinking again."

The message window sits open on my phone, face-up in the

dimly lit room, mocking me. I can't bring myself to do a damn thing about it.

"Prrrow." Jax headbutts harder this time.

I nudge him with a sigh. "You're right. I know you're right. I just…what if he's not interested?"

Jax sneezes and turns away from me. He curls up on the back of the sofa, staring at me with a pointed disinterest I've come to expect from him.

Biting my lip, I look at the phone. "Put the ball in his court." I close my eyes. "Don't take it personally if he doesn't respond."

I run through a list of things my therapist tells me to do when I get stuck in a rut like this. Deep breaths. Don't make up a story.

"Just take a breath and do it."

I type.

(Me): *Hi, Alex. Hope you're well.*

Before I can delete, I press send. The message disappears into cyberspace.

I toss the phone aside and hide my face in a throw pillow. What the hell have I done? What if he's busy? What if he *was* just being nice? What if—

Ding. The notification of a text message rises like an ominous prediction from my phone, as if in response to the sudden onset of regret and anxiety. I snatch up the phone and unlock it.

(Alex): *Hi, Jessica. I'm good. You?*

Short and sweet. I smile and reread it. Then I punch in a response.

(Me): *Still recovering from the convention. Who knew those things would give you a hangover?*

I send it and bite my lip, anticipation tingling through me.

(Alex): *Same.*

(Alex): *No one warns you about the post-con hangover. Curse them all. It happens to all of us.*

I laugh, and tension slowly gives way to a warm comfort, surrounding me like a blanket.

My heart stops when the phone rings in my hand. I jump, nearly throwing it in the process, and stare in horror at the screen. *Alex–Artist.*

"Do I answer, Jax?" I freak out and glare at my cat whose only response is a slow blink. "Shit. You're no help."

I hold my breath and accept the call.

"Hello?" I say, hoping my voice doesn't shake. Nervous energy courses through me, and I take several steadying breaths to calm the flow.

"Jessica. It's Alex. Sorry to call, but it's easier than texting for me." His deep voice rumbles through the phone, and slowly, my anxiety fades. "Did I call at a bad time?"

"No. Not at all. I'm just…sitting here, having tea with my cat."

I face-palm the moment the words leave my lips. Way to go! Now he thinks I'm some kind of loser who prefers the company of animals to people.

Shit…I do. Fuck.

"Sounds like a good time." He chuckles. "What's their name?"

"Who?" I ask, blanking for a second.

"Your cat."

"Jax." I glare at the offending feline. "He's a fat tabby who mooches off me."

"Ahh, a freeloader." Alex inhales deeply. "I know the type. The human equivalent is worse, trust me."

"You have a roommate?"

"I did," he says. "But he got married a year ago. Fortunately, my art has been selling well, so I haven't had the need to find another one."

"Do you prefer living alone?"

I settle back on the sofa and sip my tea. This is nice. I can handle this.

"That's a loaded question," he responds, and I can hear a smile in his voice. "Do you live alone?"

"I'm not sure I can answer that. You're a strange man I barely know. I could be setting myself up for a fate worse than death."

"Point taken." Alex laughs. "If it makes you feel better, most people view me as an easy target."

"You?" I mock-gasp. "But you're Daredevil."

His laughter is so deep and rich, it unleashes something feral inside me. My body warms, and my toes curl at the sound.

"Touché," he says midlaugh. "But who's to say you're not packing some secret weapon?"

The setup is too perfect, and I jump at the opportunity to use it, wondering if he'll pick up on the subtly placed detail. "You're right. I moonlight as a crime-fighting vigilante named Elektra."

"Well then, that makes us perfect for each other," he croons. "Though now I know the truth, I'm guessing you faked your near-catastrophic encounter with the escalator."

"Unfortunately, it wasn't an act. I'm a bona fide klutz." I try to joke, but it strikes true to my own ears. "I'm really good at tripping over thin air."

"Well, in this case, I'm glad. How else could I become your knight in shiny sunglasses?"

I clear my throat as emotion slowly steals my confidence. "Thank you again."

"Don't mention it." His voice lowers a fraction. "It's the

only way I can pick up girls."

This time I laugh out loud, and Jax shoots me a dirty look from his perch on the couch when I wake him.

"You have a lovely laugh," Alex says, his tone confident.

"You're a hopeless flirt," I respond as my face heats. Even though he can't see me, I know he's intuitive enough to know when he's hit his mark. "Does it work?"

"Does what work?"

"Picking up women by coming to their rescue on the escalator."

"I don't know. I've never tried before you." He whispers, "Is it working?"

"What?"

"My flirting technique," he confesses. "I'm rusty."

"It's a bit corny, but it's working."

"Good. I was worried for a minute."

"You were worried?" I blink "About what?"

"That you wouldn't call."

My heart jumps into my throat, and a thrill races along my spine. He *wanted* me to call? His vulnerability eases my tension, and I snuggle deeper into the couch, clutching a pillow to my chest.

"So you weren't just being nice?" I ask gently, almost as though I shouldn't voice the words.

"I *was* being nice…but I won't lie, I had ulterior motives."

"Such as?"

"I like the sound of your voice." The tone of his shifts deeper. "It made me curious."

"About what?" I bite my lip, waiting for his response.

"About whether there could ever be something between us." His heavy sigh echoes through the line, and my breath catches. "Call me crazy, but I'd love to get to know you better."

"Why is that crazy?" I ask. My heart pounds inside my ribs, and hope flutters in my chest like a caged bird.

"We've met only once. Had a brief connection and parted ways." He sighs. "Some people would let it go, call it a missed opportunity."

The sincerity of his words leaves me aching to reach out and grasp what he offers with both hands.

But I'm terrified. What if this doesn't work? I absolutely suck at relationships. Even though it's not what he's asking for, it's where my mind goes.

"I'm glad you texted me." Alex interrupts my rampant thoughts. "I'm not looking for anything you're not willing to give. Friendship is good, anything more would be a bonus. I just…I'd regret it for the rest of my life if I didn't take the opportunity placed right in front of me."

"I–I don't know what to say." My throat works as I struggle to find the right response. "I'm flattered. Truly. But…Alex, you should know, I'm terrible at relationships. My last one ended horribly. I'm a neurotic mess. No one wants to deal with that."

"I understand, Jessica, truly. Everyone comes with baggage. I get that." He pauses. "But I'm not the type of person who's willing to live with regrets."

I nod even though he can't see me. "That makes sense."

"Then let's start at the beginning."

A small smile curves my mouth. "Where would that be? The top of an escalator?"

"Smart-ass." He laughs. "Friends. Let's start there. See where it leads."

"Okay," I finally agree. "I can do that."

"Good." He clears his throat. "I can't promise I won't flirt on occasion."

"I can't promise I won't enjoy it." I laugh.

"So just to set some ground rules." He clears his throat again. "Can I text you?"

"Yes."

"Any time?"

"Yes."

"And calls. Do you want me to text you first?"

"Please." Relief fills me. He's the most observant person I've ever met.

"Done." He mutters beneath his breath and then continues louder. "Any off-limit topics?"

"Not that I'm aware of, but I reserve the right to not answer anything."

"Fair enough," he says. "And yes, you're allowed to ask me anything. I'll answer any question you have, including the awkward ones."

"Like how you lost your vision?" I slap my forehead the moment the words leave my lips.

"I was thinking more along the lines of sexual proclivities, but if you're dying to know how I lost my vision, I'll tell you."

"I–I wasn't…damn it. That's not what I meant." Embarrassment fills me.

"It happens. Humans are innately curious, especially about morbid topics." He sighs. "Not that my blindness is morbid. But it's not something most people deal with, which makes them curious."

"Thank you." I exhale a sigh of relief.

"For what?"

"Being candid and open. It's honestly a breath of fresh air."

"I don't deal in bullshit, Jessica. I'm me. What you see is what you get. I won't hold back." He takes a deep breath. "But I also expect full honesty on your end."

"What do you mean?" I sit up straight.

"If you're uncomfortable or whatever, I need you to tell me. Honesty is important to keep the lines of communication clear."

"I couldn't agree more."

"I think that's enough serious shit for one evening." He yawns. "Thanks again for the call. I'll catch up with you later."

I smile. "Any time, Alex."

"Same." He chuckles. "Have a good night, Jessica."

"You too."

I end the call, and it hits me.

The anxiety that plagued me all week is gone, replaced by a sense of purpose I haven't felt in a long time. Maybe this wasn't just a fluke, a random encounter.

Maybe Alex is exactly who I need in my life right now.

I cradle my phone on my chest and glance at Jax, who ruffles his fur and settles back to sleep. Maybe it's time to take a chance.

CHAPTER FIVE

Alex has been texting me every day for weeks, and I can't say I'm mad about it.

As I finish filing the last documents at the office, I double-check my watch. It's nearly four p.m., and I haven't heard from him. I frown. That's unlike him.

His messages have become an intrinsic part of my day, and I find myself anticipating them. If a text doesn't come, I'm in a funk until the little notification pings from my phone. It's as simple as him sending *Hey, gorgeous*. Perfect. Day made. Let's get shit done.

Only, I haven't heard from him today. Is he angry? Did I say something wrong? I scroll through our messages from last night. My cheeks heat at the sweet things he said. I chew on my lip. Maybe he's just busy and hasn't had a chance to text.

Is it weird to be in this comfort loop? To have become dependent on our connection? Damn it. I've told him a few times I'm not interested in a relationship. Truth is, I can't trust myself to be in a relationship. I'm too…complicated. I've been on my own for so long, and every past relationship resulted in epic catastrophe. I just—I don't want to do that to him. He's too sweet, too pure for this world. I don't want to be the reason he implodes. I can't.

So I keep him at a distance. I never text first. He's hinted about us getting together again—just friends hanging out at his studio to see his art. I want to go, but I don't want to give him the wrong impression. It's better this way.

How this man is still single, I'll never know. He says all the right things to put me at ease, and I'm comfortable chatting with him. We text a lot, and he's called a few times. It's mostly nerdy fandom stuff. A lot of our conversations are silly and benign, but I can't help feeling tension build between us.

His voice does things to me. Wicked things.

And not just his voice—it's the words he chooses. I've fantasized about it more times than I can count. His words and his voice fill my head with thoughts that are highly inappropriate for *just friends*. I've never pursued those thoughts, but I want to in the most desperate way. If the opportunity ever arose, would I be bold enough to tell him what I need? Ask him if he felt the same? The only thing I know for certain is anxious, intrusive thoughts have held me back for too long. I need to take control of my desires and my life.

I'm serious when I say I don't want a relationship, but that doesn't mean I'm not desperate for physical connection. Truth is, I love being single, but I'm starving for touch and horny as hell.

Alex doesn't ask for anything, never implies or makes overtly sexual comments. But there's always an undercurrent of tension between us, both in text messages and on those occasions when he calls. We're building a rapport. A connection. I like that he's taking it slow, letting us get to know each other. It's exactly what I need.

"You can finish that Monday, Jessica." My boss's voice pulls me from my thoughts.

"Th-thanks." I stammer, tucking my phone in my pocket. "I finished filing the stack from last week. The rest of the documents are still in the conference room."

"They can wait. You've been working hard and deserve a break." Joy, the office manager, gives me a warm smile. "Got any plans for the weekend?"

"Yeah," I hedge, not giving her details. No one needs to know I fully intend to sit on the sofa in my pajamas to read all weekend. "I'll see you next week."

Somehow, I manage to avoid all my coworkers as I gather my things and head for the door. The moment I reach my car, anxiety begins to slowly roll away. When I pull into the parking spot in front of my apartment building, it's nearly gone.

Inside, Jax swishes his tail and struts toward me with a hungry yowl.

"So demanding." I scoop him up and bury my face in his fur.

Being in my own space nearly wipes out the ever-present hum of anxiety. I carry the furry menace to the kitchen and set him on the floor before grabbing a can of cat food from the pantry. When I crack it open, his cries turn insistent.

I roll my eyes. Such a baby. Who needs a man when I have this male commanding my attention and adoration?

Ding. My heart stops. *Ding. Ding.*

Three messages hit my phone in rapid succession. I manage to set the open can of food down without spilling it all over myself, then hop over the starving cat to get to my phone in my purse by the door. Breathless, I pull it from my bag and unlock the screen.

(Alex): *Hello, gorgeous.*

His first message makes me smile.

(Alex): *My phone died.*

His second message eases my uncertainty.

(Alex): *How was your day?*

My heart melts into a puddle.

I type out a response and hit send.

(Me): *It was good*

(Me): *Missed you though.*

(Alex): *It mustn't have been that good if a message from me is the highlight.*

I chuckle, and Jax sends me a dirty look from across the room.

(Me): *Your messages have become part of my routine. Feels weird not to get one before noon.*

(Alex): *Same.*

(Alex): *Sorry if I made you worry. Damn phone bit the dust and I couldn't get to the store until after lunch to replace it.*

(Me): *I understand.*

My fingers work as I head to the couch and flop down.

(Me): *What are you up to now?*

(Alex): *Brainstorming.*

(Me): *On what?*

(Alex): *My next piece.*

(Me): *Is it for a show? Or a commission?*

I nibble the edge of my fingernail, unable to stop myself from grinning. He's adorable.

(Alex): *Just something for me.*

(Me): *I'm sure it will be beautiful.*

(Alex): *I hope so. Mindy and Sam are helping, but I'm at a loss for some of the details.*

My smile fades. I sometimes forget how reliant he is on his friends—along with his other senses—for support in his artistic endeavors.

(Me): *I'm not sure if I'd be any help, but I'm throwing the offer out there.*

(Alex): *You'll be my muse?*

Heat blooms across my face. No one has ever called me a muse. It's strange and flattering.

(Me): *If it gets you to put more beauty in the world, then yes.*

(Alex): *The invitation to come to my studio still stands.*

(Me): *Just tell me when.*

A few tense moments pass, and I wonder if I've overstepped.

(Alex): *Can I call you?*

My heart pounds, but I respond without missing a beat.

(Me): *Yes.*

On the second ring, I answer the call. "Hello."

"Hey, gorgeous." Alex's voice warms me. "Sorry. Texting gets tedious, and I'd much rather hear your voice than the animatronic one of my phone."

I pinch my eyes closed and shake my head. "You're always welcome to call rather than text." I sigh. "I'd rather hear your voice too."

"You like my voice?" He drops it an octave in a comical attempt to be seductive.

It makes me laugh. "Yes, I do. But not this Batman effect."

"You prefer Daredevil?" His voice shifts a bit, more him but still deep enough to hit the right auditory needs.

"As nice as that is, I still prefer *your* voice." I smile. "It's soothing."

"I've been called a lot of things, but never soothing."

"Well, add it to your list." I pull a pillow to my chest and hug it.

"I plan to." He laughs. "But seriously, will you come visit my studio?"

"Only if you promise not to kill me."

"I can't promise I won't kill you with kindness."

I roll my eyes.

"You're safe with me, I promise."

"Am I?" I tease, feeling bold.

"Are you what? Safe with me?" He pauses for a long

moment, and I hold my breath. "Yes."

"Why the hesitation?"

"The honest truth?" He exhales sharply. "I can't stop thinking about you."

My heart beats twice before setting off at a gallop. "Really?"

"Fuck."

The swear sounds seductive, and my body responds immediately. Rapid pulse. Stilted breath. Butterflies. The whole shebang.

"I'm trying to be a gentleman, damn it."

"What if I don't want you to be a gentleman?" The question leaves my lips before I can censor it. I barely recognize my own voice—low, breathy. Desperate.

Shit…this is not what I expected tonight.

"Jess, you're making it very hard to behave."

"I don't want you to behave, Alex." I lick my lips, emboldened by the fact that this isn't face-to-face. This kind of confident behavior is not typical for me, but I'm caught up in the moment and embrace it.

"What do you want?" His question filters through the phone with a growl.

"You." It sounds more like a plea than a confession. "I need you to talk dirty to me."

My whole body is hot and aching. I shift on the couch, unable to control the need building inside me.

"I need more. Now. Please."

"You've thought about this, haven't you?"

I can't lie to him, tell him I haven't fantasized about him pinning me to the sofa, exploring every inch of my naked body with his mouth. I moan, unable to stop myself.

"That's what I thought." He drops his voice. "If you want me to stop, just say the word."

"I won't."

He sucks in a breath. "Good girl."

"Alex."

"Yes, sweetheart?"

"Tell me what to do."

His chuckle goes straight to my clit. "I fully intend to."

Before he can say anything more, I vacate the couch and head straight for my bedroom and close the door. The last thing I need is Jax seeing me in this state.

"Are you alone?"

"Yes."

"Are you still wearing clothes?"

"Yes."

"Take them off."

I obey without hesitation. "Done."

"Lay down. Put the phone on speaker."

I follow his instructions. Desire pools in my belly, my pussy clenches. "Okay."

"Now. Close your eyes."

Everything goes dark, but I can see him. Deep in my mind's eye, I picture Alex, with his teasing smile and sinful voice.

"Touch yourself. Start with your face, then trail your fingers lower. Over your cheeks, your throat…"

I groan as I do it, imagining his fingers on my skin instead of my own.

I can't believe I'm doing this. This isn't like me, but I don't want to stop. I would die. I need this. I need *him.*

"When you reach your breasts, I want you to circle your nipples."

I suck in a breath as sensation ricochets through me.

"Now pinch them, gently at first, then harder, until you gasp at the pressure."

This feels dirty but oh-so delicious. Obeying his commands is the most natural thing in the world. A slick of arousal coats my pussy, and I squeeze my thighs together. When the pressure becomes too much, I gasp.

"Now keep going. Over your stomach. Across your hips."

His deep voice reverberates through me. It's like he's right beside me. Touching me with his words.

"When you reach the little crease where your thigh meets your torso, I want you to trace it with your fingertips. All the way down."

I bite my lip to keep from interrupting. Need pulses through me. My hips arch above the bed when I trace the crease as he instructs.

"Now listen carefully," he purrs. "With one hand, cup your pussy."

I do it and moan aloud.

His soft laugh pours through me, emboldening my actions. "Slide a finger across your cunt."

When I do it, I'm embarrassed by the noise escaping my throat and the amount of arousal coating my finger. *He* did this to me. *He* made a mess of me with only his words.

"Tell me the truth, sweetheart." He speaks slowly, deliberately. "Are you wet for me?"

"Yes."

"Taste it."

I obey, and even though I'm not sure what to expect, the action itself is erotic. Sinful.

Decadent.

"How does it taste?"

"I–I don't know." My body squirms, but I keep my eyes closed. "Different. Not bad."

"I'm willing to bet it's the sweetest pussy on the planet." He groans. "If I were there, would you let me taste it?"

"Fuck…Alex…" I whimper as my body writhes with need.

"Would you?"

"Yes."

"You want me to feast on your sweet pussy until you come." His question is more of a statement.

"Please." I slide my fingers across my sex again, wanting more friction. More everything. "I need to come."

"Stroke that clit for me." His breathy command ignites fire inside me.

I do it, and immediately, the pressure spirals higher.

"Picture me there. Touching you. My mouth on your skin. My fingers deep inside you." He keeps going, pushing me toward climax. "I'd tease you until you beg me to fill you, until you plead for me to let you come."

Panting, I gasp as my orgasm peaks.

"That's it, sweetheart. Come for me. Let me hear it."

A choked cry rips from my throat as it strikes hard and fast. My body tenses as the orgasm spirals from deep inside me, wringing every ounce of energy from the rest of my body. Sparks flash behind my lids and I whimper, my fingers slowly stroking my sensitive clit.

"Oh God." I moan as the reality of the situation takes hold.

"Not God." Alex laughs. "That was all me."

I cover my face with my arm, hoping it will hide me from my own embarrassment. I'm blushing from head to toe.

Or it could be the afterglow of the orgasm. Fuck.

"I…ugh." I don't even know what to say.

"Don't be embarrassed." His voice softens. "That was the hottest thing I've ever heard."

"What about you?" I bite my lip.

"Don't worry about me." A choked laugh fills the space.

"I…took care of it."

I mull over the implication of his words. "You came and didn't tell me?"

"Yeah….in my defense, I was distracted by your panting moans and sweet gasps of pleasure."

With a shake of my head, I grab my phone. "Just for that, I should hang up."

"But you won't."

"Why not?" I take the bait with gusto.

"Because I have a proposal."

My heart thunders in my chest. "A proposal?"

"Yes." He clears his throat. "Well, more of an invitation."

"I'm listening."

"A date." He pauses. "Come to my studio. I promise I'll keep my hands to myself unless you want me to touch you."

"Are you sure?" As much as I want this, uncertainty fills me. "About us?"

"We'll never know if we don't try, right?"

"Alex, I don't do relationships."

"I know." He sighs. "I'm not asking for anything serious…just…I don't want to regret it if we don't at least give this a chance. Tell me I'm wrong."

"You're not wrong." I heave a deep sigh. "Fine. When and where?"

"I'll text you." A heartbeat passes. "Sleep well, sweetheart."

"Night."

I end the call and drop my phone to the bed. All the air whooshes from my chest. What in the hell am I doing?

Ding. A text drops onto my phone. I open it.

(Alex): *Next Saturday. 3259 Walker Ave, Millburn, NJ.*

Fuck. Looks like I'm going to Jersey in a week. I wait for the rush of anxiety, but there's nothing but calm.

I'm skeptical. It must be the aftereffects of my orgasm. Nothing else explains why I'm actually considering this.

CHAPTER SIX

When I park in front of his building, nerves hit, butterflies taking flight in my stomach. I wonder if I'm truly insane or just careless. At this point, maybe both.

I drove two hours to see Alex.

I turn off the car and stare at the brick building on a corner lot. It's two stories with vintage aesthetics, giving me thoughts of Jimmy Stewart films and ice cream parlors. A neon sign hangs above the door, Visionary Art, blinking in vibrant green.

"I must be crazy," I mutter to myself before grabbing my purse. After retrieving ChapStick from the bottom of the bag, I pull down the visor and apply a fresh cherry coat.

With a sigh, I send a quick text to Ginger with my location. If anything goes south, I want the cops to know where to start their investigation. Not that I think it will, but a girl can't be too careful, right?

"Stop worrying. He's a cinnamon roll. Just go inside already." I scold myself for even considering Alex to be anything other than sincere in his intentions. I really have to stop watching true crime documentaries.

It's five after twelve. Shit. I'm late.

As I step onto the sidewalk, I smooth my hands over my simple sundress. Its deep blue absorbs the sunlight, and I fan myself, heading for the shade beneath the sign beckoning to me.

Another sign on the door says Closed. I frown. Did he forget I was coming? I see a doorbell beside the brass knob and push it.

Somewhere inside, a light flickers to life, illuminating the space beyond the glass. A shadow appears, moving across the floor, and a figure steps into the light.

Alex.

A smile curves my lips as he unlocks the door. He's wearing a white button-down shirt with jeans. His dark eyes crinkle at the corners when he smiles.

Adorable pops into my mind.

"Welcome," he says as he opens the door and motions for me to come in.

"How'd you know it was me?" I ask, entering the air-conditioned room.

"I'm not expecting anyone else." He shuts the door behind me. "And I recognized your scent."

"I don't wear anything with a scent. Gives me a migraine." I study him carefully and recall the details of his features from our encounter at the convention. He's more handsome than I remember. Probably because he's not dressed as Daredevil. Or because his shaggy brown hair is mussed.

"*Your* scent is unique." He smiles and changes the subject. "Welcome to my studio. I'll give you a grand tour."

Alex offers his hand, and I take it. The warmth of his palm in mine ignites a flurry of need inside me, but I suppress it. Take it slow. Enjoy the journey.

"This is the showroom." He points to fabric-covered walls positioned to create a maze throughout the room. Sunlight from outside hits the windows and highlights the white tile floor, making the space brighter.

As we wander through the room, I recognize some of the pieces he displayed at the convention. I stop short when I see the one of the woman in the park. My heart sings, and I pause to admire it.

"You really love that one, don't you?" Alex asks softly.

"How do you know which one I'm looking at?"

"Well, this is my studio. I know where everything is." He clears his throat. "Your breath caught. I figured it was because something drew your attention."

"You, sir, are far too perceptive." I nudge him with my elbow.

He grins. "Not the first time I've been told that."

"Do you get a lot of customers here?" I pivot to take in the rest of the showroom, ignoring the way his physical presence draws me closer.

"During the week, yeah. I also host painting parties, available upon reservation. They're a huge hit with the local ladies."

I spin to face him, smirking. "I'm sure it has nothing to do with the handsome artist hosting the event."

His grin turns lopsided. "Did you just call me handsome?"

"Maybe."

I try to pull my hand from his, but he holds it tighter.

"Let me show you where the magic happens."

Any response dies on a choked laugh as he pulls me to a curtained area at the back of the room. Inside, there are tables and chairs and all kinds of art supplies organized on a floor-to-ceiling shelf. We weave around the tables, and he opens the door at the back of the room.

It's pitch black.

"Alex…" I turn as he closes the door, shrouding us in darkness. "Uh, what is this?"

"Shit. Sorry." He steps to the side, and the room floods with light. "Is that better?"

I spin to find the room completely covered in paint, spatters of every color on the walls, the floors…I look up, and even the ceiling is marred by beautiful dots and swipes of paint. Along the far wall, a counter is littered with paint canisters and a coffee can of brushes. A sink sits in the center and open cabinets, full of paint supplies, run the length.

In the middle of the room, an easel holds a large blank canvas.

"This is where you paint?" I take in the space again, admiring his organization.

"Yeah." He rubs his thumb across the back of my hand. "It's nothing fancy, but it works for me."

"It's perfect." I inhale deeply, smelling stale drywall and dry paint. My gaze fixes on the blank canvas. "Are you starting a new project?"

He shakes his head. "Just finished one."

"What's this for then?" I run my fingers over the smooth canvas.

"For when inspiration strikes." He tugs my hand. "Are you hungry? I made lunch."

"You made lunch?" I gape as he pulls me to the back of the room and opens another door to a staircase.

He flips the light switch. "Of course." He grabs the rail and nudges me ahead of him. "Just follow these up, then go through the door at the top."

We make our way up the stairs, and I'm hyperaware of his presence behind me. He stays close enough for his heat to tease me. If I slip, he'll catch me. Biting my lip, I grip the rail and continue walking. When I reach the landing, I open the door.

"Welcome to my humble abode," Alex whispers in my ear.

A shiver of delight courses through me as I step into his apartment.

He skirts around me and opens his arms wide. "What do you think?"

I take in the cozy living room and kitchen with outdated furniture. It's clean and organized. My heart overflows when I see the small feast on the kitchen counter.

"It's wonderful." I lean forward and kiss his cheek, taking him by surprise.

He presses a hand to his face. "What was that for?"

"For being so perfect." I twist my hands together. "I–I appreciate the effort."

"I'm far from perfect." He laughs. "Truth be told, I'm a horrible housekeeper. Mindy helped me get the place ready. She told me I shouldn't invite you over before cleaning up."

This time, I laugh out loud. "I love her."

"I'll be sure to let her know." He heads for the kitchen. "Come get something to eat, then we can sit and talk."

He moves without prompting, knowing exactly where every item is in every cabinet and drawer. I admire how well he functions in his own space.

"You get the food." Alex hands me two plates, then grabs a bottle and opens a drawer. "Would you like some wine?"

"That sounds great." I watch him open the bottle and pour two glasses as I place a little of everything on each plate. Small sandwiches. Sliced fruit. Cheese. An assortment of rolled meats. Potato chips.

Alex picks up the glasses. "To the couch."

I carry the plates, and he follows with the wine. Once we sit, I wait for him to set down the glasses before handing him his plate.

"So how's Jax?" he asks, picking up a sandwich.

My heart flutters when he mentions my little fur devil. We fall into comfortable conversation while we eat. Whatever doubts I had about coming here turn to dust. He's just as funny and caring in person as he is on the phone. I don't know why I thought this would be weird or uncomfortable. I *like* it.

I like *him.*

Thoughts of our steamy phone conversation flit through my mind. I watch his mouth, distracted by the heated promises he made that night. When he licks his thumb, I nearly choke.

"Are you okay?" he asks, brow furrowing.

"Yeah, I'm good." I sip my wine. "Do you…can I use your bathroom?"

"Sure." He gestures toward the hallway. "Down the hall, second door on the left."

"Thanks." I head in that direction, peeking into the other rooms as I go. A bedroom. An office. A closet. Ah, the bathroom. I pull the door closed behind me and lean against it.

"Just take a breath," I mutter to myself. "You need to stop thinking about the other night."

I use the facility and wash my hands. With one final look in the mirror, I muster courage. He made a promise, but will he follow through?

I bite my lip. Desperation is painted all over my flushed skin. I'm half grateful he can't see it.

But he'll know.

Fuck. He'll *know.*

I step into the hallway and head for the living room. Instead of saying anything, I admire him, sitting patiently on the couch, waiting.

He inclines his head toward me. "Hello again."

"Hi." I lean against the wall.

Alex stands and crosses the room, stopping right in front of me. "Everything all right?"

I nod, then mentally curse. "Yeah. I'm good."

He extends a hand, and I place mine in his. "Penny for your thoughts?"

"I'm glad I came today."

"Me too." He presses my fingers to his lips.

I suck in a breath. He grins.

A wicked thought fills my head, and I can't shake it. It pushes me to action. Slowly, I withdraw my hand.

His smile falters as I step back. "Where are you going?"

"Come find me."

His laugh echoes through the room as he backs to the center of the living room. "Oh, sweetheart, I may be blind, but I can run circles in this place." His voice drops low, almost a growl. "You have five seconds to hide. One…"

Panic and anticipation infuse me as I dart forward on silent steps. My gaze lands on the small alcove in the kitchen corner.

"Two…" His voice echoes through the apartment.

"Three…"

I slide into the alcove and bite my lip, willing my heart to stop racing.

"Four…"

My eyes close. I hold my breath.

"Five." The number slips from his lips with a satisfied growl.

Every sound is amplified. A train whistle outside. The distant rumble of traffic. Music in a nearby house. The ticking of a clock on the wall.

I can't hear *him.* There's nothing but silence in the apartment. It feels like hours, but it's barely been a minute. Oh shit.

Alex. My heart thunders in my chest. Arousal boils my blood.

I open my eyes, and he's there. Tousled brown hair. Deep, fathomless eyes. Lopsided smile. He places his hands on the wall to one side of me and the cabinet on the other, boxing me in.

His woodsy-scented heat surrounds me as he leans close.

"There you are."

Any response I might form dies on my tongue as he leans closer.

"I told you before, sweetheart. Your scent"—he closes his eyes and inhales deeply—"is unique." He smiles, baring his teeth with hungry confidence. "And I'm very good in the dark."

CHAPTER SEVEN

He's close. So close I can count the crinkles in the corners of his eyes and feel the heat of his body surrounding me.

"Tell me, Jess." He licks his lips. "One word and I'll walk away."

My heart's racing, palms itching to reach for him, but I hold my ground. Memories of our phone conversation still tease me. Even now, I can't think of anything but the way his words coaxed me to the best orgasm of my life. His promises linger between us.

"Did you mean what you said…last week, on the phone?"

"That I want to taste you? Devour you? Make you come with my name on your lips?" He hums low, almost a purr. "I meant every fucking word, sweetheart."

A bolt of lust goes straight through me. I reach up to touch his face but pause halfway. "Can I touch you?"

"You may." He groans when my fingertips brush his jaw. "For the record, you never need to ask permission to touch me. My body is yours to explore."

Cupping his jaw in my hands, I slide even closer until my breath mingles with his. He sucks in a breath and holds it for a moment before closing the gap between us and taking possession of my lips with his. The kiss ignites a fire deep within me. I thread my fingers through his hair and lean into him, pressing my body to his.

Alex doesn't hesitate. He wraps his arms around me, hands moving along my spine, never stilling. He's exploring my body as he delves between my lips. His wicked tongue claims me, stroking and coaxing, begging me to open wider, to embrace sensation.

And I do.

My hands lock around his neck. He drags me from the alcove, tugging me to the center of the kitchen. His mouth on mine. His fingers biting my flesh.

Fuck, I need him. I moan against his mouth, somewhere between a whimper and a plea.

It's like he can read my thoughts because his hands slide down my hips, gathering fistfuls of my skirt. As he drags it up my thighs, his fingers tease the bared skin in its wake.

The moment he reaches the cleft of my ass, I gasp. His soft chuckle echoes in my mouth.

Alex pushes me against the counter and breaks the kiss. With a wicked smirk, he bunches the skirt around my waist, sinks to his knees, and slides my panties down, helping me step out of them.

"I—fuck, Alex." I barely have the words out when his mouth covers my pussy. My fingers tangle in his thick hair.

One hand holds my skirt while the other nudges my thighs apart. Then his tongue is there, sliding along my seam. My head lolls back, and a whimper tears from my throat as he teases my clit before sucking it into his mouth.

"Shit…" Expletives break free as he devours me, explores every slick, desperate part of my body with his sinful mouth. I grip the counter as he lifts my thigh on his shoulder and slides in two fingers.

"Are you"—I gasp when he hits that sensitive spot—"trying to make me come?"

He never breaks stride, but a solid thrum of vibration hits my clit as he growls what I can only imagine is an affirmative answer to my question. I'm close to breaking, and he knows it. When he redoubles his efforts, I shatter beneath his touch.

Sparks ignite behind my lids as I pinch my eyes closed and ride the waves of sensation. The orgasm hits like a tidal wave, ebbing with aftershocks of pleasure. Slowly, the room re-forms under my feet, and I open my eyes.

Kneeling before me, lips covered in my arousal, Alex looks quite pleased with himself. "I told you I'm better in person."

"Smart-ass." I nudge him, trying to disentangle myself from his grip.

He stands and licks his fingers before wiping his mouth with the back of his hand. "Delicious."

My face heats. "Stop."

"I'm serious." He moans as he licks his lips with deliberate sensuality. "You taste even better than I imagined."

"Alex." I want to sound stern, but it comes out breathy.

"I'm far from finished with you, sweetheart." He hooks his arm around my waist and guides me to the couch.

When he sits down, he pulls me on top of him. I sit on his lap, one arm around his shoulders, one hand pressed to his chest. His fingertips tease the skin above my knees. He nuzzles his nose into my throat.

This feels good, comfortable…but I want more. I shift until I'm straddling his thighs and rest my hands on his shoulders.

I hold my breath as he runs his hands over my thighs, under my skirt, slowly lifting the fabric as he explores my body, committing me to memory.

"Take it off," he rumbles, his voice hoarse with need.

With a little shimmy, I manage to pull off the dress and toss it on the nearby chair. He growls with satisfaction as his exploration continues uninhibited. His fingers trace my bra strap to the clasp on my spine. When it springs apart, I slide it off.

I'm naked on his lap. He's fully clothed.

My breath catches as he proceeds to caress me, his hands roaming over every inch of exposed skin. It's the most erotic thing I've ever experienced.

When he reaches my throat, I see his expression shift from need to awe. I close my eyes as he explores my face with his gentle fingertips. He's seeing me with his hands, building a visual of my face in his mind's eye. I let him take his time, savoring the intimacy of this action.

"Fuck. You're perfect." His confession rings through the quiet apartment. "Mindy said you were gorgeous, and I had a fleeting glimpse when I caught you on the escalator. But shit…I never expected…" His throat works, as though he's overcome with emotion.

"I'm far from perfect." I mimic his words from earlier, suppressing my own self-criticism. I have curves and freckles. My hair's a curly mess.

But this man makes me feel like a goddamn goddess as he worships me. I revel in his attention.

"You are to me." He groans when I rock my hips against his, feeling his erection press thick into his jeans. "Do that again, and I can't promise I'll be gentle."

My body hums at the heat in his words. "I don't want gentle."

Alex tears his hands free of my face and reaches between us to pull off his jeans. In a tangle of limbs and with a few bursts of choked laughter, he manages to kick his jeans and boxers off before positioning me on top of him again. I reach for the buttons on his shirt and slowly free them of their tiny loops. The more skin I bare, the more my hunger grows.

His heat soaks into my core resting next to him. By the time I get the shirt unfastened, his cock is insistent against my slick pussy. I slide across him.

"Fuck—condom," he mutters and swears again.

"I'm clear and protected." My thoughts are clouded, but I hear his response through my pulsing need.

"Same."

"Then claim me," I whisper.

With a curse, he grips my hips and fits us together. I gasp his name as he slides deep inside me.

"Fuck, Alex." I dig my nails into his skin and rock my hips.

His moan emboldens me. I move, stroking his cock with each motion, and deep inside me, he hits all the right spots. I cling tighter to him as we spiral into a rhythm. He thrusts up, I grind down, it's pure fucking bliss.

The pleasure builds, and I'm lost in this man.

Alex holds my hips, teeth gritted in concentration. I kiss him. He captures my lips. There's nothing but him and me and this moment.

I gasp when my orgasm peaks, stealing my breath. He holds me tight, driving deeper, harder. Clinging to him, I steady myself, riding the sensations pulsing through me.

He buries his face in my throat and groans when his own release strikes hard.

We sit, me atop him, a tangle of limbs and panting breaths. Heart to heart, cheek to cheek as the aftereffects of our climaxes leave us limp and sated.

He exhales sharply. "That was—"

"Amazing," I finish for him. "Thank you." Softly, I kiss his forehead.

His hold tightens. I sink into his embrace.

"No, thank you," he murmurs into my shoulder before peppering kisses across my collarbone.

"For what?" I ask, searching his profile.

"For this." He smooths his fingers along my ribs and back. "I've been dreaming about it for weeks."

"Weeks, huh?" I smile. "Well…I have a confession to make."

"What's that?"

"I've been dreaming about it too."

He laughs, and the sound rumbles through me. "Good thing we're on the same page."

I sigh. Yeah, same page. Pushing aside negative thoughts, I lean into the moment.

His touch on my breast distracts me and need again pools in my belly.

"I want to paint you."

"Like paint a picture of me?"

He grins. "No, paint *you*."

"Is that a thing?" I ask, breathless at the thought of my body slick with paint, the soft caress of a brush as he marks my skin.

"I've never done it, but it sounds like fun. Maybe next time…"

Pain rips through me. "Alex…I…what exactly do you want from me?"

His hands still, and he frowns. "What do you mean?"

"I told you. I don't do relationships." I try to sit up, but he holds me fast.

"So you're just going to leave and that's it?" He sighs and relinquishes control, releasing me.

When he says it like that, I sound cruel and selfish. I hang my head, insecurity rendering me unable to speak, doubt choking me.

My past relationships haunt the darkness of my mind, casting shadows on this bright, blossoming possibility. I hate that my former partners did this to me, that they made me into this terrified shell of a woman. Their demeaning words and unrealistic expectations ruined those relationships, and yet, they blamed *me* for my inadequacy, my blunders. I did *nothing* wrong, but they gaslit me. Lied to me. Accused *me.*

And the fear of being hurt, of being rejected is too strong. I wither inside at the wounds left behind, and everything inside me calls retreat. I shut down.

"I should go." I climb off his lap and retrieve my clothes.

"Jess…" His voice echoes behind me, full of pain and need. "Wait. We can make this work."

"I'm sorry." I fasten my bra and pull the dress over my head. I need to leave before I say something stupid…or break down in tears.

Panic swirls inside me like a category five hurricane, threatening to destroy everything in its path. I try to stop it, but the trauma is ingrained, no matter how hard I struggle to work through it. Pressure builds inside me, uncertainty turning into a physical presence. My chest tightens. He doesn't need to see me in this state. I knew it would end like this, with me running away before I can get hurt.

I always fall into the same trap.

Tears prick at my eyes.

This was a mistake. I didn't want to hurt him.

But it's too late.

I need to go.

CHAPTER EIGHT

Swiping away angry tears pooling in my eyes, I head for the staircase where I came in. I'm halfway to the workroom when Alex sprints past me.

He leans against the door, hands out, palms up. "Jessica, please. You don't have to leave." He clears his throat. "You shouldn't leave like this."

"Like what?" My voice cracks, and I wince.

"Angry. Upset. Frustrated." His tone is soothing and calm. Steady. Enough so, I find myself torn. "Come on, let's talk this out. We're both reasonable adults."

"There's nothing to talk about." I cross my arms, hating how vulnerable I feel right now, like he can see to the very heart of my panic.

He can't *see* it. No one can. But *he* can sense it.

"What happened just now…in there, was amazing. Tell me I'm not the only one who felt it."

"Felt what?"

"A connection between us." He licks his lips. "You have to admit, it was fucking hot."

A flash of memory swims to the surface. Alex on his knees. His mouth on my skin. His cock thick inside me as he coaxes my orgasm. I suck in a breath as my skin prickles with awareness and warmth surges through my veins.

"It doesn't matter how hot it was." I sigh, shifting my weight to one foot. "I don't do serious relationships."

"I didn't ask for anything serious." Alex drops his hands to his sides. "I have fun talking to you, hanging out with you." He runs his fingers through his hair. "Yes, we had sex, and it was amazing."

My gaze drifts lower, and I realize he never put his clothes back on. Everything is on full display. My mouth waters, but I will not be distracted. Whatever this is, we need to stop. Now.

"I told you. I don't do romantic relationships."

He inclines his head. "I understand."

"It's not something I'm interested in pursuing."

"I never suggested anything of the sort. I only invited you to come over again so I can paint you."

My eyes narrow. He's toying with me, isn't he? "You're telling me if I come over and you paint me, nothing will happen?"

"If you don't want it to, then no. I'll keep it strictly platonic."

"Putting paint on my bare skin isn't platonic, Alex."

He grins. "That's debatable."

I groan. "Did you mean you would paint *me* or *paint* me?"

"There's a difference?"

He's definitely toying with me now. Using humor to soothe my anxiety.

"Honestly, I'd like to do both, if you'll let me. And I swear"—he uses a finger to draw an X over his heart—"I'll keep it strictly professional."

A strangled laugh escapes me. "Alex…I don't—"

"You don't have to do anything you don't want to," he vows. "I'm not trying to rope you into a relationship or put a ring on your finger. I just want to spend time with you. I like you."

"You do?" His words pierce the haze of my panic, and hope takes flight in my heart.

"I do. A lot." He pumps the brakes. "But I promise, if you want me to slow down or back off, I will. Whatever you need."

My gaze drops again. "I need you to put on some damn pants."

"Shit."

Alex covers himself and runs back up the stairs. I follow him to the living room and watch him feel around for his discarded jeans. Once he pulls them on, he smirks in my direction.

"I thought it was a little drafty."

"I'm pretty sure you did it on purpose to distract me."

"Did it work?" He stops beside me.

"Maybe a little." I run my hand over my face. "But you can't keep doing that."

"Doing what?"

"Trying to make me laugh. To make me forget myself."

"Would that be so bad?" He caresses my cheek. "To let yourself live in the moment?"

"It's not only that." I lean into his touch. "I just…have a shitty track record with men, and I don't want to ruin this."

"Ruin what?"

"This." I sigh. "Us."

"How would you ruin it?" he asks, genuinely curious. "It either works or it doesn't. No one says we can't have a little fun along the way."

"How do you do that?" I stare at him in awe, my heart aching.

"Do what?"

"Stay positive and funny all the time."

"I've tried being miserable, and honestly, it was worse. So I made a choice."

"To be positive?"

"Hell no. I have shitty days." He retracts his hand, and I frown at the loss of his touch. "But I don't dwell on them." Alex closes his eyes. "If I did, I'd go insane."

"I wish I could be more like you." I admire his strength.

"You want to be a blind artist from New Jersey?"

I nudge his arm with my elbow. "You know what I mean."

"We all have our journeys." He shrugs. "Some days are harder than others, but to quote the great Joe Dirt, 'You gotta keep on keeping on.'"

I snort-laugh and slap my hand over my mouth. "You didn't just quote that movie."

"I did."

"It makes no sense."

He shakes his head. "It makes plenty of sense if you think about it long enough."

"I don't know that I want to do that." I chuckle. "It could be detrimental to my health."

"Do you want coffee?" he asks as he pulls on his shirt.

"As long as it's not from a plastic cup."

"I would never!" He grins again. "Only the best from Mr. Coffee."

"Okay." I follow him back to the kitchen, subconsciously assessing my panic. It's dulled, subdued. Interesting. My anxiety has shifted into a tentative state of being. Surprised, I embrace peace and try not to dwell on it as I slide onto a barstool across from where he's standing in the kitchen.

He moves fluidly through the room, opening cabinets, prepping the coffee maker with a liner and freshly ground beans. As I watch him work, I wonder how he got to be so confident doing everything without his sight. He did say this was his space and he could run circles around it without effort.

I want to ask questions, and he's assured me I can ask

anything…but I don't want to be rude or insensitive. Alex has been nothing but kind and considerate toward me. I really don't want to fuck things up by upsetting him. Or be a dick by saying something stupid.

"You're thinking hard over there," Alex says as he turns on the coffee maker. "Penny for your thoughts?"

"I–I was going to ask you something, but I don't want you to think I'm nosy."

"You want to know why an amazing guy like me is still single?"

My face warms, but I laugh. "I will admit, it's crossed my mind."

"Well, not to say I haven't had offers…" He strokes his jaw thoughtfully. "But nothing clicked, you know? I decided it's worth waiting for a spark."

"Yeah. I understand that."

"I take it you've been burned?" he asks softly. "It's why you don't do serious relationships?"

My throat tightens. "Yeah. Something like that." I turn away, unable to process the overwhelming emotions flooding me at his perceptiveness. Haunting memories of how hard I fought to make my past two relationships work creep into the perimeter of my thoughts. How hard I fought to make them *work* and burned myself out. Nick and Shane. Two horrible back-to-back disasters left me a burning wreck with no chance of survival. "A fling is easy. Less messy. No strings, no expectations."

"Makes sense to me." He pulls two mugs out of the cabinet.

The gentle hiss and drip of the coffee maker fills the silence between us. The aroma surrounds me, and I sigh.

"Smells good." Alex inhales deeply and groans. "If I'd lost my sense of smell…fuck, I definitely wouldn't be able to do this whole positivity thing. Can you imagine? Can't smell. Can't *taste.*

Life would be bland. It would be torture."

"It would be horrible." I nod vehemently. "I got sick last year and lost my sense of smell for a month. It was terrible. I didn't *want* to eat. Dropped ten pounds."

"Don't lose any more, please." He licks his lips. "I like everything about you just as you are."

"I don't plan to." I laugh, blushing.

"At seventeen, I got into an accident. Serious head injury. The docs weren't sure I would make it." His brow furrows. "When I woke up in the hospital, I couldn't see. My vision was gone. *Poof.* They said it will never come back."

"Oh, Alex, I'm so sorry. That must have been devastating."

"It was." He bites his lip, lost in memory. "I had a great support team. My parents. My sisters. Especially my grandma, who was damn near blind by the time she turned fifty. They came around me and gave me all the tools I needed to overcome the trauma, grieve the loss, find my purpose. They helped me rediscover art."

"You're fortunate. They must be so proud of what you've accomplished." I wipe tears away.

"They are." He pours coffee. "Sugar? Cream?"

"Cream, please." I take the mug, and he turns to open the fridge. "Were you an artist before the accident?"

"Yeah. I mean, I dabbled. It was more for me than anyone else." He smiles. "Gram loved when I would paint the flowers in her garden and hang it on the wall for her to enjoy all year."

"That sounds lovely, very thoughtful."

"Yeah." He reappears, placing the cream carton on the counter. When I reach for it, his fingertips brush mine. The now familiar fireworks build inside me. He retreats and picks up his mug.

"Can I try something?" he asks before taking a sip.

I arch my brow. "What? Something sexual?"

He laughs. "No. I'm feeling inspired." He regards the silence for a moment and smiles. "Can I paint you now?"

"Now?" I ask, nearly dropping my mug of steaming coffee.

"Yeah. I've already got an easel set up." His grin is infectious and a little mischievous. "Let's live a little."

"I don't know, Alex." I look out the window. "It's getting late, and I still have to drive home."

"You can crash here." He holds up a hand. "I have a spare bedroom. You have my word—I'll be a gentleman…unless you want me to play the villain?"

This time I laugh until my sides hurt. "You? A villain?"

"You wound me." He clasps his hand over his heart. "I can be dark and menacing."

"No, Alex." My laughter finally fades. "You are one hundred percent golden retriever energy."

"Is that a good thing?"

"It's for sure not a bad thing." I regard him for a long moment. "Fine. Let's go get our paint on."

"Yes!" Alex fist bumps the air, and I can't help but worry about what I've gotten myself into.

CHAPTER NINE

Together, we descend to the studio. The simplicity of the room's decor indicates a sense of purpose. When I step through the door, the focus is solely on the easel in the center of the space and the small table beside it. This space is exclusively for creating art.

Alex makes a beeline for the cabinets on the far wall and starts pulling containers from random shelves. I come alongside him and admire his process.

"Can I help?" I ask, unsure of what to do.

"No. I'm just organizing the paint." He lays out colors and places quarter-sized dollops on the palette.

"How do you know which color is which?" I ask, watching him work so efficiently.

"Labels." He hands me one of the containers. "There's one on each container with the color in braille and English."

"Clever." I run my fingers over the raised letters. "And how do you know which color to use?"

"I pull from memory, but that's the beauty of art—I can have fun with it. Doesn't have to be exact."

"That explains your passion for vibrant jewel and neon tones." I return the container to the table in the order he had it.

"Life is a symphony of chaos. Why not use vibrant colors to capture it?" A lopsided smile appears on his sinful lips.

"I never thought of it that way." An image of the painting I fell in love with at the convention appears in my mind's eye. The bright colors certainly capture the life of the piece, but the shadowed solitude of the lone woman still holds me enthralled.

Perhaps that's why I can relate to her. A lonely soul surrounded by the chaotic beauty of life, with all its noise and pandemonium. The painting called to me. It's as if it whispered, *I understand, and it's okay.*

"How much do you love that dress?" Alex's question pulls me from my thoughts.

I watch him select a few items from the coffee can. Three brushes and a small trowel-shaped tool.

"My dress?" I pull at the skirt. "It's one of my nice ones."

"Then I suggest you take it off."

His statement leaves me in a pool of need. I could've sworn his voice dropped an octave. He must know how much his instruction affects me.

Holding my breath, I slowly tug the dress over my head and place it on a counter. I'm in my underwear and bra, suddenly self-conscious.

"What about you?" I ask as he places paint and brushes on the table beside his easel.

"Oh, right. Almost forgot." He quickly removes his shirt and jeans, placing them beside my dress. "Thanks. I don't want to ruin that shirt."

We're in equal states of undress, and I'm overwhelmed by the warmth rushing over me, even with the air conditioning on. I fan my face.

"Give me your hand." Alex extends his in invitation.

I take it, stepping closer as he guides me toward the easel. He places me directly beside him and reaches for a brush. When he places it in my hand, I stare at him, puzzled.

"I thought *you* were painting *me*."

"I am." He clears his throat and leans close. "First, I want you to close your eyes."

With a sigh, I do it, unsure why he's asking me to do this. "Okay."

His hand covers mine to guide the brush to the canvas. It bumps with more force than I intend, nearly knocking the easel over. He reaches out and steadies it with his other hand.

"Now imagine yourself looking in a mirror." While one hand holds mine, guiding the brush, the other comes to rest on my hip.

My skin burns where he touches me. I shift my weight, and he comes fully behind me, his arms caging me. His earthy scent wraps around me, and his warmth draws me closer. I lean back. He holds me firmly in place.

Everything fades to background noise. I'm hyperaware of every breath he takes. every flex of his lean body.

I may spontaneously combust. A soft curse slips free.

He laughs, but his hold never wavers. "Relax. Breathe."

"Easy for you to say." I squirm, brushing my ass against the hard ridge of his cock. "Or not."

He groans, his fingertips digging into my hip. "If you keep that up, I'll have you on the floor, covered in paint, my cock buried inside you." He hums. "Is that what you want?"

A response lodges in my throat. If I say yes, he'll do it. If I say no, he won't.

Damn him for putting me in this impossible situation.

"Let's try something different." He lowers my hand and dips the tip of the brush into paint.

I peek, noting the vibrant shade. "Green?"

"Ah, I didn't tell you to open your eyes." He tsks and smooths his hand across my abdomen. "Closed."

A kaleidoscope of butterflies takes flight in the pit of my stomach beneath his hand. I obey, my breath coming in short pants as heat builds inside me.

Desperate desire consumes me again, an unrelenting need for connection. Something about Alex disarms me and puts me at ease. At some deeper level, I trust him. He's not like Nick or Shane or any of the men who have shown interest in me in the past. Whatever this is between us, it's a gift. A promise of something new and unexpected.

I hesitate, and he feels it.

"Do you want me to stop?" His breath brushes the shell of my ear. "If I'm crossing a line, I'll stop."

Indecision rushes through me for half a second before a certainty settles deep in my gut. Alex will never hurt me, not intentionally. This is something I need to embrace. It can't be done in half measures. I inhale deeply as he stills behind me, waiting for my response.

"I–I don't want you to stop, but…" I lick my lips, trying to find my words. "You should know, this is hard for me."

"Hard how?" he asks softly. "I won't pressure you to do something you're not comfortable with. I respect your boundaries. But I'll be honest—being this close makes it difficult."

"I know." My body hums at his touch, but the thoughts in my head spin in a whirlwind. I take a deep breath to calm them. "I want this. I want you…but, Alex, I'm broken, and I don't know how to get past it."

"I understand." He sighs. "We should stop."

"No." I stand firm, grasping his arm. "I want this. I *need* this."

"Okay." With a deep breath, his touch softens. "Why do you think you're broken?"

"I've made shitty choices in relationships over the past few years." My voice breaks. "I don't want to experience it anymore. Betrayal. Pain. Trauma."

"And you believe those failures are your fault?"

"Yes." The word echoes in the space between us.

"Ah." Alex takes a deep breath. "Can I make an observation?"

"Sure." I sniff, upset my persistent inner critic spoiled one of the sexiest moments of my life.

"I don't believe for one second *you* were the problem in those relationships, Jessica." His words make me pause. "I haven't known you for long, but I know, beyond a doubt, you are kind and considerate. You are a loyal and steadfast friend who takes pride in everything you do."

My lip quivers, and I close my eyes, taking his words and planting them like seeds in my soul.

"If those relationships failed, it was *not* your fault. It was *them*. Not *you.*"

A tear slips down my face, and his free hand brushes my cheek as though he'd anticipated it. My heart aches but also warms with his careful, considerate words.

"I meant what I said." Alex's kindness is a balm to my worry. "I'll stop. I'll give you all the time in the world, but I won't give up. I'll wait for you, because you are amazing, Jessica. Beautiful, inside and out."

"Alex." Another tear falls, and he catches it with his fingertip. "You don't want me."

"I do." His husky voice stirs the ache from earlier. "Even now, I can't stop thinking about you."

My breath catches, and I lean into his touch, pushing aside the damn persistent, intrusive thoughts.

What if he's telling the truth? What if he *does* want me?

"I'd be a fool not to fight for you, not to fight alongside you." His hand slides down my throat and across my shoulder, coming to rest on my forearm. "Tell me to stop, and I'll stop."

"Don't stop," I rasp. "I want you to teach me."

"Let's paint." His response tickles my ear, and elation fills me at the prospect of what could come next. I trust him, even though I don't trust myself. I'm stepping outside my comfort zone, determined to live. To create something out of desire rather than fear. He tightens his grip around my hand and the paintbrush tucked between my fingertips.

This time, when the brush touches canvas, it's smooth and even. With each stroke of paint, his touch drifts higher. He explores me with one hand while the other transcribes what he's discovered to the canvas. The movements make me sway, back and forth. I'm nearly limp in his embrace, following wherever he leads.

His hand closes around my breast, and he thumbs my nipple through the fabric of my bra. It tightens against his touch, and I moan, wanting more. Needing more. Higher his fingers travel until they circle my throat, teasing the sensitive skin behind my ears.

The brush moves furiously on the canvas, shifting for more paint at random intervals. At some point, he slips the brush completely from my grip. My hand falls to my side and brushes his bare thigh.

Our breaths mingle as he traces my face with his fingertips. I grip the fabric of his boxers in my fist. However this began, it has transformed into something erotic and desperate. I crave him. I want his mouth on me. His hands. I need him to explore me. To make me come.

"Alex. Please." My plea echoes through the room. Is it really my voice? The deep and desperate tone leaves me confused, but I'm too far gone to care. "I need you."

A clatter punctuates my words. Both of his hands are on me. One, slick with paint, slides over my abdomen. He turns me, and my eyes fly open. For a heartbeat, I'm captivated by his handsome face and his charming smile. It vanishes the moment his mouth covers mine.

I'm drowning in him. His hands roam my bare skin. He tugs my bra free, and I shimmy out of my panties. When I reach into the waistband of his boxers and grip his cock, he gasps, breaking the kiss.

"Fuck," he murmurs as he rests his forehead to mine. I stroke him twice, earning another deep groan before I slip the boxers down. "Shit."

I squeal when Alex grabs my waist and pulls me into his embrace. My leg kicks out and knocks over the table holding the paint. Everything clatters to the floor, my eyes go wide when paint splatters in six directions.

"I—shit!" Panic rises in my chest.

"Don't worry about it." Alex slowly lowers me to the ground. Paint smears my spine. The cool sensation gives way to heat as he settles on top of me.

He pins my hands to the floor. His mouth takes mine in a passionate kiss. I wiggle free and wrap my arms around his neck, pulling his body flush to mine while I guide his cock to where I need it.

Alex shudders when he slides into me. I tighten my hold, savoring the delightful pressure of his body invading mine.

I need this. I *want* this.

When he moves, the world coalesces into a spinning wheel of color and sensation.

I arch into him, meeting every thrust with a frenzy I can't explain.

His hand slips in the paint, and his soft chuckle is lost on my tongue as I kiss him again and again. Pleasure builds, catapulting me higher and higher until I shatter.

He follows with a deep groan when I coax his climax with a gentle bite to his neck.

"That...fucking amazing." His barely coherent words make me smile.

We're laying on the floor of his studio, covered in paint, completely drained when it hits me.

I can't walk away from him. My heart aches just thinking about it. Tears pool at the corners of my eyes. *Fuck.*

This man has flipped my world upside down. The strange part is, I think I might have feelings for him.

That can't be right. We just met. This is crazy.

Shit.

CHAPTER TEN

Somehow, I manage to get back to my feet, even though my head is spinning with uncertainty and worst-case scenarios. Alex takes me by the arm, and a wave of comfort flows through me, banishing the pesky internal criticisms.

Naked and covered in paint, it crosses my mind I should feel embarrassed or ashamed, but the expected emotions never come. Instead, I'm left wondering why there's a ball of emotion lodged in my throat, why I can't vocalize the words inside my head.

"We should shower." Alex's deep voice steals through the haze surrounding my brain.

"Yeah. I can't go home looking like a Picasso."

"I'm sure you're more of a Renoir." Alex smiles, inclining his head a fraction. "Although I like to think of you as a Vernon masterpiece now."

Heat rushes to my face as blood pulses through my veins. "So confident, it's almost cocky." I nudge him with my elbow.

"I'd say I've earned it, wouldn't you?"

"You're definitely a master, Alex." I lean close, and my breath caresses his cheek. "I'd certainly let you paint me again."

His brow arches, but his confident smile never wavers. "It's a date."

"Relentless," I tease, and this time, the jolt of apprehension never comes. Maybe I *can* make something work…at least I can give it a try. What's the worst that could happen?

You could have your heart ripped out and trampled. The annoying, persistent voice I've tried so hard to ignore rears its ugly head.

"Come on. You can help me clean up." He laughs. "The last thing I need is explaining to Mindy why there's paint in my hairline."

"Do you make all your dates shower with you after you paint them?" I ignore the sting of jealousy and how petty the question sounds.

"You're the first person I've *painted*...well, that way." He leads me to the stairs.

"Really?" I turn to study his expression, to see if he's teasing or lying. Not that I think he's capable of it at this point. I feel like I've known him a lot longer than a few weeks.

"Scout's honor." He holds up three fingers in a Scout salute. "You're the only one."

We ascend the staircase while I mull over his words.

"You were a Boy Scout?" I ask, delving into uncharted territory.

"Yup. I was close to making Eagle when I got hurt...and well, you know the rest of the story." He opens the door at the top of the stairs and gestures down the hall. "I'll let you shower first."

I pause outside the bathroom, my hand braced on the door frame. "Wait. What?"

"You can shower first." He stands in the hallway, covered in paint, completely nude, and I'm not going to lie, it's distracting. Alex has no shame in his current state of undress. It's like he enjoys tormenting me.

"Aren't you joining me?" I'm a little stunned to discover this brazen part of myself, but I embrace it, just like I've done with the rest of this journey.

He exhales sharply and runs his fingers through his paint-streaked hair. "Jess, I'm trying to be a gentleman and give you space." He bites his lower lip, letting it slide between his teeth. "If I get in that shower with you, I can't promise to keep my hands to myself."

"Good. Then don't." I step into the bathroom, hoping he'll follow me.

A few seconds later, the sound of the door clicking shut tells me I'm not alone. A shiver of need runs through me. I reach into the shower and turn on the water. It doesn't take long to warm, and steam fills the air, fogging the mirror. I catch a glimpse of myself, smeared in colorful swaths of paint, curly hair mussed and wild.

Alex leans on the edge of the counter, his expression unreadable. I cross the space between us in two steps.

"Penny for your thoughts?" I stand close, but I don't touch him. Teasing him the way he's been tormenting me.

He sighs. "I'm a no bullshit kind of guy, Jessica, if you haven't figured it out by now."

"I picked up on it." My heart pulses wildly beneath my ribs, and I clench my hands into fists to keep from touching him.

"Then you know I'll tell you exactly what's on my mind when you ask that question."

"I do."

"Good. Now get in the shower."

I blink twice, stunned by his command. "Aren't you—"

"Shower." A corner of his mouth twitches. "You have thirty seconds to get wet." His voice drops an octave. "Once I get in that shower with you, it won't be because of the water."

Fuck, who needs water to get wet when he's around giving orders like a professional Dom?

Without a word, I step beneath the hot spray and adjust the temperature. I delve beneath the water, aware it will do a number on my unruly curls, but with the amount of paint on my skin and in my hair, I guess it's a moot point now. My hands smooth over my face and hair to ensure I'm soaked from head to foot. Warmth pools between my thighs.

Three times in one day isn't unheard of, but it's very rare for me. Alex leaves me with promises of more, and my thighs clench at the thought of him deep inside me again.

What kind of woman am I becoming? A horny one, that's all I know for certain.

The curtain shakes, crinkling as it's pulled to the side. Alex steps into the narrow space. He's so close, toe to toe. His heat pulls me, even more than the warmth of the water on my spine.

He reaches out, fingers brushing my side as he settles his hand at my waist and brings me close.

"Are you wet?" His question rumbles through me.

"It's a shower. Of course I'm wet," I reply in a snarky tone.

"Smart-ass." He comes flush against me, skin-to-skin from shoulder to kneecap. His arms wrap around my waist, holding me in place. "You know what I mean."

"I do, but…" My words drift way at the insistent press of his cock against my thigh.

"But what?" He leans closer, his lips brushing my ear. "You want me to see for myself?"

A whimper escapes my throat.

Alex puts only enough space between us to slide his hand between my thighs and drag two fingers along the seam of my aching pussy. He smiles. Without a word, he slides those two fingers deep, curling them to caress the deep spot where I ache for him.

The whimper explodes into a swear followed by his name.

I cling to him, my fingers digging into his skin as he strokes me higher and higher. Heat builds, curling inside me like a hurricane expanding with intensity. His thumb brushes my clit, giving enough pressure to make me gasp.

"Fuck, Alex," I cry out as he continues with steady pressure and determination.

When I finally shatter, I collapse into him, my body shaking, my pussy twitching around his fingers. He slowly withdraws and pulls me beneath the spray of water.

Turning me in his arms, he explores my body with his hands, only breaking contact when he reaches for the soap and a clean washcloth sitting on the ledge.

With careful attention, I track his movements, committing them to memory. He's washing me. A simple act, and yet, it's so much more. He's doing the same as I am. Memorizing every moment, every curve, every whisper. It's erotic and intoxicating. I close my eyes and savor the experience.

When I think he's finished, I slip the cloth from his hand. He opens his mouth to protest, but I kiss him, stealing his words before they escape.

He groans and grasps the back of my neck, holding me in place. I soften, giving into the passion of the kiss and tasting him. He's more addictive than anything I've ever indulged in.

I press my hand against his chest.

Alex breaks the kiss and rests his forehead on mine.

"Let me wash you before the water gets cold."

With a shaky nod, he relents.

I take the suds-laden cloth to his body, and he leans a hand on the tile wall as I draw the fabric across his skin. Fuck if I don't trace every muscular line of him, especially those ligaments at the curve of his hips. He's gorgeous. Strong and lean, muscular and soft. A contradiction and a mystery. I could spend years unraveling his past, his passions, all of him.

Shaking my head, I clear my thoughts. I am *not* completely smitten with this man. I can't be.

But I *am.*

I clean the paint off of him before focusing my attention to his straining cock. Slowly, I lower myself until I'm on my knees.

"Jess, what—" His words die on a choked inhale when I take him in my mouth. "Holy fucking hell."

The water's cooling as I pull him deep into my mouth, but I keep going. It won't take long. He's on edge, every stroke of my tongue earning me a curse-strangled gasp.

His hands tangle in my wet curls, and I work what little magic I possess. This might not be my strongest talent, but I'll be damned if I let him get out of this shower without release. I've been dying to taste him, and I want to hear him cry my name when I make him come with only my mouth.

It doesn't take much to bring him to the edge, and my confidence grows until I know exactly what he likes, then I push him to the point of climax. He nudges me, and I pull back as he comes. It coats my chest and throat, but the water quickly washes it away.

"Shit." Alex tugs me to my feet and kisses me as the last of the warmth leaves the water.

We rinse off in tepid coolness, and he shuts off the tap.

Silence fills the space between us as we step onto the rug, and he wraps me in a clean towel. My brain fills the empty space with questions and uncertainty. I push the thoughts aside.

Alex grabs my hand and tugs me down the hallway to his bedroom. Nothing decorates the walls. It's a simple palette of gray and blue. The queen-size bed has a fluffy dark gray comforter.

He pulls me down onto it, careless of my wet hair and our damp towels, and wraps his arms around me.

"That was amazing," he murmurs. "Unexpected, but amazing."

"I agree." Curling against him, I sigh in contentment.

Somewhere in the back of my mind, doubt creeps in. This can't last. It never does. I bite my lip and look out the window to see the sun drifting low on the horizon.

"I should go soon."

"It must be getting late." Alex breathes deeply, exhaling a noncommittal noise. "You know you're always welcome here."

"Thank you." My heart clenches with a mixture of regret and guilt.

"Jess, I know you're not looking for a relationship, and I won't push you…" He steadies his breathing with a long pause. "But I want you to know, I'd like to make this work. I'll take it as slow as you want—just tell me. You set the pace."

"Alex, I…" My conscience caves, pushing against my reluctance, but I can't concede. "Why? I'm complicated. No. I'm a mess. You don't want to get involved with me."

"I wouldn't ask if I didn't." He kisses my forehead. "Trust me."

"Are you sure you want this?" I ask, rising to my elbow to look at him. "I mean, what if it doesn't work out?"

"Ah, but what if it *does*?" He grins, and it entrances me.

How could I not be falling for this man with all his positive, golden retriever energy?

"Besides, I like you too much to let you walk out that door without *trying*. Any man who lets you walk away is an idiot. You're worth fighting for…you're worth waiting for."

Tears sting my eyes. "Damn you, Alex." I laugh-sob and nudge his ribs. "Why are you doing this to me?"

"Because I think you and I could make beautiful art together." He beams, skin glowing, smile hopeful and wide. "What do you say? Are you willing to see where this goes?"

I regard him for a long moment, searching his handsome

face, memorizing every curve and line like an artist would before creating a masterpiece.

"Fine." I poke his chest, square over his heart. "But if you break my heart, I swear to God, Alex…"

He pulls my hand to his lips and kisses my knuckles. "Good. Now tell me you'll stay tonight."

I can't help but relent when he rises to find my mouth with his and kisses me into submission. Poor Jax will be heartbroken I'm not home for dinner, but he'll survive.

Tonight, I'm taking a chance, and heaven help me, it might be the best thing I've ever done. Or it will be the death of me. Only time will tell.

I just hope Ginger doesn't see my location and wonder if I've been kidnapped…or worse. I send her a text just to let her know I'm safe. Though I'm not sure about my heart.

I have a feeling Alex is different from the others.

I *know* he is.

CHAPTER ELEVEN

Somehow, I manage to slip through weekend traffic without incident and take the exit for to Alex's apartment-studio.

My phone rings, and I hit the speakerphone button. "I'm almost there," I say without looking at caller ID.

"Good." A woman's voice drifts through the line. "Almost where?"

"Shit." I glance at the name on the screen. "Ginger? Hey, girl. What's going on?"

"Not much. Just calling to check in." She chuckles. "I take it you're on your way to see Alex?"

"Yeah, I'm about five minutes from his place." I merge into a turn lane. A shuffling noise echoes through the phone. "Where are you?"

"California." Ginger mutters something. "Sorry, I gotta run. Kitchen emergency. This guy, I tell ya."

"Oh, that's right." I shift in my seat as I remember Ginger's new boyfriend. "How's it going?"

"It's…going." She sighs. "I promise I'll spill all the tea later. Text me when you get there so I know you're safe."

"You know it." We exchange goodbyes, and I disconnect the call.

I catch a glimpse of the clock. "Shit, it's 12:15. I'm late."

Red and yellow leaves catch the afternoon sunlight. Autumn is my favorite season in the Northeast with the color changes, crisp evenings, campfires and hot apple cider. Alex invited me to the Poconos with him and his friends next weekend, and I'm excited to take a well-earned vacation.

It'll be our first trip together. I thought I'd be more anxious, but honestly, I've felt nothing but excitement about the whole thing. His friends have been warm and welcoming, including me in their little group. It feels great to be a part of something without expectations.

Alex held up his end of the agreement, keeping our relationship fluid by giving me space when I need to recharge and allowing me to visit whenever I have time. He cares about me, and I adore him. At this point in the game, I can't understand why I kept him and the idea of a romantic relationship at a distance. I guess only my fear of a repeat of the past kept me from moving forward.

Then I remember he's not Nick or Shane. He's different. I hate that they nearly ruined my chance with Alex by poisoning my impression of what a relationship should be. Assholes.

The past three months have been long-distance. Alex and his friends came for dinner at my place once, and I drove to his a few times. But for the most part, it's been phone conversations and texting. No pressure. Conversations about random things, a little about our pasts, a lot about our plans for next year.

Alex and his crew are packing a moving van with supplies and art to tour the country, hitting every fandom convention they can. A huge anonymous donation came in last month, and Alex wants to use part of it to get more visibility. With the rest, he's planning to start an art program for disabled kids.

My heart. Seriously, he really does have golden retriever energy.

I pull up to the curb in front of his building, and the butterflies unleash in the pit of my stomach. Checking the mirror, I scowl at myself. Alex doesn't care what I'm wearing, but the nervous reaction leaves me in a panic. What the hell am

I doing?

With a deep breath, I close my eyes. *In. Out. In. Out.* Deep breaths.

After grabbing the envelope on the passenger seat and tucking it into my purse, I step out of the car. The familiar brick building is decorated with fall leaves, pumpkins, and huge bushy mums. Must be Mindy's touch. She has a gift for detail.

I slip around to a side entrance, climb the steps, and knock on the door. My heart beats like a thunderstorm in my chest. I lick my lips and wait, shuffling from one foot to the other.

The deadbolt clicks, and the door swings open.

"You made it." Alex leans on the doorframe. "I was beginning to worry you got lost."

"No, just hit traffic." I lean close to give him a chance to gauge my distance, but he already knows. Daredevil is right.

His arm snakes around my waist, and he pulls me to his chest, burying his face in the curls against my neck. "Fuck, I missed you."

I sink into his embrace. "I missed you too."

Alex finds my lips and plunders them, stealing my breath and igniting an electrical storm inside me. It flickers through my limbs, shooting to my brain where everything short-circuits. I forget everything but the man kissing me.

When he draws back, I gasp for air and sway on my feet. He holds me steady.

"Come inside." He takes me by the hand. "I have something to show you."

"You…have a gift for me?" I stagger after him as he closes the door and draws me into his apartment.

"Of course." He shoots a grin over his shoulder, steadily leading me down the hall.

"Where—?" We stop outside his bedroom, and my mouth

seals shut.

"Close your eyes." Alex's request leaves me tingling with anticipation.

I close them and clench his hand in my fist. "What did you—"

My breath halts at the faint creak of hinges. Alex leads me into the room.

"No peeking," he reminds me in a teasing tone. We stop and he comes alongside me.

"Alex, what did you—"

"Open your eyes."

"What in the—oh!" I gasp when I open them. His surprise hangs on the wall above his bed. A six- by four-foot painting in vibrant hues of neon and jewels. My heart jumps into my throat as I carefully study the painting, taking in the curves and the swirls of color.

"What do you think?" Alex asks, his voice shaking.

"It's…" My hand grasps his as tears fill my eyes. "Is that…me?"

"Yes." Alex squeezes my hand. "Do you like it?"

"Like it?" I cover my mouth with shaking fingers. "Alex, I love it."

His sharp exhale fills the silence between us, and I turn to face him, cupping his cheek in my palm.

"How…when…"

"The last couple of weeks, I worked on it." His smile warms me through. "Mindy helped with some of the finer details, but a lot was from memory."

I study the painting again, noting the nude woman lying across the canvas with a strategically draped cloth and a cascade of golden curls over one shoulder and trailing down her back. Her profile is turned to catch a hint of a smile and brilliant jewel-colored eyes.

"You memorized every curve of my body?" I ask, teasing him.

"Damn right I did." He pulls me close. "Every time I touch you, I'm sealing it away in memory. Your body." He runs his hands over my hips. "Your scent." He inhales deeply at the base of my throat. "Even the melodic sound of your voice."

He presses a kiss to my lips. I melt into him.

"Alex," I murmur against his mouth as he steals kiss after kiss.

After a few moments, I'm tangled in his web, and the need is too much to ignore.

"Wait," I press my hand into his chest, hoping to curb his interest for a moment until I can give him *my* surprise.

"What?" He breaks the kiss, breathless and confused. "You don't want me?"

"I want you." I keep space between us when he tries to kiss me again. "But I have something for you too."

"You brought me something?" he asks softly.

"Of course I did." I mirror his response from earlier and take the envelope from my purse, then I place it in his hand.

"What's this?"

"An invitation."

He inclines his head and purses his lips. "To what?"

"Read it."

Alex chuckles and tears open the letter. "How am I supposed to rea—shit…is this braille?"

Excitement floods me. "Yes."

"You…" He swallows thickly, as if choking on emotion. His fingers trail over the contents of the letter, emotion playing across his face as he scans the words with nubile fingertips. "You're inviting me to Thanksgiving." He clears his throat.

"With your family." A deep breath and a pause make my heart leap. Finally, he finishes. "As your boyfriend."

"Alex, I would love for you to come celebrate Thanksgiving with me and my family." I push through the fear and excitement pulsing through me. "They deserve to know the wonderful man who has not only captured my likeness, but my heart."

"Jess." Tears stream down his cheeks. "You just made me the happiest man alive."

I squeal as he picks me up in his embrace and spins me around. His heat sinks into me, and every apprehension I've ever had fades into the distant past.

This man knows me. This man *sees* me.

"I love you, Alex." I murmur against his lips.

"Those are the sweetest words ever spoken." His smile widens. "I love you too, Jess."

My heart nearly explodes with joy. "So you'll come?"

He sets me on my feet and cups my face in his hands, fingertips dancing over my skin. "Under one condition."

"Anything," I promise. "You name it."

"You'll spend Christmas with me and my family." He laughs, and the sound sends me straight to the moon.

"You want me to meet your family?" I grin.

"Absolutely. My mom can't wait to meet you. And my sisters haven't stopped asking me ridiculous questions about what kind of music you like and what movies are your favorite. It's annoying. Please stop them, for the love of God."

"I can't wait to meet them all." This time, I kiss him, stealing whatever rambling thoughts would spill from his mouth.

Alex groans when I deepen the kiss, and we stumble to the bed, collapsing in a heap on the gray comforter. He makes love to me hard and fast, then soft and slow, savoring every inch of my body, every sound I make.

It's heaven. Pure bliss.

I wouldn't have it any other way.

Going to that convention was the best thing I've ever done, because it put me exactly where I needed to be. Right where Alex would find me.

Tripping over my own feet, tumbling headfirst down an escalator, right into his arms. A story for the comics, that's for sure.

None of the girls will believe this one.

THE END Book 2

The Bodyguard
Fangirl Confessions
Book 3
KIRSTEN S. BLACKETER

CHAPTER ONE

I adjust the strap on my top, managing to wrangle my cosplay into place, and take a deep breath as the line shifts forward. Maybe I should have worn my *Space Vendetta* outfit today instead of this *SteamPunked* one. It doesn't matter, I'm invested. But this irritating strap just might be the thing that pushes me over the edge.

I look at the other attendees waiting to enter the convention center. Some are in costume, others wear merch from their favorite fandom. And then there are those who look like they walked in off the street on any average day. Fans come in all shapes and sizes, but few understand how important this community is to someone like me.

It literally saved my life.

No one takes me seriously. After ten years of dedication to fandom life, it still bothers me that there isn't a soul alive who understands the depth of my commitment to this community. Sometimes I take it too far, which is how I earned my nickname—Beth the Bitch—in online forums. Many recognize me as MistressViper, a title I've earned by being a *little* too critical of my fellow fangirls.

I don't mean to be this way. It's who I am. I embrace it.

Meeting our little group of fangirls at the Philadelphia convention is a huge step outside my comfort zone, and I wasn't sure I'd be welcomed by everyone in the group. Some comments I've left on the groups' fanfics were more critical than constructive. It ruffled some feathers with some members.

Seeing how I've never met any of these women in person, I may have crossed a line. Regardless, I feel like I've known them my whole life.

When we met for dinner last night, I wasn't sure what would happen. Jen didn't seem too excited to see me, and Jessica kept to herself. Vicky and Ginger welcomed me without hesitation. Madre and Ronnie were friendly but maintained their distance. Not that I blame them. I'm an acquired taste.

The strap pulls and twists against my skin when I shift my bag on my shoulder. "Goddamn son of a bitch," I grumble under my breath as I enter the narrow entrance, fumbling with my badge.

An affronted grunt rumbles beside me.

I glare at the prude asshole, but my caustic reply turns to ash.

Fuck. Not a prude.

I meet the dark gaze of a black-clad security guard with an earpiece and an unwavering frown. A quick assessment of him tells me all I need to know. This guy is smoldering hot—I'm talking five-star villain material, from his dark hair to a piercing judgmental stare. Just give him a dark cloak and a scar and he'd fit the part of every dark romance girl's fantasy.

Good thing that shit doesn't affect me.

"What?" I snap.

"The bag." He points to the table beside him.

"What about it?" I ignore his unspoken demand.

He grinds his teeth, a muscle in his jaw twitching with the effort. "Security protocol. We inspect the contents of every bag upon entrance to the convention."

With a huff, I pull the bag off my shoulder, which retwists the strap and pinches my skin in the process. I slam the bag on the table before—again—fixing my costume.

He purses his lips and opens the bag. As he rifles through my personal items with the grace of a hippopotamus performing ballet, I study his profile and mentally curse whoever thought it was a good idea to put a handsome fucker with a shitty attitude on security duty at a comic convention. This is supposed to be a happy place, but my mood is shot to shit because of this grumpy asshole. This *delectable* grumpy asshole.

I'm torn between irritation and attraction. He shoves the bag at me and jerks his head toward the entrance, telling me, without the consideration of words, I can enter the convention.

"Grumpy fuck," I mutter beneath my breath and snatch my bag.

His grip tightens as he pulls it—and me—closer. "This is a family event. Keep it up, and I'll make sure this convention is your last."

My breath catches at the implication of his words. "Did you just threaten me?"

"Not a threat. A promise." His eyes darken. "Behave, princess."

The audacity of this prick burrows beneath my skin.

"If anyone needs goddamn manners, I suggest you look in a fucking mirror."

His brow arches, amusement flickering in the dark depth of his eyes, but his demeanor remains etched in stone. We lock in silent battle for what feels like an eternity, but he finally releases my bag and turns away in dismissal.

"Next," he calls.

Heat blossoms inside me and transforms to a full-blown volcano of hate. His casual dismissal left me speechless—which is an accomplishment—but the fact that he didn't respond to my comment leaves me fuming. I stare at him for a long moment while he completely ignores me. What an *asshole*!

I stomp forward, stifling the urge to turn and glare daggers at the insufferable dickhead as I weave deeper into the crowd and pull out my phone. A text from Ginger lets me know their location. I make my way toward the vendor entrance.

Once I find a quiet spot, out of the way of traffic, I lean against the wall and scan the crowd. Irritation floods me as I switch the bag to my other shoulder. *Damn this fucking strap*, I curse repeatedly and attempt to fix it in place. Maybe Vicky has some tape or something. I don't know if I can stand any more inconveniences today. Especially one that follows me and consistently puts me in a pissy mood.

Ginger appears, her auburn waves catching the light, followed by Jessica and Vicky. I manage a tense smile and ignore my costume frustrations.

"Hey, Beth." Ginger hugs me.

We exchange greetings and sort out the details of everyone's agenda. Tomorrow, Ginger and I have scheduled events—she has a panel and I have two photo ops, one with Raven Stark, the other with Vincent Mallard. But today, we're free to roam the convention until we meet up with Madre and Jen later.

"Hey." I greet Vicky.

As we lay out our plans for the day, Vicky and Ginger to eye me suspiciously.

"Who pissed in your cereal?" Ginger calls me out.

"A handsome fucker posing as a security guard. Asshole threatened to ban me from the con." I scoff. "I'd like to see him fucking try."

Vicky's eyes widen. "He said that?"

"Yeah, kind of a dick move." I tug the offending strap again and squirm with frustration.

"Looks like you have an issue." Vicky points at my shoulder.

"In more ways than one," Ginger teases, but she sobers at

my scowl. "Sorry, it's just…only you could make an enemy the first day of a fandom convention."

I frown. "What's that supposed to mean?"

"Girl, you know we love you to death…but you can be intense. Some people struggle to know how to handle your…"

"Passion," Vicky supplies with a nod. "It's not a bad thing. You're just an acquired taste, like Jaegermeister."

"Did you just compare me to questionable *liquor*?" I gag at the thought of the taste, not to mention a hazy memory of getting shitfaced on it in my early twenties.

"We all indulged, girl." Ginger chuckles. "Anyway, I wouldn't worry about the security guard. He probably woke up on the wrong side of the bed."

"Yeah, I wish it had been *my* bed," I mutter under my breath, realizing too late it should have been an inside thought.

Ginger and Vicky share a knowing look and grin.

"Don't say anything," I growl. "Let's just check out the vendors."

"Want me to fix your strap first?" Vicky opens her bag and pulls out the sewing kit.

"I got it."

"No. You'll just stew in a miserable mood." Ginger gestures to Vicky. "Let her fix it. I don't want to hang out with Bitchy Beth all day because of a costume malfunction."

"Fine." I hand Ginger my bag and straighten so Vicky can assess the damage.

Within minutes, she's got the strap pinned in place and soft cotton fabric hidden beneath it. The irritation slowly fades, both in my mood and chafing skin.

"That better?" Vicky asks as she steps away and replaces the kit in her bag.

"Much." I smile, feeling tension ebb. "Thanks."

Vicky beams. "Of course."

"Now, let's go. There's a lot of ground to cover." Ginger links her arms through ours and pulls us into the vendor area.

My bag settles against my hip as relief fills me. It's weird how something so minute as a twisted, fraying strap can throw me into such a miserable mood.

We meander from booth to booth, taking in the awesome items for sale. It never fails to amaze me how creative the fandom community truly is. I scan items, admiring them, but nothing calls to me, begs me to take it home.

My thoughts shift, and without warning, an image of the sexy security guard pops up in the shadowy reaches of my brain. Dark hair, dark eyes, deep scowl. Fuck, he'd make a damn fine villain. But it's his voice…*fuck*, that voice could command armies. Decimate villages. Incinerate panties! I shiver at the thought, then shove the unbidden heat aside.

No, he's a first-class asshole. I should not be absently drooling over a jerk who threatened me. Truth is, this is a huge event, and the odds of us crossing paths again are a million to one. Part of me wilts at the knowledge, but I ignore it.

"You keep scowling like that and people will think you're contemplating murder," Ginger mutters beside me. "Are you?"

I snap from my thoughts and realize she's leaning close so people won't overhear. "Maybe."

"Whose demise are you plotting?" she asks with a lopsided smile.

"That damned security guard." My head aches just thinking about our earlier interaction.

"Interesting." Ginger arches a brow.

"What?"

"That some random man burrowed under your skin so easily." Ginger taps a finger on her jaw. "I've seen you take on internet trolls and convention hecklers without breaking a sweat, but this guy has you twisted up. What's different?"

"I–I don't know." I huff, exasperated he has this effect on me. "Aside from the fact that he is by far the sexiest man in this building—which is saying a lot, considering the number of celebrities in attendance. He just pushed all my buttons."

"Or you'd *like* him to push different buttons." Ginger winks.

"I wouldn't give him the satisfaction of knowing how much he affects me." I pause, inspecting a purse hanging from a rack in a neighboring booth.

"I love a good enemies-to-lovers trope."

With a side-eye at my friend, I shake my head. "You're hopeless."

"You write the best enemies-to-lovers fics," she says with a smirk. "It's only appropriate you get to experience one firsthand."

"We're not enemies, and I'll never see his surly ass again." I sniff. "End of story."

"We'll see." Ginger sighs. "Strange things happen at fandom conventions."

"Yeah." A derisive snort rips from deep within me. "We're all going to meet our husbands at a fandom convention in the City of Brotherly Love. You're a goddamn hopeless romantic, Ginger."

"And you love me for it." She blows me a kiss.

Vicky reappears after helping a cosplayer with a wardrobe malfunction, and the conversation shifts to *Throne of Ashes* as a burly cosplayer, dressed as the Forgotten Knight, stalks toward us.

I glance around, my spidey senses tingling. That guard is here. Somewhere.

I can't tell if the thought infuriates me more than it turns me on. Damn him.

CHAPTER TWO

Day one of the convention will definitely go down in the history books. It's nearly six, and there's been drama from our little fangirl group.

Jessica bailed. Big surprise. She's nice. Too nice. Not as much of a fangirl as she claims to be—it's obvious she isn't fully invested in the con or our fandom. Ginger mentioned something about her nearly falling down the escalator, whatever that means.

Vicky hit the jackpot with a cosplay disaster. Helping a random guy dressed as the Forgotten Knight and getting a picture with him had all of us swooning. If I didn't know better, I'd say the man was Jason Hunt in the flesh…but that's insane. An actor cosplaying his own character? No one would do that.

Ronnie's been distracted all day, ever since she spoke with Michael DeHart, the whole reason the *Space Vendetta* universe exists. Meeting the author of your favorite franchise is pretty awesome, but I'm more about focusing on my own writing goals. Besides, I'm not here for the *Space Vendetta* fandom as much as for the *SteamPunked* cast doing photo ops tomorrow.

Jen and Madre kept to themselves until Jen fucking disappeared! Poof, gone. Hell, don't get me started with Jen. I could tell she didn't like me the moment I met her last night at the pub. I'm sure she's fine—wherever the hell she is. Poor Madre was called to her hotel room for a family emergency.

Vicky's adjustment on my strap held, but it left a rigid piece of fabric chafing my skin. I refrain from tugging it and head for the doorway to the autograph area where Ginger said she'd wait for me. As I round the corner, I spy Vicky and Ginger near the wall. Vicky's busy rifling through her cosplay kit, but Ginger brightens when she sees me.

"I don't know if I can take any more drama today," I admit, nudging her with my elbow.

She half smiles and shakes her head. "It's been a weird day, that's for sure."

"We should go get something to drink." I rub a hand over my stomach. "And eat. I'm starving."

"Sounds like a great idea," Vicky agrees.

"Let's get out of here." I gesture to the exit, noting the dwindling crowd funneling out of the convention.

"Mind if I hit the bathroom before we go?" Ginger says.

"Yeah." Vicky puts away her kit and glances around. "Over there." She grabs Ginger by the hand and tugs her to the restrooms.

"I'll wait here," I grumble, leaning against the wall and crossing my arms.

Half-heartedly, I scan the receding sea of fans and pout. The whole day passed with not one glimpse of the grumpy guard from this morning. I huff. I don't know why I'm even thinking about him. Our interaction made an impression, that's for sure. I haven't yet decided if it's good or not.

One thing I know—I curse as I tug at the offending costume strap for the millionth time—I'm changing out of this goddamn outfit before we go for dinner. Even with Vicky's magical fix, it's beyond annoying. I might lose my shit if I have to put up with it a moment longer.

I pull aside the strap, exposing my shoulder. My skin burns at the brush of fabric, soothed slightly by the cool air. I don't have to see it to know it's red and angry as hell. I brush my fingertips over the wound, heat seeping into my skin, and I hiss. Fuck. I'm going to need ointment or something.

"Stripping at the convention is prohibited." A deep voice echoes behind me.

"I'm not stripping, asshole." I grind my teeth and turn around, ready to give this presumptuous prick a piece of my mind.

Still clad in black, wearing the exact same scowl, is the guard from this morning.

My instinct should be to apologize, but fuck him. Seriously.

I frown and lift my chin to face him fully, not bothering to cover my bare shoulder. I'm pretty slender with almost no boobs, but this costume puts them on damn good display. With my shoulder bare, it's borderline obscene, I'll grant him that. But I can't bear the touch of fabric on that spot a moment longer.

"Don't you have anything better to do than harass me?"

He folds his arms across his broad chest and narrows his dark eyes at me, searching, pinning me in place, as though he's passing judgment. I swallow hard, suddenly uncomfortable at the intense scrutiny.

So I give it right back to him. Measure for measure.

Finally, he responds. "You're lucky I'm off the clock."

"Or what? You'd kick me out for baring too much skin?" I gasp in mock horror before sobering again. "It's a fandom convention. There are people here wearing less than I am, showing way more than a shoulder."

"That might be true." He steps closer, his lips twitching. "But your smart mouth and fuck-it-all attitude tell me you're one step away from making trouble."

"Trouble?" I arch a brow at him and scoff. "You're making a fucking big leap with that one."

He inclines his head, looking me up and down once more.

"I doubt it."

"Fuck you, dickhead."

"See? That mouth is gonna get you in trouble." He shoves his hands in his pockets. "Mark my words."

The handsome fucker turns away and heads for the exit.

I stare after him, unable to believe he said those things, irritated he took the last shot before leaving.

"What kind of fucking security do they hire for these events?" I mumble.

"What's that?" Ginger asks as she and Vicky come beside me. "Did you say something?"

"Never mind. I was just grumbling." I tenderly resettle the strap in place.

"That looks sore." Vicky frowns and points to my shoulder. "I guess my fix wasn't as good as I thought. Damn. Why didn't you say anything?"

"I didn't want to steal you from the other cosplayers."

"You wouldn't have. Next time, let me know." Vicky inclines her head. "We can stop at the hotel to change before we eat. I've got some ointment you can put on it."

Relief washes over me. "Thanks. It hurts like a bitch."

"I can look at that costume for you to make sure the strap is better secured so it won't rub." Vicky falls into step beside me.

"That would be great." I sigh.

Ginger gives me a curious look as we head for the exit, but I ignore it. I don't know if she saw me talking to the asshole guard.

I'm still reeling from the strange conversation. He certainly didn't make a good impression. Part of me wonders if he'll be working tomorrow. I shake my head. *Stop thinking about him. He's a jerk.*

Another part of me, probably connected to my ovaries,

chimes in, *Yeah, a fucking hot jerk.*

Before I let that train of thought derail me completely, I turn my attention to our mission. Go to the hotel, change, hit up the pub. I need something strong.

Tomorrow, I'm set to meet one of my favorite actresses, and I won't let some grumpy-ass guard piss on my parade.

After we change and freshen up at the hotel, we make our way to the pub where we had dinner the night before. It's a cozy spot with delicious food and solid drinks.

The moment the waitress leaves with our order, Vicky sighs. "I can't stop thinking about him."

I snort into my cosmo. "Who?"

"A cosplayer." Ginger's eyes widen, and her lips curl in a sly smile. "The Forgotten Knight?"

Vicky hangs her head as Ginger fills me in on the details. By the time she finishes, Vicky's face is six shades of red.

"So did you get his number?" I ask with a grin. "It wouldn't be the first time I've heard of people with a mutual fandom bond hooking up at a convention."

"I'm not hooking up with him," Vicky protests weakly, hiding behind her mojito and sipping it quickly. Not a great idea on an empty stomach.

"Maybe you should." I smirk. "Sounds like all of us need to get laid."

"Did you get the security guard's number?" Ginger turns to me. "Maybe you two can fuck it out of your system."

I grumble at the mention of the man and play it off with a wave of my hand. "He's not worth my time." I divert my attention to Vicky. "But you never answered…*did* you get his number?"

"No." She frowns and pulls out her phone, holding up a picture of the two of them. "All I got was this photo of us together."

"Let me see." I take the phone from her and inspect the picture closely. That cosplay is damn good. Almost too good. I zoom in, looking for a flaw. Something's off. "You two look pretty cozy."

"They were." Ginger snickers before taking a sip of her lemon drop martini. "They were so cute together."

"Wait." It hits me again, this time like a ton of bricks. The floor rips from beneath me, and all thought of the sexy guard disappears like smoke on the wind. "Girl…I don't know how to tell you this, but that's not a cosplayer." I show her the photo again. "*That's* Jason Hunt."

"Get the fuck out of here!" Ginger snatches the phone from my hand and stares at the photo. "Oh. My. God. No fucking way."

Everything goes to hell in an instant. Jason Hunt was at the con, dressed as the Forbidden Knight. *Holy shit!*

I pull up Instagram to show her the impact of her encounter with Jason Hunt. Her followers are growing by the thousands. The comments—both good and bad—are compiling. As we discuss the implications of her random encounter turning social media gold, I can't help but wonder if Vicky can handle it, being thrust into the spotlight in such a way. She's the sweetest, most unpretentious member of our group, aside from Jessica. Those vultures would crush her if they ever got a chance. She's a huge fan, followed all his work, watched all his interviews. And now, she's in full-blown panic mode.

Ginger and I attempt to calm her, walking her through the steps, assuring her it will all work out, but I'm not sure it matters. Vicky is beside herself, thinking she inadvertently betrayed him by revealing his presence at the con.

No matter how hard I try to convince her it will work out

and it's not a big deal, she spirals. While we haven't known each other long, these girls are the closest I've ever had to sisters. I care about them, even if it comes across harsh sometimes. I try my best to comfort her and offer support. Ginger and I manage to convince her it will be okay. When our food arrives, we discuss the convention events for tomorrow and get a game plan in place.

To be honest, I'm thankful for the distraction Vicky's little dilemma provides. It gives me something to focus on instead of the villainous bastard who seems to be haunting my subconscious.

Later, Ginger and I sit at the bar in a little joint up the road from the hotel while Vicky recovers in her room. I cradle a cosmo in one hand and sigh.

"Now that we've put out that fire"—Ginger eyes me over her lemon martini—"are you going to tell me the truth about that sinfully dark and sexy security guard I saw you talking to?"

"I don't know what you're talking about." I ignore the heat building inside me.

"Don't play stupid, Beth," Ginger says with a wicked grin. "I saw you. The sparks flying between you could set the place on fire."

"He was being a dick." I say finally. "Nothing new there."

"He was the same guy from this morning?"

"Yeah. Fucker has some kind of chip on his shoulder." I shrug.

"Are you sure he wasn't hitting on you?"

"Hitting on me?" A scowl forms on my face as I consider her words, and I snort. "More like flexing his authority, trying to intimidate me."

"I don't know." Ginger clicks her tongue. "I saw the way he looked at you, girl. Like you're a three course meal and he hadn't eaten in a month."

This time I laugh. "You're deranged."

"I'm dead serious."

"He's just a rent-a-cop on a power trip."

"Whatever you say." Ginger throws up her hands. "But I'm telling you right now, he would have taken you against that wall if you'd shown the slightest interest."

My breath catches as the image forms in my mind. Those fathomless eyes on mine just before he pulls me into his strong arms, pushes me against the wall, captures my mouth in a sinful kiss. I blink twice, trying to wipe the vision away.

"Whatever," I say with half-hearted scoff. "He's a dickhead, and I'm not interested."

"If you say so," Ginger replies with a soft sigh before turning the conversation to Vicky's situation.

I'm relieved. Partially because I know she's right, but also because I know even if I give in, it won't last. Men can't handle me. I fucking terrify them.

Deep in the back of my mind, I picture him. Tall, dark, undeniably sexy. Something tells me he likes it on the rough side. A wicked smile curves my lips before I can stop it, and my body hums with appreciation.

Fuck. I hope I don't see him tomorrow.

CHAPTER THREE

The last thing I expected to wake up to is a red-faced Vicky barging into our hotel room a half hour until meetup time, in the same clothes she wore last night. She hooked up with someone but refuses to give us the skinny on her steamy one-night stand. Boo. I need details. At this point, I can only speculate.

Ugh. I need a pick-me-up after stewing all night in my own misery. That damn guard had me twisted in knots with our encounter after the con yesterday. Anything to shift my brain from this unhealthy fascination with a man who screams *red flag.* As I pull on a short skirt and tug a corset into place, I can't help but wonder if I'll run into him again. I'm fucking hopeless.

By the time I finish my makeup, Ginger is ready to leave. We head to the lobby to grab our morning coffee as we wait for Vicky to finish getting ready. The butterflies in my stomach take flight, climbing higher with each step closer to the convention center.

When we reach the security line, I'm prepared for confrontation. Unfortunately, a chipper blond guard with a bright smile searches my bag and compliments my cosplay.

Damn. Not a surly guard in sight.

Ginger and Vicky pause outside the convention hall where the *Space Vendetta* panel will take place, headed by the director of the franchise, John Martigan. He's a handsome devil in his own right, but I've read enough interviews to know he's a grade-A asshole who hates to have his *vision* challenged. Not that it would stop me. If I really cared about the direction of the franchise, I'd straight-up tell him to his face he lacks both creativity and imagination. He deserves to have his ass handed to him, but I won't be the one to do it because I have other plans.

I'm meeting Raven Stark today, come hell or high water. I used my bonus to buy the photo op and her autograph, and I'll be damned if anything will stop me from finally meeting her face-to-face.

"You sure you're okay by yourself until your time slot?" Ginger leans close. "We can hang out with you for another half hour."

"No, I got this." I wink. "Go. Snag the good seats up front before anyone else."

Her smile widens, and a glow of excitement brightens her features. "Oh, you know I will."

"Give 'em hell, baby." I playfully shove her.

"John Martigan deserves nothing more than a good tongue-lashing." She straightens, adjusting her blouse to reveal ample cleavage. "Which I am fully prepared to deliver."

"Thatta girl." I grin and turn to Vicky. "Make sure you record every delicious moment for me to enjoy later."

"I will," Vicky says, her cheeks pink.

After Ginger and Vicky disappear through the doorway leading to the panel, I turn and inhale deeply in an attempt to quell the nerves twisting in my gut. This isn't the first time I've met a celebrity, but it's the first time meeting *her*. I've followed Raven Stark's career for years and written a dozen and a half fanfics featuring her characters, so I might be a bit enamored.

The signing isn't for another hour, but I want to make sure I get a good spot in line. There's a decent crowd on the main vendor floor, so I take a minute to scan the directions and head for the signing rooms.

Inside the cordoned-off area, tall blue-curtained cubicles sit in rows, forming a maze through the room. Each cubicle has a sign hanging over it, showcasing the celebrity's name and a collage of their characters. A path lined with ropes zig-zags back and forth, creating a designated line for each guest celebrity.

There are a lot of fans already waiting, and some lines spill into the walkways between rows. Shit. I need to find Raven's booth.

My pace quickens as I walk deeper into the maze. Noise is muffled in here, compared to the vendor area, but the sound is still elevated enough to make my ears ring. Maybe Jessica is onto something with those earbuds she had yesterday. Regret stabs me at the memory of my interaction with her. She was uncomfortable, and I made it worse. Beth the Bitch is right.

Shoving those thoughts aside, I round the corner and scan the booths. Some names are familiar, but most aren't. I move further into the crowd. It's thicker here, harder to move without bumping into people. I can already feel my patience waning.

Toward the back of the signing area, I catch a glimpse of her name in bold white letters. *Finally.*

Muttering apologies, I shove my way through the crowd of clueless fans. They're all lost in their own worlds, some with their faces in phones, some wearing headphones and oblivious, but the groups lost in conversation and laughter leave me the most irritated. They take up twice the space they should, because they're not standing properly in line. I grumble and sidestep a swinging backpack as a fan wearing three-foot wings spins.

They clip my shoulder and knock me into a small area behind her signing cubicle. I stumble through the curtain, collapsing to the floor, tearing it down in a clumsy attempt to grab it. My head is spinning. I curse as I struggle to get to my feet. I'm uninjured physically, but my ego is bruised.

I barely regain my composure when I'm unceremoniously

hauled to my feet.

"What the hell?" I glare at the two men wearing all black, holding each arm in a tight grip.

"Ma'am, this is a restricted area," one says, his voice steady.

My gaze swings around, taking in the room. It's a staging spot where celebrities wait to be escorted to their cubicles by hired security teams. Bodyguards, for lack of a better term. A few wide-eyed celebrities stare in confusion.

"Some jackass knocked me over with his fucking wings," I grumble, trying to free myself from their grips. "It was an accident." I nod in the direction of the line still forming beyond the curtain.

"Ma'am, you'll have to come with us," the second guard says.

"You don't have to manhandle me." I jerk free, and they begrudgingly relinquish their hold, sharing a worried look.

Then I see Raven Stark, her petite figure flanked by two tall bodyguards. She looks concerned and raises her hand, but one of the guards stops her, muttering something.

"I...sorry about this." I take two steps toward her.

A firm hand clamps down on my shoulder, stopping me.

The solid impact digs into the still aching abrasion I earned from my costume. Pain flares through me, lava hot, shooting down my limbs. I see red.

Celebrity forgotten, I spin, hand balled in a fist, arm cocked back, and throw all my weight upward with a firm right hook.

It collides with the bodyguard before I can stop myself.

A collective gasp rises around me when my fist crunches his jaw. He stumbles back a half step and cradles his face in his hand.

My whole world sinks into despair. Fuck. Fuuuuck. What did I just do? Panic infuses me.

"I—shit, I..." The words die in my throat the moment he

turns, dark eyes fixed on me, blazing with fury.

I am royally fucked now.

The grumpy security guard who haunted my fantasies all night pulls his hand away from his face and clenches it into a fist of his own. Deep red stains his pale skin, a brand right where I struck him.

"I…" My throat closes at the look of pure menace etched in his stone-carved expression.

When he takes a step toward me, it takes all my effort not to shrink back. I'm not a big woman—I'm petite, wiry, fast. Having him tower over me at the moment the shame hits leaves me deflated.

The other two bodyguards step forward, but he lifts his hand, indicating they wait. Then he lowers it to wrap my upper arm in a firm grip.

"Let's go," he growls under his breath, his tone almost a dare to challenge his authority.

I grit my teeth, wanting to fight back, the desire to defend myself nearly consuming common sense. I paid good money to be here…and I fucked it up by letting my anger get the best of me. Goddamn it.

With a nod, I start walking, unable to bring myself to turn to see if Raven is watching my retreat of shame. Had this happened to any of the other fangirls, they would have been able to sweet-talk their way out of it. But not me. My mouth—and my fist—have minds of their own. It's not the first time I've made a bad situation worse, but this one will certainly go down as one of the most mortifying and regrettable.

The crowd parts for us as the surly bodyguard escorts me through the corridor. Tears sting my eyes, and I swipe them away before anyone can see. I let anger simmer, cursing myself under my breath. No one says a word as we make our way down the hall.

He directs me around a corner, and an EXIT sign lights the end of the dark hallway.

"Wait...where are you taking me?" I demand, pulling to a stop.

The guard pauses but doesn't relinquish his hold on my arm. "You assaulted an employee—in front of witnesses. Where do you think I'm taking you?"

"To jail?" I ask, uncertain.

He shakes his head and gestures to the exit with his free hand.

"You're kicking me out of the convention?" I screech.

He nods. "They have the assault on camera. By the time I reach the office, your picture will be plastered on the Banned for Life wall."

"Wait," I howl. "You can't ban me for life. I didn't do anything! It was an accident. Some jackass knocked me over, and I fell through the curtain. I didn't know the area was off limits. Fuck, you have to believe me."

"I do." He holds my gaze. "But it doesn't matter."

"Why?" I meet him toe-to-toe, indignation boiling inside me.

"Because you struck an employee."

"You grabbed my shoulder—the sore one! It was a reflex." My heart pounds in my chest, threatening to explode. I can't breathe. Tears sting my eyes. "It was a mistake! I fucked up. Tell them...please. I didn't mean to do it. I..."

"It won't matter." His eyes soften. "There's no tolerance for physical assault at the convention."

"You've got to be fucking kidding me—not even for a fucking mistake?"

"No." He finally releases me. "It could be worse."

"No, it couldn't." I wrap my arms around my body.

"I could press charges."

My horror shows, and he shrugs.

"I won't. I'm giving you a chance to walk out that door. If you stay—and the higher-ups get involved—it will be nasty."

"You're a fucking joke." I snarl. "Acting like you're doing this out of the goodness of your heart." I poke him in the chest, unable to control myself. "I wish I'd hit you harder."

He scoffs. "If you want to fight, you should learn how to do it properly."

"I know how to fight, fucker."

"Kickboxing at the local gym once a month doesn't count, princess." He nods to the door. "Now get out of here before I change my mind."

"I should've broken your pretty face." I seethe. "Fucking asshole."

"Sticks and stones, princess." He pushes open the door, and daylight floods over both of us.

I take another long look at him. Dark hair and fathomless eyes. My attention lingers on the red stain creeping along his jaw. Good. I hope it leaves a fucking mark for weeks.

"Fuck you." I toss the words at him as I spin and step into the afternoon sun.

The door clicks shut behind me, and I crumble to the ground, sobbing.

CHAPTER FOUR

A week later, I still haven't fully recovered from my altercation at the Philly Fandom Convention. Ginger and Vicky found me at the hotel bar three drinks deep at two in the afternoon. They joined me without judgment since they'd had run-ins of their own and neither really wanted to talk about it.

Not me. I was fuming, so I told them what happened. Ginger wrapped her arm around my shoulder and pulled me against her. Vicky looked downright indignant at the whole fiasco. When I explained the details—of who I hit—I saw incredulous expressions on both their faces.

They offered unwavering support and love, but it did nothing to ease the sting of my shameful banishment from the convention. I could still see the bodyguard's face as he stared down at me in the dimly lit hallway, his expression somewhere between pity and rage. I pray I never see that asshole again. If we ever cross paths on the street, I will definitely need a lawyer and bail money.

His biting words linger in my mind. *If you want to fight, you should learn how to do it properly.*

Fuck you, jackass.

I open another window on my laptop and type *learn to fight properly* in the search bar. Irritated his comment has me so riled, I skim through the results. Blog posts, how-to videos, ads for online courses, blah blah blah. None of this shit is useful. I need something in person, something intense.

After a few more failed searches, I sigh and push aside my

water bottle. This time I type *hand-to-hand combat lessons near me* and hit enter.

A map pops up, centered at my location on the outskirts of Philly. Most of the results are martial arts training centers, a few MMA-style gyms, but none of them seem to have one-on-one options. I click a gym in the next town over. The website is simple and well-organized. A picture of a worn brick building with the name of the gym painted in faded letters in the front windows sits on the main page. *The Double Tap.*

I roll my eyes. Probably some macho man joint, where they do their damnedest to make women feel out of place and uncomfortable. I nearly close the window when I notice a button on the side of the screen.

Personal Self-Defense Training Available.

Okay. They have my attention. I hit the button for more information.

Searching for a safe place to improve your self-defense skills? The Double Tap offers individualized one-on-one sessions with our trainers to improve defense skills and build confidence and muscle memory while maintaining a comfortable environment with no judgment or pressure. Our trainers work with you to get results you can be proud of. For more information, call the number below to schedule a free consultation today.

There are client testimonials, just under the phone number. I read through them.

Mitch is fantastic! I know how to handle myself in a fight now.

There is no one better equipped to teach self-defense than Scott. He's professional and flexible. Highly recommend The Double Tap to anyone searching for a place to train.

The glowing reviews stare at me. I scrunch my nose. This all sounds too good to be true—I mean, most places will post only positive reviews. But they do offer a free consultation. There's no harm in giving it a try. Right?

Before I can overthink it, I grab my phone and call the number.

"Double Tap, this is Julie. How can I help you today?"

Stunned, I blink twice before finding my words. I didn't expect a woman to answer the phone. "Uh, yeah…hi, I'm calling about the free consultation for self-defense classes."

"Oh, sure. Well, I should let you know up front, they're individual lessons with just you and the trainer. We find it's the most effective way to pick up confidence and proficiency. Once you get to a certain level, we offer open-mat sessions on Tuesday and Thursday evenings." She pauses. "Does that sound like something you're interested in?"

"It sounds perfect." I scribble some notes. "How many trainers do you have?"

"Four," she says. "Two are fully booked, but Scott and Mitch have a few openings."

"Will I meet with both of them or just one trainer?"

"We'll have you scheduled exclusively with one trainer, but emergencies do come up, and they fill in for each other if that's the case. Does that work for you?"

"Absolutely."

"Great. Do you have a preference?"

"No." I bite my lip. "Who do you recommend."

"They're both phenomenal trainers. You really can't go wrong with either. Mitch is a former Navy SEAL with a purple belt in jujitsu. Scott was an Army Ranger who led self-defense courses while he was on active duty and trained in MMA for a while."

Great. Military men. I inhale deeply. Their egos are probably as big as their heads. Not that I know any personally, except for my uncle who served in Vietnam. Those guys are just built differently. I assess my options, and with only their names and a brief synopsis of their service history, I pick one.

"Scott sounds like a solid choice."

"Fantastic..." she murmurs. "Let me just get your information, and we'll get you scheduled."

Five minutes later, Julie has all the pertinent information, and I have a meeting with Scott scheduled for eight tomorrow morning. I skim through the rest of the site, but it's bare bones, old school, and there are no photos or biographies of the trainers. It's unique but also frustrating as hell. I have no idea what I'm walking into.

But I feel good about this. Excited.

Maybe this will be a better outlet for my stress than spending unlimited amounts of time online, actively critiquing fanfics, and making enemies with grumpy guards at comic conventions.

The bodyguard's mocking comment hits me broadside again. *Kickboxing at the local gym once a month doesn't count, princess.*

We'll see about that, fucker.

The next morning, I wake pumped and ready to go. I put on workout leggings and a matching crop top. It shows a sliver of midriff and clings to my slender, non-existent curves, but I want mobility. Formfitting or not, they'll have to get the fuck over it.

Traffic keeps me on my toes, and I arrive at the gym barely a minute before my appointment. By the time I make it in the door, it's five after eight. Shit. Bad first impression.

A brunette woman wearing a cotton tank with the gym's name glances up from the computer. "Morning," she says with a chipper smile. "How can I help you?"

"Yeah, I'm Beth. I have an eight o'clock meeting with Scott."

"Welcome, Beth." She inclines her head, and her smile

brightens. "I'm Julie. Here are a few forms for you to fill out, then we'll get you in with Scott."

"Sorry I'm late," I say, taking the clipboard.

"Not a problem. Traffic can be brutal if you hit it wrong this time of morning."

Julie walks me through the paperwork. Release forms, insurance, medical information for emergencies, and a payment agreement—all fairly standard and straightforward. I finish them within five minutes, eager to get started.

"Looks like we're all set." Julie takes the clipboard. "If you head down that hall, there's a room on your right. Scott is waiting for you."

"And the bathroom?" I ask, moving in that direction.

"Across the hall, on your left." She gives me a wave. "Have fun and kick ass!"

Her positive energy hits me like a shot of Red Bull, and I take flight.

Outside the door, I pause, a slow hum of nerves twisting in my stomach. *You got this.* I breathe deeply and enter the room.

A tall man with dark hair turns from the window to face me.

"Fuck." I swear as the realization hits me like a ton of lead, straight in the chest. It's like a nightmare blooming into reality.

Standing before me is the surly, sexy security guard from the convention. Only he's not wearing all black and an earpiece. He's in a white T-shirt and a pair of gray sweatpants—which shouldn't be hot, but of course it is. I scowl when his gaze drifts down the length of my body and back up. I bristle, balling my hands into fists.

"Beth, huh?" He tilts his head to the side, studying me closely. "Assault wasn't enough, you resorted to stalking?"

"Fuck you." A wave of rage floods me, and I spin around, grasping for the door. My breath catches as I fumble for the handle, my eyes stinging. I will *not* let him see me cry. Fuck him. Fuck this. I'm leaving.

But I can't get the door open. It's jammed. I swear again.

Panic grips me, and my heart races, thundering against my ribs. Shit. This can't be happening. Of all the people in the world, why did it have to be him? Why?

CHAPTER FIVE

"Beth, I…" Scott's resigned sigh echoes behind me.

The handle beneath my palm turns, and I pull the door open. I hold my breath and step back, swiping my hands over my face and clearing my throat.

"Hey, Scott, I wanted to kno—" An interloper steps fully into the room and freezes when he sees me. "Oh sorry, I didn't realize you had a client." He holds his hand out. "Mitch Baker."

My assessment of him is quick—clean-cut, glasses, strong build. First impression—he looks like fucking Clark Kent from *Superman.* The Christopher Reeves version, not Henry Cavill. Attractive as hell.

I shake his hand. "Beth Devani."

"You're new here. Did Scott scare you off already?" he teases with a charming grin.

Why the hell didn't I pick Mitch? Then I wouldn't have this problem. I'd be totally fine bantering with this handsome nerd instead of wanting to drive my fist through the man standing a few paces behind me. I shake my head to clear the thoughts racing through my mind. "No, I just…need to use the bathroom."

"Oh, well, in that case." He sidesteps and opens the door for me. "I promise I'll be done by the time you return."

"Thanks." I step through the opening and sneak a glance at Scott before the door closes behind me. He looks thunderous.

When I reach the bathroom across the hall, I shut myself inside and collapse against the door. There's nothing but silence in the three-stalled room. At the far end sits a locker area with two showers, and it's blissfully devoid of life.

"Goddamn fucking shit!" I swear a little too loudly, and the sound of my voice echoes off the tiles. I stumble to the nearest sink and grip the porcelain with two hands, then glare at my reflection in the mirror. "This is just my fucking luck." I hang my head. "What did I do to deserve this?"

Meeting my own gaze, I assess the situation. This is unfortunate, irritating to an abnormal extreme, but what are the fucking odds of me picking the one gym within an hour of Philly where *he* works? It's almost like fate is having a goddamned field day with me. Penance for the times I fucked around and did *not* find out.

What do I do now?

I could go to the front desk, tell Julie this isn't going to work, leave. No harm, no foul. I can put Scott in my rearview and just go on with my life.

A heavy sigh rips from my chest.

No. There's a reason I'm here, a reason I chose this place. Chose that name. I don't know why or how, and I sure as fuck don't like it, but there *has* to be a reason for this. Right?

If Ginger and Vicky were here, they'd be laughing their asses off. Fuck.

After a few deep breaths, I face myself and take stock of the situation. It's fine. I can make this work. If there's anyone who I want to take my aggression out on, it's this motherfucker. I grin. Who else should handle it when he's who started this whole *learn to fight* bullshit?

I splash some water on my cheeks and fix my hair. Game face on.

Suppressing my nerves, I step into the hallway and reach for the door to the training room. Deep breath in, out. I open the door to find Scott and Mitch talking in the center of the room. They both turn to me when I enter the space.

"Great timing," Mitch says, his blue eyes sparkling behind the lenses of his dark-rimmed glasses.

"Just ready to kick some ass," I joke, coming closer.

Scott's dark eyes narrow on me as he straightens. Always assessing, that one.

"Well, just make sure you don't send him to the ER. I need him to cover my classes this afternoon." Mitch winks.

"Don't worry. I won't hurt him too much."

"Good girl." Mitch high-fives me. "Just shout if you need any additional pointers."

"Will do. Thanks, Mitch." I beam at him.

"Nice to meet you," he says with a wave. "I'll see you around."

"Looking forward to it."

He shoots me another devilish smile before leaving the room. The door clicks closed behind him, and I'm alone with Scott.

This time when I turn to face him, I'm prepared for the onslaught of emotion.

What I'm not prepared for is the look of pure, unadulterated fury on his handsome face.

"Who pissed in your cereal, sunshine?" My tone is mocking. "You look like you're ready to rip someone's head off."

"No one *pissed in my cereal*," he bites off. His eyes close for a brief moment, as though he's clearing his mind. When they reopen, his gaze is focused, resolved, but tension remains. "I just have the feeling you'd rather train with Mitch."

"He seems capable." I pace the room, purposefully circling where he stands in the center of the mat.

Scott stands still as a marble statue. I spiral closer until I stop right in front of him, tipping my chin up to study his face. Unmistakable purple and yellow hues line his jaw.

I click my tongue. "What was it you said?" I ponder the words aloud. "'If you want to fight, you should learn how to do it properly?'" A satisfied grin curves my lips. Bold as a fox in a henhouse, I run my finger along his jaw. "Looks like I left a mark."

Quick as a flash of lightning across a midnight sky, Scott grabs my hand and holds it firmly but with awareness of his strength. He strokes my palm with his thumb down the tender skin of my wrist.

"You're playing with fire, princess." He swallows hard, his dark gaze locked on me with an intensity that leaves me breathless. "Last chance to walk out the door with your pride intact."

I sober instantly.

"You weren't worried about *my pride* at the convention when you kicked me out the back door and told me I was banned for life." I pull my hand from his grip, and it slides free without effort. "So don't pretend like you care."

"Beth, I—"

I hold up a hand to cut him off. "This is fate's way of giving me a second chance."

He purses his lips, jaw clenching as he swallows.

"I want you to teach me how to fight, how to defend myself *properly*." My eyes narrow. "Then you're going to give me the chance to finish what I started."

A smile tugs the corner of his mouth, but humor doesn't reach his eyes. "You have every right to hate me." He sighs. "But if we're going to do this, you need to learn to control your emotions."

"My emotions?"

"You wear them too close to the surface. They impede your judgment. You react too quickly, let them drive your motivation, your actions. And you pay dearly for it."

His assessment hits the center of my chest with the force of a physical blow. "Are you saying because I'm a woman—"

He scoffs. "I didn't say anything about your sex being the cause of your emotional outbursts."

"But you called me emotional."

"Do you deny you react out of emotion before anything else?"

I ponder his question for a few moments. He's not wrong, but I loathe the fact that he saw through me with such ease. "No."

"Then that's where we start. When you feel a response start to pool here"—Scott presses a hand to his chest, just over his heart—"that's when I want you to step back, assess the situation, take a deep breath, and feel the emotion. Don't disregard it. *Feel* it. Explore it. Contemplate why it exists."

I snort. His words resonate, but they also leave me uneasy and unsteady—something I do not enjoy. "I thought I was here to learn to fight, not get therapy."

Scott relaxes, taking a steadying breath. "Self-defense is about defending yourself against an outside attack, not initiating it."

"Makes sense…" I nod. "But sometimes you have to strike first to ensure you don't get hurt."

"A common misconception," Scott replies softly. "Striking first only ensures there will be a confrontation, it doesn't defuse the situation."

"What do you mean?" What he says makes sense, but I can't quite wrap my head around it when I've been vulnerable all my life, relying heavily on these defense mechanisms to survive.

"At the convention…" he begins slowly, easing into the topic.

I tense, feeling that ball form in my chest. Instead of ignoring or reacting to it, I breathe, letting it settle, feeling the emotions rising around it like he told me to do.

"When I grabbed your shoulder to stop you from making a bad situation worse, you reacted. You thought you were being attacked," Scott explains carefully. "I understood your situation. I saw what happened and tried to step in, but you were on high alert, aware of the negative attention on you. At that point, nothing I could have said or done would have defused the situation. I just tried to ensure you didn't get hurt or mistreated."

"You…" I swallow the lump in my throat, and shame returns. "You tried to help me, but I made it worse."

Scott nods, his dark hair falling over his forehead. "That whole incident could have…*should* have gone better than it did."

"But I fucked it up."

"We both could have handled it better," he says with a lopsided smile.

"I—" My throat constricts, and it's hard to find the words to apologize, even though I know I'm guilty as hell. So I deflect. "Yeah, we could have."

"Shall we start over?" he asks, extending his hand.

"Do I still get to kick your ass?"

"You can try your best, but I doubt you'll be able to land a hit like you did that day."

He grins, and my world spins on its axis. His smile is fucking stunning, transforming his face from villain to hero in an instant.

I'm so fucked.

"Deal." I shake his hand and revel in the warmth of his touch. "So when do we start?"

"Next session."

I groan in disappointment.

"Don't be in such a hurry. We'll come up with a plan today. What are your goals and objectives with this training?"

"Well, I'm not exactly intimidating." I sarcastically gesture to myself.

"You're petite and slim, but don't sell yourself short. You're intimidating as hell." He snorts. "You gave me one hell of an attitude the first day of the convention."

With a scoff, I feign indignation. "You started it, grump-ass."

"I guess it was a horrible first impression, wasn't it?" He hangs his head, looking more like an embarrassed teen than a hardened veteran turned bodyguard.

"Yeah, it was."

"Good thing we're starting over." He straightens. "Now what's your main goal? What do you want to get from our sessions together?"

Aside from laid? I banish the persistent, horny voice screaming inside my head to a dark corner of my mind.

"Well, I really want to be able to defend myself, but I'm too small—"

"Weight has nothing to do with it," he assures me. "By the end of this, you'll be able to throw off a man three times your size."

"You're full of shit."

"I'm dead serious." He grins. "Wanna make a bet?"

"I'm listening."

"Give me six months." His eyes darken, and he licks his lips. "If you can't take down an opponent of that stature, I'll refund every penny."

I extend my hand. "Deal."

He shakes it. "Now, let's draw up a plan. Training starts next time."

By the time I leave the gym, my opinion of Scott has shifted from hatred to curiosity. I'm not sure whether it's a good thing. More information and accessibility aren't necessarily a positive. There's still an unhealthy amount of fantasizing going on in my head, and I'm sure it's going to be a problem at some point.

But one thing I can't argue—I need this.

So I double down.

CHAPTER SIX

Three days later, I show up for my first official lesson and nearly end up in the ER.

"You have to protect your face, Beth. This is your resting stance," Scott instructs, demonstrating by holding his gloved hands up to frame his face. "Always be prepared to defend yourself."

"I'm trying," I snap, shaking my head.

His jab slips through, grazing my cheek and knocking me off balance. Had it landed the way he intended, I would have been on my ass. I hoist my arms up and mimic his stance.

"Good." He nods. "Now plant your feet, brace them shoulder-width apart. Bend slightly at the knees…yes, just like that."

I follow his instructions and find the proper position. My tongue feels awkward with a mouthguard, heavy. It's not pretty, but it's practical and keeps me from biting my tongue or breaking my teeth. We're not wearing headgear, though he made it clear I could if I wanted.

But no, I need to feel this. I don't want padding to soften the blow.

"Now walk into it like I taught you. Two jabs, then an opposite hook. Alternate." Scott's gaze bores into mine.

Jab. Jab. Hook. Switch. Jab. Jab. Hook. Switch.

We move across the mat. When we reach the other side, we switch and he strikes while I fend off the blows with my gloves, shuffling backward. His soft grunts echo my labored breaths as he quickens the pace.

My back slams into the padded wall. He pulls a last jab before dropping his hands.

"Good." Scott takes a step back, and air floods the space between us. "You're a natural. I can't believe this is your first lesson."

Deep in my chest, my heart is racing, not from physical exertion. Fuck, he makes me work for it. Being in close proximity for an hour twice a week just might put me in an institution. His presence makes me irrational. I don't know whether it's his scent or his heat or whatever the hell voodoo he's working, but it's got me all kinds of twisted up.

"I told you, I've taken kickboxing and other classes, but nothing this intense." I blush as I think of his comment at the convention. "I need something suited to self-defense."

"Makes sense." He rubs the side of his face with a gloved hand. "Did you want to try some other techniques?"

"Like what?"

"I can show you a few moves that don't require your fists." Scott shrugs. "Have you seen *Miss Congeniality* with Sandra Bullock?"

"Who hasn't?" I laugh.

"You'd be surprised." He gestures to the door. "Mitch still hasn't watched it."

I gasp in mock horror. "He's missing out. It's a great movie."

"You can tell him next time you see him." He pulls off his gloves and tosses them to the side of the mat.

I do the same. "So are you going to teach me the S-I-N-G method?" I ask, half joking.

"If you know the movie, you already know that technique." He takes the bottom of his shirt to wipe sweat from his face, baring rock-hard abs to my view.

Holy fucking shit—he's ripped. My eyes gloss over, seeing his flesh and the dark line of hair trailing into the waistband of gray sweatpants. I lick my lips, momentarily distracted, imagining all the ways I could—

"Beth, my eyes are up here." He waves a hand in my face and points to his eyes with two fingers.

My gaze snaps up to his, and embarrassed heat floods me when I see the grin of recognition on his smug face. He knew exactly what he was doing. Fucker.

The shirt drops, hiding his abs from view. I glare at him.

"Would you rather I take the shirt off?" he asks in a teasing tone.

"No." I snap as I pull off my gloves and toss them aside with his.

"It might give me an advantage."

"You can take off your top if I can take off mine." I offer the solution simply.

His eyes widen for a moment before he laughs. "I'm pretty sure that violates gym rules."

"Why? If men can go topless, why can't women?" I ask, knowing the answer but enjoying the way it makes him squirm.

Scott rakes his fingers through his hair. "Legal reasons." He grins. "I don't think Julie would approve of a topless gym."

"Julie? The receptionist?" I ask, laughing at his reaction. "Why would she care?"

"Julie owns the gym." Scott's smirk catches me off guard. It's smoldering and coy. "You didn't know that?"

"No." I fix my ponytail. "But that only makes me love this place more. Woman owned."

"She also trains, but not as much since a shoulder injury."

"What happened?" I ask, concerned.

"Competition injury. One of her opponents got a little rough and dislocated her shoulder. Tore her bicep too. A few months ago, so she's still going to physical therapy for it."

"Ouch." I wince and grasp my shoulder. "That sounds painful as hell."

"Don't worry, I won't hurt you, princess." He motions for me to come at him.

"Firstly, I'm not worried about you hurting me." I close the gap between us. "And secondly"—I meet him, eye to eye, as I get into position—"Don't call me princess."

"The main thing to understand is distance management. Too far"—he steps back—"too close." He closes the gap, bringing us toe-to-toe before taking a step back out of reach. "Got it?"

"Like this?" I lunge forward, tackling him around the legs and knocking him back onto the mat. He slams down hard beneath me. I tumble on top of him, my legs straddling his thighs. Triumph rages through me.

The surprise on his face gives way to determination as he easily flips me over, pinning me to the mat, using his weight to press me into the floor. I wiggle, trying to break free, but he's too heavy. Too big.

Too distracting.

Fuck me.

The more I struggle, the heavier he gets. When I pant and whine with frustration, trying to push him off me, he chuckles.

"Lesson one. Be heavy." His breath caresses my cheek, minty and warm. "Next time you tackle someone, get low and smish."

"Smish?" I gasp, and he eases up a fraction of an inch. I inhale deeply to catch my breath. "Is that a technical term?"

"No, but it gets the point across." He gazes down at me,

dark eyes unfocused. "Are you okay?"

"Fine." I lick my lips, and his gaze follows the movement, his eyes turning the color of midnight. I arch against him, pushing up. "Your body is *crushing me*," I say in my best Lilo imitation.

Scott scoffs and rolls away. Once he's on his feet, he offers his hand. I take it, and he pulls me to my feet.

"Come on, princess, let's go again."

We finish the last fifteen minutes of the session, ignoring the tension pulsing between us. I manage to shake his hand and agree to another session without pinning him to the floor to have my wicked way with him.

By the time I get home, I need a cold shower and a beer to clear my head. I already feel better about my ability to trust my instincts and defend myself. But the thought of spending two days a week with Scott in an *intimate* situation leaves me breathless and a little woozy.

If he can be professional, so can I.

Can't I?

Guess time will tell. Until then, I'll learn everything he's willing to teach me.

CHAPTER SEVEN

After nearly two months of going to The Double Tap, not only do I feel stronger and more confident, I find myself looking forward to each training session.

No. I look forward to seeing *Scott*.

While our complex history still lingers in the back of my mind, I can't help but wonder if there could be something between us. He's not the asshole grump I thought he was. He's...complicated, a puzzle I can't quite figure out. I want to unravel the mystery behind the man. It's becoming an obsession. I spend hours wondering about his past and making shit up to fill in the blanks.

He doesn't talk much about himself, but when he does, I eat those tidbits up and file them away. He plays things close to the vest. I can respect that. The only problem is it leaves me craving more.

Like during my last lesson, he mentioned a brother in passing. I tried to ask about him, but he quickly changed the subject and shifted back to the lesson.

Today, I arrive five minutes early, practically salivating for my next lesson.

Julie isn't behind the counter when I walk through the door. I peek around the corner and see her working with clients in the weight room. She waves when she sees me. I smile in response and head down the hall to the training room.

My heart flutters as I open the door, and it plummets to the floor when Scott isn't there. I look around the empty room and frown before checking my phone. I'm early, but not very early. Maybe he's running late.

That's not like him. He's *always* in this room when I get here.

I toss my bag in the corner and start my warm-up stretches. This is ridiculous, getting all worked up over a guy I barely know. But I can't deny it. He's like a drug. Every damned session, the tension ratchets up another notch. I swear, one of these days, the sexual tension will explode like a goddamn fireworks warehouse.

The door clicks behind me, and I spin around, face warming.

Mitch grins. "Good. You're here." He closes the door. "Hope you don't mind—Scott asked me to step in for your session today."

"Yeah, no, that's fine." I say it casually, but inside, my gut is twisting. Is something wrong? I start running through the last session, trying to remember if he said anything about not being here.

Finally, I push aside the racing thoughts and ask Mitch directly. "Everything okay?"

"Yeah," Mitch says as he pulls off his hoodie. "Just a scheduling conflict."

"Oh, okay." My expression falls, but I hide it, afraid he'll see how disappointed I am. If he notices, he doesn't say anything.

"Don't worry." He winks. "I promised him I'd take it easy on you."

"I don't know. You've never seen my moves. *I* might have to take it easy on *you*."

"Feisty." He nods appreciatively. "I like it." He steps onto the mat, motioning for me to join him. "Show me what you got."

Mitch comes at me in a frontal attack. I sidestep, push his arm away, and pivot to place distance between us. It's a dance, this back-and-forth, the constant flux of space. I've grown used to it with Scott, almost able to predict his next move, but with Mitch, it's different. He's assessing me, analyzing my abilities as he applies each technique.

When he finally slips past my defenses, I swear. He manages to twist behind me, sliding his arm around my throat to put me in a chokehold.

A few weeks ago, I would have panicked and clocked him in the junk with a fist. While it's effective in disorienting an assailant, it's bad form to do it on the mat with your trainer. Instead, I do what Scott taught me, the reaction like muscle memory.

I step back, sliding my left leg behind his right, dip low, grab the front of his sweatpants just above the knees and pull with all my might.

Mitch tumbles back onto the mat, allowing me to break free.

"Good. Good." He laughs, lying on the mat and staring up at me. "Looks like Scott has been doing his job."

"It took me a minute to figure it out, but now I know what's coming, it's easier to escape the situation." I shake my arms and bounce on the balls of my feet. "Once I'm trapped, I'm fucked."

Mitch laughs. "Yeah, with your stature, it's hard once you're pinned, but you utilized your size well with that evasive maneuver. Sometimes, it's easier to be quick than strong."

He takes off his glasses and sets them on the window ledge. "Let's see what else Scott taught you."

"Bring it," I say, popping in my mouthguard and pulling on my gloves.

Thirty minutes later, I'm dripping with sweat. Mitch's training isn't the same as Scott's, but that's not a bad thing. He focuses on different jujitsu techniques and plays to my strengths. It complements what I've already learned. Having both of them instruct me bolsters my confidence and knowledge. I feel like fucking Rocky Balboa—all I need is a soundtrack.

"Shit," Mitch says, climbing to his feet. "You're fast."

"That's what Scott says too," I reply, retreating for my water bottle. I take a long drink and bask in his compliment.

Mitch wipes his face with a towel. He's sweating as much as me, his T-shirt clinging to his torso. I take a minute to admire his physique. He's broader than Scott, more upper-body muscle, but where Scott's face is angular and hollowed, Mitch's features are less pronounced, more subdued with a square jaw and a killer smile.

"I don't know what you're hoping to get out of these sessions, but he's definitely giving you your money's worth."

"I just want to learn more self-defense moves while gaining strength and confidence." I wipe my face with a clean towel.

"He told me about you." Mitch's eyes sparkle with mischief.

"What...about me?" Fear coils in my gut.

Mitch taps his jaw. "Said you have a wicked right hook."

Heat floods my face. If I weren't already flushed from exertion, I'd look like a cherry tomato.

"Yeah, well...it was just a huge misunderstanding."

"That's what he said too." Mitch studies me for a long moment before continuing with a laugh, "True story, when I asked him about the bruise on his jaw, he told me to fuck off. I badgered him all day until he finally admitted one of the guests at the con took a swing at him."

"He admitted a woman did it?"

"Begrudgingly." Mitch chuckles. "When I asked him what you looked like, I believe his exact words were 'she's a knockout.' He wasn't talking about your right hook."

I stumble over my thoughts, and they jumble in my mouth. He said *that* about *me*?

"He also admitted to acting like a damned asshole when you

first met." Mitch cocks his head.

"Yeah, he was a real dick." I sniff, ignoring the way my body heats at the mention of him. "Every time he saw me at the convention, it was like his personal mission was to make my life miserable."

"In his defense, he's shit with women." Mitch gathers his gear as he talks. "And his head wasn't in the game. He was distracted."

"That gave him a right to be an asshole?" I put my gloves in my bag.

"No. It doesn't excuse his behavior. He handled it badly." He shrugs. "But he was dealing with a family thing, and…well, it was a shit show all around."

"Ah." How am I supposed to respond to that? I mean, after training with Scott the past few weeks, I can see past the asshole I met at the convention, but he never offered an excuse for his behavior. He did apologize though. Fuck. Guilt creeps in at the way I gave him a hard time. Guess we were both in the wrong.

Mitch pauses beside me, resting a hand on my shoulder. "Just do me a favor and don't bust his heart like you busted his jaw, okay?"

"I–I don't know what you're talking about."

"Come on," he says, regarding me incredulously. "The tension between you two is so thick, I'd need a plasma cutter to get through it."

This time, my skin has cooled enough for my blush to shine through. I wave my hand, as though trying to push the idea away.

"Scott and I…it's not gonna happen. We'd kill each other the first week." The moment it leaves my lips, I recognize how weak I sound.

The door clicks closed behind me, and I turn to see Scott's retreating profile on the other side of the glass.

"Fuck." I frown at Mitch. "How long was he standing there?"

"Long enough." He sighs. "I'll talk to him."

"No—I'll do it."

Mitch nods, and I dart for the door. But it's too late.

Scott's gone.

Shit.

CHAPTER EIGHT

For two weeks, I stew in frustration over what happened at the gym.

I had every intention of talking to Scott the moment I saw him again, but unfortunately, life conspired against me. My office sent me on a business trip for ten days, traveling to promotional events across the country. Once I got home, I spent every waking moment compiling notes and results to present to the board of directors. Stressful doesn't cover half of it.

I *need* to go to the gym. If I don't get on the mat, I might explode. Between the hectic pace of the past two weeks and my own neuroses, I have to burn off this energy thrumming through me.

The worst part? I don't have a way to contact Scott. No phone number. No email. Nothing. The guy doesn't even have social media. He's a fucking ghost.

When I called Julie yesterday to schedule a session with Scott, she told me his only openings this week were in the evenings. Tonight at eight is later than I like to work out, but fuck—this week, I'd take a midnight appointment if it meant I could get back on the mat…and see Scott.

I walk in the door at five to eight. My body thrums with anxiety and uncertainty. What the hell do I say to him? I spent the last two weeks running through scenarios in my head, and I know I'm going to put my foot in my big fucking mouth. Again.

Julie glances up from the computer. "Hey, glad to see you." She stands up. "Scott's in the back. I'm gonna get out of here."

"Early night for you?"

"Yeah, my hubby is taking me to dinner for our anniversary."

"Oh, happy anniversary." I adjust the bag on my shoulder. "How many years?"

"Five." She grabs her purse and keys. "Don't want to keep him waiting." Julie nods toward the hallway. "Fair warning, he's in a mood tonight."

"Thanks." I wave as she heads out the door and locks up behind her.

Outside the training room door, I take a deep breath and clear my thoughts. *Just let it flow.* I step into the room, and the pulsing beat of 80s rock echoes through the space. Bon Jovi. Classic choice, which for some reason suits him. The *thunk thunk* of his fists hitting the bag matches the rhythm of the music.

Scott turns to greet me with a nod, grabbing the bag with both hands to steady it. His dark eyes and stoic demeanor betray nothing. He looks like he did the day I met him at the con. All business, no bullshit.

"Hey." I open my bag to retrieve my gear, but he stops me.

"No gloves. No mouthguard." He points to the mat. "Let's go."

"I…" My heart pounds, threatening to break my ribs. "Okay."

Scott meets me in the center, beads of sweat dot his forehead. "Show me what he taught you."

"Who?" I ask, confused.

"Mitch." The other trainer's name slips from his mouth, dripping with disdain.

I'm stunned for a moment and blink. "Wait—what the hell happened?"

"You tell me," he practically growls.

"Scott, I don't know what you heard, but you've got it all

wrong."

"No. I heard you loud and clear." He flexes his fingers. "Everything you can learn from me, you can learn from him."

"I don't understand."

Then it hits me like a ton of bricks.

"Are you...jealous?"

"Why are you here, Beth?"

My frustration returns, but this time I can see it—the uncertainty, the panic. He *is* jealous. I would have laughed, but seeing him in such a state leaves me stunned. And aroused.

"It's been two weeks of nonstop work." I level my gaze with his. "I need to blow off steam."

"That's not what I mean."

"Then you're going to have to spell it out for me, because I don't have a fucking clue what you're going on about."

The muscle in his jaw flexes, and he shakes his head. "Forget it."

"No. You started this shit." I put my hands on my hips and stand my ground. "We're both adults, but right now, you're acting like a fucking child."

"I'm—" He growls in defiance as he swallows his response.

It's obvious he's running on pure adrenaline...or emotion. Either one gives me an advantage I can use against him. He charges, and I barely have a split second to respond to his attack.

His hand wraps around my wrist, and I drop to grasp his legs and push forward in a double leg takedown. We collide with the mat, and I slip into guard position, getting heavy. He responds in a blink with a scissor sweep, reversing our positions and putting himself in mount.

He's on top, pinning me to the mat, his hands on my wrists to lock me in place. His thighs bracket my hips, and I'm hyperaware of his hard cock pressing my stomach as he leans over me. I squirm against his hold, but he's twice my size and weight and determination is etched on his face.

"Why?" he asks, the word lost in the depth of his voice.

"Why what?" I ask, breathless with exertion and need.

"Why are you still here?"

"Because I paid for a service. I expect results."

"There are hundreds of gyms and thousands of trainers." He narrows his eyes. "When you saw it was me, why did you stay?"

I lick my lips as a hundred reasons I should have walked out the door that day fly through my mind. The only thing echoing loud enough to hear is the reason I stayed.

Scott's gaze dips to my mouth, and his sinful lips part on a sharp inhale. He releases me and climbs off. Shaking his head, he reaches out an arm and pulls me to my feet.

My body trembles and I wobble. Need courses through me, but I can't—*we* can't cross that line.

"Scott, I—" When I reach for him, he pushes my hand away.

"You said it yourself." He refuses to look at me. "You and me, it'll never happen. We'd kill each other."

Shame washes over me, but it's quickly replaced by a visceral image blazing in my mind. Scott, naked, hard, on his knees, his mouth between my thighs. I moan and his gaze snaps to my face. Goddamn it.

"What a way to go," I mutter under my breath. "Fuck it."

I stalk toward him, and Scott's eyes fly wide for a moment but quickly narrow as he backs away. When he hits the wall, I cage him there, my hands on either side of his torso.

"Mitch said something that didn't make sense. Until now." I tilt my head back, rising to my full height, still a foot shorter than him.

He swallows hard, his body tense and visibly shaking.

"Do you feel that?" I murmur, leaning closer, inhaling deeply, drinking in the fear, adrenaline, and pure desire mixed with his own heady scent. "The tension pulled tight between us? It's as thick as a steel beam balanced beneath the weight of a fucking kaiju."

"That doesn't make any sense." He scoffs.

"But it does. Because you feel it too. That tension." I incline my head and smile. "I can see it when you look at me. When you touch me."

His breath catches. "Beth…we—"

"We can do whatever we want, Scott." I press my body against his, and a flame ignites inside me. "We're both consenting adults. I fail to see a problem here."

"I can't." He places both hands on my shoulders and tries to push me away.

I stand firm, unmovable, teasing him with possibilities. "Tell me you haven't thought about it, about us."

His grip on my shoulders tightens.

"I have. More than I should," I say, my hips rocking into his thigh.

"Beth, this is irrational."

"Remember the first day at the convention, when you told me to behave," I purr, unable and unwilling to stop the runaway train tearing through my common sense.

He nods.

"I thought about you that night when I took a shower, my roommate just on the other side of the door." My flesh burns, needing him to touch me, to end the torment, but he stands as still as a statue. I push harder. "I touched myself, wished it was you."

"Fucking hell, Beth."

"I came so hard, I nearly passed out."

He groans.

"But it wasn't enough." I cup him through the fabric of his sweatpants. He's fucking huge. Of course he is. "I want you. Here. Now."

A flash of hesitation passes over his face, but it vanishes in a blink.

Scott dips down, capturing my lips in a punishing kiss, and I fucking implode. His mouth is hot and desperate. He devours my whimpers, teasing his tongue over mine. Peppermint and need flood my senses. I wrap my arms around his neck and open for him.

His guttural groan ripples through me, and I'm off the ground, pressed hard to the wall, his hands on my ass as he grinds his cock against the gusset of my leggings. The friction of fabric and his length on my clit shoots my arousal through the roof, like a goddamned rocket to the moon.

I thread my fingers through his thick hair, lodging the silky strands in my fists. When I pull, his head snaps back, breaking the kiss. Midnight eyes lock on mine, flooded with desire, lost in the haze of surrender.

"Beth." A moan rips from his throat mingling with my name, and it's the sexiest sound I've ever heard in my fucking life. "Are you sure…about this?"

"If you don't fuck me, I swear to God, I will end you here and now."

"I'd like to see you try." His lips twist in a wicked grin.

I rock my hips, grinding hard into him. With building momentum, I keep pace, fucking myself against his clothed cock. His eyes roll back, and a pained groan tumbles from his parted lips.

"Are you…using me to get off?" he asks as realization

dawns.

"You won't give me what I want." I smirk, riding him harder. "So I'll take it however I can."

"You wicked little thing." He grabs my hips and spins around, taking me to the mat with a thud.

I squeal as he lands on top of me and tears at my clothes. He abandons them quickly, frustrated by the spandex. I shimmy out of my top, my leggings, my underwear. He tears his shirt off, followed by his sweatpants and boxers.

My fingers trace over his chest, down the rock-hard abs I've dreamed about for weeks. I'll savor them later, but right now, I need him inside me.

"Condom?" he asks.

I swear. "No, but I'm clear and protected."

"Are you sure?"

My body hums. "Absofuckinglutely. Unless you're secretly a male escort."

"No. I haven't…been with anyone in a long time."

"Good enough for me." I rise up and kiss him hard, pulling him closer.

He settles between my thighs, and I groan, digging my fingers into his shoulders as he slides deep, filling me, stretching me to the point I might explode. It's overwhelming—and so goddamn delicious.

He pauses, fully seated inside me. "Shit, you feel so fucking good."

I wrap my legs around his waist and urge him on with a shimmy of my hips. When he moves, I fucking lose control.

My moans echo around the walls. The sounds of our bodies, slick and frenzied, create a symphony of sex, and it only makes me hotter.

He slams deeper, harder, driving me toward release. He

buries his face in my neck, his breath coming faster.

I pivot to the right, rolling him to his back. We flip positions, still joined, and a string of curses tears from his throat as I ride his cock. His eyes roam over me, fluttering closed with a gasp when I stroke the sweet spot, just right.

He grins, placing his hands on my hips. My body trembles when he presses his thumb to my clit with gentle pressure and slow circles. As I chase my release, he quickens his pace, pushing me higher.

"I…fuck…Scott…" Incoherent thoughts spill from my lips as my orgasm rushes to the surface.

"Come for me, princess," he coaxes. "That's it, just like that."

I shatter into a million pieces as the orgasm tears through my body. He fucks me through it, thrusting and pushing me harder against his thumb. He steals every last drop of pleasure as I pant and gasp above him.

As I slowly come down, I realize he still hasn't finished. So I fuck him, rotating my hips until he grasps them with his fingertips and tips his head back in a silent gasp.

"Fuck." The guttural word fills the room with a final punctuation, and pride fills me when he comes.

I collapse onto his chest, and he holds me there, gently stroking my spine as our skin cools. I shiver, and he presses a kiss to my shoulder.

"Come on. Let's get cleaned up."

Reality crashes down around me.

"Shit, Julie is going to kill us."

CHAPTER NINE

"No, she won't." Scott laughs as he climbs to his feet.

"I hope there aren't cameras in here," I grumble as he grabs my hand and tugs me into his arms.

"Worried?" He lifts my chin until our gazes lock. "Don't be. The cameras are in the main entrance and the hallways covering the exits."

Scott presses a soft kiss to my lips, and I melt into him.

"Come on," he murmurs. "Grab your gear."

"Where are we going?" I ask, gathering strewn pieces of clothing and my bag from the corner.

He's got an armful of gear clutched against his bare chest. I realize we're both stark naked and smother a giggle.

"We can't go out like this!" I screech as he opens the door.

"Shower." He gestures to the door across the hallway. "Let's go."

I rush forward, darting across the hall and ripping open the door to the women's locker room. He flips on the light as he passes me. The door squeaks closed behind us.

Scott's halfway to the lockers at the back, and my breath catches at the sight of his muscular ass, mesmerizing me with every step. Shit. I want to sink my teeth into those cheeks.

What the hell has he done to me? One taste and I'm a goddamned horny monster now.

He disappears around a corner and the sound of running water fills the room.

Truth is, I'm dying to put my mouth all over that man's

body. Damn it. I wish we were at his place—or mine—then I wouldn't feel the pressure to hurry. I want to enjoy this for as long as possible.

After setting my gear next to his on the bench, I take a deep breath. Two towels hang outside the shower. I pause beside the curtain.

A jumble of thoughts bombards me at once. *Do it. Seize the moment. Fuck him senseless.* I shove them all aside and step into the shower.

My throat goes dry the moment I see him beneath the spray of water.

If I were a director who wanted every woman in the audience to die of spontaneous combustion, I would film this man at this moment, in all his fucking glory. A scene pops into my mind of a fic I wrote for the *Space Vendetta* fandom. Basically PWP—porn without plot—involving Commander Colton and Lynnea in a very similar situation. Only they stumble across their nemesis Ransom showering. Yes, it went exactly how you imagine it would, and it was a drabble of pure smut. I have no shame.

"You gonna just stand there and stare?" Scott asks, a lopsided smile playing on his lips.

"I like the view." All other thoughts forgotten, I lean on the wall and drink him in, letting my gaze drift across his glistening skin.

"If you want to treat me like a piece of meat, two can play that game…" His gaze smolders as he returns my heated perusal.

My body simmers, need pools between my thighs. But that could just be the mess he made of me earlier. I slide my hand over my breast, down across my stomach, and tease the crease of my thigh, so close to where I burn for him.

"Come here," he growls, reaching out and pulling me to

him.

The warmth of the water is tepid in the heat radiating from his body. He holds me against him beneath the spray, and I gasp when he dips me beneath it. I'm drenched from head to toe, my hair saturated and hanging in my face. I tip my head back to clear my view. He releases me long enough to push wet strands from my face, and I regain my composure.

Turning to face him, I poke him in the chest. "Happy?"

"You tell me?" He grins, stepping between me and the water. His hands come to rest on my hips, and he pulls me flush to his slick body. His cock presses insistently against my stomach.

"Again?" My eyes fly wide, and his soft laugh fills the tiny space.

"I told you, it's been a while." He spins me around, arms wrapped around me, holding me tight. "You bring out the beast in me."

"Don't you mean the best?"

"No." He growls in my ear, and I damn near whimper. His hand glides down my stomach to cup my pussy. This time, I do whimper, and the desperate sound echoes off the tile.

His fingers curl, sliding deep inside me as the heel of his palm grinds my swollen clit. I rock into him and groan his name.

"That's it, princess." He strokes slowly, holding me close. "Is this what you imagined as you touched yourself in the shower?"

I gasp, shaking my head, desire consuming my coherent thoughts. It's hard to think when he's touching me like this, teasing me with my own confession.

"Is it better than you imagined?" he croons in my ear, teeth nipping my neck, my shoulder.

"Fuck. Yes…" I push back against him, widening my stance

and opening for him. "Please, Scott..."

"Tell me what you need." He presses deeper, every stroke taking me higher, but it's not enough. I need more.

"I–I need to come." I rest my head on his shoulder. "Please."

He withdraws his hand, and I cry out from the loss of his touch. When I try to draw away, he pulls me roughly back to his body, grunting.

"Hands on the tile, princess."

His order echoes in my ear, making my head spin with lust.

"Spread your legs for me."

I obey, knowing he'll give me exactly what I need. Part of me wants to be a brat, make him take it, but I'm shaking, desperate for release.

I brace myself on the cool tile beneath my palms. Carefully, I widen my stance and arch my back toward him. It's degrading but oh-so delicious. Steam swirls around us, the shower raging on, but his broad shoulders block the spray.

I shiver as his hands come to rest on my hips again. One hand slides down to skim my ass and trace the sensitive seam of my pussy. I push into the touch. *Fill me*, I want to scream, but I bite my lip, waiting. My legs tremble as he replaces his hand with the head of his cock.

My body takes over, and I push back. He pulls away with a groan.

"No, princess," he murmurs in my ear. "You'll take only what I give."

Gripping my hip with one hand, he positions himself close enough to tease me. Back and forth, he slides his cock across my pussy, teasing, tempting, denying. He continues this torment until I cry out in frustration, bucking against his hold.

Scott nips my throat as he pushes deep, filling me with a

single thrust. I'm so wet, so desperate for him, the invasion is welcome relief. His satisfied groan mingles with my strangled cry.

"Is that what you want?" He withdraws to thrust deeper.

"Mm-hmm." My mind is blank. I'm reduced to whimpers and moans, sounding more like a cat in heat than a woman.

"Fuck, you feel so goddamn good like this." He takes me slowly, building momentum and pressure with every stroke.

I claw the tile, scrabbling for purchase as he fucks me with unhurried precision. He hits all the sweet spots, taking his time, and I bask in the sound of animalistic grunts and sex echoing in the narrow shower stall.

When he slides his hand between my thighs and circles my clit with two blunt fingertips, I lose what remains of my restraint. I rock my hips to the rhythm of his thrusts, meeting his questing fingers at every retreat. Inside, the spiraling vortex of my orgasm bursts free like a goddamn volcano. The force sends me reeling and my head drops back and I scream with the sheer strength of it.

Scott's own release follows with a stifled grunt.

I collapse against the cool tile for a brief moment, unable to feel my limbs. Scott gathers me in his arms and pulls me back to him, beneath the spray of tepid water.

In silence, he washes me, cleaning between my thighs with gentle caresses before taking a soapy washcloth and running it over my skin. Slowly, awareness seeps back into my orgasm-stilted body.

When he finishes, I take the cloth from him. "Turn around," I say, adding more soap to the cloth.

He obeys, and I wash the contours of his muscular back, his arms, his chest. He inhales sharply when I run the warm cloth over his softening cock.

Scott cups my jaw in his hand and kisses me, long and slow.

Unhurried, unbothered, he tastes me, as though savoring the kiss like aged wine, letting the moment draw out as we bask in the aftereffects of lust.

When he draws away, I groan in disappointment. He runs his thumb across my jaw, trailing the tip of it over my lips.

"I'm glad you came."

"Twice." I grin.

"You know what I meant."

I nod. "What can I say? You've grown on me."

He kisses me again, and we finish cleaning up.

It's not until I step from the shower that I realize what I just admitted to him—I like him. A lot.

Fuck.

Scott doesn't mention it.

We dress quickly, the clock on the wall telling us it's nearly ten.

"Shit, I gotta go." I pull on my shoes. "I'll call you."

"You don't have my number."

I unlock my phone and hand it to him. He punches in his number and hands it back to me. I glance at the screen.

Hot Trainer.

"Seriously?" I laugh and lock the phone before tucking it into my bag.

"Am I wrong?"

"I refuse to answer." I turn to leave, and he grabs me by the waist, kissing me one more time. My toes curl with the heat of it. I sway when he releases me.

"Call me later."

"Okay." I mutter under my breath as I follow him down the hallway.

His phone dings when we reach the door. A quick glance, and his demeanor shifts.

"Everything okay?"

"Fine." He puts the phone back in his pocket, but his mood has shifted.

We make it out the front door, and he locks up behind him. Like a gentleman, he walks me to my car. I toss my bag in the passenger seat and look at him.

Scott's expression is unreadable. The text must have upset him. Or maybe I did. I don't have a clue how to bring it up without sounding like a nosy shit, so I let it go. We might have hooked up, but we're not at the sharing deep emotional baggage stage of the relationship, I guess.

"Night," I say with a half smile.

"Drive safe." He closes the door and steps back.

Dismissed, I drive out of the parking lot and ignore the urge to look at him in the rearview mirror.

Something changed. I felt it. I know he did too.

But where the hell do we go from here?

CHAPTER TEN

I shoot Scott a text letting him know I got home—and that I was thinking about him. The only answer I get is a little *Read* symbol beneath my message. No reply.

The following three days between training sessions are hell.

When I show up at the gym on Friday, Mitch greets me with a grin. He covers the lesson, and while he's a great instructor, he's not Scott. I don't have the heart to ask Mitch where he is, because I know he'll see right through the mask I'm wearing.

He'll *know* something happened between Scott and me, and honestly, I'm not ready to tell anyone about it, or even think about it too much. It was just a fling. Right? Just two people with a strong attraction who fucked—twice.

Who the fuck am I kidding? This whole mess is my fault. I should have kept my distance, and now I'm, once again, in over my head and overthinking everything.

Did we cross a line? I've spent three nights running those last five minutes through my mind. Right before we left the gym, he got a text and his whole demeanor changed.

I never thought to ask him what it was. It's none of my business. But the shift in his mood left me feeling like I'd done something wrong. *That* bothered me. Still does.

Somehow I go through the motions at the gym, pretending everything is fine. Mitch assures me Scott is alive and well, but I have the feeling he's not telling me everything. "Family emergency" was the only explanation I got from Julie when I left.

Frustrated and exhausted, I head home, growing ever more

irritated thanks to weekend traffic. The moment I walk into my apartment, I toss my bag on the floor and beeline for the bathroom to take a long hot shower.

It feels amazing, but all I can think about is Scott—and the things he did to me that night. Fucking hell.

A half hour later, I crash on the couch with Chinese takeout and turn on *House*. I've seen every episode, but it's a comfort show. I adore Dr. House and his snarky attitude. Tonight, it mirrors my mood.

My phone rings, *Ginger* flashing on the screen. We haven't spoken since Philly. Every time I text her, she responds with a quick one or two words. I've had a lot happen since the last time I texted her.

"Hey, Red." I smile, setting aside my plate of lo mein.

"Hey, bitch," Ginger says with a laugh. "What are you doing?"

"Watching *House*."

"Ohh, love it."

"What are you doing?" I ask.

"Calling for an update on the hot trainer situation." She purrs seductively. "You can't tell me the grumpy, sexy guard from the con is your new personal trainer without spilling all the tea."

"I texted that over a month ago." I groan.

"Well...I was...occupied." She sniffs. "So spill it."

"Occupied?" I snort. "I'm not telling you shit until you tell me what *you* were up to."

"I can't tell you everything yet, but"—she lowers her voice to a near whisper—"I'm in LA right now working on something big."

"Girl, what the fuck are you doing in LA?" I sit up straight and mute the television. She has my undivided attention.

"Hold on." I hear the muffling of fabric and the click of a door. "Fine, you win." She sighs, and anticipation prickles along my arms. "Remember how I got booted from the *Space Vendetta* panel?"

"Yeah. We both made an impression that day."

"Well, security didn't hold me for over an hour like I said."

"I'm sorry—what?" I damn near screech into the phone. "What the hell happened?"

As Ginger launches into her story, I sit dumbfounded and soak it all in. How the hell did she keep this from all of us? I ask a million questions, and she answers most of them, promising she'll fill me in on the rest the moment she's able to do so. By the time she finishes, I'm speechless.

"And here I thought *I* had an eventful convention experience." I pop open a beer. "I'm glad it worked out for you in the end."

"Well, my life is definitely taking a new direction, that's for sure." Ginger sighs dreamily but quickly shifts the conversation. "Now tell me what's going on with the hot bodyguard."

"It's really fucking complicated." I recount the past few weeks, explaining my slow-building relationship with Scott. I tell her about Mitch, who she dubs the nerdy trainer. I laugh since I did the same the first time I saw him. The more I talk, the quieter she gets.

"I think I fucked it all up." I slump into the couch cushions and cradle a pillow against my chest.

"What do you mean?"

"We...things got a little tense at our last session, and we ended up fucking on the mat." I pull the phone away from my ear as her screech echoes through the speaker.

"You go girl!" She swoons. "How was it? Hot? It sounds hot."

"It was hot," I admit, trying not to get lost in the memory. "Then he took me to the shower…and we fucked again." I don't mean to be crass, but that's what happened.

"Goddamn, Beth. Woo! Get some, girl." I can just picture Ginger fanning herself with exaggerated southern belle flair. "I told you he wanted to hit that."

"Yeah, hit it and quit it," I grumble.

"Wait," Ginger says, stunned. "He ghosted you?"

"Yeah, after giving me his number." I explain how his demeanor changed once he received that text message. "After everything, I guess I expected too much."

"No way. You didn't do anything wrong. No expectations, no strings." Ginger's thoughtful reply lingers in my mind. "Sometimes you just need to fuck and get it out of your system. But it's not like you've been badgering him since you hooked up."

"True."

"Did you demand a ring? Call him three hundred times? Text him all night? Invite him home to meet your parents?" Ginger lobs questions rapid-fire. "No, you didn't do any of that."

"Then why the shift?" I ask, uncertainty filling me. "If I didn't do anything wrong, why the cold shoulder?"

"Girl, who the fuck knows what goes on in a man's head. They can't focus on more than one thing at a time."

Ginger has a point. It's not like Scott and I have a friendship outside of my training sessions. I know almost nothing about him.

"It sounds like he's got some shit going on in his life, and he can't juggle it."

"You think he's distracted by something else?"

"You said it yourself—both the owner of the gym and the nerdy trainer say he's dealing with family drama." She huffs a heavy sigh. "I mean, I know family drama, and sometimes that shit can fucking drain you, physically and emotionally."

"You're not wrong," I reply, remembering my own share of family bullshit. It made me not want to do anything for weeks. Fucking exhausting.

"So you don't think it's because I was a bitch to him, and he's reconsidering his life choices?" I voice my fears.

Ginger chuckles. "Girl, he saw you at your bitchiest at the convention, and he *still* wanted to bang you. I wouldn't worry about that piece of it. I think he likes your strong personality. It's just going to take time for you two to get on the same page—I mean, it's not like you've really dated…or talked. You just jumped straight to fighting, then into bed."

"Point taken." I laugh. "But what the hell do I do now? I refuse to sit waiting for him to get around to texting me."

"Then send him a message. Tell him the truth. You're into him, you'd like to see where this leads, but you're not gonna wait indefinitely. Put the ball in his court and do your thing."

"And if he doesn't respond?"

"It's on him, girl." Ginger huffs. "He's missing out because you're a catch. Sounds like you two are made for each other, you're just in different places right now. Give it some time. If it's meant to be, he'll come around."

"That sounds suspiciously like a cliché—'If you love something, let it go.'" I roll my eyes.

"It's a tried-and-true cliché because it's accurate as fuck."

"I know. It's just—fuck, I wasn't expecting this, and I sure as hell don't *need* a man." I sigh. "But it was so fucking good. I haven't had good sex in so long, I forgot it was possible."

"Well, at least you know that part of your relationship will be solid," Ginger says. "Sexual chemistry is great, but it's important the rest of your relationship doesn't cause an apocalyptic explosion."

"I gotcha." I sigh.

Through the line, I hear knocking and the sound of a distant voice.

"Shit. Hold on." Muffled voices fill the air, then she's back. "Hey, girl, I gotta run. But text me if you need moral support. I'm here for you."

"Thanks. I appreciate it."

"Keep me posted. Love ya."

"Love you too. Bye."

I end the call and stare at the television screen. I don't know how many episodes of *House* have passed since I got on the phone with Ginger, but it doesn't matter. I instantly recognize the story, but my mind is spinning, considering the good advice Ginger gave me.

She's right. I need to be open and communicate. That's not always an easy thing for me. I often demand things, but I don't think it's effective. Most people don't know how to handle my abrasive nature and brutal honesty. Which is why they call me a bitch, but is that how Scott views me?

I shake off my indecisiveness and open text messages.

(Me): *Hey. Hope everything is ok. Heard you had a family emergency. I'm here if you need anything. I enjoyed the other night, and I think we should talk about where we go from here. No rush. Find me when you're ready.*

With a deep breath, I hit send.

No response. When I check an hour later, it says *Read.*

Ball's in your court, Scott.

CHAPTER ELEVEN

After a week, I'm fucking positive Scott's ghosted me. No text. No call. Nothing.

When I finally get my ass back to the gym for my next session, Julie isn't behind the desk. I head down the hall.

After my text went unanswered, I skipped a week of sessions because I couldn't bring myself to face him, which is so unlike me. If I have an issue with someone, I typically initiate the confrontation. But for some reason with Scott, I can't bring myself to meet him face-to-face. The rejection would be too fucking much.

I have no idea if he *is* rejecting me, but ghosting someone is pretty much the equivalent of telling them to fuck off somewhere else. I'm not really in the headspace to find out.

Ginger's words repeat in my head all week, offering me some semblance of emotional support. *You're just in different places right now. Give it some time. If it's meant to be, he'll come around.*

My little internal pep talk bolsters my confidence—until I reach the door and find Mitch in the training room. I step inside and glance around. No Scott. Big shock.

"Hi, Beth! Sorry, you get me again today." He beams.

"Hey, Mitch," I say, forcing a smile. "No Scott?"

"Shit." His bright smile dims a bit as it falters. "Uh…he didn't tell you?"

"Tell me what?" My heart seizes in my chest like it's encased in ice.

"He's gone." Mitch's tone softens as though trying to ease

the blow. "He came in on Tuesday, gave Julie his notice, and collected his gear."

"What?" Panic ripples through me like an electrical current. "He just... *left*?"

"He's been going through quite a bit lately. I don't want to go into it since it's not my place to air his personal business, but yeah, it happened pretty quick." He hangs his head. "Sorry to drop this on you, I thought you knew."

"How would I know?" I scoff in disbelief.

"You two seem close. I thought maybe you two..." He trails off, leaving the implication hanging in midair.

"You thought there was something between us?" I laugh, but it sounds pained.

"Yeah, I mean, I saw you two together, saw how protective he got of his time with you." Mitch shrugs. "I'm sorry. I shouldn't have made such an assumption."

"No, you shouldn't have." I hike the bag higher on my shoulder. "I–I'm gonna go."

"I totally understand." Mitch nods. "If you need anything or want to train, just let me know, I'll get you in."

"Thanks." I leave the room, ignoring the tears burning my eyes and the bile stinging my throat. *Goddamn it.*

My hand freezes on the main door when someone calls my name. I pause and turn.

Julie jogs to the counter. "I'm glad I caught you." She reaches into the desk and pulls out an envelope. "Here."

"Thanks, Julie."

"You leaving already?" Concern etches her pretty face.

"Yeah, not feeling well. Gonna go home and rest," I lie. "Catch you later."

Once I reach my car, I tuck the letter into my bag. On the road, I turn on music full blast and let tears flow. By the time I park in front of my building, I'm numb.

It's nearly dark when I finally get out of the car and head inside. I toss my bag on the couch and grab a beer from the fridge. Cracking it open, I lean against the counter.

"What the fuck did I expect?" I ask the empty apartment and shake my head. It's not like I was expecting him to propose, but a goodbye would have been nice.

Was I wrong about him? Thinking he cared about me, that he cared about anything other than himself. Selfish fucker.

I down half the bottle before retreating to the bedroom to shower and change into my most comfortable pajamas. I play every interaction with him over and over in my mind, searching for some clue this was coming. There's nothing but a shit ton of sexual tension and unspoken hope for more.

"Fuck him." I finish the beer and toss the bottle in the trash.

Running on autopilot, I go to the kitchen, grab another beer and a half-eaten pizza in a large box, and take refuge on the couch.

For a half second, I contemplate calling Ginger to vent about the whole fucking mess. I need to talk to *someone*, but I don't have the energy. Not tonight.

My phone dings when a text message drops into my inbox. I groan and grab the duffle bag where I'd tossed it earlier. I fish it out and end up grabbing the letter Julie gave me along with the phone. The message is spam. Figures.

I toss the phone aside and look at the letter in my hand. Probably an invoice or a bill or something from the gym. When I turn it over, I see my name in chicken scratch on the pristine envelope. But it's not Julie's handwriting. I'd recognize her flowing script. This is a man's handwriting.

I tear it open and look at the signature first.

Scott.

What the fuck? I backtrack and read from the beginning of the letter.

Dear Beth,

I fucked up. I'm sorry.

By the time you read this, you've probably already imagined ripping my head off and sticking it on a pike before setting fire to my corpse. You have every right to be angry, and I'm an ass for not telling you any of this in person. Trust me, I want to. You deserve that much, at the very least.

I'm guessing you think I ghosted you. I didn't intend to. Life decided to throw me a curveball, and the truth is, you caught me at a very complicated stage of life.

We don't know each other beyond the limited interaction we've had at the gym, our messy first meeting at the convention, and…well, a night of the hottest sex I've ever had. I wanted to invite you out, get to know you, but my family had other plans for my time.

I probably should have led with the fact that I have a family. An ex-wife, her new husband, and a twelve-year-old daughter. Things have been rough lately, and that's the reason why I've been absent, distant, and irritable. None of this excuses the way I treated you. You deserve better, and I regret my behavior every day.

All that to say, I would love to start over. Can we try this again?

I'm on my way to Ohio to see my daughter, but I'd like to make it up to you when I get back to town. There are some things I want to say, but you deserve to hear them in person.

Text me if you want to meet up. Feel free to ignore this whole letter if you'd rather see me dead in a ditch.

Scott

I stare blankly at the paper, unseeing the words. My heart races, and my body refuses to move. He…he's a father?

I mean, it's not a dealbreaker, but holy shit. This explains so much. Why didn't he just tell me? I would have understood.

Part of me is pissed he didn't tell me, but then again, when did I give him an opportunity to talk about himself? We didn't talk on the mat. I paid him for his expertise as a trainer, and he gave his full dedication to that.

After reading the letter again, it hits me hard, like an uppercut to the jaw. We were both in the wrong. He didn't tell me anything. I didn't ask. Fuck.

I run my fingertips over his handwriting, pausing at his name. What the hell do I do? Text him? Ignore him?

I can't do that. Not now I have this letter. This confession.

After replacing the letter in the envelope, I set it on the table and pick up my phone. Opening the messages, I stare at the last paragraph I sent and the little *Read* beneath it.

(Me): *I got your letter. When you get back in town, let me know.*

With a deep breath, I hit send and off it goes into cyberspace.

Two seconds later, I see the *Read* icon appear beneath the message along with three dots.

(Scott/Hot Trainer): *Thank you for understanding. I'll be back in two weeks.*

My heart flutters at those words, but uncertainty filters into my mind. What if this is his nice way of telling me we had fun, but it's over?

Wait. Am I expecting him to want something more with me? Do I want something more with Scott?

I sit and stare at the painting of a cluster of roses on the wall. I don't know what I want, but I have two weeks to figure it out.

CHAPTER TWELVE

I sip my coffee and glance at the entrance of the small café for the hundredth time. We agreed to meet at five, but I got here at four, hoping to calm my nerves before he arrived.

An hour and two iced coffees pass in a blur, and I'm still a nervous wreck.

We haven't talked since the small exchange via text. He was taking care of his family, and I wanted to ensure he had the space and time to do that. Meanwhile, I took that time to figure out what the hell I want out of this relationship. I made a list of pros and cons, took inventory of my goals and dreams…hell, I even called Ginger who walked me through it all.

But the truth is, until I hear what *he* has to say, I can't really make a decision one way or another. What I do know is that we have to be on the same page. So far, our interactions have been nothing but misunderstandings and miscommunication, aside from some solid training sessions.

Two things are absolutely crystal clear. One, I like Scott. A lot. I enjoy our banter and sparring, and the chemistry between us is off-the-chart explosive.

But the second thing has nothing to do with him specifically, it's all me. I'm tired of being alone.

Don't get me wrong, I love who I am—an independent boss babe who doesn't take guff from anyone and gets shit done. But coming home to an empty house, eating meals alone, spending my free time writing smutty fan fiction isn't exactly how I envisioned my thirties. I want *more*, but my personality—

according to Ginger—is an acquired taste. It scares most people, especially men.

Scott isn't most men. He doesn't seem intimidated by me, but I can't make a judgment since we barely know anything about each other.

This is it. Make-or-break time.

The door chimes as it swings open. I glance up, only to see a couple walking through the door. The blond man holds the door for the petite brunette, who gives him a smile. They look happy. Part of my heart twists with uncertainty, and I drop my gaze to the melting ice in my glass. Is that what I want?

Another chime. I look up, and my heart leaps at the sight of Scott in the doorway, framed by setting sunlight. He assesses the room with narrow eyes until he spots me. All his features soften, and a hesitant smile steals across his lips.

I rise to my feet as he approaches the table. My heart thunders inside my chest. He looks good enough to eat. Memories of the last time I saw him flow through my thoughts, and I feel my face warm.

"Hi." He stops two feet away.

"Hi," I reply. Tension pulls between us, and I break it by closing half the space with a step closer to him.

He looks at me, thoughtful for a moment, before leaning down to kiss my cheek. The woodsy scent of him wraps me in a comforting embrace, and I sway closer, wanting to drown in it.

The soft press of his kiss lingers as he draws away. "I brought you something."

"Really?" I blink, surprised when he pulls a box out of his pocket and hands it to me.

"Before you open it, we should talk." He gestures to the counter. "Mind if I grab a drink?"

"Oh, yeah. Go for it."

"Want anything?"

"No, I'm good." If I ingest more coffee, I'll be wired for sound. I settle back into my seat as he places his order.

The box is nearly weightless and not much bigger than my palm. What could it be? Jewelry? I scoff. Such an expense is a little fast, even for us. It can't be a ring. Can it? *That* would be way too fast. A hundred rapid-fire thoughts zip through my mind.

Scott slides into the seat opposite me with a mug of steaming coffee in his hands. "Nice place. It's cozy."

"I come here a lot. The owners are friends."

As he takes a sip, his eyes drift closed in satisfied appreciation. "Good brew."

"I don't know why you're surprised. I have impeccable taste," I tease, allowing my personality to overcome the nervous flutters in my stomach.

He smirks. "Expensive taste, you mean."

"Well worth the cost, trust me." I lean my elbows on the table, studying his handsome features. "Let me guess—at home, you drink the cheapest coffee from a thirty-year-old machine?"

"You say that like it's a bad thing." He sips again.

"Not bad. Just…not surprising."

"Why's that?" he asks, inclining his head slightly, dark gaze fixed on me in amusement. "You barely know anything about me."

"I know enough. But isn't that why we're here? To get to know each other?"

"It is." He cradles the mug in his hands. His demeanor shifts from playful to serious. "The letter—I apologize. You deserved to hear it from me directly."

"I understand." I shrug, trying to play it off. "Honestly, I thought you were avoiding me after we…well, it wouldn't be the first time someone ghosted me after sex."

His brow furrows as his expression darkens. "Well, they're idiots…*I* was an idiot. You didn't deserve that. I was wrong."

I blink at the apology and the admission. It isn't often a man openly admits being wrong. I nearly make a snarky comment like *hell must have frozen over*, but I refrain. A first for me, I know, but I'm trying to be mature and not lean on my defense mechanisms.

"Thanks."

"I appreciate you giving me a chance to explain." He shakes his head and scoffs. "This wasn't how I wanted things to go between us."

My brow arches. "You had a plan, huh?"

A wicked smile curves his mouth, and I'm smitten all over again. "The moment you stepped into my line at the convention, I had a plan."

"How'd that go for you?"

"I bombed spectacularly." He ran his fingers through his hair, mussing the damp strands. "I'm not great at flirting."

"No kidding." I lean forward and whisper conspiratorially, "Don't worry, neither am I."

"I couldn't tell." He chuckles. "No wonder we started on the wrong foot."

"Yeah." I sigh, taking his hand in mine and squeezing. "Classic idiots to lovers."

"It was like the powers that be decided to make us work for it, huh?"

"Conflict makes for the best stories." My heart swells when he interlaces our fingers.

"It does."

This man with his grumpy, stern exterior truly has a good heart. I smile, allowing the moment to flow. I want to know everything about him. I want to uncover his desires, his passions, his past, his goals for the future. His everything.

"So, tell me about your daughter."

He laughs in surprise. "You want to hear about April?"

"Why wouldn't I?" I smile as relief fills his expression. "She's your daughter, a big part of your life." I pause, allowing my words to take root. "If we want to make this work, I need to know *you*. And that includes her."

Scott clears his throat and starts at the beginning. How he met his ex, Andrea, in high school and became a father at nineteen. He joined the military to provide for his wife and newborn, but the toll of military life proved too much for Andrea. His absences for deployments and training stressed their marriage to the point of breaking. After six years, they called it quits and parted ways. He got out of the Army shortly after their divorce was finalized.

Andrea and April moved to their hometown in Ohio while he found a position in Philly doing freelance security with a private company. He picked up personal training as a side gig. Even though he kept in touch, visiting his daughter twice a month, distance grew between them as she got older.

His expression twists in frustration as he explains his daughter's recent struggles.

"The last few months have been a mess, and I've been scrambling to try to figure out how to help, how to be more active in her life." His shoulders slump, and my heart breaks at the sight of this strong man struggling. "I decided to move back to Ohio to be closer to her. April needs me in her life, and I owe her that much."

Tears sting my eyes. "You're a great dad."

"I don't feel so great." He gently squeezes my hand. "But thanks."

"She's lucky to have a father who's willing to move his life around to do what's best for her. Your relationship might take work, but it'll be stronger for it in the long run," I assure him.

"Beth—these last few months, I've been torn between my daughter and the possibility of what I can have with you." He heaves an intense sigh. "The timing couldn't be worse, honestly."

"Don't ever feel guilty about putting your daughter first," I say with certainty. "She's young and impressionable, and it's important that she have her dad around to help during such a crucial time in her life."

"I feel like an asshole, leading you on." His eyes darken. "Sleeping with you, only to bail without notice."

"You need to do what's best for your daughter. I understand and appreciate that." I straighten, regarding him carefully. "I won't deny being crushed you're leaving, but I'm willing to take it as it comes and see where this goes."

His brows rise simultaneously.

"If you're serious about me—about us—then I'm willing to give this a shot. Even if it's long distance." The moment I voice the words, peace surrounds me. I shot my shot, and it feels right. My breath catches when he lifts my hand to his lips and presses a kiss to my knuckles.

"I've never been more serious about anything in my entire life."

My heart explodes with joy at his grin.

"We'll take it slow and see how it goes." I run my fingers over his. "Does that work for you?"

"Works perfect for me." He turns my hand over and presses a kiss to my wrist.

I suck in a shuddering breath as awareness courses through me, igniting a burst of need deep in my soul.

He catches my gaze and grins.

"Open your gift."

Slowly, I unwrap and open the box. Inside is a silver link bracelet with a single charm. I hold it close to read the inscription on the flat silver crown. It reads *Philly Princess* with the date of the convention beneath it.

"A memento to remember our first meeting." He pulls it from my hand and puts it on my wrist before pressing another kiss to my pulse point.

"I'll never forget." My heart flutters again as need strikes like a lightning bolt. "What about you?"

He rubs his jaw. "I carry it with me always."

I laugh. "Good."

Scott pulls me to my feet and wraps me in a hug. I lean into the embrace, savoring his heat, his comfort.

Then he whispers in my ear, "Let's get out of here."

"My place is three blocks away."

"Say less." He nudges me to grab my purse.

"Bossy." I take his hand and pull him to the door.

"And you love me for it."

"I do." My gaze meets his. "I really do."

"Good, cause I love you too."

Scott kisses me soundly on the sidewalk outside the café before taking me home to show me just how much.

CHAPTER THIRTEEN

Nearly One Year Later

"Are you sure about this?" I ask Scott as we climb the stairs to his ex's house.

"Beth, we've been over this. You're my girlfriend. We live together. Stop worrying you won't be welcome." Scott squeezes my hand and presses a kiss to my forehead.

I melt into him and take a deep breath. "Okay." Straightening, I brace myself for whatever may come.

I've met Andrea before, in passing when she brought April to Scott's place for the weekend, but this is the first time I've been to her house. I wonder if I was invited or if Scott's bringing me to solidify my presence in his life. Either way, it's uncomfortable as hell.

"What if I fuck this up?"

"You won't."

It takes me a second to realize I asked the question out loud. "Scott, this isn't a good idea."

"No. It's a *great* idea. The more they see how wonderful you are, the easier it will be. Trust me, princess." He winks and knocks on the door.

Six months ago, Scott invited me to move in with him, but that meant moving to Ohio. I thought about it for three weeks, put my notice in at work, and took the plunge. Reckless as hell, it was the best thing I could have done. There was no upward momentum at my job, and they knew I had my sights set on something bigger.

Before I said yes to moving in with Scott, I submitted my application to a dozen marketing agencies in Ohio within commuting distance to Scott's town.

Three interviewed me. One gave me the option for remote four days a week, one day in the office. I took it. The pay wasn't as good as Philly, but the possibility for growth with the company was prime.

Two months later, I packed my stuff up and moved.

Best decision I've ever made.

Our relationship grew stronger. We started making plans. And when I met April, I fell in love with the tenacious preteen who loves *Space Vendetta* as much as I do. Scott thinks we gang up against him, but deep down, he loves it.

But I'm not sure about Andrea. I think she secretly hates me. She's well within her right to have reservations. I'm trying my best, but I don't want to cause issues for Scott.

"Maybe I should go hom—?"

The door swings open, and I stop talking.

"Scott." Andrea smiles at him before turning to me. Her smile never dims. "I'm glad you came, Beth. I'm having a bit of a crisis." She grabs me by the arm and drags me into the nearest bedroom.

"I…what's wrong?" I'm uncertain what's happening right now.

"I think I fucked up." Andrea rifles through the closet before withdrawing a black garment bag. "I need your honest opinion and expertise."

"Okay…" I nod. "What's the problem?"

"I hired a friend to make a cosplay for April to wear to the comic convention in Pittsburg next month."

"That's amazing! She'll love it."

"That's exactly why I got it for her, but…" She unzips the garment bag and pulls out the costume. "I think it's the wrong character. I fucked up."

My breath catches when she withdraws a gorgeous gown for Queen Mizandi from the *Space Vendetta* series. It's a spot-on reproduction of her coronation gown, complete with accessories.

"It's fucking incredible, Andrea." I touch the fabric. "Honestly, if it were me, I wouldn't care if it were the wrong character. I'd wear this in a heartbeat."

"You would?" Andrea asks, relaxing a fraction. "Even if it's not your favorite?"

"Well…" I regard it for a moment. "Who was it supposed to be?"

"Empress Fazhailoh."

"Those are distinctly different characters with vastly different styles, but honestly…royalty is royalty. I'm sure she'll love it." I wink. "I'll be sure to plant seeds about how awesome this character is so she's more receptive, if you're really that worried about it."

"Would you?" Andrea gasps in relief. "I'm kicking myself for not verifying the information. But she always talks about how much you love *Space Vendetta,* and this trip to the convention is the event of the year. I'd hate for it to be a bust because of me."

"Don't worry." I grin. "It's a done deal. By the time the convention kicks off, she'll be all about Queen Mizandi. Trust me."

Andrea drops the garment on the bed and hugs me tight. "You're the best. Thank you."

I hug her back. "Any time."

When she pulls back, she wipes tears from her eyes. "Sorry…I'm just—I was panicking!"

"It's nothing we can't fix." I lower my voice. "We could make it even better for her, you know. I have a friend who's knows the director of the next *Space Vendetta* movie and another who's close to the author of the books. We could arrange a meet and greet."

"Are you fucking serious?" Andrea gapes at me before grinning. "I don't know where Scott found you, but damn, he picked a good one. I'm so glad. You're amazing."

"I'm just a dedicated fangirl." I laugh. "But thank you for welcoming me into your home. April is a wonderful girl, and you're a fantastic mom."

"Thanks." She hugs me again. "We should get to the picnic. I'm sure Scott and Rick are at each other's throats."

I stifle a laugh and follow her from the room once she puts the gown safely in the back of the closet.

In the backyard, I see April talking with some other girls her age and a host of guests I don't recognize. Andrea falls into the role of hostess, and I scan the crowd for Scott. He's by the grill, talking to Rick.

Neither of them is bleeding. That's a good sign.

"Hey," I say as I approach.

"Well, hello." Scott wraps his arm around my shoulder and pulls me against him. "Everything okay?"

"Yeah, all good." I press my hand to his chest.

His gaze meets mine, and everything clicks into place. This man, this family.

This is exactly where I'm meant to be, and I've never been happier.

Later that night, after Scott and I return home, he tells me to pick out something to watch as he heads into the bathroom to shower. I had jumped in the shower the moment we got home, hoping he would join me, but no such luck.

I take my time finding something I think both of us will enjoy. Then I completely abandon the idea for something I know *I* will like—and therefore, he will enjoy by proxy.

Pulling up the menu, I choose the latest *Space Vendetta* installment and press play. I pause at an innocuous background image and wait for Scott to return.

He joins me five minutes later, and I curl up beside him on the couch, ready for the fun to begin.

"What did you pick?" he asks, wrapping an arm around me.

"You'll see," I murmur into his cheek before placing a kiss there.

He groans when the intro starts, and I cackle with glee.

"You're lucky I love you," he mutters under his breath.

"I know." I wrap my arms around him, and we start the movie in relative silence.

Twenty minutes into the film, *he* shows up on screen. A secondary character no one ever pays attention to. Except me. He's my favorite. My guilty pleasure.

Simon Antilea. Pirate. First mate. Best friend of Captain Korbin Ransom.

I swear to *God* if they don't give him his own spin-off, I'll riot.

My grip tightens on Scott's arm. I've mentioned my attraction to this character in passing, but I doubt he knows the extent of my obsession. Unless he's read all my fanfics, how the hell could he possibly know?

Scott's hand rests on my thigh, drawing lazy circles on my skin just below the hem of my shorts. As I watch the drama with Simon unfold on screen, Scott's fingers slowly creep higher, until they're pressing my clit through the thin fabric of my pajamas.

I gasp, eyes glued to the screen as sensation ricochets through me. A pulse of heat vibrates through my body, making me moan.

"Is that what does it for you, princess?" Scott growls in my ear. "A tall, dark, foreboding villain?"

I whimper as he applies more pressure, just where I need it.

"You think I don't know how much you *obsess* over this character?" He nips my earlobe, drawing it between his teeth with gentle pressure.

I moan and arch my hips into his touch.

"Let me enlighten you, princess." He slides a finger beneath the fabric and touches the slick seam of my pussy. "I've read *all* of your fanfics."

"H-how?" I ask with a sharp inhale, unable to function with his hands working literal magic on my body.

"Ginger told me." His breath singes my skin, the tension unbearable. "Remind me to send her a thank-you card."

"I—fuck." My protests die when he pulls me onto his lap, straddling his hips.

Scott grinds against me, pressing his clothed erection to my aching pussy. "Tell me what you need, princess."

I thread my hands in his hair, unable to think, only to feel. "I–I need you. Now."

Scott kisses me hard, stealing my breath and my sanity. I cling to him, desperate and aching. He pulls at my tank top and shorts, nearly ripping them in the process of removing them from my body.

Naked on his lap, I rock my hips into his, leaving the evidence of my arousal on the seam of his gray sweatpants.

"Shit." He growls, pulls his garment free, and repositions me on his lap.

Now we're skin to skin. I lean back as he fits himself to me, sliding his cock against my pussy in a tantalizing dance. I grumble under my breath, trying to force his hand. But he persists in tormenting me.

"Now, princess, I need you to be honest." He barely slides his cock into me before withdrawing, earning himself a frustrated groan. "What is it about him that makes you *wet*?"

"I…I don't know." I whimper as he continues his teasing strokes on my throbbing center.

"I think you do." He rakes his teeth along the crook of my neck.

"Simon isn't a villain. He's loyal to the captain, misguided but not necessarily evil." I lick my lips, try to catch my breath. "H-he follows his own path and values friendship above all else."

"Is that what you value?" Scott kisses my jaw. "Loyalty and friendship?"

"Yes." I gasp when he suckles the tender skin of my throat. His cock persists in tormenting me with gentle caressing strokes.

"If he stood before you right now, would you fuck him?" Scott asks, his voice deep and mesmerizing.

"N-no." I shake my head.

"Why?"

"Because I belong to you."

I feel his smile against my skin. "You *belong* to me?"

"Yes." I dig my fingers into his shoulders. "I belong to you, Scott."

"Fuck," he mumbles before thrusting deep.

He fills me in one stroke, and I sigh with complete satisfaction. This is the man I love, the man I want. I grip him tight as I ride him, rocking my hips in tandem with his strokes.

I lean my forehead to his, gazes locked as I ride him, taking everything he has to offer. It doesn't take much, my body is a keg of gunpowder surrounded by an inferno.

Scott kisses me, his tongue breaking down what remains of my defenses and stealing my very soul.

I kiss him back, showing him how much I love him, love sharing this with him.

Within moments, my body peaks as the orgasm rushes forward like a freight train. Scott clings to me as it hits. A tsunami of sensation washes over me, and I bask in the glorious release.

Not far behind me, Scott chases his own release. When his orgasm hits, he swears and holds me close.

We ride out the storm together, and slowly, reality comes back into focus. The sound of the movie in the background. The soft hum of the air conditioner in the window. The harsh bite of sofa springs beneath my knees.

I rest against him, heart to heart, skin to skin, and sigh.

"I love you," I murmur, kissing his nose.

"I love you too." His lopsided smile endears me even more.

I try to move, but he holds me in place.

"What's wrong?" I ask, as the high of our sexual release dissipates.

"Nothing. I just…" He sighs heavily. "Marry me, Beth."

"Marry you?" I ask, pulling back to study his face.

"Marry me."

He's completely serious, I realize.

I wait for panic to consume me. There's nothing but certainty and peace.

"Okay." I nod. "I'll marry you."

"Really?" he asks, grinning. "What's the catch?"

"You wear cosplay at the convention next month."

"With who?"

"Your daughter and me."

"Deal," he responds without hesitation. "I'd do anything for you two."

"I know." I kiss him softly.

He turns off the movie and picks me up by the waist.

"What are you doing?" I squeal in protest.

"Taking my future wife to bed." He arches a brow at me. "You have a problem with that?"

"Not at all." I grin. "Proceed."

Our first meeting might have been bad timing, but sometimes, that's exactly what we need to find the right person at the right moment.

THE END Book 3

The Director
Fangirl Confessions Book 4
KIRSTEN S. BLACKETER

CHAPTER ONE

"Ginger, you have an unhealthy obsession with *Space Vendetta*," Vicky teases, eyeing me over the rim of her glass.

"Don't we all?" Beth half snorts. "I mean—it's why we're *here*, isn't it?"

I shake my head and laugh. "Why do you say that?"

"I heard you say something to Ronnie last night, about a disconnect between the films and the source material." Vicky looks dazed as she tries to remember. "I didn't even *know* half of what you were talking about."

"We've both been fans since the beginning." I sip my drink. "Ronnie read the books before they even considered making movies, so she's got stronger opinions than most on how they adapted the story."

Vicky is lost in thought for a moment before nodding. "Makes sense. I'd be super pissed if my favorite books were turned into movies and they didn't do them justice."

"If they fuck it up, that's where we come in." Beth winks with a maniacal chuckle. "Fan fiction is our way to correct the natural order of things."

I nearly snort my drink midsip but manage to not choke. "I mean, you're not wrong." A crazy thought crosses my mind. "Can you imagine if we actually convinced them our ideas would sell better than theirs?"

"They'd lose their ever-loving minds." Beth cackles again. "I'd be there with s'mores and a bottle of whiskey to watch the world burn."

"You're wicked, Beth." Vicky picks up a french fry. "I love it."

The two of them fall into an animated discussion about *Throne of Ashes* and how the showrunners deviated dramatically from the books. I'm not sure of the details—I haven't read the books—so I only half listen to them while I finish my burger and think about tomorrow.

Excitement thrums through me. I've been waiting for this convention for months. As soon as I found out director John Martigan would appear to discuss the upcoming installment of *Space Vendetta*, I started making plans. I've been following his career ever since I was in college. According to his wiki page, he's not much older than me, and the fact that he's already had such a strong impact on the film industry in such a short time is pretty fucking impressive. He's got a long career ahead of him, and I'm eager to see what other projects he takes on.

This weekend is my chance, my opportunity to ask him the questions burning through my mind. I'm no director—hell, I'm not even a filmmaker. But I *am* a storyteller. An amateur storyteller with no publications to my name, but I've written a pretty impressive number of fanfics over the years, as well as a healthy collection of short stories and poetry. I'd love to write a novel, but the day job keeps me pretty busy.

Not that it matters; I doubt anyone would read it. Still, I have strong opinions about the direction of the *Space Vendetta* series.

And when they open the forum to questions tomorrow, I'll be ready. John Martigan won't know what hit him after I step up to the microphone.

"Is that why you're going tomorrow?" Vicky asks, turning her attention to me.

I shake away the errant thoughts and frown. "Is what why?"

"You're still sore about the interview John Martigan did…when he said they're planning to add some fresh material to shake up the *Vendetta* series." Beth grins, savoring the absolute chaos she knows her statement will create inside me. We've discussed it before. At length and with alcohol. It wasn't pretty.

"I'm fine with them adding new material *if* it fits the narrative. I know some things in books don't translate well to film and vice versa, but I will castrate him if he decides to go completely off the deep end by abandoning canon source material. Especially if it's only to add more CGI or convoluted storylines to appease the higher-ups or sell tickets." I sniff disdainfully and take a drink.

"He's made it pretty clear what he plans to do," Beth says. "I doubt you'll be able to convince him otherwise."

"If he decides to completely fuck it up, it'll be on his head when the fans turn their backs on him. More and more studios are realizing the danger of crossing loyal fans."

"Like they care—sitting in ivory towers sipping champagne, swimming in vaults of money." Vicky snorts and crosses her arms.

Beth laughs. "Why am I picturing Scrooge McDuck?"

"Accurate as fuck." I join in with a chuckle.

"You're not going to the panel tomorrow just to rip the director a new asshole." Beth leans forward conspiratorially. "Admit it."

"Admit what?" I feign innocence.

"I'm lost." Vicky looks between us.

"John Martigan is an absolute fox," Beth explains.

"He is?" Curiosity pulling her deeper, Vicky opens her phone and types something. Her eyes widen. "Started as an actor at eighteen and found his footing as a director…one of Hollywood's most eligible bachelors. Holy shit." Vicky looks at me. "He's sinfully hot."

"He's no Jason Hunt, but that's like comparing chicken to beef. Two very different tastes."

My face slowly warms as Beth speaks. Part of me wants to hide under the table, but it's not like I'm having all my secrets revealed. Just one secret. A big secret.

"Ginger's had the hots for him for *years.*" Beth lowers her voice dramatically. "She's even written a fic or two featuring his surly ass."

"Fics about a *real person*? Is that even a thing?" Vicky blinks twice, her mouth agape.

"Oh, it's a thing. Not a popular thing for obvious reasons, but sometimes you gotta get the fantasy on paper, right?" Beth nudges me with her elbow.

I cover my face with a hand and shake my head. I'm going to fucking kill her.

"Did you publish them on Archive?" Vicky leans closer.

I shake my head. "No. I only publish stories about fictional characters."

"Can I read one?" Vicky begs. "Please. I–I'm just curious, I swear."

"Maybe." I finish my drink and push the glass away. "It doesn't matter. John Martigan may be hot, but he's got a damn temper. He's notorious for storming off if interviews get too personal. The guy has issues."

"Meh—we all have issues." Beth waves a hand as if banishing the notion to the inconsequential. "The real question is—what will you do if he answers your question?"

"What *is* your question?" Vicky asks, brow furrowed. "I missed that part."

"I have it written down back in the hotel room so I don't forget how best to phrase it, but basically, I want to know why he wants to change major plot points of the story to pander to a group of investors in suits who only care about a fucking paycheck."

"If you say it like that, he'll ignore your question entirely," Vicky observes quietly.

"I'm prepared for that possibility." I shrug. "But that's why I wrote it all down, so I can get it out quickly and at least make my voice heard."

"What if he goes supernova on you?" Beth asks, munching a chip.

"I'll give it right back to him."

"You'll get kicked out." Vicky's eyes double in size.

"They won't kick me out of the convention for asking a question." I scoff. "The worst they can do is take away the microphone. Maybe ask me to leave."

"And you're okay with that?" Beth studies me.

"Of course." I bolster my courage with a deep breath. "He needs to hear the truth from the fans. We're not interested in the same old shit repackaged and resold with a new name. We want the *original* story, told in a way that enhances the visual aspects of the universe while keeping to canon."

"You realize that means you won't get your love triad, don't you?" Beth smirks.

"That's right," Vicky gasps. "You're a huge fan of a Ransom-Lyanna-Colton triad, but it's not canon."

"They'll never put it in the series. Ever." I sigh in defeat. "It's too much for mainstream audiences—they'd never accept it. I've come to terms with that simple truth."

"It would be fucking epic on so many levels," Beth admits wistfully. "I mean the hate-fucking alone would—"

"Don't tease me right now." I press a hand to my heart. "It's one of those things I know will never come to pass, no matter how much I wish it into existence."

"Does it happen in the books?" Vicky asks.

"No." I pout. "But I'm sure Ronnie told Michael DeHart all about the idea when she met him today."

"Who's Michael DeHart?"

"The author of *Space Vendetta*. He started it when he was in his early twenties. Once the books took off, he was slammed with offers to make films based on the novels." Beth pops another chip into her mouth. "His main caveat was he had to be part of the process to ensure they stick to his vision."

"But didn't you just say the director is changing things?" Vicky looks perplexed again.

"He is," Beth clarifies.

"I'm so lost." Vicky hangs her head.

"It's complicated." I explain in the easiest way I can. "The first studio sold the rights, and a new contract was drawn up. They threw Michael DeHart under the bus by adding a disclaimer that the director has ultimate decision-making over the final product."

"Fucking bullshit," Vicky exclaims, slapping a hand over her mouth when patrons at a neighboring table turn to stare. "Sorry."

"It *is* bullshit, and that's exactly why I'm going to the panel tomorrow." I straighten, filled with righteous indignation and holy purpose. "*Someone* has to put John Martigan in his place."

Beth bursts out laughing. "I'd *love* to see that."

"Come with us," Vicky says.

"I can't." She frowns. "Photo ops are at the same time as the panels." Beth winks at Vicky. "Just promise you'll record the whole thing for me."

"I can do that." Vicky shoots me an apologetic look and crosses her heart. "For fangirl use only."

"I *want* the whole world to see it." My heart races at the thought of blasting my confrontational encounter with the director of *Space Vendetta* all over social media. I take a steadying breath. It'll be fine. He'll ignore me like he does anybody who asks questions that challenge his position and authority. I plan on knocking the big fucking chip off his broad shoulder and walking away with a smug smile.

Serves him right.

"I'll drink to that." Beth orders a round of tequila shots.

Vicky groans. "Last one. I need to get to bed. I'm fucking exhausted."

"Okay," Beth relents.

After our shot, we cash out and head back to the hotel. The moment I get to our room, I slip into the shower, desperate for a few moments of peace.

I love these girls to death, but it's been a whirlwind of activity today. Between Vicky's run-in with Jason Hunt, Jessica's panic attack, Ronnie's strange disappearance, and Beth's rollercoaster mood thanks to a grumpy security guard, I've had to run interception all day. It takes a toll on a body.

The hot spray soothes my nerves. A good night's sleep will set things right. Tomorrow I'll finally have my chance to confront the one man who's not only inspired my creativity but has haunted my fantasies for years.

I just hope I can keep it together long enough to get the question out. Honestly, I'm afraid if he makes eye contact with me, I'll spontaneously combust. The last thing I need to do is pump up his over-inflated ego.

Bring it, Martigan.

CHAPTER TWO

My hand shakes as I step into the auditorium. The panel doesn't start for thirty minutes, but I want to be sure to get a good seat.

"You got this." Vicky takes my hand and squeezes, her smile radiating confidence. There's a soft glow to her this morning…probably due to her late night activities.

When she arrived at our room this morning, Beth called her out for wearing the same clothes as last night. Not to mention the rosy hue to her cheeks and the bashful smile she wore while hedging around our questions. She hooked up with *someone* last night, and while I have a hunch about who it might have been, I have no proof.

A sexy night with Jason Hunt would be the stuff of fangirl dreams, but Vicky's not like that. She's private. Beth and I exchanged a look at her vehement denials, but we ultimately dropped it. When she's ready to spill the tea, we'll be here. Fortunately for her, Beth has her photo op and I have my panel. It's enough to distract us from pulling her into the café across the street to grill her until she breaks and spills the dirty details of her mysterious hookup.

Beth left us at the doorway with a wink, wishing me luck. I wish she could have stayed to run interference for me if I need it. Vicky will do her best to keep me on track, but she's not as ferocious as Beth—there's a reason Beth is called Mistress Viper in the online forum.

"There's someone over there with a clipboard. Let's ask if

we're in the right place." I nod toward a blonde woman across the aisle.

"Hi," she says as we approach. "Can I help you?"

"Yeah, is this the room for the *Space Vendetta* panel with John Martigan and Michael DeHart?"

"Sure is." She beams at us. "There's still plenty of seats. Welcome."

"Are they doing a question and answer?" I ask as a flutter of nervous energy swirls in my stomach.

She checks her clipboard. "Yes…but they're taking names and drawing at random to give everyone a chance."

"Oh." My heart drops like a rock to the pit of my gut. "Right."

"Would you like to add your name?"

"Sure." I clear my throat. "Ginger Darling."

"Is that your real name?" She meets my gaze, her own eyes sparkling.

I nod.

"That's gorgeous."

"Thanks," I say.

"I've got you down. If you want to find a good seat, they're filling up fast."

With a flashing smile, I thank her and turn. Vicky's already found a few open seats near the stage. She grins and points.

"Ronnie's already here, and it looks like she's saved seats." Vicky takes my hand, and we wind our way through the growing crowd.

"Glad to see you made it." Ronnie takes her purse off a chair and a notebook off another. "Had to fight to keep these, but it was well worth it."

"Thanks," I say, sliding into the one beside her. "We're running a little late." I exchange a look with Vicky, who blushes at my comment, so I shift the conversation. "I'm surprised to see you here. Thought you were heading home this morning?"

"I was going to, but when I heard they'd added Michael to the panel, I didn't want to miss it." Ronnie tosses her dark ringlets over one shoulder. Vibrant red lipstick and winged liner give her a femme fatale vibe. All she needs is a pencil dress with kitten heels, and her curvaceous beauty would be the talk of the convention.

"Didn't you meet him yesterday when he was signing books?" Vicky asks.

"I did." Ronnie's grin widens. "He invited me to come to the panel today, said it might be something I would enjoy."

"Wow. That's awesome," I respond. "You two must have hit it off."

"After the fangirling wore off…yeah, I guess we did." Ronnie waves a hand. "But anyway, enough about me—Vicky, what happened yesterday? I saw your post blow up on Instagram."

Vicky relays the story, and we fall into easy conversation while we wait for the team of volunteers to prepare the stage and do a sound check. We're moments from showtime, and I'm sweating bullets.

Finally, Ronnie turns to me. "Moment of truth, Ginger. Are you gonna ask him?"

I take a deep, steadying breath. "Damn right I'm gonna ask him."

"Good girl." Ronnie takes my hand. "We're right here with you. Fangirls united."

A chuckle escapes me. "He's not getting away from this convention unscathed. He needs to know what his decisions cost true fans of the series."

"As long as you don't threaten his ass, you should be fine."

Ronnie smiles reassuringly.

"Okay. I won't vow to hunt him down and castrate him if he follows through with his plan." I incline my head but allow a sadistic grin to overtake my innocent expression. "The implication will remain."

"You're playing with fire, Ginger." Vicky sighs. "Just stick to the script."

I pull the slip of paper from my purse and silently read it over and over, committing the words to memory even though I'll have it in my hand.

The chatter around us fades into a round of applause as the panel emerges from the curtains surrounding the stage. We're in the front row, and I have a perfect view of the neat line of chairs on stage.

As the guests arrive, I note Michael DeHart as he steps from behind the curtain. He waves, wearing a bashful smile as the crowd goes wild. He takes the seat directly in front of us, his gaze searching the crowd. It stops cold on us, and a genuine smile breaks across his handsome face. He winks at Ronnie before turning his attention to the other panelists joining him on stage.

The crowd erupts in a cacophony of cheers, whistles, and applause when *he* steps onto the stage. John Martigan. My breath catches in my throat at the sight of him. He strides across the stage, larger than life, broad shoulders filling a tailored Armani suit, his thick dark hair falling in waves around an angular face. Smile wide, eyes narrowed against the stage lights. He waves his impossibly large hand and picks up the microphone on his chair. His biography says he's six three, and even though I'm five eleven, I feel like he'd tower over me. It could just be the stage and his presence…but I doubt it.

I swallow a lump rising in my throat as the panel guests settle into their seats. He's fifteen feet in front of me, his dark gaze drifting across the crowd. The moderator introduces everyone and begins the discussion, leading the conversation and lobbing softball questions to the panelists, asking for details on upcoming projects.

Vicky and Ronnie follow the volley of dialogue, their attention pinging between the guests and the moderator. My attention is fixed solely on John Martigan, who hasn't yet answered a single question or added his thoughts to the mix. Strange.

He sits with his legs crossed, arm in his lap, microphone clutched in his fist. His gaze remains above the crowd, scanning but pleasantly impassive. He appears to be listening, but I recognize a glint in his eyes, the kind that appears when someone isn't paying attention. I spend a lot of time in corporate America, and I've attended enough meetings to be able to recognize when someone's zoned out.

Finally, the question-and-answer portion arrives. I sit straighter, smoothing my hands over the bold and bright neon colors of my skirt. Good. I want to be sure he sees me in the dim light.

I squirm with anticipation as they call on audience members to ask questions. The first is nothing but flattery and a silly question about the release date. The second is even more ridiculous, something about a crossover between *Space Vendetta* and a completely unrelated series. The third question proves more interesting since it pertains to the timeline of events within the series.

"Our next question comes from…Ginger." The moderator scans the crowd, shielding his eyes as though searching. "Where are you, Ginger?"

"Here." I stand, stuffing down nervous energy threatening to make me puke. I clutch the paper in my hand as I meet John

Martigan's eyes.

A volunteer with a microphone takes me by surprise. He holds it out, urging me to speak.

"Hi, this question is for the director." I struggle to keep my voice sweet and neutral, but it trembles regardless. "Mr. Martigan, you've made quite a name for yourself in the film industry, and to this point, you've done admirably well in keeping the *Space Vendetta* films true to the source material."

John Martigan leans forward, both feet on the ground, his narrowed eyes locked on me. I note the way the muscle flexes in his jaw as I continue.

"As a fan of both the books and films, I—and many in the fandom—are concerned with your most recent interview in *FilmTalk* regarding the vision you have for the direction of the upcoming films. It seems like you've decided to *adapt* the source material to suit the whims of the studio and box office rather than remaining true to the creator's story." In my periphery, I notice Michael DeHart cover his mouth with a hand and shift in his seat, but my attention remains riveted on John Martigan, whose demeanor has darkened with each word I utter. "Do you have any intention of following the books or are you going to screw it all up?"

A chorus of shocked gasps, low murmurs, and a smattering of applause rises from the crowd. It quickly dims as the director lifts the microphone, his gaze seeming to purposely avoid me.

"There's always a flux between the books and the cinematic experience." He offers a half smile, but it doesn't reach his eyes. "Michael and I have discussed this."

"Yes, but in your last interview, you said there would be *significant* changes to some of the characters and to events that take place later in the series. Exactly how far do you plan to deviate?" I place my hands on my hips.

"I'm confident any adaptations we make to the story will enhance the experience." He nods as if to punctuate his declaration and end the discussion completely.

Michael DeHart remains impassive beside him, his hand firmly set over his mouth, his eyes wide.

"So you admit it?" I grab the microphone, holding it in place.

The volunteer looks around uncomfortably.

"Admit what?" Martigan's attention snaps to me again.

"That you sold the fans out." My tone is sickeningly sweet. "How much did you get for your soul, Mr. Martigan?" I deepen my voice an octave. "I hope it's worth it. Fans have long memories, sir."

John Martigan's expression devolves into a whirlpool of panic before shifting to a tight mask of irritation, then indifference. He nods once and drops the microphone to his side.

A pair of men in black polo shirts stamped with "security" move in front of me, blocking my view of the stage. The volunteer with the microphone skitters away. Around us, the crowd bursts into activity and conversation.

"Come with us." One of the guards gestures toward a side exit.

"You can't be serious?" Ronnie stands. "She just asked a question."

"Don't make a scene," the other guard says. "Let's go."

"Fine." I grind my teeth, striving for some semblance of decorum, and turn to Vicky and Ronnie. "I'll text you. Finish the panel."

They blink at me in horror, ready to come to my defense, but I hold my hand up.

"Don't worry. I can handle this." Straightening, I exit the

room, one guard ahead of me, one following.

Behind me, pandemonium erupts as the crowd devolves to chaotic shouts and boos. I hear the moderator attempt to wrangle them back to order and continue the panel discussion, but he fails miserably.

I grin as the doors close. *That's what you get, Martigan. Fuck around and find out.*

My pride shifts to uncertainty as a guard steps into my path, his hand pressed to his earpiece. I pull up short.

"Come with me." He directs me down a hallway…away from the exit I anticipated.

"Wait. Where are you taking me?"

The guards say nothing, and panic takes hold of me. Mouth dry, heart pounding, head spinning, I wonder what line I crossed. What are they going to do to me?

"Am I being arrested?" I ask warily.

Neither guard responds, which fuels my harried thoughts. Fuck. Fuckity fuck fuck. I should have toned down the question. I worried the director would flip his shit, but I'd never anticipated this. Damn it.

At the end of the hall, they open a door marked Security Holding and motion for me to enter.

I stop outside the door. Panic turns to terror in my veins.

"I–I'll leave the convention. Please."

"Inside." The guard pins me with a stern look. "Now."

With a huff, I enter the room, cringing as the door clicks shut behind me.

A choked gasp tears from my throat when it locks. I pinch my eyes closed.

Shit.

I'm going to jail, aren't I?

CHAPTER THREE

Five.

Ten.

Fifteen minutes pass.

My leg bounces beneath the table at a frantic pace. I glance at my phone and scowl at the time—not to mention the distinct lack of reception in this room. That's when I start to wonder if this is a holding cell for criminals as they wait for the police.

Shit. I chew my fingernail and run through the morning's events again. I didn't threaten anyone. I didn't incite a riot. Hell, I thought my question was tame—though I should have stuck to the script still clutched in my hand rather than running wild.

I snap my gum and curse again. The adrenaline from sitting anonymously in the crowd has worn off, and the reality of my actions are crashing against me in wave after wave of anxiety-inducing nausea. Fuck.

A million questions and possible answers race through my mind at hyper speed. What happened to Vicky and Ronnie? Are they being held? Do they know where I am? Is this all some kind of conspiracy to keep the media at bay?

With its stark white walls, distinct lack of decoration, and absolutely no windows, the room closes in. There's a table and two chairs, and it looks exactly like the interrogation room in a detective movie. The kind where they bring the murderer in to grill them for hours, playing good cop–bad cop until the suspect breaks and confesses to the crime.

I whimper. This isn't good. My brain is making shit up to

counter the lack of information, and it's driving me bonkers. If I don't get out of here soon, I might lose my mind. The least they can do is tell me what I did wrong instead of holding me here without a valid reason.

Another two minutes pass, and I'm nearly to the point where I'm going to bang on the door, demand an attorney or something. That's when the door latch clicks, and the only exit swings open in invitation.

I'm on my feet in two seconds, ready to bolt, but *he* walks in.

John Martigan.

His dark eyes fix on me, and I sink back into my chair, folding my arms across my chest. His gaze briefly dips to my breasts, like my movement amplified their presence, but he looks away and clears his throat. The door closes behind him with a decisive snick of the lock sliding into place once more.

"Didn't get enough earlier and came back for more?" I ask sweetly. "You must be a glutton for punishment."

The director clears his throat again and slides into the chair opposite me. "I believe you're confused as to *who* holds the power here."

"What do you want?" I lean back and glare at him, ignoring the heat building inside me.

He's right there on the other side of the table. Only three feet separate us. I can count the freckles along his cheek and nose. From this distance, I'm able to make out the distinct color of his eyes—a warm mix of chocolate and bourbon.

I lick my lips as desire consumes me. I've harbored this crush for years, but seeing him here in this room, staring at me with a mix of curiosity and distaste…it's enough to make me squirm.

Can he tell how he affects me? I push aside the question and face him with my most impassive expression.

"You knew that would happen." He rubs a hand across his jaw and leans forward, elbows on the table. It wasn't a question. "Yet you did it anyway."

"I have no idea what you're talking about." I toss my hair over my shoulder.

"Was your intention to get me to react?" He holds my gaze, but I only blink at him as the words slowly sink into my mind. "Were you trying to bait me? To catch me in a moment of weakness so you could go viral and boost your social media ratings?"

I scrunch my nose in distaste at his accusation. "Is that what you think that was? A stunt to boost a social media account?"

"You came to that panel fully intending to ask that question." His gaze narrows. "You *knew* it would cause a riot."

"You're fucking delusional." I scoff. "It was hardly a riot."

"They're *still* wrangling the crowd in an effort to control the damage you caused."

I lean forward, matching his stance, bringing us dangerously close. His cologne drifts over me in a sultry caress. I shake my head, refusing to be distracted.

"You mean the damage *you* caused when you refused to answer an honest question and had security drag me out of the room."

"An honest question?" He snorts. "I highly doubt that. Judging from the tone of your voice when you asked, I'm willing to bet you spent hours, if not days, crafting the question in a way you knew would garner a reaction."

"It worked, didn't it?"

"Not quite, sweetheart."

"Don't fucking call me that, you chauvinist prick." I slap my hands on the table, nails scraping the top.

"What would you prefer?" His grin widens. "Red?"

Fury blasts through me in a rush of indignation. I shoot to my feet and lean across the table to grab his tie in my fist. "You haven't earned the right to call me anything—especially that."

"Well, I wouldn't have started with it if you'd provided your name." He rises, meeting me in the middle.

"So you weren't paying attention, otherwise you'd know my name." We both lean over the table, breath mingling, my hand still fisted in his tie. Tension pulses between us as silence stretches. My brain short-circuits over the whole situation, strained as it is.

His voice dips to a deep base, low and throaty, sexy as sin. "What would you prefer I call you?"

His tone reverberates, so deep and dark and sinful, I blink twice, unable to comprehend his words. His voice has no right to sound this fucking delicious. Not now. Not ever.

"Ginger." My name slips free before I can stop it. Fuck. No! Don't concede to him. Ever.

"Ginger," he repeats.

My name sounds absolutely filthy on his lips.

I scowl. "I demand you release me. I've done nothing wrong."

"Is that so?" He remains still, his gaze flicking to my grip on his tie. "If you persist in being obstinate, I can have you permanently banned from future conventions."

"You won't." I jerk my hand back as though burned. "If that were the case, you'd have had me escorted from the premises."

"True." He's close…too close, and it takes all my effort not to react to his proximity. The last thing I need to give him is more ammunition to take me to court—or worse.

"You can't keep me here forever." I glare at him. "Look.

My question wasn't revolutionary. It wasn't meant to incite anything, especially a riot." I grit my teeth. "You're only a few decisions away from fucking up a perfectly good franchise—one that could earn a lot of money while remaining true to the source material and keeping the fans happy." I sigh, exhausted. "Don't fuck this up. That's all I'm saying."

Martigan's eyes narrow, searching, inquisitive for a long moment. Almost too long. My breath stutters when he finally straightens.

"I see." He pulls back, slowly fixing his tie, smoothing it against his chest, and withdrawing with an audible whoosh of energy. Whatever tension had blossomed between us vanishes.

I stand up and blink twice. What just happened?

Before I can respond, he steps toward the door and knocks twice.

"Wait here." He indicates the chair with a brusque nod.

The door opens, and he steps out.

"Wait," I call, shooting around the table just in time for the door to slam in my face. "No! Come back here, you bastard!" I curse, slamming my closed fist against the door.

Tears spring to my eyes as I pace the room. My agitation is double what it had been when they first locked me in here.

"I'm not a fucking criminal. I demand you release me this instant!" I beat on the door until my hands ache. "Goddamn it!"

I lean against the door, my chest heaving, head aching. Why the hell did he leave me? Why am I still here? I curse repeatedly, wondering what the fuck happened.

What little conversation we had led to no resolution, and still, he just abandoned me here. Like a common fucking criminal. Asshole.

I pace the room twice more, chewing on the edge of my fingernail and running the conversation through my head, over and over again. Did I say something wrong? Did I somehow incriminate myself?

My breath catches when a thought slams into me. Was he recording me? Trying to trick me into confessing something? I scan the room, noting the absence of cameras or mirrors of any kind. Which doesn't actually mean much in this day and age. There are a hundred sneaky ways to trick someone into a confession and get it on film.

I pray Vicky and Ronnie are advocating for me, trying to find out where they took me and why. But I'm not holding out much hope of them finding me. These people have too many connections, and it would take forever to find an advocate to even start looking for me.

Shit.

The more time I spend in this room, the more my anxiety grows. Maybe I should have asked something different.

But that wouldn't be fair. Not to me. Not to the hundreds of thousands of fans who want the promises of Michael DeHart's *Space Vendetta* series and not some half-assed, money hungry interpretation of events in the books.

A sob catches in my throat. This wasn't what I'd intended—not even remotely—but I couldn't let it go. Not when I love this series so much. Not when I know what it could be if the director just *listens to reason.*

Fat chance of that happening now. I had my opportunity to convince him to change his mind, and I blew it. Maybe it was the way I phrased the question. Or the tone I used.

None of it matters. Not now.

John Martigan made his opinion known, and unfortunately, it left me in a very uncomfortable position. The question remaining—am I ever going to get out of this room? More concerning—am I going to face charges for what I'd done? Will

I be able to attend another convention?

I swear again, multiple times, before I let the tears fall freely.

CHAPTER FOUR

My panic and fear burn down to a smoldering fury. I angrily swipe tears away and square my shoulders before marching to the door.

"You can't hold me in here," I shout and again beat my fists against the wood. "Open this goddamned door, right no—"

The door swings open mid-hit, and I stop my fist from colliding with the person on the other side. A surly guard stands before me, her eyes narrowed. I drop my hand and tug my dress into order.

"Am I free to go?"

"Not exactly." She gestures toward the hallway where three more guards wait.

"You're *escorting* me to the exit?" I scoff. "Four guards? This is a little extreme, don't you think?"

"Come on." She steps aside so I can walk through the doorway.

Two of the guards shift out of the way when I approach. The third turns to take the lead while the woman follows behind me. They form a circle around me as we reenter the crowded convention hall.

Curious gazes follow us. I half expect one of the guards to ring a bell to announce my shame to the gathered masses. Everyone we pass stops to watch the procession. Whispers flow through the crowd. Some pull out their phones and snap a picture or document this unexpected event with video. I have no doubt it'll be all over social media by dinner.

Instead of hanging my head and hiding my face, I tip my chin high and gather what remains of my pride, carrying it like a banner as we weave through the convention center.

John Martigan did this to me. He doesn't have to actually press charges. This is my punishment, being forcibly escorted from a fandom convention after publicly humiliating him on stage—and on livestream. If I ever see him again, it will be too soon. I'll probably murder the bastard.

My gaze skims the crowd as we pass. I keep praying to catch a glimpse of Vicky, Ronnie, or Beth. I reach into my pocket and tightly grip my phone. Part of me wants to send a text or call them. But the last thing I need is a video of me falling flat on my face, trying to text while being escorted from the Philadelphia convention by four guards.

By the time we reach the exit, any shame I felt has turned to righteous indignation. I need to find the other fangirls. I need a plan. John Martigan will not get away with this.

The guards lead me out the door and guide me down a walkway to the street. I stumble over my own feet as we approach the curb.

A black town car is waiting, complete with tinted windows and a driver standing beside the sleek ride. It looks like part of the presidential fleet. He steps forward and assesses me as the guards disperse. "Ginger Darling?"

"Yes." I stiffen, ready to bolt.

The driver nods and opens the back door.

I hesitate, my senses on full alert. "Am I being kidnapped?"

He shakes his head, and a small smile curves the corner of his mouth. "Please."

I pull out my phone, ready to hit the emergency call button should the need arise. As I slide into the car and my eyes adjust from the bright sunlight outside, I realize my mistake.

"Fuck," I mutter as I settle into the leather seat beside John Martigan. A wave of unease washes over me and mixes with the undeniable pull of my long-standing attraction to the man. This combination of emotions leaves me unsteady.

The door closes, encasing us in the air-conditioned interior. A tinted privacy barrier separating the driver from the passengers slides closed before I can tell the driver to let me out.

I slump against the seat as the car pulls into traffic. My heart pounds, and I glance at the phone clutched in my hand before surrendering to the undeniable pull of his presence. When I look at Martigan, I find him relaxed, resting his jaw on his fingertips, studying me.

"Decided to kill me, have you?" I quip, unsure if I can trust him. Or myself.

He lowers his hand and inclines his head. "Actually, I have a proposition for you."

"A proposition?" I fold my arms across my chest, leaning as far away from him as the car allows. "If this is some kind of sexual thing, you can fuck all the way off."

"Hardly." His dark eyes glitter with amusement. "Considering your literary proclivities, I'm not surprised that's the direction your mind went."

My head snaps up. I open my mouth to ask what he means, but he stops me with a raised hand.

"First, this conversation is not to be repeated to anyone outside this car, is that understood?" Martigan's gaze bores into my soul.

Reluctantly, I nod. "Fine."

He settles back and withdraws his phone from his jacket pocket, then unlocks it to read what's on the screen. "Ginger Darling. Marketing director for DragonFire Publishing Incorporated. Thirty-two. Single." His gaze quickly rakes over me. "Interesting."

A lingering heat simmers in its wake, making me shiver. I shove it aside. "What's interesting?"

He continues without answering. "Standard social media accounts…boring." A smile blossoming on his full lips makes him more sinfully attractive than before. "There it is. *StarShipper*."

My heart stops beating when he says my pen name on FandomFics Archive, and ice flows through my veins, freezing the breath in my lungs. I stare at him, unable to speak.

His brow arches as he scrolls, his amusement growing. "Well now, this explains so much."

I stare, unmoving as he reads through the titles of all the fan fiction I've ever posted online. There's no connection between my social media accounts and my fan fiction page. No one in my real life even knows I write fan fiction. The only people who know are the fangirls in our online forum—and they don't have any connection to my everyday life.

My mortification grows as he selects one of my *Space Vendetta* fics, "Her Wicked Pirate," and proceeds to read aloud from a random location in the document.

"'I moan with unrepressed delight as Korbin presses his open mouth to my aching clit.'"

Martigan's deep voice echoes through the car, and the words combine with his sinful inflection to set my body on fire. Heat burns in my cheeks as he continues.

"'My pussy aches for him, even though everything about this is wrong. He's my enemy, Colton's enemy. Thinking of my lover as his enemy fucks me with his tongue is sobering.'" Martigan clears his throat and looks over the phone at my horrified expression. "I will admit your prose leaves me…wanting."

"Fuck you." I huff. "There's nothing wrong with writing a little smutty fan fiction to blow off steam. Anything can sound pornographic when you read it out of context."

"You misunderstand." John returns the phone to his pocket, his attention fully on me. "I'm impressed by your body of work. And by the quality of your writing."

"Then wha—" Realization slams into me with the force of a freight train. Did he imply my writing gave him a hard-on? I clear my throat and try *not* to look at his lap. I redirect the conversation to his original statement. "Are you sure this isn't some thinly veiled sexual proposal?"

"Believe me when I say it most certainly is not." He pauses. "After doing some research, I've come to the conclusion your question today was not a publicity stunt."

"No shit." I snap, ignoring the flood of emotions and arousal thrumming through me. "I told you that earlier."

"You did." He exhales sharply. "You're a talented fan who is dedicated to the integrity and success of the fandom."

"I would have told you *that* if you had just listened to me."

Martigan studies me with a strange expression for a long moment—assessing, unreadable before it vanishes completely. "You're right," he finally says. "My apologies."

"Wait." I blink twice. "What just happened?"

"I overreacted." He runs his hand through his hair, mussing the thick, dark waves. "You had every right to ask that question. Fans should never be ignored or dismissed."

"I…" Words lodge in my throat, dying before they can escape my lips. "What about the panel? The commotion?"

"My error in judgment has been rectified." He holds my gaze steady, his voice strong, his words sincere. "I've already issued a statement addressing it as a misunderstanding and assuring fans of the *Space Vendetta* franchise I will be taking a new direction to ensure the films closely match the source material."

"Y-you are?" I stare at him, completely bewildered. "What's the catch?"

"No catch." He smiles, unleashing another wave of fluttering inside my chest.

"Why this sudden change of heart?" I wait for the punchline of this obvious joke.

"Your question sparked a much needed conversation between fans and creators." He sighs. "As much as I thought I knew about this fandom, I was wrong. Thank you for showing me the error of my ways."

"Is this a joke?" I pause and glance around, waiting for the big reveal. "Am I being pranked?" It's only us. No cameras, no fanfare. Nothing. "You're serious?"

"As a heart attack." He nods, flexing his hand against his thigh.

My eyes widen at the sheer size of his hand in contrast to my own. I suck in a deep breath. "I'm not allowed to tell anyone about this conversation?"

"No." He regards me with a somber look. "I have already issued a public apology. But this—I wanted to issue one directly to you without the prying eyes of the press."

"And your proposal?"

"A truce of sorts." He clears his throat. "I want to ensure no animosity remains between us after my apology."

"Why?" Confusion swirls within me.

"Your insight led us to this moment. I handled it poorly, but it opened my eyes." He taps his fingers on his leg. "You may be just what I need."

"What you…need?" I parrot, even more lost than before. "You're not making sense."

"I know. Again, my apologies." He shakes his head and taps

the glass partition to signal the driver. "I have a few things to take care of before I say anything more."

I growl in frustration. "Look, if someone had told me today was going to be like this, I would have laughed in their face. I don't regret asking my question, and I'm glad it triggered this change of heart. But I'll be honest, I have no idea what I'm doing here now."

"You'll see."

"You are the most confounding man I've ever met." I throw my hands up.

"I get that a lot." He grins. "I've been told it's part of my charm."

"Somehow, I highly doubt it," I grumble.

The car rolls to a stop.

"I'll be in touch," Martigan says as the door opens.

"Sure." I climb out of the car.

His voice drifts from the interior. "Remember our deal."

"How could I forget?" I respond with mock sincerity.

My legs wobble as I turn and stare at the hotel where I'm staying. How the hell did he know? Without a backward glance, I head for the entrance. The director's words spin in my head, distracting me. Somehow, I manage to make it to the bar and slide into a seat without colliding with anyone.

Once I have a lemon drop martini in front of me, I pull up my fangirl group text and send a message.

(Me): *I'm at the hotel bar. Needed a break. Xoxo*

A flurry of texts come through, and even though I assure them nothing happened, they know I'm lying. John Martigan's words drift back to me, and I swear. Why does he want me to keep our conversation a secret?

I sigh and sip my drink, lost in thought. That's not the only question burning me up.

What did he mean, *I'll be in touch*?

A delicious shiver of desire snakes through me as I imagine the implication of such a statement. The memory of him reading my fic aloud, the tenor of his voice, deep and seductive and unwavering, lingers like the familiar strains of a favorite song…it leaves me breathless, unsteady.

I push it away. There's no way he's interested in me. Not after this fiasco.

CHAPTER FIVE

Nearly a week later, I'm still stewing over the confusing encounter with John Martigan. It burns like hell, but I've managed to keep my end of the bargain. Not a soul knows of our conversation—neither conversation. Except, of course, for the guards and chauffeur. Though they weren't privy to the details, and I feel a distinct lack of control.

When Vicky and Ronnie found me at the bar, I told them what I could, and it aligned with what they'd seen. My question ignited a firestorm against the director and other panelists. They told me Martigan vacated the stage shortly after I was escorted from the room, and the panel continued without issue.

But the conclusion of the event left me stunned.

Vicky showed me a video she'd recorded of John Martigan taking the stage once more, issuing an apology to fans, and vowing to do right by the source material. He shook hands with Michael DeHart and left amid a flurry of flashing lights, applause, cheers, and controlled chaos.

My head ached at his transition from the man I confronted to this calm, collected director.

True to his word, John Martigan attempted to heal the wound he'd caused by deviating from the original *Space Vendetta* timeline. Not that he'd done it yet, but the simple fact of discussing possible alternatives left the fandom in an absolute tizzy. Including myself.

I open my laptop and pull up contracts and marketing files for new authors joining our publishing house. They need to be finalized and emailed by noon, and I can't spend my time running the events of last week through my head on a loop.

One of the benefits of my job is to work from home most days. I function best in my own space, shrouded in comfy sweats and jamming to 80s rock. My hair bobs in a topknot as Bon Jovi streams through the speakers.

Unbidden, John Martigan creeps back into my mind. This guy is like a goddamned earworm. I can't shake him no matter how much I attempt to distract myself.

His presence left me trembling and hyperaware of my physical reaction. It's strange though—no matter what happened between us, how tense it got, I never felt threatened or unsafe. Weird. I'm not afraid of the infamous director, but I'm not an idiot. He's more powerful and intimidating than I could ever dream of being.

That's one major reason I've kept my mouth shut. Even though Vicky and Ronnie begged for details, I told them nothing happened. A *huge* lie. But I can't say anything. To anyone. Ever. Damn him.

The soft patter of rain taps on my window as I shift my focus back to the tasks at hand. There are at least twenty emails waiting for me in my inbox. I'll tackle those after lunch. Right now, I have to send these documents out and make sure I have everything ready for the staff meeting tomorrow morning.

A text comes through with a *ping* on my phone. I glance at it. Vicky.

(Vicky): *Hey, girl. Just checking on you.*

I type out a quick response.

(Me): *I'm fine. How are you?*

(Vicky): *Did you see Martigan's announcement?*

My body tenses and my heart races as I open a new window and search for his name. Sure enough, it's in the entertainment headlines.

I read aloud to myself, breath catching. "Director John Martigan delays filming to renegotiate script and casting for upcoming *Space Vendetta* installment." I blink and reread the headline twice before continuing through the article. "Citing artistic conflicts, Martigan calls for a delay to ensure the franchise is on track."

Holy fucking shit.

I grin. The bastard actually did it.

Vicky texts me again.

(Vicky): *Looks like you made waves at the convention. Congrats, girl.*

(Me): *Thanks*

I send my reply, then scroll down the rest of the article. I'm halfway through it when the phone rings.

I answer, expecting one of the authors with questions about their marketing resources. "Ginger Darling, Director of Marketing, how can I help you?"

"So professional." A deep voice reverberates through the line. "A vast difference from the hellcat who blindsided me in front of an entire convention."

My breath catches again, but I recover quickly. "If this is who I think it is, you must be a glutton for punishment." I pause. "I just saw the article in *Entertainment Times*, Mr. Martigan."

"Just following through on a promise."

"And what was that?" I lean back, putting the phone on speaker.

"To ensure the fans are heard." His voice fills my apartment, almost like he's standing beside me.

"On behalf of the fandom, thank you. But don't think this puts you in my good graces."

"A personal apology wasn't enough?"

"It helped," I say. "But it seems I've become infamous for

confronting the director of one of the most famous franchises in history."

"You knew exactly what you were doing when you took that microphone, Ginger." A haggard chuckle escapes him. "And I'm glad you were brave enough to do it."

Warmth simmers through me, settling deep in my bones and taking root. "You didn't call to shower me with flattery." I sigh. "What do you want?"

"How far are you from the city?"

"From Manhattan?" I straighten and calculate the distance. "Three hours. Why?"

"I'd like to meet you for dinner Saturday."

I scoff. "So you can kill me and toss me into the Hudson?"

"That would be a monumental waste." His voice lowers. "No, I have a business proposal to discuss, and I prefer to have the conversation in person."

"Is this like the proposition you never got to mention in the car?"

"Yes, well…I spoke out of turn then, but I assure you, I'm fully prepared to discuss this at length. If you're willing and able."

"I'm able, but the willing part is where I'm a little murky." I lick my lips. "Why me?"

"Come to dinner, and I'll explain it to your heart's content."

His sinful proposition is a temptation I don't need in my life, but curiosity wins out. "Fine." I click my tongue. "When and where?"

"I'll have my assistant send the details over via email this afternoon."

Part of me wilts, knowing this is nothing more than a professional exchange of ideas—a business meeting—and not something romantic. I shake my head. Beth is right. I'm a fucking hopeless romantic.

"Which email address would you prefer I have her use?" he asks, breaking my thoughts.

"Ginger dot Darling at contact dot com." I give my independent address, the one I use for business outside the publishing house, not my personal one. That would be dangerous.

"Got it." He hums in thought for a moment before continuing. "I can have a car meet you at the station if you take the train."

"I can handle the city." Defensiveness kicks in, but I manage to stop it from taking over. "Thank you though. That's very thoughtful."

"You're welcome." A long silence stretches between us. "Until Saturday then."

We exchange pleasant goodbyes, and I disconnect the call, staring at my blank phone screen. What the hell just happened? I replay the conversation, and still, nothing connects in my mind.

Did that just happen?

I open my email to find a new message from Martigan's assistant with a time and location for dinner on Saturday. That was fast. Too fast. My brain spins.

I unlock my phone and pull up Vicky's contact. She answers immediately.

"Hey, girl, what's up?" She sounds breathless.

"Sorry to bug you. I just…" I bite my lip, wondering whether I can relay this information. Shit. "I just got off the phone with John Martigan."

Silence for the space of three heartbeats. At the other end of the line, I hear a murmur and a door closing. Vicky unleashes on me, her voice a screech vibrating through my living room.

"John Martigan?" She huffs. "I knew you were keeping something from me. Spill it. Why the hell is John Martigan calling you?"

"I–I can't share all the details—not yet—but when I can, I'll tell you the whole story, I promise. Suffice it to say we had an exchange at the convention, and now he wants me to meet him for dinner in the city."

"Whoa. He asked you out to dinner? Did you guys hook up or—"

"No, nothing like that. It's a business dinner. He has a proposal he wants to discuss in person."

"Oh." Disappointment echoes in her tone, but it's quickly replaced by a hopeful bounce. "When is this dinner?"

"Saturday at seven."

"Where?"

"The Plaza Royale."

"Fancy." She clicks her tongue. "Any idea what it's about?"

"Aside from our conflict concerning *Space Vendetta*, no."

"Ginger, I know you can't tell me details, but you know I'm freaking out over here with you keeping me in the dark?"

Disappointment fills the pit of my stomach. "I know. I'm sorry."

"Did he flirt with you?" she asks carefully.

I ponder the question, remembering the sinful way he read those lines from my fanfic. I shake my head. "No, I…I don't think so."

"Damn." She sighs. "I was hoping he wanted to seduce you."

"He's not the type," I say. "I mean, I've watched dozens of interviews with him. He doesn't really date, and when he does, it doesn't last long. He doesn't even have a type that I can tell."

"I mean—you're smitten with the guy, you would know."

I run a hand over my face, warmth sinking into my palms. "Don't remind me."

"Does he know the extent of your obsession?"

"Geezus, Vicky, you make it sound fucking wrong. I'm *not obsessed* with John Martigan."

"If the shoe fits, lace that bitch up."

"I'm not obsessed."

"Fine." A pause. "Where was he born?"

"Allentown, Pennsylvania. November 19, 1980." I groan at the way the response drifts from my tongue without thought or hesitation.

"Obsessed," she repeats with a laugh.

"Fuck you, Vicky." I inhale deeply to clear my head. "There's no way he knows, and I'm not going to tell him. So there."

"If he invites you to his room, will you go?"

"Vicky!" A million indecent thoughts fly through my mind, along with a resounding *Yes*.

"Girl, I'm just playing devil's advocate here. You need to be prepared for all eventualities." She sighs. "If this is a business thing, you need to get your hormones under control."

"I know." My heart hammers in my chest. "What the hell am I doing? This is crazy."

"It's not crazy," she assures me. "Just follow your heart and trust your gut. I'll be your backup if you need me. Okay?"

"Okay." I inhale a steadying breath, then exhale. "Thanks, Vicky."

"You're welcome, but I'm going to demand every detail the moment you get home."

"I expect nothing less." I laugh. "Maybe you tell me who you hooked up with at the con and we'll call it even?"

"I'll think about it." A nervous laugh escapes her. "Gotta run. Love ya."

"Love you too." I disconnect the call and toss my phone

aside, staring at the screensaver on my laptop.

How the hell am I supposed to work now? Fuck.

I do what I normally do when I can't focus. I cpen a blank document and write until I can focus again. Five thousand words and one smutty fanfic featuring John Martigan later, I dive back into my checklist for work.

CHAPTER SIX

As the elevator rises, I smooth my hands over my emerald green velvet dress. A nervous habit. The sensation of the fabric helps to soothe my anxiety, but I'm still twisted tight, a tangle of Christmas lights with no hope of salvation.

What the hell am I doing? My mind spun with reservations on the train into the city. Curious glances came my way, but I only clung tighter to the bag on my shoulder.

John Martigan's assistant emailed me the day after his call with more details, including a note to pack clothes, which, at first, seemed like a blazing red flag, but then I read on. He insisted I stay overnight and booked a room for me at the hotel.

Vicky said he was just being a gentleman and didn't want me traveling late. But I can't shake the feeling that there's more to this gesture than goodwill. I appreciate it—don't get me wrong—but it still sets off warning bells.

I make sure to share my location with Vicky and my brother. If anything goes sideways, I want someone to know where I am. The overactive imagination of a writer kicked into full gear and drove me to leave a note on my kitchen counter with all the details of the evening's plans. It includes a printout of the email from Martigan's assistant outlining the invitation and pertinent information.

Knowing I've protected myself as much as I can gives me the boost of courage I need to climb into the black town car waiting for me at the station. If Martigan tries to pull any shenanigans, I'll have the upper hand.

A flicker of uncertainty brushes my mind and alights on my heart. I shake my head to free the complex tangle of thoughts as the elevator comes to a stop. There's no turning back now. I already claimed my room overlooking Central Park, safely stowing my overnight bag and checking to ensure I'm presentable. I thought I was ready, but the moment I step from the elevator car, my heart beats wildly and my hands shake. I can do this.

The Rooftop Courtyard, a lavish, gilded restaurant comes into view, and I'm stunned at the opulence of the setting. I feel like I've stepped through time and come out in Old Hollywood. I half expect to see Humphry Bogart, Cary Grant, and Jimmy Stewart having a conversation at the bar while stunning starlets—Laruen Bacall or Katherine Hepburn—linger beneath chandeliers with cocktails. It's amazing, and I soak it in like a sponge, basking in the ambiance, letting it fuel my courage.

I roll my shoulders, straightening as I approach the maître d'. His gaze slides over me in a courteous manner, and he smiles.

"Good evening, madam," he says, his voice a silky mask of politeness. "Will you be dining with us this evening?"

"Yes, I believe I'm expected. Ginger Darling."

"Of course, Ms. Darling." He bows slightly with a sweep of his arm. "If you'll follow me."

All of the tables are full, and I ignore inquisitive glances from patrons as I pass. I don't know how Martigan managed to secure a table for us. There isn't an empty seat in the entire restaurant.

We round a corner, and tucked away from prying eyes in a small alcove overlooking the park sits John Martigan at a table for two. He stands when he sees me, nodding to the maître d' before turning to me, his eyes dark in the dim light. "You look positively ravenous."

"Don't you mean ravishing?" I ask, fighting a smile.

"That too." He grins and pulls out the chair for me. "But to be honest, I'm sure you're hungry after traveling."

"I'm used to it." I slide into my seat, aware of his presence thanks to the lingering woody scent of his cologne mingling with a crisp, clean bite of soap.

"Being hungry?" He returns to his seat with a soft chuckle.

"Traveling." I unfold an ivory napkin and place it in my lap.

"Of course."

"Mr. Martigan," I begin, folding my hands and meeting his gaze. "What am I doing here?"

"Straight to business." He sighs. "Can we have a drink first?"

"If you insist." He flags the waiter and turns to me. "Ladies first."

"I'll have a lemon drop martini."

The waiter nods and turns to Martigan.

"Old-fashioned."

After the waiter leaves, we fall into silence as I look at the menu. My mind is spinning. What is this all about? If he thinks he's going to seduce me…well, he'll have to try a hell of a lot harder. Even though I've harbored an alarmingly persistent crush on him for years, I can't ignore what happened at the convention. Apology or not, I'm not the type who forgets. He's going to have to work hard to gain my trust.

The waiter returns with our drinks, and we order dinner.

Martigan lifts his glass in a toast. "To fandom."

I arch a brow but say nothing and clink my glass to his. The tart sweetness of the drink is perfect, and I sigh in delight.

Martigan clears his throat and shifts, pausing for a moment with the glass halfway to his lips before taking a drink. He sets it aside. "You are quite the enigma, Ms. Darling."

I incline my head. "That makes two of us, Mr. Martigan."

"John, please."

"If you insist." I take another sip of my martini and place the glass on the table. "Well then, John, what is it you wish to discuss?"

He leans back in his chair, regarding me with a pensive expression. Finally, he replies, "At the convention, you asked a question—one I anticipated, but you phrased it in a way that…well frankly, it left an uncomfortable impression on me."

A wicked smile curves my lips. "Are you saying I left a mark?"

"In more ways than one." He taps a finger on the table. "I have a problem, Ms. Darling. One I think you may be able to help solve."

My interest is piqued, but I resist the urge to lean forward, not wanting to seem overeager. "Ginger," I say simply. "It seems silly to try to remain professional when you've already uncovered my scandalous secret."

"Writing spicy fan fiction is hardly scandalous." He smiles, and a pair of dimples appear—a rare occurrence, I think. "But that's precisely the reason I wish to engage your aid."

"Aid?" I study him. "In what?"

"I would like to hire you as a consultant on the upcoming *Space Vendetta* film."

My hand shakes. I stare at him. My jaw is slack in stunned surprise. "You want to hire *me* as a consultant?" I scoff. "Why not ask Michael DeHart? He wrote the fucking series, for God's sake."

"I've spoken with Michael." He sips his drink, so casually, it's almost as though we're discussing the weather and not something monumentally life changing. "I showed him your work, and he agrees—you're the perfect solution."

I eye him suspiciously, even as my breath catches in my chest and my heart shudders, skipping three beats. The mix of emotions surging through me ranges from total elation to utter horror to complete skepticism. It loops through me like a goddamned out-of-control tilt-a-whirl. I think I might be sick.

I take several deep breaths. In. Out. In. Out. Finally, I'm in control.

"What do you mean 'the perfect solution?' Was there a problem?" Realization dawns when he shifts in his chair. "That's why you didn't want to answer my question. You were already getting pushback over the last film and the interview discussing upcoming installments. The changes you wanted to make created a rift."

He inclines his head but says nothing for a few tense seconds. "Your question at the convention put me in a hell of an uncomfortable position. One I was unprepared to face in the spotlight of the panel."

"And yet, you walked away still employed."

"Of course. I have a contract." His focus intensifies. "But I didn't walk away unscathed."

"I'm sure." I admire the strong line of his jaw, the muscle twitching beneath his skin. "But you can't blame that on me."

"I'm not. It was a powder keg from the beginning. But you, Ginger…" He sighs deeply. "You struck the match."

"And that means I'm the best person to help put out the fire?"

"Yes," he replies without hesitation.

The waiter arrives, which interrupts our conversation, but it does nothing to alleviate the tension vibrating between us.

I admire the food before me—a delightfully aromatic dish of crab-stuffed salmon, caramelized onions with brussels sprouts, and buttered roast potatoes in a cream sauce. My mouth waters with the first bite, and when I glance at my companion, his gaze is fixed on me, his attention divided between my mouth and my eyes. Warmth pulses through me like lightening, and suddenly my hunger shifts to something more carnal.

A reminder of my decade-long obsession with this man fills my mind, making my face warm under his scrutiny.

"How is it?" He picks up his own fork and knife.

"Delicious," I say between bites. This time, I allow the fork to linger on my tongue and slowly draw it from between my lips.

John's eyes go from mahogany to midnight. I shiver with delight, knowing I have *some* kind of effect on him. He drops his gaze to the steak on his plate. A silent calm settles between us as we eat. Random pleasantries escape, but business is a topic untouched as we finish our meal. Even then, he seems unhurried to resume the discussion.

When the waiter returns, I decline dessert, even though the tiramisu looks tempting. John charges the meal to his room and eyes me across the table as the waiter leaves.

"Are you certain you don't want dessert?" He smiles, and it transforms his stern expression into something friendly and approachable.

"I couldn't possibly eat another bite." I run a hand over my stomach and notice his gaze flicker at the motion.

"Then allow me to tempt you with something sweeter." He rises and offers his arm.

A flurry of butterflies unleashes in my chest, swirling and stealing my breath. "I…are you attempting to seduce me, Mr. Martigan?"

"Why?" A lopsided smile steals across his sinful lips. "Do you *want* to be seduced, Ms. Darling?"

This time my breath catches fully, and I purse my lips to keep from confessing the truth. I do want him to seduce me.

Every moment spent in his company makes it harder to remain indifferent, impartial. The infatuation I've harbored for *years* has nothing on this new blossoming emotion. Something I don't need. Something I don't want.

Or do I?

Summoning every ounce of restraint I possess, I stand and tilt my chin to meet him eye to eye. "You, sir, are the devil."

"Temptation is the sweetest sin." His voice is low and brims with dark promise.

I slide my arm through his and wait for regret and panic. Neither comes, and I pray my instincts are right, because if my hormones have taken over, I'm completely fucked.

CHAPTER SEVEN

Tension simmers between us as he leads me from the restaurant to the elevator. He keeps me close and presses the button for his floor. He releases me, but I can feel the gentle pressure of his hand and the muscle beneath the fabric of his clothed arm.

My pulse races, increasing with each floor, like a speedometer in a sports car. Up and up, faster and faster. He must sense it, because he's as calm and still as a statue. I glance at his hands, balled at his sides. He releases them, stretching his long fingers. Neither of us make an effort to fill the silence, and it stretches tight, like a rubber band about to snap.

We reach his door. It's the penthouse suite, of course. He unlocks the door and pushes it open, holding it for me to enter. I cross the threshold, unsure what to expect. My heels are unsteady in the plush carpet, so I reach down to slip them off.

I spin in the center of the large space, complete with a desk and chair overlooking the city and Central Park. A sofa and two wingback chairs sit around a coffee table. To my right, a large door leads to what I assume are the bathroom and bedroom. The soft glow of lamps is warm and inviting.

My gaze fixes on the large windows, and I try not to notice my own reflection. Instead, my attention shifts to the world outside, the city shrouded in shadow, glittering with light. John's reflection steals my focus as he comes alongside me.

I turn to face him. "Your room has a better view than mine."

"I doubt it." His gaze remains fixed on me.

Whatever witty response I had dies in my throat at the need etched on his handsome face.

"Would you like something to drink?" John steps away, shaking his head and breaking the spell.

"No. Thanks." I clear my throat. "But I'm curious as to why you brought me here?"

"Dessert. Have a seat." John gestures to the sofa. "I'll be back in a moment."

With a sigh, I settle on the couch, my hands splaying over the soft fabric. This place really is high end, and it makes me self-conscious. What am I doing here?

A vivid reminder floats across my brain. John Martigan wants *my* help. A hundred possible scenarios fly through my head at lightning speed. Before I can focus on them, John returns with two folders and places them on the coffee table.

"What are those?"

The top file is thin, almost empty. The second is three inches thick and bound. My curiosity stirs.

"Open the first one." He sits in a chair, his expression impassive.

I pluck the thin file from the stack and open it. A standard NDA. My gaze snaps up to his. "What the hell is this?"

"Before I show you anything else, you need to sign this." He cocks his head.

"Why?"

"Because I want to show you something only a handful of people have seen, and in order to do so, I need you to agree that what we discuss—what I show you—doesn't leave this room."

I lick my lips, all nerves. "You make it sound so sordid."

"The studio is very protective of their property. And rightly so—they paid a lot to secure the rights to this series." He leans forward, resting his elbows on his knees.

"How are your interviews with the media any different from someone spilling the details of what's in those documents?" I eye him suspiciously.

"The interview was preplanned, and my answers were approved by the powers that be ahead of time."

"Unlike my question and your response," I say, half teasing.

John doesn't smile.

I grab my purse from the edge of the sofa, pull out a pen, scan the document, and sign once I've established there isn't anything suspicious or harmful. I place the file back on the table and turn to John.

"Show me what you got."

He stands, taking the thick folder with him. "Come here."

I stand and round the sofa, shuffling closer as John opens the file and organizes the papers in neat piles on the desk, each labeled in bold italics. *Main Story Arc. Side Character Development. Main Character Development. Subplots and Red Herrings. Conflicts and Resolutions.*

One paper sitting on the smallest stack catches my full attention. *Romantic Subplots.*

My gaze snaps to his, and a slow smile appears on his lips. "Is this all for the *Space Vendetta* series?"

"Yes. It spans the contents of all twelve of Michael DeHart's novels for the prequel and continuing sagas." He pauses to take a deep breath. "This is the continuity bible for the series, vetted and confirmed by Michael for use in construction of the films."

"Canon?" I ask, my voice shaking.

"For the most part, yes, but we added some things to expand the subplots and overall story arc. It's not always easy to translate from novel to film. There has to be flexibility and an element of unpredictability."

I nod, understanding the complexity of the problem. "Was the creator also included in the incorporation of new elements?"

"Every step of the way."

My brow furrows. "Then why did you do that interview. Why did you say those things? Was any of it true?"

"Some of it was true," John admits with a shrug. "But there were already rumors about the films straying too far from the source material. The studio wanted to stay ahead of them, so we spread a little discord of our own by reinforcing the idea that there were differences in the upcoming films."

"And you didn't think fans would react negatively to that?" I frown, narrowing my eyes.

"Any attention on the film is marketing to promote it. The more people talk about it, the more visibility it gets." He leans into my space, his voice lowering to a devastating baritone. "Thanks to your little confrontation at the convention, *Space Vendetta* is trending on all social media platforms."

"You used me to promote your films?" I growl.

"I...seized an opportunity." John regards me for a heartbeat before continuing. "You had every right to ask that question, and I added fuel to the fire by creating more conflict."

"So your reaction on stage was ingenuine?"

"My reaction was one hundred percent authentic."

"Then why did you have me removed?" I fold my arms across my chest, wishing I was wearing a wrap or a sweatshirt, anything to shield myself from his view.

"That was for a purely selfish reason." He steps closer, and I suck in a breath. "You challenged me in front of everyone. Something so rare deserves investigation. Protection." He presses his lips together, as though uncertain whether to say more.

"Why me?" I ask, my voice trembling. "There are hundreds of fangirls who are more dedicated and knowledgeable. Why not ask them to help you?"

"Because none of them dared to do what you did." He reaches out and catches a lock of my hair between his fingertips. "You reminded me *why* I took on this project in the first place." His whiskey gaze penetrates my soul. "Passion."

"You have no idea who I am. You know nothing about me."

"That's not true." He drops his hand to his side. "I researched you, Ginger Darling, and I wouldn't ask you to do this unless I believed you were capable."

"Reading the extensive collection of fan fiction I've written and stalking me on LinkedIn does not mean you know me."

My breath catches. My body hums with awareness. He's close, *so* close. And yet, he doesn't close the gap between us. He lingers. Watching. Taking my measure. I swallow a lump of uncertainty choking me.

This can't be happening. He—*this*—it's not real. It's a ploy, an illusion. If I concede, it will all vanish. He'll use me without hesitation.

Won't he?

"You're right." He leans closer still. "I don't know you." His breath caresses my cheek. "But I want to know you, Ginger. If you'll let me."

"I know seduction when I see it."

"Am I tempting you?" he asks, his tone reverberating through me. "Even a little?"

I lick my lips, heart beating in frantic rhythm, mind spinning out of control. "Tell me your favorite ship."

My question is frivolous, stupid, but I want to torment him. I *need* to know, even though it changes absolutely fucking nothing about the urgency coursing through me at this moment.

"Ransom and Lynnea." His gaze locks with mine. "The villain and the morally gray bounty hunter." He rests his hand at my waist, and a shiver of desire races through me, raising gooseflesh along my bare arms. "Colton is too good, too pure. He's idealistic. A golden god of perfection. What he has with Lynnea will never work. But Ransom is her match in every way. They deserve each other."

"H—" Everything is scrambled in my head, and it's hard to find words, let alone vocalize them. "How would that work? It's already been established Lynnea and Colton are connected romantically."

"Are you saying it's impossible to put them in a romantic situation?" John inclines his head, his gaze searching, burning with heat.

"You could…but fans of the series might riot." I swallow hard, ignoring the scent of him curling around me like a warm, comforting blanket. "They love Colton."

"They love Ransom too." His grin widens. "Just like you."

"I…" My mind goes blank. I completely forgot he read my fanfics. He even read some of my stories about the three main characters in a poly romance. "How would that even work?" I shake my head. "It's impossible."

John catches my chin in his hand, his thumb stroking my jaw. "Let me show you."

"Sh-show me?" I stutter, confusion and desire boiling inside me as I lean into his touch.

"Close your eyes." He coaxes me into compliance, and I obey. "Picture the scene—Lynnea corners Ransom in the cantina. He's confident, cocky, riding the high of his last heist. He knows she's hunting him for the bounty at Colton's order, but he's just lounging, sipping his drink, watching her approach, his eyes hooded. He relishes the coming confrontation."

I gasp when his touch disappears. My eyes fly open.

A devilish smile curves his full lips. He's close—so fucking close. I've dreamed of this for years, but never have I ever envisioned myself in this position. Here and now, I can't bring myself to care. I fall into the role with ease.

"You're coming with me, Ransom." I tilt my head, lifting my jaw a fraction.

"Ranger." He moves deeper into my space, the hem of my gown brushing his black trousers. "Join me for a drink first?"

"Only if you surrender."

"Surrender?" John traces fingers along my jaw, down my throat, along my bare collarbone. I shiver. "I will gladly surrender to you, my warrior queen."

"I'm immune to your charm, Ransom."

"Are you?" His fingertips slide over my chest, brushing a nipple, continuing until his hand comes to a rest on my hip. He pulls me flush to him, and I'm keenly aware of every hard inch of him pressed against my stomach and the vee of my thighs.

"Colton will have your head for this."

"Let him come for me himself." His grip tightens around me. "Until then, I'll gladly endure his punishment for a taste of pleasure."

"Ransom, we can't…"

"That, my dear, sounds like a challenge," John murmurs, any remaining words lost as he closes the distance between us and kisses me.

CHAPTER EIGHT

My world implodes. John's mouth on mine, his presence filling my senses, surrounding me. His arms embrace me, keeping me flush to him. I should protest, but my surrender is effortless. His kiss is an invitation, and I comply without hesitation.

I wrap my arms around his neck, and he groans. A smile tugs my lips, breaking the kiss for a half second before he seizes the opportunity to plunder my mouth. He tastes like whiskey and temptation. His warmth surrounds me as passion flares into friction, igniting a deep desire, one I've tried desperately to suppress.

His kiss is even better than my overly romantic imagination concocted during sleepless nights and silly daydreams. John Martigan, master storyteller, proves yet again that he knows exactly how to capture his audience. I melt deeper into him and savor the sensations crashing over me like waves on the shore.

I thread my fingers through his hair, tightening my hold, earning a deep rumbling growl from John.

His hands roam over my back until one cradles the back of my head, mimicking my own motions, tangling in my curls. He pulls, and a delicious pressure tugs my scalp.

I gasp, breaking contact.

"You have driven me to madness." His murmured words whisper against my kiss-swollen lips.

"Are you still playing Ransom?" I ask, dazed with need coursing through my veins. "That sounds like something he would say."

"Point taken." His choked laugh sets my body aflame. "Not Ransom."

"Oh." My face and body burn with equal parts shame and desire.

"The moment I saw you in the audience, I…" He shakes his head, laughs self-derisively. "It sounds so cliché, but you immediately captured my attention with your vibrant dress and deep auburn hair, those wide green eyes bright with indignation as you asked your question."

"That's quite the admission." I tease a finger along his jaw, noting the tension beneath my featherlight touch. "But you're not the only one with a confession."

"Is that so?" His thumb caresses the pulse at my neck.

I briefly imagine his hand wrapped around my throat. A necklace fit for a fangirl. My breath hitches.

"Yes."

"Are you going to enlighten me?" He leans closer, his lips brushing the shell of my ear. "Would you prefer I draw it from you between gasping moans?" He presses a soft kiss to my pulse point before drawing back, his eyes dark and intense. "Your choice, kitten."

From any other man, the endearment would sound trite, childish. But from John…it triggers something carnal in my soul, leaving me a quivering mess of desire. A whimper escapes as he strokes my cheek.

With a deep breath, I rise, meeting him eye to eye. "I want you to work for it."

"If you insist." John spins me in his embrace, one arm banded around my waist, hand splayed across my stomach while the other catches my throat with gentle, measured pressure.

My head lolls back on his shoulder, and I let my eyes drift

closed.

"Tell me if it's too much, kitten." His body melds to mine as I relax in his hold. "Just say *vendetta,* and I'll stop."

"Don't stop." The plea breaks free before I can silence it.

His soft laughter travels through me in measured vibrations.

"Good girl."

Oh fuck. He really has read all my fanfics. I've been told many times by my fellow fangirls I have a praise kink, but I've never experienced it like *this* before. Not in this way that leaves me aching and wet and fucking feral. Damn him for unleashing yet another layer of fantasy.

Those masterful fingers tighten around the base of my throat with just enough pressure to make me gasp and squirm.

"Too much?"

I shake my head.

"You like that, don't you, kitten?" He whispers into my temple. "That's the thing about fan fiction—it allows us to play into the fantasy, gives us an opportunity to toy with things that otherwise elude us. Sometimes, it's just a way to purge the story in our heads…but then there are glimpses of what we truly desire woven into the safety net of the written word."

How is he so confident? So aware? "Ho—how do you—?" I gasp as he cuts me off with a finger to my lips.

"You're not the first fan to explore such things through fiction." His hand slides along my throat, down to the velvet covering my breasts. He slips deftly beneath the fabric and palms my heavy breast in his massive hand.

A gentle squeeze makes me arch my back against him. I suck in a breath, basking in a spark unfurling in the pit of my stomach. The warmth of his hand kindles my resolve, and I push deeper into his palm.

"So needy, kitten." He circles my nipple with his thumb

before withdrawing his hand. "Tell the truth." His voice deepens as his hand drifts over my torso before slowly gathering the fabric of my skirt higher, inch by inch. "What will I find waiting for me?"

My breath hitches again as he exposes my thighs and arranges my skirt around my waist. Cool air brushes the damp fabric covering my pussy. I'm torn between embarrassment and arousal. He's pushing me, teasing with words and measured actions. He cups the heat between my thighs, and I squirm.

A moan tears from my chest as his fingers slide beneath the fabric, a quiet, gentle exploration igniting a riot inside my body. I buck my hips toward his touch, needing more than he's offering.

"You're positively dripping." His groan sends a shockwave through me. "Is this what I do to you?"

"Yes," I say between gasping breaths.

He delves deeper, one lone finger teasing my pussy.

"Do you feel that?" he asks, grinding his rock-hard cock into my backside. "It seems you have a similar effect on me."

"John...please."

"Shh, I'm not finished with my interrogation." John withdraws his hand, and a chasm of emptiness consumes me.

I sway, and he catches me by the waist.

"Hands on the table."

I obey his instructions and look over my shoulder at him. His expression is a mixture of determination and desire. He slides my skirt even higher, pooling it above my waist, and hooks his thumbs in the waistband of my panties, slowly lowering them to catch at my ankles.

I'm exposed to him. Cold air licks my aching pussy but does nothing to soothe the heat building inside me.

He leans back, his gaze raking over my body in this

submissive position.

"You're so beautiful," he says, smoothing his hand over my ass. "Fucking perfect."

He withdraws his hand and brings it back down against my flesh with a soft smack. A sting of pain rips through me, followed by a burst of pleasure.

I gasp and bite my lip.

"Goddamn it, John." I curse when he does it a second time.

"Do you want me to stop?" He runs a finger along the wet seam of my pussy, barely grazing my clit.

"Fuck." I choke on a gasp and push myself into his touch.

He withdraws completely.

"You're a goddamn tease."

"Tell me something I don't already know." He spanks me again, alternating sides with each strike, soothing with gentle strokes.

"I—" The confession lingers on my tongue for a moment, and a whimper rips free when he does it again. I whine as tension spirals higher, my body pulsing with the need for release. "I've had a crush on you for years…fucking years." One tear slides from the corner of my eye, then another. "I want this—I want you. Please."

"Good girl." John groans, his hand sliding between my legs. He nudges my thighs apart, hindered only by the fabric at my ankles. His fingers slide deep inside me, his thumb circling my clit. Slowly, he moves, fucking me with two fingers gliding over sensitive flesh.

"Fuck!" I cry out as pleasure consumes me.

"That's it, kitten." He pushes deeper, draping his body over me, his cock digging into my hip. His hand rests over mine on the table, our fingers intertwining as he thrusts deeper, quickening the pace. "I'll give you what you need."

I cry out again, unable to remain silent a moment longer. Not when he's unraveled me with such precision.

He shifts his thumb over my clit, and sparks ignite a pulsing flame. My body tightens around him as my orgasm takes hold, ripping through me with the force of an explosion. Panting and gasping, I ride the waves of sensation until he slowly withdraws his hand.

Without moving, he manages to tug down my dress, covering my trembling exposed body. He gathers me in his embrace. I rest against his chest, my cheek pressed to his warm shoulder as he rubs my bare arms.

For several moments, we say nothing.

I can barely think, let alone process what just happened. Somehow, I manage to pull back, just enough to meet his dark gaze.

He reaches up and runs the pad of his finger beneath my eyes. His brow furrows.

My mind is jumbled, and I struggle to read his expression. Is he disappointed? Angry?

A sudden flare of embarrassment strikes me. "I…need a moment."

"Of course," he says, releasing me with reluctance. "The bathroom is through there."

I nod. "Thanks."

A few unsteady steps remind me of the panties around my ankles. I kick them off, stooping to pick them up before disappearing through the bedroom. Once I'm alone in the bathroom, I lean on the sink and stare at my reflection.

Hair wild. Mascara smudged. Skin flushed. Lips kiss-bruised.

Oh my God. I look like I've been thoroughly fucked, which is only half true. What the hell just happened? What have I done?

I hang my head in a flood of shame, followed by a choked laugh.

My fantasy. It *really* happened.

Holy fucking shit.

Reality hits. What must he think of me? I quickly fix my makeup and hair. I use the toilet and consider putting my panties back on, but they're absolutely soaked. I toss them in the trash and wash up.

I manage to wrangle myself into some semblance of order before returning to the living room. The moment I see John standing by the window, looking out over the city, my heart constricts. Is this just a fling? It can't be real. Fantasies *aren't* reality.

He turns and smiles when he sees me.

I clear my throat. "W-were you serious?"

"About what?" He comes closer but keeps a respectable distance.

"Having me as a consultant for the series?"

"Absolutely."

"Even after…" I let the implication drift off.

"Ginger, I've read your writing, seen your passion firsthand. You're a natural storyteller. I don't know many who have the stones to do what you did at the convention. You're exactly the type of creative we need to make this series better."

"You're insane." I shake my head.

"That's what they keep telling me."

"What about this?" I gesture between us.

"What do you want it to be?"

"I don't know." The words are hollow. I know exactly what I want, but I'm not ready to explore it. Not yet. Not with my nerves still so raw from pleasure at his hand.

"There's no need to rush." He takes my hand and kisses my fingertips. "I'm a patient man."

I laugh, partly from nervous energy but mostly at the way my body reacts to his touch. I'm completely fucked. This man has ruined me.

And I enjoyed every fucking moment.

"Why don't you get some rest?" He releases my hand, and I frown at the loss. "You can let me know when you're ready to discuss it."

"When do you need to know?"

"Just text me whenever you're ready."

"Okay." I nod and step closer.

He inhales sharply as I press a kiss to his cheek.

"Thank you," I whisper against his skin.

"Good night, kitten." He steps back, tense, but I see his smile. "Dream of me."

I laugh and gather my bag. His words ring through my head as I retreat to my room on the twelfth floor.

But there's no sleep. All I can think of is John and the proposition before me.

Fuck.

CHAPTER NINE

When I check out of my room the following morning, I find a surprise waiting outside the hotel. Another black town car. The driver opens the door. I heave a heavy sigh and climb in. On the leather seat lays a single deep maroon peony and a note.

Thank you for a lovely evening. I look forward to our partnership. The driver will take you home, however far that is. ~John

I fold the note and tuck it into my purse.

The driver rolls down the partition. "Where to, miss?"

Twisting the peony stem between my fingers, I give my home address. He nods and rolls the partition back up. The blossom has a faint scent, sweet and delicate, not overly fragrant like a rose. It's funny, I would expect roses from John, not a peony. They're my grandmother's favorite flower, and I always admire them in her garden. It's a refreshing gift—and quite thoughtful. I tuck it safely into the corner of my bag, allowing the massive bloom to peek out the top.

I spend most of the trip on my phone, searching for as much information as I can about John Martigan. It's a waste of time, honestly. I already know everything I can find on the internet. I'm hunting for something I'll never find in a public forum.

This tells me everything *he* wants the world to know about him; *I* want to know who John Martigan really is. After the glimpse he showed me last night, I'm even more invested than before. He doesn't know the extent of my fangirling, but I'm pretty sure he has an idea.

The real question is—can I trust him?

I consider texting the fangirl group to ask for advice, but the NDA pops into my mind and I don't know if it extends to the events of last night as well. I decide to test John instead. I send a text.

(Me): *Thank you for the ride home.*

His response comes through almost immediately.

(John): *You're welcome.*

(Me): *Silly question.*

I'm trying to keep the text light and vague, but I have to know.

(Me): *Does the NDA only cover anything related to* Space Vendetta *or does it extend to us?*

I cringe but hit send anyway.

(John): *The NDA pertains to the studio and the project only.*

(John): *Should I be concerned?*

(Me): *No, I just want clarification. Thank you.*

Feeling bold, I add a grinning devil emoji at the end and hit send.

(John): *Behave, kitten.*

A bolt of need shoots through me at those two simple words. How does he do that so effortlessly? I'm aroused and concerned by how easy it is for him to affect me.

I wait until I get home to pull up Vicky's information. It's Sunday afternoon, so she should be home. Uncertainty gnaws in my gut.

"You safe?" Vicky asks via greeting.

"I'm fine. Home now." I collapse on my sofa.

"So I see," she says. "I'll stop stalking you now."

"I appreciate it."

"How did it go?"

Vicky won't pry, but I need to vent. I know I can trust her, especially since she still hasn't told any of us who she hooked up with at the convention. She can keep a secret.

"It's complicated," I mutter. "Dinner was great. He was the perfect gentleman."

"But?"

"But I don't know what he wants from me." I sigh.

"I don't understand." Vicky clicks her tongue. "He invited you to dinner, paid for a hotel room, and you're confused about what he wants?"

"It's complicated, trust me."

"Did he do something illegal?" Vicky immediately gets protective. "I don't care who he is, if he—"

"He didn't do anything illegal." I stifle a laugh. "The opposite."

"The opposite?" Vicky snorts. "Now *I'm* lost."

I groan in frustration. "Listen, I can't discuss some things, but I promise, he didn't cross any lines I didn't want crossed. Okay?"

"Holy fuck," Vicky nearly shouts. "You slept with John Martigan?"

"Vicky!" I cover my face with my hand. "No, I didn't fuck John Martigan." I bite my lip and add, "I came *really* close."

"Girl, what the hell happened last night?"

"We had dinner, he invited me to his room, we talked." I pause for a moment. "And then he sorta…bent me over the desk and made me come harder than I've ever come in my entire life. So…there's that."

"Oh my God." Vicky's gasp echoes through the line. "You hooked up with John Martigan."

"No, Vicky, we didn't have sex. Things just…escalated…and then it was over." Disappointment fills me at the thought. I push it aside.

"Uh-huh." Vicky sounds unconvinced. "I'm gonna need more."

Skirting around my *Space Vendetta* conversation with John, I fill Vicky in on the details of the evening. When I tell her how it ended, she seems almost disappointed.

"The real question is—why did you stop?" Vicky asks, cutting straight to the heart of it all.

"I…" A heavy sigh bubbles from deep in my chest. "I don't know if this is real, Vicky. Can I trust him? Can I trust what I'm feeling right now?"

"Ginger, take a deep breath."

I follow her instruction, and tension slowly ebbs from my shoulders. "I don't know what to do."

"Can I tell you a secret?" Vicky practically whispers the question.

"I just told you a *huge* secret, so yeah, I think we're good."

"Well, you know the mystery guy I hooked up with at the convention?" Vicky's voice shakes.

"The guy you won't tell us anything about?" I tease her. "I remember."

"It was Jason Hunt."

"Get the fuck out of here!" I gasp, surprise and elation filling me. "Girl, how the hell did you hook up with Jason Hunt and not tell us?"

"It just…happened." Vicky's confession rings in my ears. "He texted me after dinner, and I met him in the bar. We kissed, and then—well, we hooked up."

"And you're just telling me *now*?"

"I didn't want anyone to know. I mean—it was a one-night stand. It's not like we're dating."

"But…Jason Hunt?!" I stammer.

"Yeah. I know."

"And you didn't tell us." I act hurt, but honestly, I'm just flabbergasted.

"It's not like I'm ever going to see him again," Vicky says. "He's in Hollywood, and I'm…well, I'm here. This isn't the movies. I mean, even if he wants to make it work, it's just not realistic."

"First of all," I tell her, summoning my most mom-like tone, "good on you for seizing the moment and embracing your pleasure." I soften my tone a smidge. "And secondly, don't you ever sell yourself short. You're an amazing woman, who is worthy of love and adoration. If he can't see how fucking fantastic you are, then he's an idiot, and fuck him."

"I appreciate the kind words, Ginger, but there's no way in hell Jason Hunt wants me." She sighs. "And you know what? I'm okay with it."

"Have you spoken to him since the convention?" I ask, my heart breaking for her.

"No." She shifts the conversation back to me. "Listen, what I'm getting at is, I know what you're going through. Having a sexy romp with a guy you've been fangirling over for years is like icing on a cake. You just have to know there are trade-offs. That's not to say it won't work out for you and Martigan."

"But that's just the thing, Vicky—I don't know what I want with him." I groan in frustration. "He's amazing. So different from the way interviews and media portray him. There's a hidden side to him. I saw it."

"Well, what is your heart telling you?"

"My heart is telling me to take a chance and go for it." I bite the edge of my nail. "But my gut is telling me to slow down and be careful."

"What's the worst that could happen?"

"Absolute annihilation of my heart and soul." I embrace

this extra melodramatic part of myself. "I might never recover."

"I doubt it'll be that bad." She laughs. "But you're right about one thing."

"What's that?"

"You're not going to get out of this unscathed. It's too late for that. The moment you stepped into that theater and asked that question in front of an entire fandom, your fate was sealed. No matter what happens next, Martigan left his mark on you."

"So what are you saying?" I ruminate on her words, letting them sink into parts of me I refuse to reveal, or even acknowledge.

"I'm saying—run with it. You have no idea how this will end."

"But…what if everything blows up in my face, and I'm left with nothing but heartache?"

"That's the chance you take," Vicky says sagely.

"When did you get so wise, V?" My heart feels lighter, even though I'm no closer to an answer or a direction about which path to take.

"You're the wise one," Vicky says with a chuckle. "I'm just taking a page from you."

"You're right." I sigh again. "What are you going to do about Jason Hunt?"

"Nothing."

"Nothing?" Surprise feels like a punch to the gut. "Why?"

"It doesn't feel like the right moment. I don't know how to explain it."

"No…I get it." My head spins. "I appreciate you walking me through this. I'm no closer to a solution, but at least I can rest and look at it logically."

"Good luck. Maybe you should write to purge some of your thoughts."

"That's not a bad idea. Thanks, V."

"Anytime. Keep me posted, will ya?"

"You too." We say goodbye, and I end the call.

Nothing about this situation feels wrong per se, but it leaves me on unsteady and unfamiliar ground. If I agree to help Martigan with the upcoming film, I'll be putting myself in a situation outside my control. And now, knowing there's sexual attraction simmering between us, I don't know if I can maintain a professional boundary with him.

I want both him and the job. Is that too much to ask?

It must be, because I just can't see a way around it. If we explore whatever is burning between us and it fizzles out, it will ruin the whole deal.

And John Martigan isn't interested in a relationship. He only wants what's best for his film and his career. If I'm going to be a part of that, I need to set some boundaries.

After what happened last night, I'm not sure I have the strength to say no to him.

CHAPTER TEN

Two weeks. That's how long it takes to build the courage to call him.

After my chat with Vicky, I weighed the pros and cons. Hell, I even made a list. She didn't know the details or his offer, but I was more concerned about this blossoming physical connection to John.

He never mentioned a relationship. The chemistry between us is off the charts, but I'm not foolish enough to assume he wants something permanent or romantic with me. It could just be an indulgence on his part. Wouldn't be the first time a Hollywood hotshot got some nookie, then bounced.

Although in his defense, he doesn't have that reputation. If he did, the tabloids would be all over it. He's hot and popular—any wisp of gossip about him is front page news. Fortunately, the incident at the convention flew under the radar since they kept my identity under wraps after the panel. Part of me wondered what the media would do with the information if they actually had the truth of that encounter.

All things considered, though, I can't say no to his offer. Working alongside him to ensure the *Space Vendetta* fandom gets the series they want, a series true to the source material, that is worth it.

As for him and me…well, I still need to figure that out. What do I want from John Martigan?

I pull up his number on my phone and take a deep breath. I'm halfway through writing a text when I remember how much he dislikes texting. It's not something he told me, but I saw it in an interview. Grumbling, I delete everything and hit the call button.

He answers almost immediately. "Hello, Ginger."

A rush of warmth consumes and flusters me. His voice triggers a flood of need and desire. Shit.

"Hello, John." I try to play my emotions off.

"I was wondering if you'd ever call."

I bristle at how easily he prods my uncertainty. "I've been busy."

"Understandable." He pauses. "Have you considered my offer?"

"Yes." I clear my throat. "But I have questions."

"I expect nothing less. Let's hear them."

"Will I be required to travel?"

"Yes. You will come to Los Angeles to help adjust the script to suit our needs and address inconsistencies."

"Fair enough. I'll require lodging, transportation, and a daily allotment for meals."

"Noted and agreed." He continues, "Anything else?"

"If I'm to be a consultant, I want my name in the credits."

"I'm sure that can be arranged."

"My consultation fee is three thousand a week."

John chokes. "Three?"

I grin at the unsteadiness in his tone. "You're right—that's too low. Five thousand is more realistic."

He grumbles under his breath, and my smile grows wider. Too bad I didn't do this in person, I would have enjoyed watching him squirm.

"Anything else?"

"Yes, I want it all in writing." A sense of power infuses me at his scoff.

"That might be tricky, but I'll see what I can arrange." He sighs. "I'm almost scared to ask if that's all again."

"For the moment, that should suffice."

"Very well." The distinct sound of a pen scratching paper filters through the speaker. "I've made note of your requests."

"When will you need me in LA?" I ask, nervous energy bubbling inside me.

"This weekend. I can have you fly out on Friday."

"So soon?" My body hums with anxiety. I wasn't expecting it to be this quick.

"Is that a problem?" he asks, his unyielding confidence returning.

"No." I swallow hard.

"Good. Pack for an extended stay. Anything else you might need, you can get here. Better yet, email my assistant a list, and she'll make sure you have what you need."

I glance at the calendar beside my computer. Today—Tuesday—stands out in bold letters. Fuck. This isn't how I envisioned this conversation, but I'm committed now. There's no turning back.

"My assistant will send your travel information, and a car will meet you at the airport with—"

"John," I interrupt him.

"Yes?"

"Thank you."

"For what?"

"For listening to the fandom."

"This may be hard to believe, but I was a fan long before I was a director." He huffs a half laugh. "I understand more than most how important it is to get things right."

"Yes…well…" I drift off.

"Is there something else you want to say?"

"A-about that night…at the hotel, I…" My words fail, and I lapse into silence again.

"We can discuss it when you arrive Friday." His voice deepens. "But you should know, I haven't forgotten, kitten. How you taste, the sweet noises you make. They haunt me."

My breath catches at his candidness. Heat rushes through me. I can feel the blush rise on my fair skin to betray how much his words affect me. Good thing there's no one here to see it.

"I look forward to seeing you Friday."

"You too." I end the call, unable to slow the racing of my heart.

I'm going to LA to work with John Martigan on the new *Space Vendetta* film.

Holy. Shit.

The week passes in a blur of activity. I'm fortunate my boss is willing to grant a leave of absence. While I feel guilty about my evasive explanation, I can't tell anyone exactly why I'm going to LA. I give a passable reason and promise myself I'll tell them the moment I have leave to do so. It's taking all my effort not to scream it from the rooftops, but I can't. That alone makes me miserable.

My consolation is that John Martigan will be at the other end of this flight.

Somehow, I manage to not overpack and drag my large suitcase to the check-in line. Once it's in safe hands, I adjust my carry-on over my shoulder and head to the gate. The monotony of travel puts me in a funk, and I mentally review the list of things I needed to do before I left. Nothing sends up a flag.

I sent a list of required items to Steph, John's assistant. She's wonderful and included the address and pictures of my housing, as well as a list of nearby restaurants and stores.

Nope, I'm set.

But as the plane takes off and creeps across the country, uncertainty digs its talons into my brain. What if this is a mistake? No one knows the truth of why I'm here. I lied to everyone—well, I didn't lie, but I wasn't honest. I couldn't be honest. Damn that NDA.

Is it really the NDA stopping me from telling them? Or is it my own insecurities?

What if this fails? What if it goes sideways? What if Martigan just wants to use me?

I suck in a breath and put in my earbuds. After a few minutes, I'm lost in an audiobook from an indie author I picked up at Jen's recommendation—*Queen Takes Hook* by Kirsten S. Blacketer. God, I love some good steamy pirate fun, especially a Captain Hook retelling. I'm a sucker for a morally gray villain.

When the plane finally lands, I practically sprint down the gangway and through the airport to the baggage claim. I wrangle my bag from the carousel and head to the pickup area. There's a group of men in suits with signs.

Ginger Darling. I spy my name right away, then look at the man holding the sign. He's wearing sunglasses, but I recognize his face. John Martigan.

"You said there'd be a car waiting," I say with a grin as butterflies take flight in the pit of my stomach.

"Yes. *My* car." He takes the handle of my large suitcase. "Let's get out of here."

We make it through the chaos of LAX and spill into the sunshine. I pause beside the BMW as he loads my luggage before opening the door for me.

I slide in, my fingertips caressing the leather seats, still cool from the air conditioning. He climbs into the driver's seat and slips the car into gear, weaving around cars with the ease of someone accustomed to the insanity that is LA traffic. I grip the door handle and mutter a prayer.

John chuckles. "No time for regrets."

"No, but if I survive, I may reconsider my involvement."

Once we're on the highway, I relax. John knows how to drive. He's smooth and focused. I melt into the seat to admire the view flicking past my window. It's vastly different from the East Coast. I shift beneath the warm sun shining through the window even though the car interior keeps me cool.

"How was your flight?" he finally asks.

"Uneventful." I look at him and admire his profile. "Thank you, by the way."

John clears his throat, looking uncomfortable. "Don't thank me yet."

Fear unravels the excitement coiled inside me. "What do you mean?"

"I..." He bites back a reply and swears. "There are still some details I'm working out with the studio."

"What do you mean?" I scowl, folding my arms across my chest.

"I mean—the studio rejected my proposal to bring you on as a consultant." He sighs, glancing at the mirrors before merging to take the exit. "No credits, no contract."

"No contract." Anger bubbles inside me. "You might as well turn around and take me back to the airport."

"Ginger, just wai—"

"I'm not doing this shit for free, John." I growl as fury consumes me. "I took an unpaid leave of absence from my job to help *you.*"

"I know."

"We had an understanding. I told you exactly what I need to make this happen, and you couldn't even tell me they rejected it *before* I dropped everything to fly across the country and save their asses."

"I can explain…just—I didn't want to do this over the phone. Or in the car." He glances at me, eyes hidden behind sunglasses. "We're almost there. Thirty minutes, and we can discuss it."

My mood darkens with every mile. I curse myself for believing this could actually work. For thinking he respects me, desires me. Nothing about this situation shows even the smallest amount of respect. If it's too good to be true, it probably is. Fuck him.

I pull out my phone and start looking up flights to return home. I can't stay here. Not now. Not after this bombshell. Tears prick my eyes, and I swipe them away. He will not see me cry. I refuse to let him have that satisfaction. Bastard probably gets off on other people's misery.

We enter a neighborhood lined with thick green trees, palms and hedgerows full of lush foliage and flowers. It's like something out of a movie. He drives deep into the tangle of streets and stops at the end of a gated drive. Slowly, the gate swings open.

I glare at him. "I thought you were taking me to my apartment."

He sighs again. "Yeah, about that…"

"I swear to God, Martigan." I envision sixteen different ways I could end his life without having it lead back to me. With three deep breaths, I control whatever outburst had been lingering on my tongue.

"My place is big enough for both of us. You'll have your own space."

"I'm *not* staying with you." I grit my teeth, even though my body betrays me with a hum of appreciation at the thought of being in close proximity to John. I'm too pissed off to let my hormones fuck me over with insatiable demands. "I've already booked a return flight."

John winces, and guilt stings me. I haven't booked anything yet, but he doesn't need to know that.

The car rolls to a stop in front of a large home, midcentury modern with eclectic touches of contemporary architecture and technology. I barely have time to admire the house and landscaping before I open the door. Heat hits me in a wave, pushing me back against the BMW. Hurt and betrayal sting like bile in the back of my throat, choking me.

"Ginger." A car door slams behind me as I stalk toward the house.

I'm halfway to the front door when John catches me by the wrist.

"What do you want?" I spin around, tearing my arm from his grasp.

He throws his hands up in surrender, but he's close. So close, his scent wraps around me, and I'm transported to the hotel room that night. My body responds, and I clench my thighs together to alleviate the ache.

"Listen, I'm on your side. I…" He rakes his fingers through his thick hair, and it falls in waves over his forehead. "I fucked up, I realize that. But give me a chance to explain before you leave." He pulls off his glasses, his dark eyes pleading. "Please."

My heart softens the smallest fraction, and I nod. "Fine."

A smile blooms on his lips, and he moves to the front door, pushing it open with a flourish. "Come on in."

With a defeated exhale, I cross the threshold while my little fangirl heart takes flight.

CHAPTER ELEVEN

I spin as I walk through the house, unable to believe it's real. This is a *Space Vendetta* fan's wet dream, a goddamned museum dedicated to the films. Every surface is an homage to the series. The decor, tasteful and well-planned, reflects the fandom in its entirety. Vintage-style posters in sleek frames line the walls. Glass cases showcase props from the films. Even the furniture compliments the displayed items.

My heart flutters with every step as I take it all in. I run my fingers over a glass cabinet with Ransom's carbine blaster from the first film. "This…" I swallow a laugh and turn to John. "This is your collection?"

John stands on the landing inside the door, hands in his pockets, watching me. His smile widens. "I told you—I was a fan before the films."

"Understatement of the century." I gesture around me. "And here I thought *I* was obsessed."

"One of many things I adore about you." John's soft confession fills the space between us.

I step toward him, my fury now a fraction of what it had been in the car just moments ago. I don't relinquish it, but it no longer drives me.

"I'm still pissed, John." I stop an arm's reach away. "You made a fuckton of assumptions to bring me here without confirmation of my requests."

"I realize that, and I apologize." He keeps his hands in his pockets and halves the distance separating us. His expression softens, his eyes clear and contrite. "But I have a solution if you're still willing to work with me."

"I'll need an extra thousand a week." I sniff. "Especially if you expect me to stay with you." My face heats at the wolfish smile curving his mouth. "That sounded wrong. Fuck."

"I can't do an extra thousand a week, but I can make it up to you."

"How?" I ask, squinting at him in suspicion.

"Full access to filming as my personal guest."

I tap a finger on my jaw. "I'm gonna need more."

"How about a dinner party with Michael DeHart, Commander Colton, and Captain Ransom?" He grins at my obvious response.

"Yo-you're joking, right?"

"Nope. Tonight."

"Get the fuck out of here." I press a hand to my chest, my excitement bubbling to the surface. "You're serious?"

"Deadly." He reaches out to touch a stray curl at my temple. "I know this isn't going the way you wanted it to, but for what it's worth, I'm glad you're here."

"Are you?" My body hums with need.

"I am." He sighs. "C'mon, I'll show you to your room."

John leads me down the hallway to a small suite, immaculate and styled similarly to the rest of this *Vendetta* house. I take in the king-size bed next to a wall of windows overlooking the backyard. A small veranda lays just beyond a sliding glass door, and I note the deep greens and browns mixed with hues of gray and blue.

I turn to face him. "This is your room?"

"It is." He shrugs. "I figure giving you the master suite is the least I can do."

"And where will you sleep?" I ask, eyeing him with mischief.

"Guest room down the hall."

"You didn't lure me here to seduce me?"

"No. But I won't lie—the thought has crossed my mind." He chuckles. "I'll have your bag brought in. Shower, rest, do whatever you need. Dinner is at six."

"Okay," I manage, breathless and torn. I want him, but I'm raw from the rollercoaster of emotions. "And thank you."

"You're welcome." John presses a kiss to my knuckles and leaves me alone with my thoughts.

I stare at the closed door, and a strange sense of peace settles over me. I'm here. I'm making the best of it.

Determination takes over. I find the spacious bathroom and marvel at the huge shower for a moment before undressing. If I'm having dinner with Colton, Ransom, and Michael DeHart, I need to look my best.

Deep down, though, I know I'm doing this for John. Be still my fangirl heart.

CHAPTER TWELVE

I'm not sure what I expect, but it certainly isn't an amazing evening in the company of some of the most talented people on the planet. The actors who portray Colton and Ransom are absolute gentlemen and indulge all of my questions. Michael DeHart adds commentary when he finds it prudent, but he's rather reserved. Which doesn't surprise me; most authors are.

I'm a fangirl, but being in the presence of the author, director, and leading actors of the series I fell in love with ten years ago is almost too much to handle. None of the other fangirls will believe this.

By the end of the evening, I'm comfortable in their presence. They even ask my opinion about the series and how fans view the characters. I do my best to be honest and open without inflating their egos. They handle it well. When the subject of fan fiction arises, I hide a blush behind my lemon drop martini.

John gives me a knowing look but offers no details. My part in the fan fiction arena of the fandom is not something I hide, but I don't usually share it with people I've just met. Especially when it reflects the characters they portray on screen and the fantasies they inspire. Nope, I'm not touching that with a ten-foot pole. This evening is too perfect to ruin it with *that* conversation.

What surprises me most is John's quiet reservation. He plays host well, but from the moment his guests arrive, he places me at the center of their attention, allowing me to bask in the moment. He watches the evening unfold, listening, only adding his opinion when asked.

As dinner gives way to drinks and dessert, I become increasingly aware of his gaze on me. He indulges in only one drink, and I limit myself to two. I can't blame this swirling heat on alcohol or on the company surrounding us. It takes all my effort to refrain from reaching for him while we laugh and share stories.

Fascinating as our guests are, I find my expectations shift as the hour grows late. By midnight, we've bid them goodnight and John has walked them out.

Exhaustion tugs at me, but that subtle hum of desire pulses deep in my chest. It only strengthened through the evening. Whatever residual anger remains simmers on extremely low heat while an inferno of need rages through me. I want him, and it's damn near impossible to ignore it any longer.

I pace the room, stopping to gaze out the dark window. I see nothing but the gentle sway of palm trees as I will my body under control.

"You've enchanted them," John says behind me.

I turn to him, a smile on my lips. "Of course I did. I'm an extremely charming individual."

"You're terrifyingly adept." He steps into the room. "They were singing your praises."

"As they should." I move closer to him, the two of us inching together with measured steps. "I'm a goddamned delight."

"An irrefutable fact." John stops in the center of the living room.

"I'm glad you agree." I stop a breath away from him. His scent curls around me like a warm blanket. My restraint grows thinner with every heartbeat.

"I do have one complaint."

Those dark eyes fix on mine.

"Only one?" My pulse thrums.

"You didn't tell them about your fanfics." A sinful grin sets my panties aflame. "I'm sure they would have enjoyed it if you'd read a selection aloud."

Heat burns my face, but I stand unwavering. "Those stories are for *fans*, John. It would be highly inappropriate to read smutty fanfic to the actor who portrays the character in the story. Don't you think?"

"Flattering, more like." He strokes his jaw. "If you wrote something about a character I played and read it to me, I—"

"You'd file a restraining order on me." I finish his statement with a soft laugh. "Those stories are part of *fandom* space. We would never presume to extend the fantasy to reality."

"Even if I want to cross that line?" he says, voice deepening.

"You have no idea what you're asking for, John." My breath hitches as he leans closer.

"Oh, but I do." His eyes drop to my lips, then back up, holding my gaze, as if waiting for permission. "I know *exactly* what I want."

"I guess you'll have to settle for little old me."

"Settle? No." His exhale caresses my lips. "You are the center of every one of my thoughts, every fucking fantasy. I've done nothing but replay that night in New York over and over in my head, dreaming of what could have been."

"You still want me?" I whisper.

"With every fiber of my being."

"Cliché but effective." I kiss him, hard and fast, needing his touch on my skin. His breath in my lungs. I crave him like air, even though I shouldn't.

John crushes me to him, his arms a band of steel holding

me in place. His mouth slants over mine, and a hum of satisfaction rips from his throat as he tastes me.

"God, I missed this." His fingers thread through my hair, massaging my scalp as he tightens his grip. "For weeks, I thought I'd imagined that night," he murmurs between questing kisses. "But your taste, your scent, the press of your curves…I can't purge them. You drive me mad with desire."

"John…" I encircle his neck with my arms and press my body fully against him. "Show me what I do to you."

"Fuck."

He grabs me by the waist and lifts me into his arms. I squeal in surprise as he carries me from the room.

Excitement floods me, my thighs already slick. The moment he touches me, he'll know just how much power he has over me.

I whimper as realization washes over me. I'm at his mercy. Shit.

But he took such good care of me last time.

John sets me down, and I wobble. He catches me, pulling me to him, one arm around my waist, one cradling the back of my head, tangling in my hair. Those sparkling whiskey eyes burn into mine.

"Last chance, kitten." He licks his lips. "Tell me what you want."

"I want you."

"You can do better than that." He grins. "You work with words. Tell me *exactly* what you want me to do to you."

My breath stutters, but I gather my wits enough to respond clearly. "John, if you don't fuck me, I swear I will haunt you in this life and the next."

"Threats work too." He kisses me, stealing any snarky reply from my lips.

Our tongues dance as his hands roam over me. Slowly, he

gathers handfuls of fabric and begins undressing me. The zipper trails along my spine as he slides it. The sundress slips from my shoulders, past my waist, ending in a pool around my feet. He makes quick work of my bra and tosses it aside. My nipples pebble in the cool air, but they harden even more as he stoops to drag his tongue across their peaks. My fingers thread through his hair, holding him tight.

His hand glides over my hips, down to slide between my thighs. He groans and looks at me, eyes midnight and sparkling.

"You're so wet for me, kitten." He presses his fingers to my clit, and I rock against him with a gasp. A needy moan bubbles from my throat as he moves the fabric down and drops to his knees.

I brace myself on the bed as he lifts one leg, parting my thighs wider. A brush of cool air followed by his warm breath touches my aching pussy.

I bite my lip. I want his mouth on me.

An electric shock spirals through me as he presses the flat of his tongue to my clit. He kisses it, his warm mouth welcoming and intoxicating. My thoughts spiral to nothingness. All that's left is this man, his wicked mouth, the pleasure building like an avalanche inside me.

John teases with his tongue, tasting, searching, tormenting. My fingers tighten in his hair as my orgasm builds. When he presses two fingers deep inside me, I nearly combust. He hums with delight, and my hips buck in response. I'm a goddamned powder keg, and he's the lit fuse.

"I…John, plea—" My words spill out, incoherent, muddled. "Fu-fuck me. Please."

With one last deep kiss to my throbbing clit, John slowly rises and pushes me onto the bed. I watch him slowly strip. My overheated body cools in the air, but the chill does nothing to quell the molten heat flowing through my veins. Every inch of my skin burns for his touch.

When he tosses the last of his clothes aside, he stands before me wearing only a confident smile. My gaze drifts to his cock, proudly standing at attention against the pale skin of his stomach.

"See something you like?" he asks.

"It's hard to tell." I lick my lips. "Come closer, let me explore."

He growls as he climbs onto the bed, his body covering mine in a series of languid but powerful movements. A predator claiming his prey.

I sink into the bed beneath him and sigh in delight as his heat penetrates me. Chest to chest, his heartbeat mirroring mine.

Then he kisses me, settling between my thighs, his cock hard against my pussy.

I reach between us and grip him in my fist. He hisses in a breath and swears.

When our gazes lock, he looks positively feral. "You asked for it, kitten."

"Please," I murmur, my thoughts vanishing as he replaces my grip with his own before plunging deep into me. A strangled gasp rips from my throat at the invasion. My brain turns to gelatin as he moves. "Fuck me."

John groans in approval and withdraws slightly before thrusting deeper. With every movement, my body tightens, spiraling higher and higher. I need this. I need *him*. My fingernails dig into his shoulders as I brace myself for each delicious onslaught.

His pace quickens, and I shift to meet his frenzied thrusts, arching my hips, rocking my body against his, needing more friction, more sensation.

Lost in the torrent, I kiss him, hard, nipping his lip between my teeth. He pulses inside me. I tighten around him in response.

He pulls back, slipping from my pussy, and I whine in frustration.

Without missing a beat, John flips me onto my stomach, hooks one arm around my waist to bring me to my knees, and pulls my back against his chest. He drives into me from behind, one hand still around my waist, palm encasing my breast while the other holds my hip in place as he pounds deep into me.

Sweet fucking mercy. His cock hits every sensitive bundle of nerve endings I didn't know I had. I thrash toward him when his fingertips circle my clit.

"Come for me, kitten."

My hips move of their own volition as he continues to fuck me with long strokes, his fingers applying gentle pressure in rhythmic circles.

I shudder when my orgasm hits like a bolt of lightning. Body trembling, I lean into John as he continues his torment, drawing every last drop of pleasure from my body.

"Good girl," he murmurs, teeth scraping my bare throat.

He pulls out and takes himself in hand. I feel the heat of his cum on my back as he takes his own release.

Hearts still racing, we catch our breath. He captures my jaw in his hand and turns my face to tenderly kiss the corner of my mouth. I practically purr in satisfaction.

"Stay here," John says, pressing another kiss to my bare shoulder.

He climbs off the bed and retreats to the bathroom. When he returns, he cleans me with a damp, warm cloth and tucks me beneath the blankets.

I grab his hand and pull him into bed beside me. He settles there and tugs me against his chest, cradling me in his embrace. Silence fills the room as we recover from our highs.

"I forgive you," I mumble. "But don't think I'm going to forget."

"Valid." He presses a kiss to my forehead. "So are you gonna stay?"

"I'll stay." I nestle deeper into him. "Someone needs to keep you in line. This fandom needs me."

"So do I."

The words barely register as I drift off to sleep, content with the knowledge that I'm exactly where I need to be. Working on a film for my favorite fandom with the director I've fantasized about for most of my adult life.

Weird how that works out.

CHAPTER THIRTEEN

Several Months Later

Filming officially begins in January, and I'm already freaking out. While things with John and me are good—better than good—I still can't help feeling like an outsider. In the writing room, on set, at parties and events…it's unsettling how much I shrink into myself. Which, if anyone knows me, is not who I am.

I sink deeper into the sofa and stare at the TV. *While You Were Sleeping* plays with the volume low, and Christmas lights from the tree nearby reflect on the screen. I don't need to hear the show to know what's going on. It's my favorite Christmas comfort movie. I sigh and pull the plush blanket tighter around me as I watch Sandra Bullock clock Bill Pullman in the face with a door. I smile. This whole movie is a spin on the misunderstanding trope, which I typically hate…but here, it works perfectly.

Misunderstanding. The story of my life.

Last night John took me to a holiday party in the Hills. I recognized quite a few names, and while the fangirl in me wanted to socialize, something held me back. Probably the feeling that I was candy dangling from John Martigan's arm and no one knew who the fuck I was. No one dared say it, but I could see the question in their eyes. *Why is she here?*

John introduced me as his girlfriend, but I could see no one believed it. Why should they? He's an award-winning director, and I'm…well, I'm me. Fabulous and amazing, but that means nothing in Hollywood.

"This is the tenth time you've watched this movie." John

comes around the couch and slides into the seat beside me. "Come here."

I shift positions to curl myself against him, draping my legs across his lap and resting my cheek on his shoulder. "You shouldn't hate this movie. It's a classic."

He chuckles, and the sound vibrates through me. "It's a great movie. I won't deny it. But it's not my top Christmas movie of all time."

"Let me guess. *It's a Wonderful Life*?" I nudge him in the ribs.

"Also a fantastic film and a classic Christmas pick, but no."

"*How the Grinch Stole Christmas*, the Jim Carrey version?"

He shakes his head.

"You're not one of those guys, are you?"

"What guys?" He smirks.

"The ones who think *Die Hard* is a Christmas movie?"

He rolls his eyes. "It *is* a Christmas movie. It takes place at a Christmas party." A teasing scoff breaks free, followed by laughter. "And while it's a must watch on Christmas Eve, it's not my favorite."

"I give up then." I study his profile. "What's your favorite holiday movie?"

"*A Christmas Story*."

"I should have guessed you're a Ralphie fan."

"I had a Red Ryder BB gun and everything."

"Of course you did."

We lapse into silence, watching the movie. After a few comfortable moments, nagging frustration settles again inside my chest, heavy and persistent.

Finally, it bubbles over into words. "John, when the movie begins filming…" I bite my lower lip, uncertain of how to phrase this. "What happens next?"

"Well, it will go—"

"No," I cut him off. "With us?"

He shifts to face me. "What do you mean?"

"I'm here to help you with the script. When that's over, my job is done." Sadness fills me. "I…well, I'll go back home."

His brow furrows as a frown forms on his lips. He's lost in thought, so I push forward.

"These last few months have been amazing. I've learned so much, met so many amazing people." Emotion chokes me. "But this can't last forever."

"It can," he says slowly, forming the words as realization brightens his expression. His whiskey gaze locks with mine. "Stay."

"What do you mean *stay*? I can't just drop everything I've ever known to come live in sin with you, no matter how fucking wonderful that sounds." I sigh. "It's just not realistic."

"Okay, then." He pulls me fully into his lap, so my thighs straddle his and we're chest to chest.

I brace my hands on his shoulders and ignore the insistent press of his cock through his sweatpants, right against my center. His countenance turns from playful to pleading.

"Marry me."

For a moment, I think I heard him say *Marry me*, but that would be crazy.

I blink, shoving at his arm playfully. "Don't tease like that."

"I'm not teasing, kitten. I'm deadly serious." His hold on my hips tightens, fingertips biting my skin through the fabric of my lounge pants. "I'll ask again. Ginger, will you do me the honor of being my wife?"

"You're not joking." My breath catches, my heart beating a thousand miles an hour.

John shakes his head, a lock of dark hair spilling across his forehead. I push it aside and cradle his face in my hand.

"This is crazy." I can barely breathe. "It feels right, but holy shit, it's absolutely insane."

"Why?" He cocks his head, and his eyes sparkle. "We've known each other for six months. Worked together." His voice deepens. "Played together."

A shiver of desire races through me.

"I fail to see a problem."

"We barely know each other, John." I suck in a breath. "If we rush off and get married, it'll be all over the tabloids the next day."

"First of all, I know enough about you to know I'm willing to tie my life to yours." He pulls me closer, our breaths mingling. "You're a caring, passionate woman who's dedicated to her fandom, friends, and family. You don't take shit, you always build up those around you without concern for how it will benefit you."

My heart warms at his words, and tears fill my eyes. I swipe them away with a laugh.

"As for the paparazzi, they can go fuck themselves."

I choke on another laugh.

"Seriously, who cares what anyone else thinks? This isn't a film I'm directing for someone else and promoting according to a contract. This is my fucking life, and for the first time, I know exactly what and *who* I want." He cradles my cheek in his palm. "I want you, Ginger Darling. I want you in my life and in my bed from now until I take my last breath."

"Goddamn it, John." Tears start anew, and he brushes them away with the pad of his thumb.

"Is that a yes?"

I kiss him, hard and fast, letting my emotions take control. He crushes me to him, opening his mouth and tasting me. I surrender to him completely, writhing against his solid body, wanting more.

Now.

John obliges with unbridled enthusiasm. He pulls my sweatshirt off, shifting his attention from my mouth to my breasts. I cry out as he pulls a nipple between his teeth, gently suckling. I thread my fingers through his hair and tighten my hold, not wanting him to stop but needing him elsewhere.

"John…please…" I whimper as he hooks his thumbs into the waistband of my pants and tugs them down. Somehow, I shimmy out of them, giggling and moaning in equal measure at the delirious absurdity of it. Naked, I settle firmly on his lap and grind my pussy against the seam of his sweatpants, leaving it wet.

"Impatient." He pulls his pants down to free his cock, grips my hips, and pushes into me with a single thrust.

A satisfied groan rips from deep inside my chest, and my head falls back. This feeling of fullness, of warm completion…it's unlike anything in the world. No amount of addictive substance could ever compare. I rest my hands on his shoulders as he moves.

My head snaps forward, and my eyes meet his. They hold me captive, brimming with desire and admiration. He wants to marry me.

"I–I love you, John." The words mingle with the sexual haze surrounding us.

He stills, reaching up to cradle my face and draw me to him, placing a kiss on my parted lips. I melt into him as he deepens the kiss, still rocking his hips, driving my pleasure higher. When he breaks away, he touches his forehead to mine.

"I love you, Ginger." He shifts our positions, laying me on the sofa and covering me with his warm body.

This time, when he pushes into me, I relax into his frenzied movement, meeting him thrust for thrust with a rhythm that makes my head spin. I'm so close.

"Come for me, kitten." He shifts his hips, angling for every motion to brush my sensitive clit.

My nails dig into his skin as the orgasm slams me. Soft, gasping breaths escape to tangle with ebbing sensation as my climax fades.

John swears as he moves to pull out. I wrap my legs around his hips and hold him inside me, wanting all of him.

"Fuck, Ginger," he bites out as he comes.

We lay there, entwined on the sofa, our breaths slowly resuming an even rhythm. He kisses me softly before climbing off and disappearing down the hall. I lay there, too sated to move. John returns with a damp cloth, and as he cleans me, a warm bubble consumes my heart. He helps me dress, then dons his own clothes before settling on the couch and pulling me against him.

The movie is still going. Sandra Bullock's character tearfully leaves a chapel as all hell breaks loose with Peter and Jack's family. I sigh, knowing how hard it must be to make such a decision. John gently strokes the inside of my wrist.

"New Year's Eve," I say, breaking the silence.

"What?" he asks.

"Let's get married New Year's Eve." I look at him. "We can start the new year fresh."

His eyes glint with what I can only assume is joy. "That sounds perfect."

"I'm so glad I asked about our future now." I wrap my arms around him, laying my head on his chest.

John laughs and kisses my brow. "Me too, kitten. Me too."

THE END Book 4

The Author
Fangirl Confessions
Book 5
KIRSTEN S. BLACKETER

CHAPTER ONE

I squint in the dim light of the Irish pub and search for a familiar face. Not that it will make a difference, since I've never met these women before.

"Ronnie?" A cute brunette pops up beside me, her bright eyes and friendly smile relaxing me immediately.

"Yeah," I reply.

"Vicky. I go as JustMyStarShip." She hugs me. "I'm so glad you could make it."

I blink at the unexpected contact, then hug her back. "Me too."

She withdraws, beaming, and points to a clustered group of women at the far end of the restaurant. "Come on, the girls are dying to meet you."

They all turn as we approach, and introductions are made. I've spoken to all of these women in our online forum, and it's nice to finally meet the fangirls in person. It's not hard for me to remember names once I put a face to them. I greet each in turn before sliding into a seat beside Jessica.

As we wait for the server to make the rounds again, I scan the group. Ginger, Jessica, and I sit on one side of the table with Beth, Madre, Jen, and Vicky opposite. It's a cozy spot, a perfect setting for a fun first date. I take in the details, already mentally outlining a story to use this setting.

Everyone breaks into little side conversations, and Vicky turns to me as Jessica decides to bounce out early.

"So how was the trip from St. Louis?" she asks before

sipping her cocktail.

"Uneventful." I skim the menu to find something tasty, but first, I need a margarita. "I did manage to finish the next chapter of my new *Space Vendetta* fic."

"Really?" Vicky grins wickedly. "Are we going to get spice with this next update?"

"Girl, it's a slow burn. You don't get any spice in the first dozen chapters." I laugh. "I promise it's coming. Pun intended."

"Oh, I can't wait. I love the combo you've got going on," Vicky says. "There aren't enough fics for that pairing—Jastin and Rayina are, like, the perfect duo."

"Yeah, it's a shame we've never seen them together in the films." I sigh.

"Oh, are you talking about your latest fic?" Jen jumps into the conversation, her eyes bright.

"Yeah."

"I love the idea of that pairing." Jen nods. "It's a shame the author doesn't read your fics to get ideas for the next book."

"They interact a little in the books but nothing romantic." I wince. "Sorry, spoilers."

Jen waves her hand. "It's okay. You're our go-to for source material since you've read all the books."

"Yeah, and all the fics ever written for the series," Vicky adds.

My face heats, but I brush it away. "What can I say? I'm a dedicated fan."

"Well, if you're such a huge fan, you would already know Michael DeHart has been added to the roster for the *Space Vendetta* panel Sunday, as well as for a book signing tomorrow." Vicky winks.

"Get out of here!" I pull out my phone and check the Instagram page for the convention. Sure enough, there's been an update to the roster, and Michael DeHart, author of the *Space Vendetta* series, will have a table open for a short time on Saturday. "Holy shit."

"I know, right?" Ginger jumps into the conversation. "Looks like he's a surprise last-minute addition. It's so cool."

"Are you going to try to find him tomorrow?" Vicky turns back to me.

"Hell yeah!"

My excitement is momentarily derailed by the realization I didn't bring any books for him to sign. Shit.

"I don't have anything for him to sign."

"I'm sure you can think of *something* he can sign…" Ginger gives me a bawdy wink.

Just the thought has my body overheating, and I fan myself. "The last thing I want is to get kicked out of the convention because I asked him to sign my boobs. This is a comic convention not a rock concert."

"Who says it can't be both?" Beth smiles wickedly.

"It can, but it would be a good way to get kicked out." I turn to Ginger. "I will not be one of those fangirls who accosts the author of *Space Vendetta* just because he's the ultimate hottie—drop-dead gorgeous *and* talented as fuck."

"No one at this table is advising or encouraging you to rub those sexy curves all over him." Ginger sips her lemon drop martini.

"While I'm sure he'll appreciate the view"—I smooth my hands over my chest—"according to the interviews I've watched and articles I've read, he's notoriously shy and typically doesn't do big events. An open signing is a huge win for fans."

"I've heard the same," Ginger adds. "All we need is an overzealous fan overstepping boundaries and fucking it up for the rest of us." She glances teasingly at Beth.

"What? I'm not going to cause a scene this weekend." Beth says, indignant. "If we need to worry about anyone, it's you." She points at Ginger.

With a mock gasp, Ginger feigns insult. "I told you. I'm not going to do anything stupid. I'm just going to ask a single question."

"Sure." Beth laughs. "I know you better than you think I do."

The waiter's return dissolves the conversation. After everyone else orders and I ensure he knows I want a spicy jalapeño margarita, he asks if I want anything else.

"Your phone number?" I tease, unable to control myself. He's cute but not really my type; I just like keeping people on their toes.

He stammers for a moment, looking flustered.

I laugh. "I'm just messing with you."

"Good, because that would be hard to explain to my girlfriend." He sighs with a wobbly smile. "I'll get your drink and put the orders in."

"Thank you," Ginger calls after him before turning to me. "Oh my God, Ronnie, I can't believe you did that."

"Did what?" I ask innocently. "It's just a little harmless flirting."

"Are you going to do the same thing when you see Michael DeHart tomorrow?" Ginger asks, her green eyes fixed on me, long lashes fluttering.

"You should." Madre looks up from her phone. "Please. I live vicariously through you guys."

"I forgot," Ginger says with a gasp. "Madre's our only *taken* fangirl."

"How long have you been married?" Jen asks.

"Twenty years next fall."

"Holy shit, I didn't realize you'd been married that long." Ginger nods appreciatively. "Bravo."

Madre heaves a dramatic sigh and laughs. "You guys make me feel so fucking old."

"You *are* the oldest in our group," Beth points out. "Hence the name—Madre."

"If you were my kid, I'd ground you forever." Madre laughs at Beth's horrified expression.

"Seriously, what's your real name?" Ginger leans forward.

I know it, but I don't out her to the rest of them.

I guess I lied earlier. Madre is the only fangirl I've met in person, but only because I saw her at the airport on the way here.

"Bonnie," she says.

"Bonnie suits you," I say with a smile. "What I really want to know is how you got pulled into the *Space Vendetta* fandom when you're so obviously obsessed with *Throne of Ashes*?"

"Yeah, I've wondered the same." Jen turns to her.

"I love both and found them around the same time." Madre smirks. "But *Throne of Ashes* has dragons and magic, and something about those two things captures a piece of my heart."

"You've written over thirty fics for that fandom alone," I say, skimming the list of her contributions on the FandomArchive. "That's dedication."

Madre laughs. "My list of fics is nothing compared to yours, Ronnie."

"Wait, how many fics has she written?" Vicky asks, curious.

"Holy shit." Ginger claps a hand over her mouth. "Sixty-seven—and that's only for *Space Vendetta*."

The rest of the girls stare at me in disbelief.

"What?" I ask. "Trust me when I say I don't hold the record. That honor goes to VendettaDaddy—they've written eighty-one fics."

A ripple of murmurs runs through the fangirls.

"Some aren't very long, but that writer knows the fandom and the source material better than anyone." I've read every single fic, and I've been a fan of their work from the beginning.

"Even you?" Beth asks.

"Even me. Whoever they are, they're hardcore."

"Not like VSpaceV," Madre says.

"Wait." Ginger holds a hand up. "Why is that name familiar?"

"VSpaceV was on a different fandom site. There was a huge scandal with one of their works. It upset a lot of fans, and they got massive hate." Madre looks between me and Ginger. "They took everything down and went silent."

"How many fics did they have?" My curiosity grows. I thought I knew everything there was to know about the *Space Vendetta* fandom, but this is the first time I've heard of this scandal.

"Not nearly as many, but the material was so raw, so visceral, it caused an uproar." Madre pauses as the waiter delivers my margarita.

"When was this?" I sip, and the tequila and spice of the jalapeño warms me through.

"Back when the internet was still young and more like the Wild West." Madre eyes each of us in turn. "Probably before some of you were born."

"We're not *that* young." Jen laughs.

"Still." Madre shrugs. "Most people don't realize Michael DeHart didn't create the *Space Vendetta* universe, though he turned it into what we know it as today."

"His dad came up with the idea." I add this little random piece of trivia that really doesn't impress anyone. "They worked on it together when he was a kid. His dad got inspiration from an old comic books with a similar title, and Michael wrote the books. Both are used in the creation of the films."

"Really?" Jen stirs her drink. "I didn't know that."

"It's not typically advertised." I frown. "His dad died when he was eighteen, just after Michael published his first book. So he took on all the creative processes and grew the series to what it is today."

"That's an impressive feat." Ginger lifts her glass in salute. "To the creators of *Space Vendetta,* the fandom that brought us all together."

"I'll drink to that." I raise my glass to hers, as do the other girls. We drink, and right at that moment, our food arrives.

I'm starving, and the burger on my plate looks amazing. The rest of the meal passes in relative silence as we dig into our food.

Afterward, we head back to the hotel where we all decided to stay. It's two blocks from the convention center and within walking distance of almost anything we could possibly need during our weekend in Philly.

My room is two doors down from Ginger and Beth. Madre and Jen are also sharing a room, though I'm not sure where Vicky and Jessica are. I decided to get my own room since I like having space to decompress after big events.

Tomorrow is going to be amazing. I'm so stoked to finally see Michael DeHart in person. He's such a huge influence on my own writing, and—I'm not going to lie—I've had a crush on him for ages.

Michael DeHart shouldn't look as good as he does. He should be paunchy and balding with glasses, but he's not. The man is a goddamn adonis with an inverted triangle–shaped torso telling me he works out that upper body and can probably bench more than my bodyweight. He's impressive as hell. I'm curious to see if pictures and videos do him justice.

All I have to do is stay calm, don't fangirl *too* hard, keep my inside thoughts in my fucking head, and we'll be golden.

He's an author, Ronnie, not a rockstar. Don't scare the man.

CHAPTER TWO

Day one of Philadelphia Comic Convention is off to a rocky start when I damn near lose Jessica in an escalator accident. I swear she was right behind me, but by the time I turn around, trapped in a sea of people, I see her still at the top being held by—is that Daredevil?

Well, shit. Put that on my bingo card of things I wasn't expecting to see today. It's an adorable meet-cute for a fanfic though. I file away the mental note.

When she finally arrives at the bottom, I reach out and rest my hand on her arm. "Oh my God, I saw the whole thing. Are you okay?"

"I'm fine," she replies, still swaying a little.

"Good thing Daredevil came to your rescue. There's something about a man in a mask, isn't there?"

Jessica looks dazed, a far-off glaze in her eyes. "Yeah. There is." She adjusts her earplug.

"Maybe you'll run into him again." I nudge her. "Did you get his number?"

"No." She shakes her head. "I didn't even get his name."

"Well, in a getup like that, he'll be easy to spot." I wink. "We'll find him."

"What if he doesn't want to be found?"

"Honey, he's wearing a red bodysuit. Trust me, he *wants* to be seen in this crowd." I push my curls behind my shoulder, wishing I'd pinned my hair up this morning. It's getting warm.

"If he were Deadpool, I'd agree." Jessica scans the crowd

as we enter the vendor area. "But we're talking about Daredevil."

"Look, girl, if he doesn't come looking for you, he's blind. You're a knockout!" I take in the cute blond girl-next-door vibe she's rocking and offer a comforting smile. "Men."

Her face turns red, but she smiles.

"First time at a con?" I ask her, stopping to inspect a Funko Pop! figurine.

"What gave it away?" She laughs.

"Nothing gave it away…" I pause, unsure of how to word it. "I can tell you're overwhelmed by the crowd."

"A little." She sidesteps a cosplayer with giant wings. "I'm working through it."

"Well, if you need a break, let me know."

"I appreciate it." She rests a hand on my shoulder before retrieving a map from her bag. "Where's the authors' booth?"

My heart does a little hop. "I think it's on the other side of the room."

"Let's head that way then." She takes my arm, and we peruse booths as we walk.

Excitement bubbles through me with each step. I'm going to meet Michael DeHart. Holy shit. I spent extra time on my hair and makeup this morning—not that it matters, but I want to make a good impression. Instead of wearing cosplay this weekend, I chose to rock vintage-style jeans with a loose *Space Vendetta* T-shirt.

Through the crowd, I spot his name hanging above the table. A tangle of nerves pulls tight in the pit of my stomach, and I wonder for the hundredth time if I'm going to ruin the illusion I have in my head by actually meeting him. Some fantasies are best left in imagination.

No. I'm doing this. I *need* to do this. I have questions, damn it.

I do a little squeal-hop when he comes into view, sitting behind the table, smiling at passing attendees. Jessica gives me a little nudge to step forward. Nervous flutters unleash inside my chest, and I press a hand to my heart.

"You got this," I whisper to myself as I approach his table. "Just be your awesome self and don't be inappropriate."

He looks up as I approach, his smile sincere. "Hi, I'm Michael."

"Ronnie." I shake his hand, and his touch sends a shiver of awareness through me. *Keep it together, girl.* "If I'd known this would be a historic event, I would have been better prepared."

He blinks in confusion, his smile faltering. "I'm sorry?"

"You don't often do signings." I gesture to his setup. "I would have brought my collection for you to sign, had I known."

Michael chuckles softly. "Oh yeah…well, it was kind of a last-minute decision." He pauses to regard me for a long moment. "Sorry, for a second, I thought you were coming on to me."

"And if I was?"

He swallows hard and looks hesitant. "I don't mix business with pleasure."

My heart sinks a little, but I smile and wave a hand anyway. "Neither do I."

Michael's shoulders relax.

"Now that we've cleared that up, I was wondering if I could get a picture with you."

"Sure." He stands and comes around the table to stand beside me. Shit. I barely come up to his shoulders, and he smells so fucking good.

I manage maintain my composure for the picture and keep my hands to myself as he retreats to his seat behind the table.

"I have a proposition for you."

He laughs again. "You have a way of phrasing things so it sounds like innuendo. Has anyone ever told you that?"

"Oh yeah. It's part of my charm." I toss my hair over my shoulder, trying to look cute and nonchalant. I'm not sure it works, considering the suspicious way he's still watching me. "It's not really a proposition—more like a serious question."

He leans forward, elbows on the table, game face on. "Ask away."

"How do you feel about fan fiction?"

His brow furrows. "In general?"

"Well…I'm curious how you feel about fan fiction based on your world." I hold my breath, unsure whether I really want to know the answer.

Michael taps the table with the pen he's holding. I can almost see wheels spinning in his head. When I'm positive he's not going to answer, he sighs.

"I'm not against it." He leans back in his chair; those blue eyes fix on me. "Fans are entitled to have fun with their favorite characters. Not all stories go the way we'd like, so it's a great way for people who are invested in the plot to play out those what-if scenarios."

"That's why I enjoy it."

"Do you just read it, or do you write as well?"

"I…both." I shift my weight to the other foot. When did this conversation drift to me? "Do you read fanfic of your own work?"

A shy smile appears on his lips, making him even more handsome. "I don't know if I can answer that question."

Confused, I lean on the table, arching a brow. "What do you mean? You either read it or you don't."

"You really want to know?" He glances to the left, to the right, like he's making sure no one is listening.

I follow his gaze and nod. "I wouldn't have asked if I didn't want to know."

He leans forward. "It depends."

"On what?" I ask, coming even closer. I feel like we're exchanging gossip about someone who could walk into our conversation at any moment.

"The tags."

I snort-laugh. "Seriously?"

"I'm deadly serious." He laughs. "Remember, I wrote the source material these fics are based on, and there are some strange pairings…not to mention, some pretty explicit kinks I'd rather not read."

"Are you kink shaming?" I ask with a laugh.

"Not at all." He lifts his hands. "I would never yuck someone's yum, but there are some images I don't need in my head."

I ponder his comment for half a second before nodding. "I get that. There are some I avoid just because they're…well, they're not my jam."

"Exactly." He again taps the table with his pen. "So are you going to tell me how many fics you've written?"

"Over a hundred, at least." I chuckle when his eyes widen. "Most of them are for *Space Vendetta*, but I've dabbled in other fandoms. Most of those were fix-it fics."

"Now *I'm* intrigued." He holds my gaze, and I swear he's staring into my soul. "You know I have to ask…"

"Ask what?" I lick my lips.

His eyes dip at the motion but soon recapture mine. "What pairing is your favorite in the *Space Vendetta* fandom?"

"Created by you or the fans?"

"Either."

I think for a moment, even though I already know which

pairing I ship to the heavens. I sigh and bat my lashes. "Don't hate me."

"I don't think that's possible." Michael smiles. "Humor me."

"Ransom–Lynnea–Colton."

"A poly enemies-to-lovers romance?" He chuckles. "I wasn't expecting that."

"What did you expect?"

"Ransom–Colton is the most popular." He shakes his head. "Personally, I think while it's a steamy combination, they'd probably kill each other within a week."

"I don't know. I've read some really good fics with that pairing and neither of them die in the end." I smirk. "At least not in a literal sense."

"Of course." A hint of pink tinges Michael's cheeks. "So have you written that poly pairing?"

"Quite a few." I nod fervently. "It's not easy to write, and I know my work isn't at the same level as some on FandomArchive."

Michael takes out his phone. "What's your pen name?"

"You can't be serious?" I gape at him. "I…you don't want to read my fics."

"Why not? You've captured my curiosity."

I stare at him for a moment, wondering whether he's joking. Finally, I relent. "Okay, but I'm not nearly as talented a writer as you are."

"Only one way to find out." He opens the search box on FandomArchive. "Name?"

"NoticeMeSenpai." I spell it out for him.

He reads, and I see him smile.

"Bookmarked." Michael looks at me again. "I'll read some of them tonight."

"Sure you will." I roll my eyes.

"Are you going to be here tomorrow?" he asks.

"Yeah. I'm going to the *Space Vendetta* panel."

"Good. I'll give you my thoughts afterward." He tucks his phone away.

"I didn't come over here to convince you to read my fan fiction, you know?" I shake my head at him.

"Then why *did* you come over here?" Michael relaxes against the table. His bicep steals my attention for half a second, and I clear my throat.

"There's a fic I read a while ago, and I…well, I think you should read it." I bite my lower lip, unsure about bringing this up.

"Why?" He grins. "Is it spicy? Gruesome? Did they write the characters better than I do?"

"Not exactly, but…" I lean forward, inadvertently giving him a good view of cleavage in the process. I press my hand over my chest, and his gaze returns to my face. "I think it had a better grasp of the characters' relationship development. Honestly, I think you should read it."

"Are you saying it's better than what I write?" He stares at me, amused.

"No, it's just…I think it would have been a better direction for the story overall."

"I should be insulted," he says with a laugh. "But you have me curious." He pulls out his phone again. "Fic title and author name?"

"'The Revolutionary' by VendettaDaddy," I say, reciting from memory.

His fingers hover over the phone screen, and his head snaps up.

"Have you already read it?" I ask tentatively.

He looks…uncertain?

"No, but I've heard of it." He tucks the phone back into his pocket and clears his throat. "I take it you're a fan of this author?"

"Oh yeah. I've read all their work." I feel a blush heating my face.

"I see." Michael taps the pen on the desk. "Well, I'll read this after I finish yours and let you know what I think."

"Are you blowing me off?" I ask, sensing a shift in his demeanor.

"No, ma'am." He softens. "I promise. I'll let you know what I think of both."

"Okay."

A group of fans descends upon us, pushing me to the side. Michael greets them and shoots me an apologetic smile. He writes something on a paper and slides it to me across the table before turning to the new arrivals.

I pick up the card. There, next to the phone number, is a note. *Text me after the panel tomorrow.*

When I look up, he's fully dedicated to interacting with his fans. I tuck the card into my bra and retreat from the table in search of the other fangirls.

They're never going to believe this.

CHAPTER THREE

The first day of the convention is winding down, and I'm still humming from my interaction with Michael DeHart. I'm dying to talk to someone about what happened, but this isn't the time or place.

I slip out of the convention early and grab a sandwich from a shop in Reading Terminal Station, which has, by far, the best food selection in Philadelphia. After some Danishes this morning, I can't stop thinking about all the options there.

I slide onto a stool and cozy up to the narrow counter. The chatter and noise create a bubble around me, and I can't think. Which is good. Right now, the last thing I want to do is overanalyze. I order a cheesesteak, fries, and a Coke. I'm fucking starving, and I can't wait for the fangirls to finish up their rounds. But now, I need time to eat…and time to chill.

When I pull out my phone, I'm tempted to look up the fics I told Michael to read. I had a plan when I went in there today, but something tells me I bit off more than I can chew. He seemed almost pleased when I showed him those stories. Which is weird. I don't think many authors like seeing fan fiction set in the world they created. Maybe he's right though—it's the perfect space for fans to blow off steam when authors and filmmakers fail to hit the right notes.

With a huff, I open the fangirl group text.

(Me): *Grabbing dinner at RTS, anyone want to catch up at the hotel rooftop bar at 9?*

(Ginger): *I'm game.*

(Beth): *Same.*

(Vicky): *You guys enjoy. I'm gonna crash early.*

(Jessica): *Sorry, guys, I'm heading home. Been a long day. Enjoy the rest of the convention.*

(Madre): *Thanks, everyone, gonna pass. Family emergency, gotta put out some fires.*

Everyone replied except Jen. Weird. She doesn't seem like the type to ghost us, but I overheard Ginger say Jen peaced out early. I wonder what happened.

My food arrives, and I dig in. It's fucking delicious. One of my favorite things is trying local eateries whenever I visit a new city. This one definitely makes the cut.

Once I finish, I grab a few pastries for tomorrow and head back to the hotel. My phone pings, and I check the email notification. My current fanfic obsession has updated with a new chapter. I cannot get enough of it. It's the author I told Michael DeHart to read. I hope he sees the update.

I kick off my shoes and curl up on the bed with my computer. The update is two chapters. *Wow.* I expected only one, but now I'm super happy I'm taking the time to read this. I want to be prepared for my conversation with Michael tomorrow…assuming he actually follows through with his promise to read it.

My heart stops.

Shit.

He promised to read *my* fics too. I bury my face in the pillow and scream. He has my name. There's nothing stopping him from reading all of my fics if he wants to. Holy hell. I don't know if I can face him tomorrow. There are some very loose interpretations of his original material in my stories.

Pushing my concern aside, I dive into these new chapters, and everything fades into the background.

I'm riveted, completely captivated. There's no other word for it. Whoever this author is, I will read every fucking thing they ever write. I don't care if it's a grocery list or a fucking how-to manual. They are an absolute gem.

And I feel vindicated giving this information to Michael DeHart. I feel like combining his creation with this unique character twist from VendettaDaddy would make for an epic film experience.

I glance at the clock. "Fuck," I say to the empty room. It's nearly eight thirty. I need to get ready to meet the girls at the bar. After touching up my makeup and putting on some comfortable flats, I steal a moment to type up a review of the new chapters. It's simple and flattering, but seriously, if I ever met this author in person, I might die.

Then again, I thought the same thing before I met Michael DeHart, and I'm still kicking. Although my heart may never be the same. He looked so good, smelled better than I imagined, and, *ugh*, even the banter was top-notch.

I grab my purse and head to the elevator. As I punch the rooftop button, I stare at my reflection in the door and straighten my top. *It's not like you'll see him in the hotel.* I scoff at my overzealous imagination.

The doors open and I step out, checking my phone—it's just before nine.

Inside the enclosed area of the rooftop bar, there are only a few tables taken, and the rest of the room is fair game. I snag a booth in the corner, opposite the main entrance. The bartender nods as I slide onto the bench.

A few seconds later, a server appears—a cute brunette with a short bob. "Here's some menus. Kitchen closes at ten, but the bar is open til midnight." She smiles. "What can I get ya?"

"Spicy margarita, bonus points if you can do jalapeño-pineapple."

"No problem."

"Oh, and a few friends will join me."

"I'll be back when they get here then."

I grin. "Thanks."

Ginger and Beth arrive shortly after my margarita does. The server pops over as they're sitting down, and they place their orders.

"Ladies, how was your first day of the con?" I sip the delectable drink.

They share a look and spill all the tea. I missed out on a whole cosplayer debacle, only to find out it was really Jason Hunt in costume! Holy shit, no wonder Vicky tapped out early. Poor girl. Getting put under a microscope on social media so quickly can cause whiplash.

I'm still spinning as Beth tells me about her encounter with a grumpy security guard, though she begrudgingly admits he's a stone-cold fox. "Too bad his shitty personality fucks it all up," she says with a huff.

Ginger seems worried the convention is too much for Jessica, and I agree before relaying her near-death experience on the escalator and the subsequent encounters with her Daredevil hero…who happens to be a blind artist. Again, not on my bingo card for today, but at this rate, my card is going to be fucking full.

How much crazy shit can go down in one weekend?

"Madre sends her regards." Ginger sighs. "It seems her youngest had a run-in with some jerk at a local ice cream shop, and she needed to talk to mom. Guess it turned into a buddy watch of their favorite cartoon while eating junk food kind of night."

My heart softens toward Madre. She's the best of us. A dedicated wife and loving mom, balancing work and a personal life full of anonymous fan fiction. I aspire to be half the woman she is.

"What happened to Jen?" I look between Ginger and Beth. "She's the only one who didn't respond."

"I don't know." Ginger shrugs. Beth does the same with an added eye roll. I know those two don't really get along. Beth can be harsh in her criticism, and I think Jen is so new to the fandom scene, she still takes it personally.

"She left without anyone knowing?" I frown. "Did something happen?"

"I guess she spoke to Madre before she got on a bus to go home. I don't know exactly what happened, but it was around the time Nicholas Hughes was signing autographs." Ginger sips her lemon drop martini.

"She couldn't handle it," Beth says offhandedly.

"Handle what?" I'm curious.

"Being here but knowing she wouldn't actually meet him." Beth shakes her head. "A rookie mistake."

"It's not a mistake," Ginger clarifies. "I just don't think she was ready for the onslaught of feels. I mean, we've all experienced it, but this isn't our first comic convention either."

I nod in agreement, and Beth reluctantly joins in.

"So," Ginger says, turning to me, eyes aglow, "I want to hear everything. How did it go with Mr. DeHart?"

I recount the interaction as best as I can. Ginger praises my obvious restraint, and Beth asks a few questions. On the whole, they're invested in how the fan fiction conversation will play out now he has my input. Not like it will matter, but I took a chance, and I'm damn proud of myself.

"So you gave him your pen name?" Ginger practically bounces in her chair.

"Yup."

"That's so exciting!" Her exuberance is contagious.

"Do you think he'll actually read it?" In her typical way, Beth is skeptical. "I mean, guys like him have more important things to do than read fan fiction. Especially when it's about their own work."

"He said he enjoys some fan fiction." I shrug. "Who knows what he'll think of mine?"

"You told him about VendettaDaddy's latest piece?" Ginger asks.

"I did…" My expression falters, and both women exchange a look.

"What? What is it?" Ginger leans forward, invested.

"When I mentioned the title and author, it seemed like he recognized it."

"Maybe he did," Ginger says.

"Yeah. Maybe he's already read it and hated it." Beth inclines her head. "What if he just didn't want to hurt your feelings?"

"He could have been honest." I bristle, then think more about it. "But I get it—he's in front of fans all weekend, he has to keep up appearances."

Ginger nudges Beth and scowls before turning back to me. "Are you going to talk to him again?"

"He said he wants to connect after the panel tomorrow, but I don't know how it's gonna happen." I bite my lip. He gave me his number to text him, and I want to spill but hold back because it feels like some kind of sacred pact between the two of us. If I reveal his secret, the whole fandom will come crashing down.

"I guess we'll see what happens." Ginger sighs.

We finish our drinks and retreat to our rooms, ready to crash before another big day of events. When I reach my room, I get ready for bed and curl up under the blankets.

But I can't sleep.

With a huff, I pull out my laptop and open the fanfic again. There's a comment under the review I made earlier.

Love your enthusiasm. Thanks for the support. – VendettaDaddy

Holy shit, VendettaDaddy replied to my comment.

They *never* reply to comments.

Ever.

I've been following this author for years, and this is the first time I've seen them interact with readers at all.

I decide to scan the new chapters again. They take a different avenue than the original story, but it still aligns with the universe. Almost like a split timeline—a what-if moment followed through writing.

Then I see it. I must have skipped it the first time, but it's there in black and white.

"The name of the cantina is *Ronnie's*?" I mutter. "No way."

I search earlier chapters of the fic, and the name doesn't appear anywhere until this most recent installment. And sure as shit, it's my name.

I read the description of the character who owns the bar. It's less than a sentence, but I can't believe I fucking missed that too.

Raven curls, tied loose, and smoking hot curves that could thaw a pirate's heart.

There's no fucking way.

I bite my nail. It can't be.

That fucker is writing fanfic of his own fucking books!

Michael DeHart is VendettaDaddy.

Now I really can't sleep. I also can't text anyone, and I can't call for backup. I don't want to jinx this. It's a dream so delicious I want to stay and enjoy it a little while longer. So instead, I stare at the ceiling and ponder what the fuck this means.

CHAPTER FOUR

I hit the convention before the rest of the fangirls, mostly because I'm anxious to get to the panel and reserve the best seats. But I have an ulterior motive. I'm hoping to catch a glimpse of Michael DeHart before the panel. I know it's a long shot, but after what I think I uncovered last night, I don't trust myself not to out him in front of everyone.

After a quick loop of the convention floor, I discover he's not here yet and isn't scheduled to be seen until the panel at eleven. I begrudgingly retreat to the auditorium and find prime seats near the stage. Alone, I munch on the pastry I bought yesterday and sip a lukewarm latte from the hotel.

My mind spins as I wait. There has to be a reason why Michael DeHart is writing fan fiction of his own books. I mean, he's the author. If he wants those scenes in the books or to take the plot in a different direction, why doesn't he just write it that way?

I'm so confused. And the worst part is, I can't bring myself to tell any of the fangirls what I found. It's so farfetched, no one will believe me.

Or maybe he doesn't want anyone to know…but then, why would he put such an obvious clue in the fic for me to find? I groan. No, I can't tell anyone. Not yet. Not until I talk to Michael.

His hesitation bothers me, because—what if he doesn't want anyone to make the connection? He doesn't tell his fans he has dozens of *Space Vendetta* fan fiction available under a pseudonym. Honestly, fans would eat that shit up.

Sitting in a nearly empty auditorium, I realize I have no solid facts to back any of this up. I'm making a—highly educated—guess because a random background character seems to describe me. Plenty of people have curly black hair and curves. It doesn't mean anything. It's a long shot. I could be completely off base, looking for things that aren't really there. Things I really desperately want to be there.

What if it's just coincidence? Everything. The description. The comment. The way he reacted when I gave them the name of my favorite fanfic author. All of it, just a pile of coincidences.

I can't confront Michael DeHart with coincidences. I need to do more research, more reading. Or I can wait until after the panel, when he said we could talk, and just fucking ask him. That would be the mature thing to do, right?

I can't seem to calm the trembling in my hands. This could all go terribly wrong. I mean, it's not like I have a relationship with this guy…or even a budding friendship. No. He doesn't know me from Adam, and I know nothing about him that he hasn't carefully curated and shared with his fans. I could blow my opportunity of a true connection with Michael on a hunch. I've seen enough detective movies to know I don't like the odds.

I glance at my phone. Thirty minutes to showtime. There's a steady flow of guests coming in to fill the empty seats. I've had to shoo away a few people who tried to snatch the two seats I reserved for Ginger and Vicky.

Conversation slowly filters in around me, and I stand up, looking around the auditorium in search of their familiar faces. I spot them speaking with a volunteer holding a clipboard.

When they finally turn toward me, I wave, catching Vicky's attention.

Vicky has her trusty cosplay medic kit slung over her

shoulder, and Ginger lights up the room in an 80s neon dress with matching fingerless gloves. They both glow. Excitement flows through me as they move through the crowd.

I debate telling them my theory but decide it's best to wait until *after* I speak with Michael.

"Glad to see you made it." I grab my purse off one chair and my notebook off another. "Had to fight to keep these, but it's well worth it."

"Thanks," Vicky says, sliding onto the chair beside me. "We're running a little late. I'm surprised to see you here. Thought you were planning to head home this morning?"

"That was my original plan, but when they added Michael to the panel, I didn't want to miss it." I toss my hair over one shoulder.

"Didn't you meet him yesterday when he was signing books?" Vicky asks.

"I did." My grin widens. "He invited me to come to the panel today, said it might be something I would enjoy."

"Wow. That's awesome." Vicky smiles. "You two must have hit it off?"

"After the fangirling wore off…yeah, I guess we did." I redirect the conversation with a wave of my hand. "But anyway, enough about me—Vicky, what happened yesterday? I saw your post blow up on Instagram."

As Vicky relays her story and the volunteers finish prepping, I notice Ginger nervously checking the stage. I can't help but feel the same nervousness.

"Moment of truth, Ginger. Are you gonna ask him?" I throw the question out there.

"Damn right I'm gonna ask him."

"Good girl." I take her hand. "We're right here with you. Fangirls united."

She laughs. "He's not getting away from this convention unscathed. He needs to know what his decisions cost true fans of the series."

"As long as you don't threaten his ass, you should be fine." I smile, thinking the exact same thing about Michael DeHart.

"Okay. I vow not to hunt him down and castrate him if he follows through with his plan." Ginger's innocent expression shifts to evil genius. "The implication will remain."

"You're playing with fire, Ginger." Vicky sighs. "Just stick to the script."

As though summoned from my thoughts, Michael DeHart steps from behind the curtain. My heart rate doubles, hammering in my chest. He's wearing a similar outfit to yesterday—casual light blue button-down shirt and khakis. His overly mussed blond hair looks like he's been running his fingers through it. His bashful smile makes him look more like a boy-next-door than a reclusive forty-year-old writer.

The cheers grow louder as he crosses the stage, finds his seat, and turns to the audience with a nod and a wave. When he sits, his gaze scans the crowd. I watch the way his blue eyes dart back and forth until they fix on me. A genuine smile breaks across his lips, making him even more handsome. I reflexively grin and savor this unexpected connection.

The crowd goes wild when John Martigan steps onto the stage. I don't look in his direction because Michael is still staring at me. My friends are focused on the director, but I only have eyes for the author.

And while the attention is off him, Michael winks.

He fucking winks at me, and my hormones lose their ever-loving shit.

He turns as the rest of the panelists join them on stage. The crowd is wild and ready, and I'm on the edge of my seat.

The moderator introduces everyone and begins the discussion, leading the conversation with the panelists, asking about upcoming projects. I'm taking notes, my head swiveling back and forth between the guests and the moderator. Probably a bad idea to sit this close because I'm getting whiplash. But it's worth it in the end, because every time Michael answers a question, his attention lands on me for a breath before going back to the moderator.

Eventually, the question-and-answer portion begins, and Ginger has her chance to ask John Martigan her explosive question. Tension fills the room, thick and heavy. Everyone watches the volley of words bouncing back and forth between Ginger and Martigan with weighted anticipation.

I'm tempted to watch the exchange, but my eyes are fixed on Michael, who looks like he wants to crawl under the stage. He covers his mouth with his hand, and his cheeks are stained pink from what I can only guess is second-hand embarrassment.

I can see Michael's discomfort at the scene playing out before him. He's a private person and doesn't like to cause waves or drama. He looks like he hopes the floor will open and swallow him whole. Or that everyone will forget he's there all together.

"So you admit it?" Ginger grabs the microphone from the shaking volunteer.

"Admit what?" Martigan replies.

"That you sold the fans out?" Ginger's voice shifts, and I swear it's like watching a villain's origin story unfold. "How much did you get for your soul, Mr. Martigan? I hope it's worth it. Fans have long memories, sir."

Everything happens in a flash, and before I can blink, two security guards move in front of Ginger as the terrified volunteer skitters away. The audience bursts into conversation around us.

"Come with us." The guard motions to Ginger.

"You can't be serious?" I stand, ready to defend her honor. "She just asked a question."

"Don't make a scene," the other guard says. "Let's go."

"Fine." Ginger turns to us. "I'll text you. Finish the panel."

We try to speak, but she brushes us off with reassuring words before they lead her from the room. "Don't worry. I can handle this."

Absolute chaos erupts around us as Ginger is taken out. Fury races through me. I can't just stay here while my friend is hauled away like a goddamn criminal. I know she told us to finish the panel, but fuck that. I have to do something.

I spin to find Michael looking at me, his face pale, his expression apologetic. The moderator scrambles to regain control of the crowd.

"Come on." I tug Vicky's sleeve.

We head toward the exit, and I glance over my shoulder at Michael. He mouths something, but I'm too far away to make it out.

Once we reach the hallway, I pause against the wall "Well, that's gonna be all over the internet in five minutes."

Vicky is pale beside me. "Going viral twice in one weekend has to be a record, huh?" She pulls out her phone and checks the tags for the convention. "Shit. Look at this." She shows me her phone.

Sure enough, #VendettaShowdown is trending with clips of Martigan facing off against Ginger.

"What else could possibly go wrong?" I mutter to myself.

I text Beth, but there's no response. "Come on. We need to find Ginger."

Together, we go to the main security area and demand to see our friend. They stare blankly at us.

Finally, one speaks up. "Are you with the girl who took a

swing at a security guard in the off-limits area behind the photo ops?"

Vicky and I exchange a look. There's no fucking way.

If I were a betting woman, I'd put all my money on Beth being the center of that exchange. What are the odds of two of our friends being ousted the same day of the same convention?

"She's gone." The guard looks pleased with himself.

We thank them and leave, intent on searching the whole convention center until we find our friends. It's not until an hour later that I get a text from Beth, followed shortly by one from Ginger. We agree to meet at the bar in the hotel. When we walk into the lobby, I realize my mistake.

In all the commotion I forgot to text Michael after the panel. *Fuck.*

My one chance to get answers in person, gone.

I tell Vicky to go ahead and pull out my phone. I saved Michael's number last night, but I didn't have the courage to use it. I don't know if I want to after all that happened today.

Pushing aside my hesitation, I type a quick message.

(Me): *It's Ronnie. NoticeMeSenpai. Sorry about today.*

The message is marked *Read*, but there's no response. Not that I actually expected one. I stare at the phone, hoping for something. Even a *Fuck you* would be nice, but there's only silence.

I sigh and toss the phone aside. Damn it, I really need a drink now.

CHAPTER FIVE

I don't know why I expected him to respond. Maybe deep down, I thought we had a connection. I mean, his expression changed instantly when he saw me in the audience at the panel. He fucking *winked* at me.

Then shit hit the fan, and I haven't heard a damn thing since.

I flop down on my couch in a comfy sweatshirt and pajama bottoms. It's Saturday night, and I have a date with some steamy fan fiction. I open my tablet and find the bookmark leading me to "Silent Moon." It's one of VendettaDaddy's older titles and one of my favorites. I open a new page in my notebook and grab a pen.

It's been three weeks since the convention, and outside of work, I've been reading a shit ton of fan fiction. Everything by VendettaDaddy and some other authors with a similar writing style.

I have a notebook dedicated to the things I've uncovered, lines that fit the writing style of Michael DeHart. Direct quotes from the books, twisted just enough to sound original. I write down everything in different categories. After reading all of VendettaDaddy's fics, I'm certain of two things. One, I fucking love their work. Two, there's not a doubt in my mind this author is Michael DeHart.

The craziest part is VendettaDaddy hasn't updated since the convention. No notes, no notifications, radio silence. I've been watching closely, waiting for an email about an update. Some people might view this as an unhealthy obsession, but I feel like I'm a detective close to solving the biggest case of the century.

Most of the fangirls think I dive too deep into the meaning behind stories. But I like the complexity of storytelling. Even if the author didn't mean to write it a certain way, they created something with invisible and unintentional layers. Their subconscious jumps in to add a depth we as readers don't always consider. I like finding those hidden depths.

Maybe that's why I loved my English classes in college. I especially enjoy literary analysis where I can do deep dives into literature most people only enjoy at a superficial level. Granted, the educational establishment doesn't consider genre fiction to be any kind of literary mastery, but it influences entire generations and leaves a mark on society whether it has "literary merit" or not.

I list the films and the books in a spreadsheet, and whenever I find a connection, I note the fic and date it was uploaded, then I correlate it to the film or the book. There are several instances where a story deviates from the book material, making it seem original. Only it wasn't because it's used in the film. The problem with this is timing. In every instance, the film hadn't been released when the fic was updated, so those little changes were foretelling the film adaptation. I find another instance and mark it down.

"That makes six so far…" I chew on the end of my pen. "In the grand scheme of things, it's not a big deal. Maybe they just got lucky…but maybe…"

I decide to take a chance and leave a comment on the chapter in question. It's been out for ten years and barely gets any hits anymore, but I'm hoping VendettaDaddy will pick up on my hint.

Before I can second-guess myself, I put it out there.

(NoticeMeSenpai): *This is one of my all time favorite fics! It's always a treat to revisit when I'm in a funk. You have a talent for capturing the characters in a way that feels genuine. I just realized something though, and it has me wondering—did you know the movies would steal this scene for the third film? Hope you update your latest fic soon.*

I post it and move away from the screen, searching for the latest fic, the one where he talks about the raven-haired bombshell in the cantina. I question the wisdom of what I'm about to do but opt to take the chance. What's the worst that can happen—he ignores it?

I find the last chapter and open the comment box.

(NoticeMeSenpai): *This last update has me on the edge of my seat. What happens to the raven-haired bombshell we met in the cantina? I'm dying to know.*

After I post, I close the window. Exhaling sharply, I refocus my energy into something creative. I've ignored my own fan fiction for far too long, so I turn on a movie I've seen a hundred times for background noise and open the Word doc holding my latest story.

This one is a modern alternate universe with an enemies-to-lovers vibe. I made Colton and Lynnea rival coffee shop owners in the same neighborhood. It's cliché and fluffy, but I like it. Sometimes we need a familiar and fun escape to get us recharged and back in the groove.

I dive in, enjoying the characters' banter and sexual tension. Finally, I hit my stride and words are flowing.

Ping.

An email hits my inbox. I ignore it.

A few seconds later, another *ping* makes me stumble over a word. I grumble as I minimize the window and open my email folder. FandomArchive notification.

Holy shit. *Two* notifications from FandomArchive.

I open the first message. *VendettaDaddy has responded to your comment.*

My heart does a little fluttery flip in my chest. I close my email and reopen FandomArchive. Sure enough, I have two notifications. I open the first, and it's a response to my comment on "Silent Moon."

(VendettaDaddy): *I'm so glad you enjoy it. It's one of my favorites too. These characters are like old friends, so easy to write. That's quite an interesting theory—I'm sure you've got a hundred of those, don't you? I'll update mine when you update yours.*

I stare at the response and half choke with laughter. "You snarky little shit."

Instead of replying right away, I open the second notification. This response has my body humming and my mind racing.

(VendettaDaddy): *A fascinating side character, isn't she? I'd also like to know more about her. Do you think she'd be willing to talk to me? Maybe buy me a drink, tell me all her secrets? I feel like she deserves her own story, don't you?*

My heart fucking stops. It's him. There's no denying it.

I pull out my phone and open the text app, quickly searching for the last message I sent to Michael.

(Me): *Michael, stop playing games. I know it's you.*

The message notification shifts to *Read*, then the dots appear. I wait, squirming in my seat, unable to control the excitement thrumming through me.

(Michael)*: I was wondering how long it would take you.*

(Me)*: Take me to what?*

(Michael)*: Text me.*

Confusion and frustration pour through me in equal measure. I texted him that day, did he forget?

(Me)*: I texted you after that shit show of a panel.*

(Michael)*: I see that now.*

A pause before another message pops up.

(Michael): *In my defense, a lot happened that day, and it kinda got away from me. Doesn't excuse me being a dick and not responding though. Sorry about that.*

I can sympathize. That whole event turned into a circus. I didn't even stick around for the rest of the panel to see how it played out. My goal was to take care of my girl, but everything went sideways there too.

(Me): *You're forgiven but only because of the unexpected chaos. I had no idea Ginger's question was going to blow everything up like that.*

I slip into the kitchen and grab a drink while I wait for his response. It comes quicker than I expected.

(Michael): *Can I call you?*

My mind blanks as I stare at the four words on the screen. H-he wants to call me. Maybe this is a good thing? I don't know. I wasn't expecting any of this.

(Me): *What? No hot date keeping you up late on a Saturday night?*

(Michael): *Yeah, but she won't get off my lap, and it's making it hard to type.*

(Me): *You better be talking about a cat.*

(Michael): *Oh, the jealous type. I like it. Btw my mother's beagle takes offense at your assumption.*

(Me): *Please tell me her beagle's name is Snoopy.*

(Michael): *Close. It's Lucy. Now, about that call?*

A laugh escapes me, and I hit the call button. The line rings twice before he answers.

"Thank God. I was beginning to lose feeling in my arm from trying to text around her lazy body crushing me." He takes a deep breath. "Hello, Ronnie."

"You remember my name." I pop the cap on a Coke and retreat back to the couch. "I'm impressed."

"I remember a lot of things." Michael chuckles. "But your name reminds me of the Archie comic. I always liked Ronnie best. Please tell me it's short for Veronica."

"It is." I curl up on the couch and put the phone on speaker, then rest it on my chest. "I was always more of a Betty fan, personally. Hot take, but Betty and Jughead were always endgame for me."

"You have a lot of interesting hot takes." Michael's voice is deeper than I remember. "You know I have to ask—how did you know it was me?"

"What was you?" I sip my drink, acting coy even though we both damn well know this is turning into a flirtation.

"How long did it take you to figure out I write as VendettaDaddy?" Michael's voice is damn near sinful over the phone. He should narrate his own books; they'd be thirst traps in a week.

"Well, you have a horrible poker face," I tease, ignoring the way my blood simmers at the sound of his voice. "The moment I gave you the author name for those fics, you looked like a deer caught in the headlights. Granted, you recovered quickly, and I didn't think anything at the time, but later…yeah, it was a dead giveaway."

"Quite the little detective," Michael says with a laugh.

"But the update to your fic the day we met, where you mention a raven-haired bombshell in Ronnie's cantina…" I tsk. "It was a little heavy handed, don't you think?"

"I don't know, I thought she fit the scene." Michael hesitates for a moment before adding, "You were the perfect inspiration for a character meant to distract our hero from his purpose."

My heart thrums. "Are you saying I'm distracting you?"

"No. I'm saying you're a beautiful and welcome distraction."

Michael's words ring in my ear, and I'm overheating.

"I thought you didn't like to mix business with pleasure, Michael?" My voice drops into a sultrier range.

"Am I your employer?"

"No."

"Are you my employer?"

"No."

"Good. There's no conflict of interest." Michael sighs on the other end of the line, and I imagine him stretching like a panther, pleased with himself.

"Let me get this straight." I put the brakes on because this could quickly get out of control. "Are you hitting on me?"

"Maybe. Is it working?"

"That's beside the point." I shake my head. "What do you really want?"

"The million-dollar question." Michael laughs. "Honestly, you intrigue me. You're gorgeous, witty, quick on the draw, and talented as hell. It's an intoxicating combination, and I want to know more about you."

"Does this have anything to do with me figuring out your deep dark secret?"

"Honestly, I'm impressed anyone figured it out after all these years. I wasn't open about it, but it seems like you did some extensive reading to find the clues I left—albeit inadvertently, in some cases."

"The scenes from your fics that were in the films? I knew it!"

"Most people don't make the connection, especially since they don't look at release dates of the fics versus the films." Michael makes a noncommittal noise and presses forward. "Where do you live?"

"Why?" I ask, suddenly suspicious. He's gorgeous and I would jump him in an instant, but that doesn't mean I want him to know every detail of my life. Not yet at least.

"I'd like to meet in person, maybe have coffee."

"And you're willing to fly here to make that happen?"

"Wherever *here* is, yes," Michael says with confidence.

"North of Saint Louis, a town called Alton, Illinois."

"Are you free the weekend after next?"

His voice lures me into temptation, and I'm weak, so fucking weak.

"Yeah."

"Good. I'll fly in and get a car. Give me a time and place, and I'll be there."

"Promise me one thing?"

I hear his deep inhale through the line. "Anything."

"You'll update your fic this week and post it before our date."

"Your wish is my command." Michael laughs again. "I gotta take Lucy for a walk. She's impatient."

"Well, thanks for this. I was worried you would ghost me."

"Not a chance. See you in two weeks, Ronnie."

"Good night, Michael." I hesitate before calling out, "Keep him in line, Lucy."

His laughter is the last thing I hear before the line goes silent.

I stare at my phone. Did that really just happen?

Holy shit. I have a date with Michael DeHart in two weeks! It's my ultimate fantasy come to life.

Reality sinks into my silly brain, and the high I'm riding turns into a free fall. Oh fuck. What if this is some kind of sick joke? What if he gets off on leading on fans?

No. I've been a fan long enough to know he's not that type of person.

And I'm a firm believer in giving people the benefit of the

doubt.

But I'm questioning my life choices.

I'll sleep on it and see where I am in the morning. Tonight, I'll take it as a win and celebrate it as such.

CHAPTER SIX

I spent the whole night tossing and turning. I love sleep. I can sleep anywhere, anytime. But last night, I could *not* turn off my brain. My conversation with Michael replayed, over and over, in my head.

Am I crazy? Obviously, I'm not the only one who felt the instant connection. That explains the tension humming through the phone last night. I could have talked to him for hours, but I have a million questions I'd rather ask in person than over the phone or via text. No, I want to look into those baby blues and lose myself in his company as I pick his brain.

Geezus. I'm falling apart. I barely know this man. Yeah, I've been low-key obsessed with his work for years, but we've only spoken twice and met once. We can't jump into a whole relationship with only off-the-charts chemistry? Can we?

By five a.m., I give up all pretense of sleep and start my day. I spend a few hours cleaning my apartment, doing laundry, deep cleaning the bathroom—things I've been putting off for far too long. And I have Michael DeHart to thank for kickstarting my anxiety into overdrive so I'll try to drown it out with menial tasks.

I collapse on the couch around noon, starving and depleted of motivation. My apartment has never looked so fucking great, and I bask in it for a moment before nagging uncertainty resurfaces with a vengeance.

Fuck it, I need to talk to *someone* about this.

Running through the fangirls, I settle on Ginger. She's the glue of our group, always lending an ear and offering support. I haven't spoken to her since we had cocktails in the hotel lounge after the panel from hell.

When I open my text message app, I see Michael's name and my heart flips. I need to get this man out of my system. This is getting out of hand. Once I have Ginger's text thread open, I send her a heads-up to see if she's available.

(Me): *Hey, are you busy?*

A few seconds pass, then her response pops up.

(Ginger): *Hey! Not busy at all. What's up?*

(Me): *I need to talk if you have time. Something happened.*

I barely hit send before my phone is ringing.

"Girl, you can't send a text like that. If it's an emergency, just call," Ginger says, her tone panicked.

"Sorry, didn't mean to freak you out," I assure her. "It's just…I have a problem, and you might be the only one who can talk me through it."

"What's the problem, darlin'?" Ginger asks. The panic in her tone is gone now, replaced by curiosity.

"So you remember my whole run-in with Michael DeHart at the convention?"

"Yeah, you two kind of connected over fan fiction." Ginger pauses. "Why?"

"Well, after the whole panel explosion—"

"I'd hardly call it an explosion."

"Girl, it was full damage control after they led you out of the auditorium. Vicky and I spent an hour looking for you, only to find out Beth was kicked out of the convention for assaulting a security guard." I scoff. "I'd say we left a mark."

"Well, it's been fixed now, so no harm, no foul."

"Wait." I stop her. "What do you mean *it's fixed*? Shit like that doesn't just *get fixed* without some major damage mitigation." My mind spins at the possibilities. "Did you strike a deal with

John Martigan? Is that why he issued a public apology and backtracked his changes to the new film?" I damn near screech into the phone.

"I–I can't discuss it."

"Ginger Darling, you're holding out on me." I jump to my feet and pace the living room.

"I'm holding out on everyone." She hisses. "Listen, when I can talk about it, you and the other fangirls will be the first to know. I promise. But just trust me, I can't talk about it right now."

"Fine." I huff, irritated she's keeping secrets from me—from us. "Whatever it is, it better be worth it."

"Oh, it's fucking worth it." She's damn near purring. Now I'm even more curious. "But tell me what's going on with you and Mr. DeHart."

"It's complicated."

"Then start at the beginning," she says. "I've got all day."

"Okay. So you know how we talked about fan fiction at the signing?"

"Yeah."

"Well…" I hesitate for a moment. "I gave him a recommendation for a fic I knew would work perfectly in the upcoming film, even though it deviated from the original material."

"Oh, yes, I remember you telling me about it. Wasn't it 'The Revolutionary' by VendettaDaddy?" Ginger sounds intrigued.

"Yes. I gushed about it, but it was weird because he gave me the strangest look when I told him the title of the fic and the author."

"So?" Ginger asks.

"I didn't think anything about it until later when I was reading an update." I put her on speaker and pull up the fic in my notes. "Have you read the latest update?"

"No, but you won't spoil anything for me. What did it say?"

"He was referencing a new secondary character in the cantina Ransom frequents. Here's the quote, 'Raven curls, tied loose, and smoking hot curves that could thaw a pirate's heart.'"

"Uh…wait. No, that doesn't make sense…" Ginger murmurs under her breath. "Wait, are you implying what I think you are?"

"I'm not *implying* anything, Ginger." Excitement floods me, and my heart races. "I'm telling you Michael DeHart writes fan fiction of his own fucking books."

"No fucking way." Ginger squeals into the phone. "That's insane, and you're basing it all on a single quote in a recent update. You don't have proof."

I grin. "That's where you're wrong."

"What the hell are you talking about?" Ginger sighs.

"Okay, well the quote was the first clue, but what about the name of the cantina in the fic. 'Ronnie's'? The name wasn't even mentioned until the update where he mentions the raven-haired beauty."

"Circumstantial," Ginger says simply.

"When I got home from the convention, I reread every fic written by VendettaDaddy. I made notes for lines and scenes that sounded like Michael's writing."

"Honey, it's fan fiction—we borrow the creator's words all the time." Ginger tries to convince me I'm wrong.

"True. But do they use those words *before* they're in the creative works of the original author?"

"What do you mean?" Ginger asks, her interest piqued further.

"I mean, there were lines in the fics from the *film* versions, only they were posted long before the films released."

"You're kidding me?" Ginger sounds incredulous.

"I'm not. I have the receipts." Then I drop the bomb on her. "But those don't matter."

"Why not?"

"Because Michael called me last night and admitted he writes fan fiction as VendettaDaddy."

An unholy screech from Ginger makes my ears ring. "He called you?"

"Actually, I called him."

"You had his fucking phone number?"

"He gave it to me at the convention, on the first day."

"And you conveniently forgot to fucking mention this delicious little tidbit?" She's about to implode, I can hear it.

"With everything going on, I didn't want to add to the chaos. I'm sorry."

"It doesn't matter now. What does matter is you spoke to him last night?" Ginger's excitement bleeds into her tone. "What did you talk about?"

"I called him out on being VendettaDaddy." I frown. "He didn't try to deny it, and he was impressed I figured it out."

"And that's all?" Ginger sounds disappointed.

"Of course that's not all." I sigh. "I wouldn't have called you in a freaking panic over just that."

"Well, no, I've seen you handle online bullies and trolls without effort." I hear the tapping of her nails on a table through the phone. Suddenly the sound stops. "Did he flirt with you during this call?"

"A little." I bite my lip. "He…well, he offered to fly here to meet me for coffee."

"Wait." Ginger actually squeals this time, her delight infectious. "He offered to fly halfway across the country to meet you for *coffee*?" The word drips with innuendo.

"Why are you saying that like a euphemism?"

"Because it is, darlin'. That man isn't flying to catch up about fan fiction over coffee. No, ma'am. He's hoping this turns into something more."

Dear fucking space Jesus. I…does he really want to have sex with me? I mean, I wouldn't say no—that *would* be crazy—but my conscience doesn't allow me to be a wham-bam-thank-you-sir kind of gal. I like to be romanced, and I'm not scared of commitment. But is that what I want from *him*?

I nervously lick my lips. If anyone can help me figure this out, it's Ginger.

"I don't know about this, Ginger. I'm not a one-night stand girl."

"None of us are, until we're faced with a unique fine-as-hell proposition, looking like he just stepped out of our wettest dream."

Her words make me chuckle, but they make sense.

"So if John Martigan asked you to meet him for dinner, you would?"

Ginger goes strangely silent, then she clears her throat. "Yes, I would."

"And would you sleep with him after that one date?" I ask sincerely.

"Damn it, Ronnie. Why did you turn this on me?" Ginger swears and mutters beneath her breath, and it makes me laugh. "I'm not in your situation to gauge the mood. If the vibe's off, no, probably not. Doesn't stop me from thinking about it."

"Makes sense." I flop back against the cushions. "Do you think I should cancel?"

"No, don't cancel. You've already done the work, why not enjoy the payoff?" She purrs. "Maybe he'll take you to dinner too, make a whole day of it. I mean, he's already in town to see you."

"You're right." A couple of ideas for things to do pop in my head. Things that don't involve fucking. "I'll see if we can spend the whole day together."

"Then, if the vibe is right, you'll know if you want to go all the way."

"Why do you make this sound so sordid?" I ask with a snort. "We're just meeting up to discuss our mutual love of fan fiction."

"Honey, if you believe that, I have a bridge in Brooklyn to sell you." Ginger laughs. "But seriously, just enjoy your date. Who knows? Maybe something unexpected will come from it. Just be yourself, and be open to a new experience."

"You don't think he's trying to lure me into some kind of sex cult, do you?"

Ginger's laugh fills the line. "You and your wild imagination. That's what makes you a fantastic author, you know that, right?"

"You're a fantastic author too, don't forget." I join the laughter. "That makes us equally crazy."

"Excentric, darling, not crazy." Her voice softens. "And don't worry, I'm here if you need me. Just send me a text if you need to be rescued. I'll call with a family emergency."

"You'd do that for me?" My heart aches at her kindness.

"Of course. We have to do this shit for each other. It's the only way to stay safe out there." She continues, "Have a safe word in your text window ready so all you have to do is hit send."

"Like 'pineapple?'" I chuckle.

"Exactly. We'll use that." Ginger sighs. "I'll admit, I'm a little jealous. You're going on a date with Michael DeHart. You'd better call me the next day with all the juicy details."

"You know I will." I smile as a weight lifts from my shoulders. "Thanks, Ginger. I owe you."

"Anytime, girl, and you don't owe me a thing."

"I'll keep you posted," I say, boosted with confidence.

"You'd better. Love ya."

"Love you too."

We exchange goodbyes, and I end the call.

Imbued with a new sense of purpose and determination, I text Michael.

(Me): *About our date. Let's spend the whole day together. I want to show you around town.*

A few minutes later, his response appears.

(Michael): *I look forward to it. I'll text you when I arrive. Send me the first stop.*

My heart does a little flip. I can't believe I'm actually doing this.

CHAPTER SEVEN

I glance at the clock behind the register at the small coffee shop, and the nervous excitement that's been humming through me the past two weeks becomes a constant buzz in my ear. My leg taps beneath the table. I start to fidget. He told me he'd be here at noon.

Instead of harping on the time or who I'm about to meet, I focus on tangible things in the room. The leather of my chair. The paper cup beneath my fingers. The gentle rock music playing through speakers, occasionally garbled by the rumble of the coffee grinder. The sweet, earthy scent of coffee and rich pastries.

This is my favorite spot, not too busy and off the beaten path in Alton. So many good memories here—meeting friends, writing sprints to finish a fic. I figure this is the best place to meet Michael. It's public but not overly busy, and it has a writer's energy.

This whole scenario feels kind of crazy, like the plot of an alternate universe fanfic or something. I have no idea what to expect, but I plan to enjoy it regardless. Ginger's words linger in the back of my mind. *He's not meeting you just for coffee.*

I chuckle. She's got a wild imagination, thinking he'd fly from Los Angeles to St. Louis just for a piece of this. I mean, he's Michael DeHart, he could have coffee with any fangirl his heart desires.

But he chose me. I bask in the possibility for a few seconds, and my heart takes flight. Why was our connection so memorable he's willing to go to such lengths to pursue it?

Good thing I have a whole day planned to keep us busy.

The door opens, and I turn to find the man of my fucking dreams walking through the doorway. Goddamn. My jaw drops as he enters the shop, and I take in the full picture. He's wearing khakis with sneakers and a light blue polo that clings to his broad shoulders and chest like a wet T-shirt. Holy shit. I mean, it's damn close to indecent. How dare he come in here looking like a three course meal and a late night snack?

His blue eyes fix on me, and he grins.

My ovaries do some kind of little dance while my mind screams "Take me, I'm yours." I manage to compose myself enough to stand when he approaches the table.

"Ronnie, you look gorgeous." He takes my outstretched hand and kisses the back of it. What kind of chivalrous bullshit is this? Thank you, I'll take another.

"Th-thank you." My tongue trips over the words. "You look…good."

"Just good?" He arches a brow. "Guess I'll have to try harder next time."

Next time? I shake my head to clear my thoughts. *Get it together, girl.*

"Would you like some coffee or something to eat?" I gesture toward the menu over the counter. "They have delicious sandwiches here. I thought we'd grab a bite before heading out."

Michael deviates his attention from the menu to my face. "Head out?" He smirks. "Where are you taking me?"

"The community park. There are some nice trails, and it's not too hot today. It's pretty this time of year."

"Sounds like fun." He turns back to the menu.

I step forward, getting ready to order a club sandwich when I feel the heat of him surround me as he steps in line behind me.

"How's the turkey melt?" he says against my ear.

Gooseflesh breaks out over my skin, and I swallow an involuntary moan. This fucker knows exactly what he's doing. I manage to ignore the heat racing through me and reply.

"It's good, but if you're craving something hot, the Reuben is divine." I add extra emphasis to *divine*, and judging by his sharp inhale, I think I nailed it. Two can play this game, sir.

We place our order, and Michael insists on paying. I let him, since technically he initiated this date. Is it a date? We never established what this is supposed to be, but honestly, does it matter? I mean, he called it a date in his text message. It might as well be a date with all the sexual tension simmering between us. I'll savor it while it lasts.

After exchanging small talk about his trip and the weather, we enjoy our sandwiches and coffee. It's nice. Relaxed. Like two old friends catching up after years apart. I try not to ask too many personal questions. I'm enjoying how the details of our pasts slowly unravel, like a candle melting rather than a kid ripping open presents on Christmas morning.

When we leave the coffee shop, Michael holds the door for me as I step into the humidity. It always steals my breath, but today, I'm not sure I can blame my breathlessness solely on the weather.

"Is it within walking distance?" Michael asks, taking in the area.

"No, we'll have to drive. My apartment is a block away, so we can grab my car and go to the park from there."

"No need." Michael unlocks a car nearby. "We can take my rental."

I glance at the car and laugh. "Really? You needed a Mustang convertible?"

"What?" He shrugs and gives a charming little grin. "It was

all they had left."

"Sure." I shake my head as he opens the door for me. I climb in, and damn, it feels nice. My little Ford sedan is roomier, but when he starts the Mustang and the rumble hits me through the floorboards, I sigh. A girl could get used to this.

Michael looks at me from the driver's seat. "You good?"

"Never better." I clear my throat. "Just go straight until you reach the stoplight."

Somehow, I manage to keep my shit together for the duration of the drive. He maneuvers the car well, mindful of the directions as I give them. We make a decent team, and once we reach the community park, he finds a shady spot to leave the car.

He takes in everything as we meander down a nature path. It's quiet today. There's a festival down by the river that's drawn most of the crowds. I considered taking him to it, but I wanted a spot where we could talk yet still be in public.

As expected, the conversation turns to writing, and I'm humming with anticipation. He tells me about his early career, how much he loved creating the *Space Vendetta* series. He admits to dabbling in other genres, but nothing else felt comfortable. His father originally came up with the idea for the series, and they did a lot of brainstorming to build the world. It ultimately became his after his dad died, and he threw himself into his writing.

"I'm sure he'd be proud of you, seeing how far you've come with *Space Vendetta.*" I offer the small consolation.

"Yeah. I do have a few regrets."

"Regrets?" I ask as we stop beneath a pagoda by the pond.

He leans on the pillar. "Yeah. If I could do it over, there are some changes I would make."

"Like what?" I rest against the railing and search his face.

There's a far-off look in his eye, but it shifts as he turns to me. "When my series was picked up for publication, I made some concessions, things the publisher didn't like about the direction of my story. If I wanted it published, I had to make those adjustments."

"What?" I huff indignantly. "That's bullshit."

"That's publishing." He shrugs. "I didn't let it drag me down too much. They let me keep the major things I wanted, but a few minor details were scrubbed."

"Why didn't you put them in anyway?" My rebellious nature kicks in.

"It wasn't worth the battle." His smile widens. "Besides, isn't that what we have fan fiction for?"

"You wrote those fics because the publisher wouldn't let you put the scenes in the books?" I gape at him, impressed as hell. "I'm sure they *loved* that."

"They have no idea. I've never told them. In fact, I've never told anyone." He reaches out to pluck a stray leaf from my hair. "Until you."

"You didn't tell me. I figured it out." I narrow my eyes at him. "The girl in the cantina, you knew I'd find it."

Michael nods. "I'm sure you would have figured it out eventually anyway, but when you came to my table and told me there was a fanfic you thought would work well in the series, I knew you were a kindred spirit."

"Why's that?" I ask, mesmerized by his revelation.

He takes a deep breath. "Because that fic was originally part of the series. I had to cut it during edits, and it broke my fucking heart to deviate from my plan. I loved the subplot so much, but my publisher thought it was too risqué since the books had been opted for film."

"I knew it." I'm a jumble of emotion, but excitement wins. "I knew the moment I read it that it fit perfectly in the world you created, like those two pieces were meant to be together."

"That's why I trust you with my secret." Michael takes a step closer. "You understand the story and how it all ties together. You see the potential."

My heart flutters as his scent fills me—a warm woodsy cologne mixing with the earthy scent of the gardens around us. I straighten, my body humming with need. I want him to touch me. Kiss me. Something. Anything to end this building tension.

I hold his gaze and lick my lips. "Can I tell you something?"

The sky blue of his eyes darkens. "Anything."

A strange boldness creeps over me, and I lean close, placing my hand on his chest.

His sharp inhale tells me all I need to know. He feels the same fucking thing. He feels this desperate simmering attraction between us.

"I love reading your fics, not just your books." I press my hand more firmly against his racing heart. "I think your fics are raw, unfiltered, sexy as hell."

"Sexy, huh?" His voice rumbles through my touch.

"Most men aren't very in-tune with their characters' emotions during sex scenes, but you find a way to weave everything together and balance it."

His body tenses. His eyes shift to midnight.

"I–I can't tell you how many times I've thought about them…" I let the implication dangle in the air.

"Ronnie, you can't leave me hanging like that." His voice is low and deep and sexy as fuck.

I rise on my tiptoes and lean even closer. "I think about them when I touch myself."

A growl rumbles from deep in his chest, and he catches me by the waist, pulling me against him. I clutch his arms to hold myself steady.

"If we're being honest here, Veronica, I have a confession of my own." He leans down, his lips teasing my ear. "I can't tell you how many times I got off reading your work. The sinful, sexy actions of my own characters, taken in a direction I could never have dreamed, and yet, it felt right, like an extension of my own subconscious."

I squeak, unable to form a coherent thought.

Oh, fuck. I think we just crossed a line.

I've never been more relieved.

"When I saw you at the convention, I couldn't stop staring. You looked good enough to eat." His lips tease my ear as his confession wrecks my self-control. "But when you told me your pen name—the author who wrote the fics I adore—I'd never been more turned on in my entire fucking life."

"Michael," I murmur as he draws back. Our eyes lock, and I'm drowning in him. "If you don't fucking kiss me, I might explode."

"If I kiss you now, I won't be able to stop." Michael wraps his hand around the back of my neck. His thumb brushes the pulse point in my throat. "If we were somewhere private, I would show you exactly what I think of while I read your fics."

Evidently, I forgot we were in public, in view of everyone walking the trails. Shit. I manage to wrangle my hormones under control and withdraw from his embrace.

"Come on," I say, grabbing him by the hand. He links his fingers with mine as we trek back to the car.

Michael asks for directions, and I give them. It's the only conversation we can muster.

My body is a live wire. I'm so close to combustion, one touch could set me off. Judging by the tension in his shoulders and his steady breathing, he's also struggling to keep things under control.

We pull up in front of my building. As I unlock the front door, I look at Michael.

"What about dinner?" I ask, eyes wide. "I had it planned."

"I can think of something better than dinner." Michael pins me against the door, his expression ravenous.

"What would that be?" I say, pushing the door open behind me and slipping down the hall.

"Dessert." He closes the door and stalks closer. I'm fumbling with my keys but manage to find the right one as I reach my door.

Michael cages me against it, leans into me. I want to surrender. My hand shakes as I slide the lock free. The door opens, and I barely step forward before Michael catches me by the waist, spins me around, and kisses me like he's a starving man and I'm the first sweet he's tasted in his entire fucking life.

CHAPTER EIGHT

Oh, sweet fucking mercy. His mouth slides against mine, and all coherent thought leaves my brain.

I wrap my arms around his neck as he pushes me into the apartment and kicks the door closed behind us.

My fingers thread through his hair. So soft, so thick. His breath brushes my cheek as he draws back, just enough to take in the space around us.

"Bedroom?" he asks, peppering kisses along my jaw in slow succession.

I disentangle myself from him to find my bearings. Grabbing his hand, I tug him to the bedroom, just off the living room. His eyes are hot, dark, fixed directly on me, and I've never felt so goddamn sexy.

Seizing the moment, I slip my shoes off and begin a slow striptease.

His gaze follows me, predatory and ravenous.

I slide my shorts off, stepping out of them as I back away.

With every step I take, he closes the gap with one of his own, stalking me closer to the bed.

I revel in the power I have over him. I have his undivided attention, and it's playing into every fantasy I've ever had. For years, I was self-conscious. Curvy girls aren't attractive, they said. But the way Michael devours me with his eyes proves that's a fucking lie.

He's about to pounce, I can sense it.

Slowly, I tug my shirt over my head. My breasts bounce. A

groan slips from him.

I make the mistake of laughing, and he's on me in an instant.

Michael snatches me by the waist, his body pressed against mine from hip to shoulder. His heat sinks into me, and I can't wait to have him on me, inside me.

"You look like one of those pinup girls from the fifties," Michael whispers in my ear, his mouth leaving heat in its wake as it trails across my jaw and lingers against my throat. "It's driving me crazy."

I chuckle, but it dissolves into a moan as his teeth rake over my pulse. I'm fucking soaking wet, and once he realizes, it'll be game on.

He runs his hands over my hips, teasing bare skin as he hooks his thumbs into my panties and tugs them off. He sinks to his knees, dropping slowly, pressing kisses to my breast, my stomach, my thigh. Then he's looking up at me, my panties around my ankles, and he grins.

"Michael," I murmur.

He grips my ankles, both hands sliding up my legs in a tantalizing journey over my skin. My legs part, and his expression never wavers. Fingers brush the seam of my pussy. His eyes drift closed.

"You're already wet for me."

He opens his eyes and pushes a finger inside, deep. I whimper.

"So fucking wet."

My legs tremble, and the breath in my lungs catches as he brings his finger to his lips, licking it clean.

"Fuck, baby, you taste so sweet." He stands, pulling off his shirt and tossing it aside.

I'm distracted by the sheer breadth of him. His broad shoulders taper to a narrow waist, and I run my hands over his washboard abs, up across his chest.

He toes off his shoes and removes his khakis in less than a second.

“On the bed, vixen.”

My eyes snap to his at his sinfully appropriate pet name. Something melts deep in my chest. I obey, giving him a full view of my ass as I climb onto the bed.

He pins me on my back to the mattress, hands around my wrists, eyes locked. I swallow hard. My body instinctively arches toward his.

His skin is hot where we touch. His bare thighs slide against mine, creating a delicious friction. He kisses me again, a tangle of desire and desperation.

He somehow manages to remove my bra and palms my breasts. His thumbs brush my nipples, and a zing of longing ignites a hum in the pit of my stomach.

His fabric-covered cock rubs my clit. I grasp the waistband around his hips, needing nothing more than to have him deep inside me, right fucking now.

Michael catches my wrist. “Not yet, vixen.” He smiles against my lips. “Let me give you what you need.”

He thoroughly explores me. His hands drift over my body, molding to every curve, squeezing, taking in every part of me. His mouth follows, leaves nothing untouched.

I’m thrumming with need and impatience.

My thighs part as he slides his hand between them, cupping my pussy. He inhales deeply before his mouth descends on me, and everything around me shatters into nothingness. He sucks me into his mouth, his tongue dancing over my clit, fingers teasing my entrance. There is only him, that wicked mouth, those goddamned talented fingers. My entire existence is rewired in this instant.

I arch my hips against his mouth, and he redoubles his efforts. He devours my pussy, worshipping it with every stroke of his tongue. Two fingers slide deep, filling me. He moves them and finds the sweet spot that makes my toes curl.

A gasp rips from my throat as the first flutters of my orgasm take flight. He continues, focusing everything on my pleasure. I run my fingers through his hair, careful not to pull too hard or grind myself into his face.

He moans. A ripple of excitement tumbles through me.

He shifts his pace slightly, and then hums, long and deep. The sound reverberates through me. My breath catches in my chest as the orgasm rolls over me, an insistent relief that leaves me boneless on the bed.

Michael rocks back, a slick grin on his wicked mouth. He wipes it away with the back of his hand.

"You look like a Colton, but deep down, you're a Ransom," I murmur, half dazed from my climax.

He laughs, but it fades as he covers me with his body. Chest to chest, thigh to thigh, he meets my gaze, cups my face in his hand.

He kisses me, and I taste myself on his tongue. It's incredibly sexy.

I inhale sharply, and he deepens the kiss, rocking his hips toward mine. His thick bulge rubs my swollen clit, and I gasp into his mouth.

"Condom?" he asks.

"Top drawer." I motion vaguely to the left.

He moves away for half a breath, but before I have time to miss him, he's back. He makes quick work of removing his underwear and sliding the condom on. Then he's between my thighs, begging for permission.

Like he fucking needs it.

I wrap my legs around his waist, and he pushes inside me. One thrust, sliding so fucking deep, I swear I see stars.

My fingers bite into his arms, keeping me steady. I'm afraid I'll float away if I don't. He feels so fucking good.

Then he moves, and my world shatters again. Sensations tumble through me, and I drown in him.

Michael fucks me slowly, his kisses tender and gentle.

I want more. I want to *feel* everything.

"I won't break," I murmur against his mouth as my hands slide down to grab his ass. "I need you to fuck me."

In response, he growls and thrusts into me. The momentum shifts, and I cling to him as he pushes harder, faster, pressing me into the mattress, stealing my breath with every kiss, with every delicious, punishing drive of his cock. I hold tight.

Then, without warning, Michael slows to a stop.

Before I can protest, he rolls, and I'm on top, straddling his hips, his cock pushing even deeper. My eyes drift closed at the fullness. I bite my lip and reopen my eyes to meet his gaze.

His hands slide up my hips, teasing the weight of my breasts. He gives them a gentle squeeze and pleasure shoots straight to my core.

"Ride me." He licks his lips, pupils blown wide, desire painted all over his tanned skin. "I want to see your face as you take your pleasure."

Something warm and gooey unlocks inside me, but I don't want to look at it too closely. Not right now. Instead, I focus on his words and rock experimentally.

His grip on my hips tightens. I keep moving, back and forth, round and round. Finding the motions that make my body sing, the ones that earn a satisfied gasp from Michael.

I'm learning his expressions, his sounds, and when I hit his sweet spot, I know immediately and use it to my advantage. I fall into a delicious rhythm, and we're both slick with sweat and panting. He runs his hands over me, eyes dazed with need.

He's close, I can tell.

I lean back, using my body as leverage with every stroke. Michael presses his thumb to my clit in gentle circles, and a cry rips from me as my climax hits. Harder than before, it rushes through me like a tidal wave, leaving me soaked and heaving against him.

I barely register my surroundings, but I see an expression of pure bliss on his face. Lip tucked between his teeth, eyes closed, his own climax pulls him beneath the waves.

Sated, I try to shift my weight off him, but he pulls me down and presses a kiss to my lips.

"That was pretty fucking amazing," Michael says softly.

"Yeah, it was." I lean back to study his face. "Thanks."

"For what?"

"Coming to Alton."

He grins. "You're welcome."

"Ginger was right."

His brow furrows in confusion.

"My friend Ginger said you weren't flying halfway across the country just to have coffee and take a walk in the park."

His laugh rumbles through me, and I can't stop a smile.

"She was right."

"You planned to seduce me this whole time?" I ask, pretending to be insulted.

Michael holds me tightly to him. "I planned to seduce you the first moment I saw you."

"Mighty bold of you, sir. I could have been a psycho."

"I was willing to take the chance." He kisses the tip of my nose. "Glad I did."

"Smart-ass."

I climb off him and head for the bathroom. He follows and disposes of the condom, then comes behind me, wrapping his arms around my waist as we face the mirror.

It's oddly domestic. Sexy as hell. I could get used to this.

My heart clenches at the question of what happens next.

"Let's shower and then grab some dinner." He kisses my temple.

"Then what?" I ask, turning to him. "What happens next?"

"I was thinking I would stay the night, make love to you a few more times, and tomorrow, we hop on a flight to LA?"

Michael's words slowly sink into my brain.

"You lost me at that last part." I shake my head. "We? As in you and me?"

"Yeah." He runs his fingers through his hair. "I know it's last minute, but I promise it'll be worth it. Will you come to LA with me? Just for a couple of days."

I do some quick mental math and realize I have plenty of comp time at work. They won't die without me in the office for a few days.

When I nod, relief fills Michael's face. "You'll come?" he asks, seeming to need to hear the words aloud.

"Yeah—" I don't get to finish the sentence because Michael is kissing me again.

I fall into his embrace and again surrender to his charm. After he coaxes another orgasm out of me in the shower, we make it to dinner.

This whirlwind romance has my head spinning, but I will enjoy every fucking minute because there's no telling how long it will last or what's waiting in LA.

All I know is, I'm falling in love with Michael DeHart, and the last thing I need is a broken heart.

CHAPTER NINE

The flight to Los Angeles passed without incident, though I found it difficult to keep my hands to myself on the plane. Michael booked two first class tickets, which must have cost a small fortune, but he didn't even blink.

We sipped champagne and shared earbuds as we watched a movie on his phone. It was strange, this level we've unlocked in our whirlwind romance. I'm not uncomfortable with it. In fact, I'm strangely at ease with the possibilities.

My boss had no issues with my last-minute time-off request, especially when I reminded her I had a shit ton of time accrued and deserved this. She pried, trying to get an explanation about why I needed the sudden break. I threw out the family emergency excuse, and the questions stopped. I hate lying, but I don't need the nosiness right now. Not from her, and certainly not from my gossipy coworkers.

It took me practically no time to pack. Michael assured me I only needed enough clothes for a few days, and anything I forgot, he would gladly pick up if I found myself in desperate need.

I tried to contact Ginger, but she didn't respond. I wanted someone to know where I was, so I sent a text asking her to call me when she could. It wasn't until the flight took off that I realized she wouldn't be able to get ahold of me for a few hours. All I could do was pray she didn't freak out when I didn't answer my phone.

When we finally land in LA, Michael puts on his backpack

and carries my suitcase off the plane. Once we reach the terminal, he takes my hand.

"Freaking out yet?" He leads me through the crowds.

"Not yet." I glance around, taking it all in. The farthest west I've ever been is Colorado. California has always been a distant land, a fairy tale place with a price tag too high for me to pay.

A car is waiting for us. Michael slips his arm around me in the back seat as we head to his home.

"I hate driving here," he confesses. "One of the perks of having money is hiring a driver. I don't know what I would do without Mack."

The driver tips his head toward us through the rearview mirror. "Likewise, sir."

"Stop it, Mack. Ronnie doesn't need a show." He grins. "We're old friends. He bailed me out years ago, when I first got to LA. A cab driver in Hollywood. I offered him a job, and he jumped at the opportunity."

"So do you keep a full staff?" I ask, wondering how rich he really is. Not that it matters, but it must be expensive as hell to live here, let alone have a personal driver.

"No. Just Mack." Michael blushes. "I clean my house, cook my own meals. My mom didn't raise me to rely on someone else. Having a driver is an indulgence, one my mom doesn't really appreciate, but on days when I'm stressed out, it's worth its weight in gold."

"Your mom sounds like a smart woman." I take his hand and lace our fingers together.

"She is." Michael leans back and looks at me. "I'll be honest, I didn't think you'd come."

"Why not?" I suppress an urge to flirt with him. There's no divider between us and Mack, and I don't want to make the poor man uncomfortable.

"Because most women I know don't like surprises." Michael regards me for a long moment. "You seem to live for the moment. I like it."

"You like that I have no self-control if adventure calls?"

"I think you know what you want and what you don't." He leans closer, his voice lowering. "You take control. That's sexy as hell."

"Well, it's hard to say no to my standing crush since the tender age of sixteen."

His brows shoot into his hairline. "You've had a crush on me for how long?"

I mentally do the math. "Fifteen years, give or take. I fell for you the moment I saw your picture on my brand-new copy of the first *Space Vendetta* novel."

His cheeks turn a lovely shade of pink. "Goddamn it, Ronnie. You're making me feel old."

I reassure him with a pat on the hand. "We're not that far apart—I'm thirty-four."

"I'm forty-one." He rakes a hand over his face, which only deepens the pink to a deeper shade of rose.

"Damn. You've reached retirement age, might as well put in for social security." I laugh at the murderous look he gives me.

"Don't start." He digs a finger into my side, finding the one spot more ticklish than my feet.

I squeal, squirming in my seat as he relentlessly runs his fingers over the ribs on my side.

"Okay, okay." I put my hands up, breathless from laughter. "I'll stop."

"Good." He tucks me against his side, and I lean my head on his shoulder.

Mack shoots us a look in the mirror and shakes his head. He must think we're insane.

I can't bring myself to care. This feels good. Comfortable. Easy. I'm going to enjoy every moment, soak it up with the California sunshine.

Michael asks about my job, my family, my brother—who is also a huge *Space Vendetta* fan and gamer—but when he asks about my fellow fangirls, I hesitate. Not because I don't love them, but because it's a different kind of bond. A sisterhood. A community of fans and creatives who share pieces of themselves behind the safe wall of our fandom group. I don't want to cross any lines. I give him a basic rundown of the girls and their interests.

"Your friend at the convention, the one who stood up to John at the panel?" Michael whistles low. "She's a firecracker."

"That's Ginger." I smile at the memory. "She knows as much as I do about the *Space Vendetta* universe. When she heard they were going to change some major plot points for the upcoming film, she lost her shit."

"Going up against Martigan like that took guts." Michael blows out a breath.

"Ginger never backs down from a challenge." Pride fills me. "She's the best, and she takes no shit."

"I like her already." He laughs. "Does she know you're here right now?"

"No." I pout. "I tried to text her but no answer." I take my phone out of my purse and check again. No messages. Damn it. "Nothing. I hope everything's okay."

Michael rubs his thumb over the back of my hand. "I'm sure she's just busy. She'll call when she's free." He grins. "Think she'll freak out when you tell her?"

"Probably." I laugh; I can almost hear her reaction now. "She'll curse me and wish she was here. Probably so she can throw something at Martigan."

He tries to smother a laugh behind his hand, but I see it.

"Oh." He directs my attention to the scenery outside. "We've arrived."

My jaw drops when I see the house. It's a cute bungalow surrounded by trees and flowers. As we pull into the driveway, I catch a glimpse of the backyard and a pool. It looks like a little slice of paradise. I instantly fall in love.

"It's gorgeous," I say, gasping as I step from the car. "Like your own little jungle oasis. You can't even see your neighbors."

"That's exactly why I bought it." He takes me by the arm. "Come on, let me show you around before our guests arrive."

"Guests?" I pause on the step just outside the door, blinking. "What guests are we expecting?"

"That is a surprise." His eyes gleam with excitement. "Trust me, you're gonna flip out."

"If you got Commander Colton and Captain Ransom to join us for dinner, I cannot be held accountable for some of the things I know will come out of my mouth." I stare at him, half-stunned. "Seriously, if you hadn't notice, I don't have a filter."

"One of the many things I admire about you." Michael gives me a quick kiss and tugs me over the threshold into the house.

The moment we step inside, I'm more in love than I was before. The living room decor is simple and elegant with dark wood and cream draperies. A large flatscreen TV sits on the far wall with two loveseats positioned to face both toward the television and each other. There's a bookcase against the opposite wall with books by a variety of popular science fiction and fantasy authors. I pause to read the titles.

"Do you want something to drink?" he asks from the arched entrance to what I assume is the kitchen.

"Sure." I look up at him. "Surprise me."

With a wink, he disappears from view.

I take my time wandering around the room. I stop in front of the fireplace to admire a large painting of a golden hawk in flight over an endless forest shrouded in mist and fog with the spires of a castle in the distance. A vase of silk roses sits on the mantel, almost like it's a protruding piece of the painting. The strange effect has me mesmerized.

"Your sparkling water," Michael says beside me.

I nearly jump, my heart racing at his sudden appearance.

"Holy sh—" I breathe deeply and take the glass. "Thank you."

"Sorry, didn't mean to sneak up on you." He glances at the art I'm admiring. "There's something surreal about this painting."

I turn back to it. "Yes, there is."

"A friend of mine painted it before I published my first book." Michael smiles. "He read the very first draft, and this popped into his mind."

"This?" I squint at it. "It looks more fantasy land than alien planet."

"Who says alien planets don't look like fantasy landscapes?" He chuckles. "But you're not wrong."

"I'm rarely wrong." I wink and sip my drink. "Just giving fair warning."

"Noted." He studies me for a heartbeat. "Look at the painting again."

I do as he directs, taking in details, searching for hidden depth or meaning. There are other features hidden in the forest and fog. Buildings. A waterfall. Small figures. A moon obscured by clouds. I lean closer, inspecting the spires of the castle towers.

I gasp, my heart leaping. "Ransom's pirate banner." I turn to Michael, who is positively aglow.

He nods. "What else?"

My attention lingers on the golden hawk for a heartbeat longer than I can explain. It finally clicks. "The golden hawk is the same as on Colton's uniform."

"You're halfway there." He nods again. "Say the first thing that pops in your mind."

The pieces all slide into place, and I gasp. "Holy shit."

Michael laughs. "Say it."

"Your first draft of *Space Vendetta* wasn't science fiction, was it?" I cover my mouth. "It was *fantasy*."

"Good girl." He wraps his arm around my waist, plucking the drink from my hand and setting it aside before pulling me into his embrace. "I knew you'd figure it out."

I press my hand to his chest, my heart racing at his proximity, his touch. "Why did you change it?"

Michael shrugs. "I don't know. It felt like the right decision." He sighs. "Everyone who read the first draft said there was something missing. It just didn't *feel* right, you know?"

I nod, understanding exactly what he meant. "What was the original title?"

"Don't laugh." He eyes me seriously for a moment before the boyish grin appears again. "The original title was *The Ballad of the Wicked*."

I consider it for a moment. "It's...catchy."

"That's a nice way to put it." He catches my chin and tips my face up. Heat flushes through me, and I suck in a breath as he leans down to kiss me.

My arms wrap around his neck. I lose myself in him. He deepens the kiss, I lean my weight into him, needing to be closer. Needing—

The doorbell breaks our sexy interlude.

Michael draws back, disappointed, but it's quickly replaced by excitement. "We'll continue this later." He disentangles himself and clears his throat. "They're here."

I smooth my hands over my cheeks, an attempt to tame the heat lingering there. Whoever is on the other side of the door will know exactly what we'd been up to the moment they see me.

"Hey, glad you could come on short notice." Michael swings the door open and gestures for his visitors to enter.

I nearly fall over.

"Ginger!" I rush to my friend as she walks in the door. "What the hell are you doing here?"

She catches me in a huge hug and laughs.

Before she can answer, I see the other guest and immediately round on her. "You're here with John Martigan." I pull her to the side. "You've got some explaining to do, girl."

"I know. I know." Ginger laughs, hugging me again. "I wanted to tell you, but I had to wait." She looks bashfully at John, standing beside Michael, both of them watching us in amusement.

"Okay, now I feel like the odd one out." I pout. "Did you know what was going on here?" I ask Michael and gesture between Ginger and John.

"Not until last week." Michael nudges John with an elbow. "This guy is full of surprises."

"Wait." I glance between them for a moment as realization hits me. "You two aren't at odds like the press claims?"

"I told you," Michael mutters to John. "She's quick as a whip."

"She did figure out your little secret, didn't she?" John asks, elbowing Michael in retaliation. "I guess you've finally met your match."

"I guess I have." Michael grins, reaching out a hand to me. "Come on. I've ordered pizza. It'll be here soon, and we can catch up."

"We have so much to tell you," Ginger says as she takes John's arm and leans into him.

"Yeah the hell you do." I wag a finger at her. "You'd better not skimp on details either. I need to know exactly what happened to you at the convention. I thought this fucker threatened you?" I look at John. "No offense—this was before."

John holds up a hand. "None taken. I know our public personas can be a little…much."

I scoff. "Understatement."

"I promise, I'll tell you everything." Ginger eyes Michael's hand holding mine. "You need to do the same."

"Deal. We're gonna need something stronger than sparkling water, Michael."

"Don't worry, I've got other drinks." He leads the small group to a cozy kitchen, where we scrounge up passable cocktails just in time to hear the doorbell for the pizza.

The evening turns into a wonderful reunion, full of humorous recollections of the comic convention and the men's reactions to Ginger's question. The subsequent fallout and everything it set in motion.

I can't believe how much has happened in these last few weeks.

Most of all, I can't believe it's led me to this moment. I look at Michael who's explaining his favorite fandom pairing that deviates from his books.

This man. This beautiful, creative, clever man.

I think I'm head over heels in love with him. And I can't think of a single reason why it's a bad thing.

When the evening ends, we walk Ginger and John to their car and wave as they drive out the gate.

Back inside, my attention drifts to the painting. It's been in the back of my mind all night, a nagging thought that just won't let go. I cock my head and look closer, searching for things I might have missed.

Then I see the signature at the bottom.

J.M.D.

Michael wraps his arms around my waist, holding me from behind, and his warmth sinks into me to create a comfortable cocoon of muscle.

"Your father painted this." I say the words softly, almost with reverence.

"He did." Michael kisses my cheek. "You really are the most intuitive person I've ever met."

"I just have an eye for detail."

"Is that so?" He kisses a trail down my neck, lingers on my bare shoulder.

"Mmm." My eyes close.

"Now that I have you all to myself, I'd like to show you something else."

"What's that?" I ask, my voice hoarse.

"My bedroom."

He sweeps me into his arms, bridal style. I cling to him as he carries me down the hall and into his room.

I might as well admit it to myself. I love this man, and that might just be the craziest thing ever.

CHAPTER TEN

Michael carries me to the farthest bedroom. The oak furniture and dark fabric are almost an extension of the jungle outside the windows. He sets me on my feet, and I spin around, taking in this part of him. I want to soak all of him in, then maybe this emotion holding my heart in a chokehold won't feel so strange.

"You certainly have a thing for the outdoors." I step out of his reach.

"It's my dream to become a hobbit." His eyes are dark, fixed on me, full of hunger, curiosity, and something I can't quite place.

"Don't you mean a hermit?" I ask, trailing my fingers over the comforter.

"No. I mean hobbit." He runs his hand over his jaw.

"Tolkien." I nod, finally understanding his draw toward fantasy. "You're certainly not built like a hobbit—far too tall…and broad…and handsome."

"Tall, broad, handsome."

Michael remains still as I walk around the room, touching everything, as if committing it to memory.

"Sounds like you're describing a romance hero."

"I would have to add *brooding* to the list for that to be true." I regard him for a moment, allowing my gaze to skim his body in a slow deliberate display of appreciation. "You might be reserved, but one can hardly call you brooding."

"I can brood."

A laugh bubbles from deep inside me, and he frowns.

"Michael, I like you as you are. You don't need to brood for me to want you."

"You *like* me." He steps forward, but I'm rooted to a spot beside the bed. "Is that why you tease me?"

"I don't tease you." The words barely escape my lips when I'm overwhelmed with the need to touch him.

He reaches out, brushes his thumb along my jaw, places his hand at the nape of my neck. His fingers tangle in my hair, and a breathy gasp slips free without me realizing.

"You do tease. Every moment in your presence. Every touch. Every glance. Every word from your sinful lips." He exhales sharply, and I see his resistance crumbling. "Every thought of you leaves me in a state of perpetual agony." He grinds his hips against me, his hard cock unmistakable beneath the soft fabric.

"You don't need to brood when you say things like that." I slide my hand down his chest, his abdomen, and rest it on the unmistakable ridge of his erection.

"Fuck." He sucks in a breath through his teeth. "I'm making your character a goddamn seductress."

"My character?"

Realization makes me grin, and I stroke him. He shivers beneath my touch.

"You mean the raven-haired beauty in the cantina?"

He gives a shaky nod.

"Does she have a name?" I sway gently, torment him with a featherlight caress.

His grip on my neck tightens. "Ronnie."

"Who will she seduce?" I smile at the effect my touch and words are having on him. He's barely holding on, waiting for me to give permission. That knowledge reinforces my determination to draw this out. I want him on his knees, begging for release.

I lean closer, my voice barely above a whisper. "Does she want to enchant the brilliant commander with her wicked talents?" My pressure on his cock increases, and he groans. "Or does she have her heart set on the charming devious captain?"

"She—fuck, Ronnie…I—"

A guttural growl rips from deep in his chest when I unfasten his khakis and slip my hand in to wrap around him. His words fade as I sink to my knees and free him, appreciating the sight of his glorious cock.

A surge of power rips through me when I take him in my mouth and his string of curses fills the silence. I tease his cock with my tongue, sucking him deep, only to withdraw slowly, my teeth gently raking his skin. His fingers tighten in my hair as his hips move.

I hold him steady, my hands on his thighs, his cock on my tongue. I slide my hands up to grasp his ass and take him as deep as I can, nearly hitting the back of my throat.

"Shit."

He fumbles for words. I keep going, unwilling to give in.

"I…Ronnie, stop."

I pause and look up at him, my mouth still full. He curses again.

"As much as I'm enjoying this, I have plans for you."

I withdraw slowly, circling the head with my tongue before relinquishing the hold. He twitches at the sensation.

"You didn't answer my question," I say as I rise to my feet.

"I don't know the answer yet." Michael steps free of his pants and pulls his shirt over his head. "I'm sure you can tell me which man she prefers?"

It doesn't take much to pull the silky top over my head and toss it aside. I hum thoughtfully as I unclasp my bra. His gaze follows my movements, dark pupils blown wide.

"I guess that depends," I murmur, as though seriously contemplating the question. I'm more invested in teasing him than getting an answer. "What's her motivation?" I look at him over my shoulder as I unbutton my pants and push them down my hips. "What does she want from her lover?"

Michael doesn't move. He remains as still as a statue.

I prowl closer, swaying my hips.

His hands clench tightly into fists by his side.

God, I love this little game we're playing. My body vibrates with the need for him to touch me, to fuck me. But he's holding back. He *wants* me to torment him until he breaks.

"What do *you* want?" His voice is hoarse.

"Me?" I circle him—not touching, only admiring. His scent wraps around me, and my resolve wavers. "I want *you*, Michael. In my life. In my bed. I want you inside me. I want us so tangled up in each other, there's no way to separate one from the other. I want something I'm not sure is possible…or wise. I want to be reckless, even though it just might implode."

He meets my gaze, and my breath catches. His lust-hazed expression darkens, and something flickers behind his eyes.

Suddenly, I panic. I crossed a line. I went too far.

Did I just fuck up and say too much? Shit.

"I…sorry." I back away, drawing my lower lip between my teeth.

Michael grabs me by the waist and pulls me against him. His mouth crashes down on mine, and whatever worries were beginning to form dissolve in pleasure. He tastes me, tongue delving between my lips, plundering and punishing.

I clutch at his arms, rake my fingers through his hair, rub my body against his. He sets me on fire. I want it to consume me.

Entwined together, we stumble to the bed, and Michael goes down first, taking me with him. He pulls me to the center in a tangle of limbs and moans. He's kissing me as though I possess the very air he breathes. I let him take what he needs because it fuels my desire.

As he's settling between my thighs, he stops with a curse.

"What?" I ask, momentarily stunned, aching for him to fill me.

"Condom." He barely gets the word out.

"Fuck it." I grind my pussy into him. "I'm clear. I'm protected. Just fuck me."

"Are you sure?"

"Yes." I groan. "Please, Mich—"

He thrusts deep, and whatever voice I have devolves into a guttural groan of delight. I wrap my legs around him to bring him closer. He moves, rotating his hips, and pleasure spikes through me.

Then he fucks me. Slow at first, but I claw at his shoulders, whispering in his ear.

"Take it. Don't be gentle." I purr as he quickens his pace. "That's it. Fuck me, Michael. I want you to claim me, make me yours."

"Goddamn it, V." He growls. "If you keep talking like that, I'm going to come."

"Do it." I stroke the fine hair at the nape of his neck, let my nails scrape his skin. "Fill me up. Let everyone know this pussy belongs to you."

"That filthy fucking mouth of yours will be the end of me." Michael swears and kisses me hard.

It doesn't take much more to tip us both over the edge. When my climax hits, I pull him into the storm with me, and he tumbles into his own release.

As the haze of our orgasms wears off, Michael rolls to the side, brings me against him, and kisses my shoulder.

"Shower?" he asks.

"Sounds delightful." I follow him to the bathroom despite my still trembling legs. He washes me thoroughly before pinning me to the wall, his hand firm against my throat as he makes me come twice on his fingers.

"Good girl." He kisses me with a tenderness that leaves my heart aching.

It's not until later, when we're lying beneath the blankets in the dark and a breath away from sleep, that I ask the one thing I've been dreading.

"What happens next?"

Silence swallows my question.

"Stay with me." He kisses my bare shoulder and holds me tighter. "Stay as long as you want."

"I can't just leave my life in Alton—my friends, my family, my job." Heaviness weighs me down.

"I understand. We'll figure it out." He exhales, his breath caressing my skin. "I like you. A lot." He sighs. "More than a lot."

My heart squeezes. "I feel the same."

"Let's give it some time." He strokes a hand over my hip. "You visit me when you can, and I'll come visit you. We can take it slow."

I scoff. "Jumping into bed together is not taking it slow."

"No, it isn't, but I don't regret anything."

"Me either." I sigh. "Long-distance relationships are hard."

"True, but you're worth it." He kisses my neck. "I'd do anything for you."

A tingle of warmth and certainty flows through me at his words.

"Same."

I swear I hear *I love you* as I drift off to sleep.

After I wake the next morning, we part ways at the airport, and the sinking feeling I expected never comes. Instead, I'm full of optimism.

If this is real, it'll find a way to work. I know it will.

CHAPTER ELEVEN

A Little Over One Year Later

Michael sits on the sofa, legs propped on the coffee table, computer in his lap. I'm curled up beside him, reading on my tablet. It's the most domestic fluff I've ever experienced, and I adore it.

I'm not going to lie. The past year of doing the long-distance thing has been rough, but it gave me the time I needed to assess what I really want in life. We spent two weekends every month together, one in LA, the other in Alton. He took me to Thanksgiving with his family, and I had him join my family for Christmas.

When Ginger sent an invitation to the latest *Space Vendetta* event in LA, I nearly died. A fantasy come true—walking the red carpet with the man of my dreams. I practically fall over myself in my rush to show Michael the invitation.

"I don't attend those events. Too many cameras, too much noise." He looks up from his computer and sobers instantly at my incredulous expression. "But if you want to go, I'll make it happen."

"Good, because all the fangirls will be there." I frown as I think about it. "Well, they're all invited. I think Madre has plans with her family that weekend, but everyone else should be coming. Ginger rented a huge house for all of us to stay and hang out. It'll be a blast."

I'm about to leave him to his own devices, but Michael

makes a long-suffering noise and sets aside his laptop. He takes my hand and pulls me into his lap.

"I'm sorry. I forget this is all new and exciting for you." He holds me close. "I've spent so many years avoiding promotional events for the films, it feels weird to suddenly be invested again."

"I know you're a private person, and I get it. Being the center of attention isn't your jam." I boop his nose. "But the good thing is, they're not there to drool over *you*. Just the actors who play the characters you wrote."

"Gee, that makes me feel better. Thanks, babe." Michael half sighs, half laughs. "They're definitely going to notice the smoking hot bombshell I bring to the red carpet."

I press my hand to my chest. "*Moi*?"

The mischievous grin on my lips makes him arch a brow. "What kind of chaos are you planning?"

"Nothing." I tease my finger along his jaw, which is clenching at my evasiveness. "I promise."

"Ronnie, we're already going to be the center of attention when I show up with *you* on my arm. Please don't make us front page news."

"I wasn't planning on it." I squirm in his lap, but he pins me in place.

"Then what *are* you planning?" His blue eyes narrow suspiciously.

"Well, I was hoping we could dress in cosplay." His eyes widen with panic. "Not like, full cosplay, but you know, little nods to our favorite characters."

The panic slowly ebbs in his expression, but he still looks uncomfortable. "I don't know. It's a formal event, V."

My heart flips when he uses the pet name.

"What about this, we design something that fits the theme and intent of the event, but we put our own flair on it?"

"Such as?"

"We incorporate details of our fan fiction characters." I hold my breath, waiting for his response.

Michael blinks twice before bursting into laughter. "You know, that's not the craziest idea I've ever heard."

"Only the fangirls will understand the subtle nod." I bite my lip. "What do you think?"

"I think you're going to do what you want." He softens, and I sink into him. "Just keep it minimal, that's all I ask. I'm not competing with Hughes for the cover of *Celebrity Gossip*."

"Thank you." I kiss him in excitement. "I love you."

"I love you too, V." He cradles my cheek in his hand. "Did you think about my offer?"

"To buy a place in the mountains and become hobbits together?" I nod. "Of course, but I think it's impractical."

His expression falls. I feel guilty but only for a moment.

"We could never be true hobbits, only sad imitations." I smile when his skeptical expression meets my gaze. "The actual problem will be finding a job."

Michael brightens. "I can write anywhere, and you don't have to work if you don't want. I'm sure we can find something."

"Maybe I'll write a book," I say in jest.

"You should." He pauses, his attention fixed on the far wall for a moment, like he's lost in thought.

"Is something wrong?" My brow furrows. "I was just kidding."

"No." He snaps back to reality, meeting my eyes again. "I think you *should* write a book. In fact, why don't we write something together?"

"Together?" I stare at him, stunned. "Are you serious?"

"As a heart attack." He shifts in the chair, positioning me so we're face to face. "We *should* do it. Create whole new worlds, explore unexpected tropes, turn the industry upside down. As a team."

"What if it flops?"

"Who cares? We'll put it out there for whoever wants to read it, just like we do with fan fiction."

"But you're an established author with a reliable track record, they'll never go for this. I have nothing published."

"That doesn't make you any less of an author." He hooks a finger under my chin. "I've read all your fics, and I adore your writing."

"You do?" My heart swells with love and pride.

"I always have. Even before I knew *you*, I adored your work. That's why I was momentarily stunned when you told me your pen name the day we first met." He grins bashfully, a lovely pink on his cheeks. "I was as starstruck with you as you were with me."

"Stop it." I can't take this overload of emotion. "You're gonna make me cry."

"Happy tears only." He grins, and I'm swept away by how amazing he is and how fucking lucky I am.

I nod with a sniffle.

"So what are we writing?" He looks like a kid on Christmas morning, brimming with energy and excitement. "Space Pirates?"

"You've already done that."

An idea hits me, and I can't suppress a giggle.

"This is scary. What's going on in that head of yours?"

"I'm thinking we should try a space fantasy—other worlds, strange creatures, magic. Lots of sex. And of course dragons." I rub my hands together gleefully.

"I think those are overdone." Michael bursts my bubble.

"Space fantasies with lots of sex?"

"No, dragons." He kisses my cheek. "Although I like where this is going. We can brainstorm later."

"Why not now?" I ask, my mind spinning with endless possibilities for characters and civilizations across the galaxy.

"Because I have another question."

"I already said I'd move to the mountains, become a hobbit, and write smutty space fantasy with you. What more could you want?"

"I want you to marry me."

My whole body goes rigid. "What did you say?"

"V, I want you to marry me."

"That isn't a question."

He chuckles. "Veronica, would you do me the great honor of becoming my wife?"

"You're not on one knee."

"Do I have to be on my knee to ask this particular question?"

"I adore when you're on your knees." I purr, warmth swirling in the pit of my stomach. "But I'm quite comfortable where I am, so I'll let it pass."

"So sassy." He leans closer, his lips a breath from mine. "Will you marry me?"

"Of course I'll marry you." I wrap my arms around his neck and close the distance to his lips.

He kisses me back, and all the pieces fall into place. I'm blissfully happy.

"I hear fangirls make the best wives," Michael murmurs against my mouth. "Guess we'll have to compare notes with the other couples."

"Guess so."

"Now come here and let me show you an idea I have for a scene in our upcoming best-selling novel." He runs his fingers through my hair.

"So confident." I sigh. "But that's why I love you."

"I'm glad someone does." He sighs in relief. "I love you too."

When he kisses me, he takes his time, exploring, savoring. I melt into him, and for the first time in my life, I'm glad I did something reckless. I wouldn't be here if I hadn't been willing to push the boundaries just a little bit.

Sometimes the best decisions can come from the strangest fangirl fantasies.

THE END Book 5

About the Author

Kirsten S. Blacketer

Kirsten S. Blacketer is a multi-published indie author of both historical and contemporary romance. When she's not writing, she homeschools her two children and enjoys time with her family. In those moments of freedom, she devours romance novels while sipping a glass of wine. Age has only shown her that writing villains can be just as fun as heroes. Her next life goals are to write a New York Times Bestseller and one day have Adam Driver play a starring role in a film version of one of her books. A girl can dream, right?

Read more at **http://kirstensblacketer.com.**

Also Writes as Jen Bradlee

Other Books by Kirsten S. Blacketer

Craving 1985 Series

When I Found You
Can't Fight This Feeling
She Gives Love a Bad Name
Owner of a Lonely Heart
Just What I Needed

Historical

An Irresistible Shadow
A Shadow's Kiss
Mississippi Moonshine
Deceiving the Earl
Jewel of Winter
At Winter's Demand
Under Winter's Control
Seducing Winter's Gentleman
Stealing the Widow's Heart
Seduction on the Alpine Express
Temptation on the Alpine Express

Contemporary

A Lockdown Love Affair
A Holiday Love Affair
Mistletoe and Mistakes
Confessions of a Fangirl
Confessions of a Gamer Girl
Confessions of a Glamour Girl

Fantasy/FairyTale

Curse of the Huntsman's Jewel
The Huntsman's Revenge

Pirate Fantasy/Historical

Queen Takes Hook

Paranormal Historical Monster Romance

Death and Desire

The Society of Wanton Widows

A Late Victorian Series Coming 2026 from Dragonblade Publishing

www.ingramcontent.com/pod-product-compliance
Lightning Source LLC
Chambersburg PA
CBHW030341310726
48979CB00001B/135

* 9 7 8 1 9 6 6 9 0 5 2 0 2 *